STONEBEARER'S APPRENTICE

SHADOW BEARER TRILOGY, BOOK TWO

JODI L. MILNER

To Tim
May your adventures be as big as your imagination.

CHAPTER ONE

There are hurts only time can fix. To Katira, healing was a matter of finding the proper treatment, whether it was stitching tidy lines of sutures or applying soothing sanaresina balm that left her fingers smelling of pepper, camphor, and waiting. If an injury was properly cared for, in time the discomfort faded away.

It had been five weeks and three days since Mamar died in Amul Dun's infirmary. And time, that persistent thief, continued to tick by in a constant stream. During those first raw days she thought her grief would wear her down to nothing, and she would crumble away like a riverbank in a flood.

Time proved that wrong as well. While her loose clay and sand might have washed away, it left behind strong sturdy stones. Just as massive quarried granite blocks made the walls of her new home strong, the sturdy stones of Mamar's love and teachings helped her to build herself again.

Or at least that's what Katira told herself as she flung the wet rag into the bucket of soapy water to rinse it before drawing it out and wringing it again. Much like sorrow, her anger flirted dangerously close to the surface. At least the tower's miles of elaborately patterned mosaic tile didn't care if she took out her frustration on it.

She scrubbed the hundreds of tiny tiles in front of her until they gleamed, then moved to the next section, and then the next, and the next. Working helped her forget. The harder the work, the easier it was to ignore how worry and the ache of loss fought for her attention.

Papan, curse the man for his stubbornness, was doing the exact same thing. She knew, because she learned it from him. Despite all that had happened, he threw himself into the work at the tower like an anchor being tossed off a boat. He was determined to hold Amul Dun firmly where it needed to be despite how fast he sank.

She shifted the bucket back another few feet and rinsed the rag again before tackling the next section of floor. Had this been any other day, her friend Isben would have been doing chores somewhere else in the tower or performing his apprentice duties. He'd worked closely with Master Regulus for so long that he'd let himself believe that the longer his master lived after his ordeal at Khanrosh, the better chance the man might make a full recovery. He'd been crushed when the old man passed yesterday.

Once Katira finished cleaning the tile in that hallway, she would go check on him.

She'd be the hand he could hold onto while his own flood took him, as he'd done for her those weeks ago after the death of Mamar. He stayed with her when she felt she was being swept away bringing parcels of cheese, mugs of hot sweet tea, and a comforting shoulder to cry on. She owed him no less.

The midmorning bell tolled. The sound echoed off the

mountain and filled the air with its sonorous tone, another reminder how time kept passing, regardless of her actions.

A skittering tapping sound came from the end of the hall closest to Papan's apartment. Katira paused to listen, rag dripping above the tile. In the weeks she'd lived and worked in Amul Dun, she thought she'd learned all the different sounds of the ancient tower, but this one was new. It reminded her of something she couldn't quite put a finger on.

The sound tapped closer.

She hurried to her feet, rag and bucket forgotten. Papan had told her over and over that Amul Dun was safe. Nothing could sneak past the glyphs woven into the walls. But this sound wasn't safe. She'd heard it before in Khanrosh where she'd come face to face with that demoness, Wrothe. It meant danger.

She grabbed the solid wooden bucket. Maybe this was a rat. Maybe she was letting her imagination get the best of her. All the same, she wasn't going to face whatever it was empty-handed. Papan's oft repeated saying came to mind, 'to do nothing is death.' She refused to do nothing.

She stepped back, putting more space between herself and the sound. Half the long hallway separated her from where Papan sat studying a stack of papers Bremin had delivered that morning.

Even on bright days, this hallway faced away from the sun and tended to be dark. Shadows puddled around the base of each thick curtain bordering the windows. Another nail scratched on the tile, louder this time. Shadow hounds couldn't come here, it wasn't possible.

Possible or not, a shadow broke free of the wall and crossed the brighter shaft near a window, followed by a second. The glint of sharp teeth caught the light as they passed.

Fear's icy nails dragged down her back. She'd faced such hounds before. These were creatures of magic and could only be killed with magic. She was defenseless.

The closest hound gave a low growl. This was no fantasy conjured up by her mind. The hounds were here, in the tower, hunting her.

She stumbled backward, desperately needing to get further away. "Help! Papan! Somebody, help!" Her shout rang off the solid walls filling the space.

The first hound leapt for her. She dodged away, swinging the heavy bucket at its face. The bucket passed through the hound as if it were no more than smoke, useless. It would only slow her down. She dropped it and bolted away from the hounds, away from Papan, feet pounding against the tile. The skittering of claws followed her, drawing ever closer.

A hound leapt up with a snarling growl and snapped at her arm. Its teeth grazed the skin, leaving a stinging line as she jerked away.

She kicked at it. Her foot passed through the creature like smoke.

"Papan!" she yelled. "Help!" This far away she feared he couldn't hear her through the thick door.

The second hound rushed forward, snarling and snapping at her ankles. As she jumped away, the first knocked her to the floor from behind. She scrambled to get to her hands and knees, to crawl away, to keep those snapping jaws from reaching skin.

"Papan!"

This was it. She pressed her head into her arms, trying to cover herself and keep them from getting to her face and neck. Teeth sank into her exposed arm, biting down and ripping the skin.

Katira screamed at the sudden sharp pain and swung her fist, this time making contact. It let go with a yip. Enough time for the first hound to dive in and bite at her other arm. It grabbed and pulled, shaking its head back as if she were nothing more than a rodent it was killing to eat.

Heat blossomed inside of her, wild and alive. It filled her, stretching through her chest and extending up her neck and down her arms. The hounds released their hold and flinched back at the sudden glow of the lines on her arms.

It had happened like this only twice before. The first time she'd worked herself into a violent rage when she believed that villain Surasio had murdered her parents. Then next time was when Isben told her Mamar had died and her grief at the sudden news exploded from her. Isben had been there and stopped her both times before she could hurt herself.

He wasn't here now.

The power seized her, filling her mind with a deadly calm. Deep beneath its weight, Katira knew she should be afraid, knew she should try to stop, but it was like she was watching herself from a distance.

The two hounds grew bold once more, eager to take their prize. As the first charged, jaws ready to snap, Katira extended a hand. A raw torrent of light shot from her palm and gathered around the hound, freezing it place. Its jaws snapped shut and its snarls stopped short. The power brightened, tightening and burning until all that was left was ash.

Katira's heart hammered, rabbit-fast and strained. Her power retreated within her, making the darkness of the hall even darker in contrast. A different heaviness pressed its weight against her, that of the hound's venom coursing through her veins.

The last hound fell back, teeth bared, and ears flattened to its head. It circled her as if weighing the risk of attacking. She extended her arm, unsure if there was still power there, if she was strong enough to cut it down should it attack.

The door to their rooms opened with a bang. Papan burst out, cane clutched in one hand, bright sword glowing in the other. He flowed into action without question, closing the distance between them in a limping sprint and cutting down the remaining hound with a single swinging arc of his sword.

The heat inside Katira dimmed and winked out, leaving a vast emptiness. Katira's vision blurred and she curled up, pressing her cheek against the cool tile of the floor. Sounds came and went, too muffled to hear. Papan called her name. A nagging ache spread from where the hound's teeth had cut her.

Papan's sword clattered to the ground as he knelt beside her and shook her by the shoulders. "Katira? Can you hear me?"

She could only nod. The ache of the venom pressed against her lungs and heart.

"This will only take a moment. I promise." He placed his hand against her neck. "You need to trust me. You'll be okay."

The hallway spun as Katira struggled to breathe. She reached for Papan's hand, desperate to cling to something.

The warm flow of his power pressed through her, seeking that hidden place where hers had retreated, and coaxing it to return. Katira shivered as the first pain of summoning broke through.

"Breathe through it. Let it pass. Let it move through you." Papan coached, his voice soft and gentle.

Katira followed his guidance, sucking air through her teeth against the burn. The lines on her skin wavered back to life. As she did, her awareness of him opened like a window. She found a surprising calm, much like the odd calm that had seized her moments before. That calm allowed him to focus on what needed to be done.

Beneath it hid the truth. Fear laced tightly around his heart and prickled his skin. He was scared at what had happened, scared he might not be enough to help her, scared at what this attack meant. He nudged at her reserve of power, encouraging it to spill. She held his hand tighter as she let it fill her.

"Good, there you go." Papan continued. "Let the Khandashii overflow from its channels and neutralize the venom."

Deeper, behind his fear, hid something else he didn't want anyone to find. Dark threads, like fine roots, clung to his edges and stretched through him like a net — too thin to be noticed at first glance, but deceptively strong nonetheless. Before she could see more, another surge of his power pulled her back.

As much as she trusted him, she'd never done anything like this before. After she'd been bitten in Khanrosh, Issa had cleansed her. She didn't remember enough to understand what was needed. Bright stars burst at the edges of her vision.

"Stay with me," Papan urged. "Keep breathing."

The gentle flow of his power changed and became insistent. It pushed at that well of power inside her, forcing more to spill out. The burn grew to a blistering flame. She arched against the intrusion, trying to get away.

He pushed harder, forcing the flame to fill her. "Only a little longer. Don't fight it."

Katira's sight darkened as the flood hit its peak and lingered one, two, three long seconds before ebbing away and retreating back to its hiding place.

Papan withdrew his hand from Katira's neck head and sagged against the nearby wall, panting. "By the Stonemother's throne, what happened here?"

The question hung unanswered. The sounds surrounding her continued to mix and blur. If he said anything else, Katira didn't hear it. She couldn't keep her eyes open. While the creeping ache of venom was gone, a deeper fatigue dragged her down.

Papan helped her back to their rooms and set her into one of the comfortable chairs by the fire. With a steady hand, he wrapped makeshift bandages around the worst of where the hounds had dug in.

As he tied off the last one, he grabbed his cane. "This needs better care than what I can give. I'll be right back. I promise."

With the fog muddling her head and all her strength drained away, Katira couldn't bear the thought of being alone. Shadows lurked in the corners of the otherwise cheery sitting room. Any of them could be hiding another monster.

"Don't leave me."

He squeezed her hand and his fingers trembled as he let go. "I have to, I won't be long."

True to his word, Papan returned quickly with Cassim, the healer, in tow. The bulky man was red-faced from trying to keep up. A basket of supplies dangled from one elbow, and his white robe hung crooked off his wide frame. The front of his dark hair stuck up from where he wiped his forehead with his elbow.

He bustled into the room and set down his basket on the table. "Okay, General, why am I here?" he asked, searching the room for his patient. "If this is something simple, I'll not be pleased. I've said it before, if they can walk themselves to the infirmary, then let them. Save me the trip."

Papan gestured to Katira where she sat by the fire. "It's more complicated than that, I'm afraid."

Katira gave a small wave from her warm chair, glad to see someone she knew and trusted.

"So, it's you then." He smiled and crossed the room. "What can I do for you, Katira?" His eyes widened when he saw the blood-soaked bandages hastily tied around her arms. His tone instantly changed to one of concern. "How did you manage to do that?"

"Just lucky, I guess?" Katira offered, not ready to explain.

He shook his head and clicked his tongue. "Between you and your father, perhaps it's best if I stayed with you for the trouble you seem to get in." He puffed out a breath and held out a hand. "Come over to the table where the light is better. I'll get you patched up."

Katira took the healer's hand, glad to have him to lean on. The fog and fatigue were fading, but she didn't trust her legs yet. He guided her to one of the chairs before sliding the other chair closer with a foot.

On the other side of the room, Bremin let himself in as if he'd been expected. Behind him came none other than Lady Alystra, Amul Dun's very own High Lady. Papan gave a respectful bow before ushering them into the small adjoining study and shutting the door.

Cassim quirked his head to the side. "Well, this just got a lot more interesting. Exactly what's going on?"

Katira shrugged. "I'm not sure. Didn't expect that either." She tugged at the messy knot on her bandage, eager for him to get started. "Honestly, Cassim, if it wasn't on my arms, I'd have you leave the basket, and I'd take care of this myself."

The comment brought Cassim back to why he was there. "I know you would. That's not the point." He plucked out several rolls of bandages and set them on the table. "Honestly, there's not much to do around the tower most days. Master Firen has had me digging my way through the library studying historical healing glyphs out of dusty books and scrolls day in and day out for the past week. Can I tell you how frustrating it is to know all this stuff and never have the chance to use it?"

"Sounds interesting," Katira offered. Studying in Amul Dun's renowned library sounded slightly more gratifying than carrying laundry to be washed or floors to be cleaned. She sucked air between her teeth as he untied the first makeshift bandage.

"It's boring. At least now we have the new weapons to study from Khanrosh. Before that, it was even more boring." His eyes narrowed as he studied her arm, as if he couldn't quite believe what he saw. "This... this is a shadow hound bite," he stammered. He grew suddenly serious. "Start at the beginning and don't leave anything out. What happened?"

Katira glanced over to the door where her father had disappeared. "Not sure what to tell you. I was out in the hall and two hounds came out of nowhere."

He blinked in surprise. "Here? In the tower? That's impossible." His hand tightened around her wrist. "There are glyphs in place that prevent them from entering."

"Yet here we are." She flexed her hand with a wince.

He immediately loosened his grip and made quick work untying the other bandage. "Sorry. It's upsetting, that's all. It also explains why *they're* here." His gaze flicked to the shut door. "You mind if I delve these? I'd hate to miss anything important." As he spoke, he removed his stone from around his neck and bound it to his palm.

Katira's stomach fluttered. "Go ahead." It was still so new to be working around people who could use their magic for healing. All her training with Mamar relied on analyzing injuries with sight and touch alone.

Cassim placed his fingers on either side of the torn skin and a gentle warmth spread between them. Back at the ruins, Isben had done something similar when he had thought Wrothe had hurt her. The warmth faded after a few moments.

"Nothing surprising. All traces of the venom are gone. Just like I like it." He tried to give her a reassuring smile, but the shock of learning about hounds in the tower clearly unnerved him. "Had it been a shallow cut, I'd bandage it and let it be. We heal fast enough, it's usually better that way. But these are deep and ragged enough I'd best knit them back together for you."

"I guess stitching isn't an option around here?"

Back in Namragan, she would have used a needle and gut to realign the torn edges. While she didn't relish the thought of getting stitches, the familiar method was all she knew.

Cassim made a face. "Why on earth would anyone want that? For starters, this hurts far less and will leave a much smaller scar. You'd be hard pressed to find anyone in Amul Dun who even knows how to stitch up a cut." He placed his fingertips back on either side of the wound. "With your permission, of course."

Katira nodded and fought the urge to look away. She had trained her whole life to patch up wounds like this, but the thought of watching the power work on her own skin made her stomach turn. She forced herself to watch anyway, needing to know how it worked.

Again, gentle warmth gathered around the wound. This time the flesh began to tingle. The tingle grew into an itch, which grew into a pinch. She grimaced. The edges of the wounds pulled together under the dance of light coming from Cassim's fingers as he worked his way methodically from one tear to the next.

"Almost there. Hold still just a touch longer." Cassim pressed down on her arm to pin it to the table.

The pinching continued another few uncomfortable moments before the final dance of light finished. Katira looked at her arms in wonder. All that was left of the bites were fresh pink scars.

"There we are. All done. Those will be a bit tender for a few days." He held up one of the clean bandage rolls. "Keeping it covered helps." As he worked, the corner of his mouth drew into a smile.

"Listen. If you want to see me, all you have to do is come visit. There's no need to get hurt." He tied off the last wrap and tucked the remaining bandaging supplies back into the small basket before tapping her arm. "Leave that on for a couple days, it'll keep you from picking at it." He then laughed through his nose and shook his head. "I suppose you know better than that."

Each careful wrap of the bandage felt smooth and tidy under Katira's studied fingers, certainly better than Papan's quick wrap or what she would have been able to do herself.

Behind the closed study door, Katira could only hear murmurs of conversation. She wanted to be in there; surely she had a right to be. The attack had happened to her.

Cassim readied to leave, then stopped short to look at one of the dried bundles of herbs on a shelf. "You studied with Mistress Mirelle for a long time, didn't you?"

Katira jerked at the unexpected mention of her mother.

While her grief had eased over the weeks, it certainly wasn't over.

Cassim pinched the bridge of his nose. "I'm sorry, I'm so stupid. Forget I asked, please."

"Don't apologize. It feels like everyone is afraid to talk about her. Sometimes it's nice to remember that she lived." Katira walked closer to the shelf and found him studying a dry bundle of Mamar's favorite healing herb, sanaresina. "What would you like to know?"

"She taught you herb craft, right?" He touched one of the fallen leaves.

"Of course. Ever since I was old enough to work a mortar and pestle, she showed me how to grind herbs and concoct medicines. I was going to start my own shop one day when she thought I was ready." She glanced out the window toward the mountains, toward home. "I guess that won't happen now."

"Not for a few years at least." Cassim sighed. "Remember, Mirelle was an Amul Dun trained Healer, like myself. She started here before going out to have her own little shop. You can do it too, if you wish, after you pass the tests."

Cassim's words were comforting, but they made it clear how much about her new life she still didn't understand. She had never heard mention of any sort of testing before. She wasn't sure she liked the sound of it. Before she could ask him about it, he turned to leave.

"I should head back before Master Firen starts to let his imagination get the best of him." Cassim set the basket into the crook of his elbow. "When the General rushed in needing a healer, he didn't explain anything. If I don't get back soon, Master Firen will come to see what's going on. From what I've seen, those lot might want to keep this quiet. You okay if I go?"

Katira liked talking to Cassim. She'd have him stay longer if it were possible. "I guess so. It's just, I have this whole new life to figure out. There's so much I don't know that it feels like I'm falling, but I don't know when I'll hit the ground."

"That's a bit dramatic, but it sounds exactly like how I felt all those years ago when I first came here. Learning that you are different and having your whole life uprooted is hard. Don't let anyone tell you otherwise. But don't forget, you belong here. One day it will feel like home. I promise."

"How long did it take you?"

"Years. I won't lie. But I'm stubborn like that. Having something to focus on can help." A hopeful gleam filled his eyes. "Perhaps you could teach me about different herbs and how to prepare them?"

The idea filled her with joy. "Of course. I would love to do something I'm good at."

"Then it's done. I'll speak to Master Firen. I'm sure he'll agree."

Cassim excused himself, leaving Katira with a difficult decision. Should she knock on the study door, or sit out by the fire and wait? No, waiting at a time like this would make her crazy. But, barging in on Papan and the High Lady in a secret council also felt wrong.

She had to talk to someone and they might be hours. Isben still needed her, too. There hadn't been anything like this in the tower the whole time she'd been here. The chances of another attack so soon seemed too small to consider.

CHAPTER TWO

earing a hole in the barrier separating the surreal dreamspace from the waking world was like killing. The ragged edges thrashed like a wounded animal. Loose threads whipped and flailed in sizzling arcs through the surreal grey space between worlds.

Ternan never thought he'd be dragged there again. With Wrothe's defeat at Khanrosh, he'd hoped she'd be trapped in the place plunged even deeper behind the shadow barrier, that of the mirror realm. It would be that much harder for her to reach him. But she'd always been a cunning one. Paired with her rage, it was a powerful combination.

The threads at the corner of the tear merged as the barrier fought to heal itself. Wrothe uttered a stream of curses vile enough to curdle milk. She drew more of Ternan's power and combined it with her own to maintain the glyph wedged in the gap.

"Let it close," Ternan yelled over the noise and the violent ache pressing at his temples. "Nothing else can be done."

"Silence." Anger whipped around her like a tempest. "We're so close." She never could accept failure, on her part or anyone else's. Killing Katira was part of a personal vendetta. The girl had foiled her plot in Khanrosh and hadn't paid for her insolence.

A dangerous hunger sparked in her eyes when Jarand rushed into the hall. Katira might have tried to kill her, but Jarand was the one who struck the final blow that sent her back to the mirror realm. He was weak still, perhaps the remaining hound would be enough to kill him as well.

Whatever hope Wrothe had for success was cut down as easily as the hound by Jarand's blade.

The tear snapped its jaws shut without warning, the force of it throwing both Ternan and Wrothe back a few steps. Red sparks chased over the spot, patching and weaving the injured barrier shut. It reminded Ternan once more how much the shadow barrier acted like a living thing.

"How?" Wrothe's anger echoed off the grey walls of the dreamspace hallway. "How can that untrained little girl defeat one of my hounds?" The question wasn't directed at him. She paced back and forth, eyes wild. Ribbons of unchecked raw power shot around her. Should any of those ribbons seize him, she might rip him apart on accident.

He put more distance between the two of them, stepping closer to where Jarand knelt next to Katira. Seen in the dream-space, they were only shadowy representations of how they appeared in the waking world. "What does it matter to you anyway? Nothing from the mirror realm stays dead for long. You'll have your precious hounds back in the course of a few hours." Ternan leaned in and studied the lines of Katira's face. "Besides, she isn't little or defenseless. We saw her courage at the ruins."

"Don't mention the ruins, ever. It took weeks to recover my strength after that idiot stabbed me." She absently rubbed at the spot on her stomach as she remembered. "It's your fault my escape from that stupid stone prison failed. Had you come for me, instead of your underling, none of that unpleasantness would have happened."

Ternan bit his tongue. Above all else, he had to stay calm. Here in the dreamspace, she could still hurt him. "I've explained this. I couldn't be the one to release you from your prison." He held up his blackened stone. "You made that decision when you twisted my power all those centuries ago." He gripped his stone in his hand, bracing himself for what he had to say next. "My favorite apprentice is dead because of your scheming."

To Ternan's surprise, Wrothe's anger suddenly faded. The flailing ribbons retreated to the small flow of power holding him there. She would soon tire and have to let him go. "Great plans require great sacrifices."

Seeing this, he dared to continue. "That's only fair when both of us pay the price. You've paid nothing while *my* people have been both hurt and killed. I've sacrificed plenty for you. You got what you wanted. You're out of your prison. How have I benefitted from any of this?"

"I thought you loved me. You said you wanted to be with me."

Ternan couldn't tell if the hurt in her eyes was real or another plot to manipulate him. She'd done it so many times. He couldn't fall for it.

"You used me. That's not love. And worse, you used your power to bend my thoughts, make me serve you. You made me believe the peace you offered me was real. Jarand's not the idiot. I am."

She came closer to him and laid her head on his shoulder. At one time he took comfort in such gestures. That was before he learned how she could influence him. A surge of longing pierced him. Unbelievable.

He shrugged her away and the longing faded as quickly as it came. "No. That's not going to work. I know your tricks."

She crossed her arms over her chest and pouted. It amazed him that she'd lived well over a thousand years and still thought this childish act worked on anyone. "The mirror realm isn't my home. It never will be. I won't stop until I find a way to return to the waking world permanently."

Jarand's shadowy figure helped Katira back into their quarters. "Then why hurt children? This insane anger of yours makes that goal much more difficult. I can't help you find and test new glyphs if the High Lady suspects you are still a threat. If they catch you, they'll bind you back into an eternal prison like before, and if they do, I won't be able to get you out."

Her pout deepened, and she turned her back on him. "I'm removing obstacles. It's strategic."

"You're hunting them because you're still angry with me." He grabbed her by her shoulders and turned her back around. "Even after all these years, you haven't forgiven me for the part I played when you were bound to that prison. Don't play innocent with me. Letting Regulus die, wanting to have Jarand for your own, trying to kill his daughter, this is all part of you punishing me still. If I wasn't bound to you as your link to the outside world, you'd kill me too."

"You don't honestly think I'd hold a grudge like that for centuries. Do you?"

"Yes. You would. And you have. You forget, I can tell when you are lying."

Her childish act disappeared, and a dark cruelty returned.

"Fine. I want to hurt them and you are going to make it possible. When can you help me open another tear?"

Her sudden change forced a squeak out of Ternan. Times like these were when her insanity became the most dangerous. He tripped backward, barely catching himself before falling. "I won't. You need to stop this madness."

"I allow your resistance, but no one tells me what I can or can't do." Wrothe came closer. Sparks of power flashed over her extended palm.

"It won't work. The girl is on her guard now." Ternan scurried further back. "Leave her alone. There's got to be another way to get what you want."

A bolt of power arced past Ternan's ear and exploded against the wall behind him. "When?"

He yelped and shuffled back until his back met the wall. "I refuse. You forced my hand to try this attack. I won't do it again."

She studied the artful glowing swirls of the dark lines at her wrist as she calculated and planned her next move. "Two hounds wasn't enough. Next time it will be four, plus my wolf."

"This needs to stop." Ternan's mind raced to find a reason valid enough for her to consider. "You risk everything if you strike again, especially so soon. I know Lady Alystra. If she suspects there is a threat, she won't rest until she puts a stop to it." He paused to let the idea sink in.

Wrothe didn't look up. He wasn't sure if she was even listening at this point, or if all reason had abandoned her.

"What's more, she's got Bremin. He was there at Khanrosh. He's seen you. It's only a matter of time before they link these attacks to you. You will tip your hand too early."

"They underestimate me." She came closer and caressed the smooth dark marble of the wall next to where he stood. "I want all of this. Both in the mirror realm and in yours." She sighed. Her shoulders softened and her head lowered. "You are trying to manipulate me. I don't like it." Chains of glyphs formed around her. The crimson dress she favored melted into a pale-yellow robe. Her raven black hair shortened and curled.

The sight dried Ternan's mouth. "Please don't," he pleaded. "Not again."

Wrothe transformed, taking on a different face, one she had no right to wear. One which brought him more anguish than any other. His long dead companion from ages ago, Evangeline, stood before him. It wasn't her, but Ternan's heart couldn't tell the difference. Wrothe knew how lonely the empty years left him. She had taken advantage of his weakness, made him love her. At first, he welcomed her presence. It was nice to once again have a connection to someone he believed cared about him. He knew better now when he was truly trapped.

"Why do you give so much of yourself to things you can lose?" Wrothe used the warm tones of Evangeline's voice. A short-bladed knife appeared in her hand.

"This isn't fair." A new sense of fear leapt into his throat. "All I wanted was for you to see reason, to see how your anger destroyed any chance of reaching your goal."

"I don't ask you to think. I ask you to do, and yet you challenge me." She set the blade against the pale flesh of her wrist and cut a long thin stripe.

Ternan reached out to stop her. She fixed him in her gaze, and her influence poured over him once more. This time, instead of desire, frozen terror built in the base of his spine, preventing him from touching her.

"Tomorrow evening. Will you be strong enough by then?" Her voice had gone as cold as his terror. Coming from Evangeline's body, it shook him.

"It's too many."

She lifted the blade and brought it down once more, this time across the meat of her forearm.

"Stop, please!" He reached out, desperate to take the knife away, to stop up the flow of blood.

"Will you be ready?" She held the blade to her throat.

The sight snapped his mind. He couldn't watch any more. "Three, I need at least three days for what you plan to do. Just stop."

"That's better." The blade disappeared. The cuts shrank into themselves. Wrothe eased back into her usual form. "Rest. I'll come for you."

The dull greys and blacks of the dreamspace faded into the familiar furnishings of Ternan's private office as Wrothe unbound him from the unnatural space. After being with her, the dark shadows gathering around his desk and the stacks of books perched like gargoyles on the edges of his many shelves were too much. He threw back the heavy curtains covering the lone window, swung back the creaking shutters, and let the crisp cold air hiding behind them swirl into the room.

CHAPTER THREE

*I*n the small study, Jarand gripped the edge of the desk that filled half the room as he waited for Bremin and Lady Alystra. The shock of the attack had faded, leaving him weary, hurting, and with so many questions. He'd promised Katira that Amul Dun was safe. In all his years of service as Guardian, he'd never heard of anything dangerous breaking through the wards and glyphs. Someone had failed in their duty, and he wouldn't rest until he found out who.

Lady Alystra eyed him cautiously as she entered, as if measuring what she'd heard against how he appeared. She arranged the folds of her deep grey woolen dress and sat straight backed in the padded armchair. Even without her formal robes and emblems, she radiated firm control.

Bremin circled behind her, preferring to stand. He gestured to the remaining chair, which Jarand took gratefully. Killing off the hound had strained his back injury from Khanrosh. The nerves running down his leg protested his every movement loudly.

"You're upset," Lady Alystra stated simply.

Jarand's hand gripped tighter around his cane, fighting the urge to become angry. It would be so easy. "I have every right to be. Amul Dun was the last safe place. Nothing should have gotten in here. Not even shadow creatures. Something is horribly wrong."

"Be assured that this has taken us by surprise. Until today our defenses have worked perfectly." Lady Alystra didn't sound surprised in the least. But her shoulders sat high and tight and she couldn't keep her fingertips still. She was truly bothered.

Bremin set a hand on her shoulder, which she covered with her own. "Did you get a chance to investigate the hallway?" he asked.

Jarand shook his head. "Only to be sure they were gone. My first concern was Katira. I sought you out as soon as she was safe."

"So you can tell us nothing of where they might have come from or how they got in." Bremin furrowed his brow. "I'm surprised. I'd have thought figuring that out would be of greater importance to you."

"It's not too late. The moment we finish here I can perform a more thorough examination. If power was used, the residue will still be there." The anger Jarand wanted to keep under wraps grew more insistent. His daughter could have been killed, and here they were chiding him on an oversight? Ridiculous. "I took the best course of action. Preserving life comes first."

Lady Alystra's head lowered a fraction. "You've changed. You know that, right? Raising Katira has softened your hard edges. Before, you would have done all in your power to ensure the safety of Amul Dun first. Tactically, it would have made more sense. A breach within these walls puts everyone who lives here at risk."

"Don't." A trickle of rage leaked into Jarand's voice. "Don't you dare. I wasn't going to let her die so I could examine a hallway. Not after everything we've been through. Not after Mirelle." Speaking her name stopped him short. He hadn't said it aloud since her passing for fear it wouldn't feel the same. He was right, it didn't.

"Easy, Jarand," Bremin said, always the peacemaker. "No one is accusing you of anything. You suffered a significant loss. We can't expect you to come away from that unchanged. Perhaps we've asked too much of you these past weeks. Perhaps you need more time before you take up your former responsibilities in the tower. We can grant you that, if you need it."

There was the friend that Jarand needed. Caring, yet straight to the point. In seconds, Bremin managed to give Jarand space to think, acknowledged his struggles, and offered a solution. Even then, the gentle offer felt like a slap. It was Bremin's way of telling Jarand that he agreed with Lady Alystra. He'd failed to ensure Amul Dun's safety.

The thought galvanized him. He needed to prove them wrong. Not only for the safety of the tower, but to prove to himself that he was still worthy of the respect his title granted him.

"That's not necessary." Focusing on what needed to be done pushed the raw emotion aside. He would deal with those feelings later. For now, he had work to do. "I'll mobilize a unit of the Guardians. They can investigate the protections here and in the other halls and ensure they are still in place and adequate. They need to know about this incident anyway.

Should something else break through, I'd prefer them to be ready."

Lady Alystra drew herself up as if hefting the weight of responsibility back onto her shoulders. "I agree, the protections must be inspected. However, for now I ask for you to keep this quiet until we know more. The stability of Amul Dun is still too delicate in the aftermath of Khanrosh. We can't jeopardize our image further with something that might be an isolated event. The other three Stonebearer Towers believe Amul Dun is the seat of our strength. They are loyal to us because of it. If they learn how weak we are, we risk losing them."

Jarand leaned heavily into his hands, his elbows resting on his knees. "But what if this isn't an isolated event? What if Khanrosh was just the beginning?" His shoulders sank at the thought.

"Your concerns are noted, General. For now, you will lead a private investigation here and see where we stand. I need someone I can trust who knows what failure looks like." She released Bremin's hand and leaned forward. "I can trust you, can't I?"

Jarand looked up and his gaze met hers. Despite her outward calm and her stern rebuke, fear hid in her eyes.

"Of course, my lady." He pressed his fist to his heart in a salute. "I'll see it done."

Bremin and the High Lady saw themselves out. The second they were gone, Jarand let his head fall into his hands as the enormity of his task dawned on him. Should he fail to find how the hounds got in, should he miss something, the whole tower would be at risk. Lady Alystra trusted him. He prayed that was the right choice.

CHAPTER FOUR

*K*atira rested her head against one of the two carved pillars flanking the library doors. When she'd first set out to find Isben, the exhaustion caused by the attack felt no worse than what she'd had after a bad night's sleep. However, after walking half the length of the tower, all she could think about was a comfortable chair.

It didn't matter. In a few minutes, she'd be deep inside the quiet of the library's tall bookcases, sheltered nooks, and Isben's arms. Being with him brought a peace she couldn't find anywhere else. With Master Regulus's death, he would be hollow and aching. If she could do anything to bring him some relief, she would.

She leaned her whole weight against the carved panels of the library door before they sighed open and admitted her into its depths. Overhead, windows circled around the rim of the vaulted ceiling sending down bright shafts of light where dust motes danced.

Down the center aisle of the library, a series of tables slumbered, some blanketed in papers, pens, and books, some bare and exposed. Between each sleeping table clumped small clusters of comfortable chairs hunching around power-fueled braziers. Open flame had been banished from the library centuries ago after an abandoned candle had ignited an entire history of books.

Katira wormed her way back through studies of the Roshiian languages, passing the histories of the ruling families of Fordzala, until she reached Master Regulus's personal alcove hidden behind the collection of histories of Amul Dun. Here, the southern facing windows caught the warmth of the sun in the afternoon and made it the perfect place to hide with a book.

Sure enough, Isben's woolen coat lay wadded up on one of the nearby chairs. Deep inside the alcove, Isben rested his head in the crook of his arm and, just like the tables, was deeply asleep. Sunlight sparkled in his golden hair and made his angular jawline seem too severe for his face.

Beneath his arm, several pages of Master Regulus's notes were trapped and in danger of being drooled on. The rest of the pages perched in a messy pile near the edge of the table, too close to his sleeping elbow for comfort. One startled awakening and they'd be knocked to the floor.

She scooted herself onto the bench next to him, being careful not to make a sound. Sleep blunted the sharp edges of loss, and he'd be feeling that loss keenly. With care, she rescued the pages from under his arm and scooted the pile into a safer place. When he didn't wake, she selected the page he'd been looking at and began to read.

Master Regulus's words scrawled in all directions. Katira squinted to make out what it said. Ever since they returned to Amul Dun, the man had written like a man possessed. He started at first light and pushed through to evening when sleep cast its spell on him. Most nights, Isben practically had to carry the man to bed.

From what Katira had seen, the pages spoke of what happened at Khanrosh, and Master Regulus's dealings with Wrothe. Master Regulus was a historian, and it made sense that he would try to make peace with himself by writing about what he had seen. As for Katira, it was still too soon to relive that experience. She set the page down.

Isben's hand flexed as he woke. He rubbed at his face and stretched before blinking his eyes. Sleeping on his arm left a series of folds from his sleeve imprinted on his cheek.

He smiled when he saw her. "Sorry, must have nodded off. How long have you been here?"

"Not long. I wanted to check on you. You doing okay?"

He ran a hand through his hair, smoothing down the side where it stuck up. "Didn't know what to do with myself. I figured I'd see if I could make any sense of what he was so desperate to write."

Katira handed him the page she'd taken and he returned it to the stack.

"And?"

"I didn't get very far. Most of this was written in a terrible rush. I did learn that for all of these weeks, he was hiding how much Wrothe hurt him, I guess to spare me the worry. The fool knew he was dying all along, but he had to finish this first." He sniffed and straightened the papers in the stack, reverently aligning the edges. "Guilt ate him up. He blames himself for everything that went wrong at Khanrosh and with Wrothe. I can only hope writing this helped him make some sense of it."

"Do you think he found some peace, in the end?" Katira

inched her hand along the edge of the table to be closer to his, an open invitation should he want something to hold on to. Whether he acted like it or not, the redness around his eyes told her how he was hurting.

"I'd like to think so." Isben's hand curled into a fist. "Still would have liked him to have told me what was really going on. We could have done something for him. Saved him, maybe."

Katira took his hand and coaxed it around hers. "He lived long enough. Had he wanted to be saved, he would have done it. He didn't do this to hurt you."

"He should have explained that to me." Isben touched his apprentice stone before letting his free hand fall into his lap. "It would have made a difference."

"You still haven't told me how you are doing." She traced circles on the back of his hand. "You okay?"

"It's weird. I keep thinking I'll see him here writing when I turn my head." He shifted his gaze to the now empty workspace. "He's gone, but it's like I can't believe it yet."

"I know how you feel. Sometimes, I catch myself looking for Mamar when I have a question. Part of me won't let go of her."

Isben nodded and leaned into the padded backrest of the bench with a sigh. Warm afternoon sunlight crawled across the table touching the pages and their intertwined hands. The world would keep spinning, regardless of what happened. People would come and go in their lives. People would die. All they could hold onto was that moment and being together.

Katira considered telling him what had happened with the hounds. He'd find out eventually, and if he didn't hear it from her, he'd be upset. But was it worth disrupting this small moment of quiet? He was already dealing with so much, it didn't seem fair to shift the focus to herself and make him worry.

At the same time, it frustrated him that Master Regulus had hidden the truth. Just as she gathered up the courage to tell him, Isben broke the quiet with his own question. "How about your father? Yesterday had to have been hard for him, too. He and Master Regulus were close."

The moment vanished. She knew Isben would ask about Papan. In his mind, he was this legendary figure straight from the stories Isben loved so much.

All it meant for her was that her father was that much harder to talk to. Despite his assurances, the healer in her felt something was wrong. Mamar's death had shattered something inside him. But instead of searching out the sharp broken pieces to put back together, he swept them into a hidden place. Master Regulus's death tossed those pieces out in the open again.

Perhaps that darkness she'd seen in him was his attempt to pull those pieces together again? It didn't feel right.

"He'd want me to tell everyone that he's doing okay. Deep down, I don't think he is. Even before yesterday he was struggling. He struggles to sleep. He barely eats." She took much needed comfort in the warmth of Isben's hand around hers. "I don't know what to do. I'm worried about him."

"Have you told anyone?"

"He wouldn't want me to. He's always been one to lick his wounds in private. Besides, who would I tell?" Helplessness poked at her insides.

"He has friends here. People who have been through this. They can help." He turned to face her. "You can't do this alone. It's too much. It's okay to ask for help."

Katira drew up a mental list of everyone at Amul Dun

who she could talk to, and it was distressingly short. Cassim rose quickly to the top, and as a healer he might have better insights than most about healing from grief. Then, there was his companion Issa, who Katira hadn't learned until later was the Captain of Lady Alystra's personal guard. Both she and Cassim had been with Papan during the war years.

Another name added itself to the list. Bremin. Of course. She'd seen how Papan greeted him when he showed up in Namragan those months ago. They acted more like long-lost brothers than friends. Talking to him felt right, except for one small thing. Here at Amul Dun he served as Master Advisor, the standing second in command to Lady Alystra herself. It was a position of both power and visibility. As such, it earned him more respect than she'd seen given to Papan as General. Surely he'd be too busy with his other duties to take the time to talk to her.

Isben sat quietly as she thought, but her silence finally got the best of him. "I'd give anything to know what you're thinking about right now."

"It's just that you're right." A bitter laugh escaped. "Why are you always right?" She leaned her head against his shoulder. "I should have done this weeks ago. I feel so stupid."

"Don't say that. You were doing what you thought was best. You know your father better than most, you know how he prefers things. But you also know when something's not working. If Master Regulus was still around, I'd suggest talking to him." He furrowed his forehead and turned his attention back to the stack of notes. "Wait. I think Master Regulus wrote a few things in here intended for your father. Now is as good a time as any for him to read them. He might find something in there that is helpful."

Katira scooted the pages closer, trying to read the scrawled text once more. If these notes had an explanation, perhaps something that justified how Master Regulus's actions lead to Wrothe's release from her prison, they might help Papan understand the truth behind what had happened. It might relieve some of the guilt she knew he carried.

"Do you think he could? I mean, these are your master's private papers. Does that go against his wishes?"

Isben shook his head. "He was a Seeker. He thrived on information. These notes were meant to be shared. I only wish that he'd given me better instruction on what he wanted me to do with them now that they're finished. Maybe your father could help with that. He's bound to know better than I do."

He plucked a spool of string from one of his pockets and tied the pages into a tidy packet. "You should still talk to someone, besides me, of course. Promise me you will?"

"I will, I promise." She hugged the pages to her chest as she stood to leave the table. "What about you? Will you be okay if I go for a while?"

The corners of his eyes pinched with a sadness he didn't try to hide. In the next few days the ache of his grief would blossom like a bruise. Katira didn't want to leave him, not when the worst of it was yet to come.

"I feel better now that those are being taken care of." He waved her off when he noticed how she hesitated. "Go, I'm fine."

Katira hurried from the library. The sooner she could convince Papan to read the pages, the better.

Katira leaned in close to hers and Papan's apartment door and listened for the quiet murmurs of voices. Should he be in a meeting, she didn't want to disturb him.

Hearing nothing, she opened the door and leaned in. No one sat at the table near the window in the sitting room, no voices came from the small study. A creak came from the room they'd repurposed into her bedroom.

Inside, Papan sat on the narrow bed. In his lap he held one of Mamar's many journals. In the whole tower, this was the place her presence rang the loudest. The room used to be Mamar's private study and still held many of her things.

Katira sat on the bed next to him and set the pages down on the edge of the cluttered bedside table. "I didn't expect to find you in here. Everything okay?" It felt like a stupid question.

He shifted on the bed, as if he meant to leave. "I was looking for something, thought it might be in here. Now that you're back, you probably want me out of here."

Katira shook her head. "It's okay. This was Mamar's space long before I came, it will always be hers." She glanced up at the shelves holding everything from books and journals, to jars of powders with tidy labels in Mamar's familiar hand. "I like it this way. Stay as long as you need."

He settled back onto the bed. "Where did you get off to? I didn't expect you to leave so soon after what happened."

"I needed to visit Isben. He's all alone now."

"That was kind of you." He patted her knee. "But stupid. The halls hadn't been checked. More of those things might have broken through. You should have stayed, or at least waited for me to take you."

"But I thought..." She trailed off, realizing she hadn't thought about it at all. The possibility of there being more of those monsters left her cold. She hugged her arms around herself gingerly. "Is the tower safe now?"

"I thought I knew." He rubbed at the back of his neck. "Nothing should have gotten through, but when I checked I found things that I couldn't explain. I'd prefer you not to be alone until we clear this up. Isben too, if he can help it."

He motioned to the bundle of pages. "What do you have there?"

She lifted the bundle on her lap and angled it so he could see. "Something I think you need to read."

Papan's breath caught in his throat and he leaned closer. "Are those what I think they are?" He ran a finger across a few lines of text as he read, not waiting for her answer. "I thought for sure the Seekers in the library would have taken these already. How did you get your hands on them?"

"Isben had them. Master Regulus forgot to tell him what to do with them. Isben thinks you should read them and I agree. Of everyone here at Amul Dun, Master Regulus meant for you to see them. I'm sure of it."

Papan let out a breath and withdrew his hand, balling it into his lap with the journal he'd been holding. "It's funny what people choose to leave behind, isn't it? It's worse with Stonebearers. We live so long that sometimes we forget that someday we'll be gone. Regulus was a rare one. He had weeks knowing he wouldn't make it, and what did he choose to do with that time? He wrote a book."

"Well, what would you do if you knew you were going to die?" Katira asked, suddenly curious.

"Never thought about it." He tapped the pages thought-fully. "I suppose I'd try to write letters to the people I loved. Something for them to remember me by, I guess. No, that doesn't seem right. I'd try to spend as much time with them as I could. Create one last good memory."

She set the pages in his lap. "You and Master Regulus were close. This feels like it's his letter to you. Will you read it?"

"Of course. But not right away. I need some time before I think I can face this." He gave the pages back. "Could you put these on the table for me?"

The memory of those branching dark roots lacing through him flashed through her mind again. It wasn't like him to put aside things that might be important. The sooner she could talk to someone the better.

CHAPTER FIVE

When Papan offered for her to accompany him to the High Lady's office, Katira jumped at the chance. Where the High Lady was, Bremin would be also. Now all she needed was an excuse to talk to him in private.

After spending all day in quiet, the noise and constant flow of people in and out of the immense main hall jarred Katira's senses. A tall guardian with a precisely trimmed dark beard saluted Papan as they crossed through the archway and into the hall. The fading light of the afternoon caught on his gleaming breastplate and royal blue gambeson.

Another pair of Guardians flanked the hallway leading to Lady Alystra's office and private quarters. Katira tried to remember if she'd seen this many posted Guardians around the tower before, or if she was only noticing them for the first time because of what happened. They too gave Papan a sharp salute.

As they drew closer to crossing the threshold into the next hallway, Katira spotted Isben's familiar blond curls.

She tugged on Papan's elbow. "Is it alright if I go talk to Isben?"

Papan's eyes darted to where she saw Isben exiting the hallway that led to the southern wing. He smiled. "Yes, as long as you promise to stay here until I finish. I won't be long."

"Thank you." She gave a small formal curtsy as he'd taught her and made her way across the wide floor. Isben carried a tray laden with a large gleaming tea service. When he spotted her, he turned her way, being careful not to upset any of the delicate porcelain cups.

He waited to speak until they were nearly shoulder-to-shoulder. "Well? Did you give him the pages? What did he say?"

"Forget that for a moment." She adjusted one of the crooked teacups. "Why on earth are you delivering tea? I thought they'd give you a break for a few days."

"One of the library Seekers found me, insisted I get back to work." He adjusted his grip on the tray, causing the cups to rattle against each other. "I didn't have the heart to explain who I was." Isben's chin quivered briefly. "I think I finally understand why you kept working through your first few weeks. It helps you forget and makes it easier to pretend things are normal. That's why you did it, isn't it?"

Katira pushed down the knot of emotion. "I suppose so. Although I doubt I realized it at the time."

"Does it get any better?"

She reached up and straightened where the edge of his light grey apprentice tunic had folded in. "With time it's easier. I promise."

Isben looked up, as if searching the hall for someone. "You came down here with the General. Did he read some of the pages?"

"He refused. It's so unlike him. I thought he'd stop everything to see what was in there. I'll keep trying, I promise."

Isben shifted his hands on the tray once more. "What about the other thing?"

"What other thing?" Katira asked.

Someone cleared their throat behind them, making her jump.

"I hope I'm not disturbing something important." Bremin spoke in a quiet, gravelly voice Katira always found soothing. "I can come back another time."

Instead of the ceremonial robes many other Stonebearers favored while in the tower, he sported a simple well-made linen shirt with a subtle purple collar over dark close-fitted trousers.

"No, sir." Isben said, giving a respectful bow of his head and lifting the tray as an explanation. "In fact, I best get going." He turned on his heel and made his way across the wide hall.

"He's a funny one. Are you two still spending time with each other?" Bremin stepped into the spot where Isben had been standing and clasped his hands behind his back. "I wanted to see how you were after what happened. You'd left before I had a chance to talk to you."

Katira felt her cheeks go pink. While he didn't intend it, he poked at the hornet's nest of not one, but two sensitive subjects. Her insides filled with an uncomfortable buzzing. Yes, she liked Isben, but that was none of his business. And yes, she'd been foolish to go out alone. "You didn't come to talk to me about boys. Did you?"

"There's that fire of yours. With all that's happened, I was worried we might have lost it." He studied her with eyes she knew missed nothing.

Katira suppressed a groan. "Are you always this insufferable?"

"Alystra would say so." Bremin chuckled to himself. "It's probably why she likes sending me away to gather information for her as often as she does." He gave her another measured look and the mirth faded back to concern.

She'd promised Isben. The moment to ask if they could talk presented itself to her, but she still had to be brave enough to take it. Her fist knotted itself in the fabric of her skirt. Why was this so hard?

"I was wondering if I could have a moment of your time, in private."

The corner of his mouth tugged into a smile. "Certainly. I have a few questions for you as well. Come with me." Bremin cocked his head toward the hallway where Papan had gone. "We'll use my private study."

Katira followed him down the lushly carpeted hall to a doorway she hadn't noticed before. The small study suited him. Simple, elegant, understated. And cold. The room's fireplace appeared to not have been used for years. She shivered and regretted not bringing a shawl.

"I'm not in here much. Sorry about the chill." He tossed a handful of kindling on the grate and took a flint to it. "Have a seat." Bremin gestured to one of a pair of comfortable armchairs facing the fire.

Tongues of flame licked up around the dry wood and soon warmth reached out into the room. He leaned a few more sticks of wood over the kindling before joining her in the other armchair. Katira fumbled with her fingers, lacing and unlacing them in her lap, unsure of how to start.

Bremin broke the silence. Direct as always. "How is he?"

The question caught her off guard. She had expected him

to make more small talk until she was ready to tell him. Diving right in like this made a brand-new knot tie itself in her throat. She swallowed hard past the lump, but it refused to budge.

"That bad, then." Bremin's forehead knotted as he watched her carefully. "It's okay to be upset, you don't need to hide it from me."

Even with Bremin's permission, Katira absolutely did not want to cry. "I'm worried. I thought for sure I'd see him start to improve by now." She took a deep breath and blew it out. "He's hiding it too well when he's around the other people here, but he can't hide it from me." Her breath shuddered in her chest.

"It's okay. You're safe to say what you need to here. Let it out." He leaned closer to her, with his elbows on his knees. "Knowing you, you've probably been trying to carry this weight all by yourself for far too long."

Hearing those words broke the dam holding back all the pain she had tried to hide for the past weeks. On top of all the grief of losing Mamar, worrying about Papan was too much. Her shoulders shook, and she let the sobs come. Bremin set a hand on her knee, letting her know she wasn't alone. That single point of contact anchored her into the present and gave her something real to hold onto.

It had simply been too long. For weeks she'd been gathering up the hurt she couldn't show around Papan. It wasn't healthy, she knew that, but it worked. Her pain had lessened over the passing weeks. She'd assumed Papan's was doing the same. However, when she got that glimpse of his mind, when she saw that darkness, it scared her.

Her hand brushed against the elaborate leather knots of the bracelet on her wrist. Each precise knot and familiar braid bumped under her fingers. The tears slowed and stopped.

Elan had given her the bracelet on their last perfect night in Namragan. The Harvest Festival was in full swing around them with the lanterns lit and the village square overflowing with music and food and people laughing. She traced one strand with a finger. The bracelet represented another loss, another reason to grieve.

Bremin used it to artfully steer the conversation to safe ground, giving Katira a chance to regain her composure. "Elan's a good lad. Did he tell you that we spent several days together chasing your trail when Surasio had you?" He rubbed his chin. "Took all I had to keep him from running himself to total exhaustion. He couldn't stop worrying about you."

A flutter of mixed emotions filled Katira thinking of Elan. The love they had shared was filled with peaks and valleys, but it was theirs. Sending him home was one of the hardest things she had ever had to do.

"I'm glad you had the chance to meet him. He was good to me." She shifted her gaze out the window of the small office looking out over the statue-lined courtyard. "I hope he finds someone who makes him happy."

"You two left on good terms, then?"

"Yes. I suppose so." She touched the locket at her throat where she kept his picture and wondered if Elan still wore its twin. It was her last gift to him before sending him home.

With her calm restored, Katira was ready to face talking about Papan again. "Is there anything you can do to help my father?"

"Grieving is tricky business. It's important both you and Jarand get the help you need. I've seen other Stonebearers fade like this after losing their companions." He touched the stone hanging from a fine chain around his neck. "We must respect his need to grieve. But if the process stalls, if he falls in too deep, which he might have, we must help him find his way back again." He pressed his lips together in thought. "Allow me to discuss a few ideas with Alystra. I'll get back to you with what we come up with."

Katira wiped at the tears on her face with the edge of her sleeve. Bremin had voiced her worst fear and was already thinking of ways to help. It was more than she could have asked for. "Thank you." The simple words didn't feel adequate enough to express her gratitude.

"No need to thank me. I should have sought you out days ago." He tugged his pants straight and stood from his chair. "Alystra prefers me to wait until people ask for help. She's right. If people aren't ready, my meddling tends to cause nothing but irritation. I'm glad you didn't wait any longer." He offered her a hand. "We'll talk again, soon. Until then, take care of yourself."

"I will, I promise." Knowing she had someone on her side, someone she could trust, lifted a heavy weight from off her back and she stood taller. Both she and Papan would get through this, she would make sure of it.

Bremin escorted Katira back out into the carpeted hall just as Papan exited through the set of larger doors where he had met with Lady Alystra.

Behind him, Issa shut the door harder than necessary and followed him as he made his way down the hall. Her brilliant blue doublet was thickly quilted and stiff, reminding Katira of the armor she favored. At her side, the fastenings of her sword clicked a rapid staccato against the metal studs in her belt.

Whatever they'd talked about in there must have been serious. The scowl on Issa's face could summon a lightning storm.

Katira joined them as they walked, not daring to ask how anything went. At times like these, it was best to wait until Papan chose to talk.

Issa held her silence until they were well away from the beehive of activity buzzing around the High Lady's office. When she did, her words were strained and quiet. "No one, including Lady Alystra, has been able to tell me anything useful." Her gaze flicked to Katira. "I need to know what happened."

"I've told you everything I gathered from my investigation." Papan paused as someone walked past. "If you need to know more, Katira might have a few additional insights. She was there."

Katira stopped midstep. He couldn't honestly want her to relive that nightmare. Not here, not out in the open.

"It's okay." Papan pivoted back to face her. "She only needs a few details. Answer as best you can."

Issa locked her arms behind her back and waited for Katira to catch up. "We'll start with an easy one. Where were you when you first saw them?"

Katira noticed how Issa carefully avoided mention of the hounds. If the warrior woman was exercising caution, she would as well. "The second-floor northern corridor, halfway down the hall."

"Good." Issa nodded her approval. "How many were there?"

"Two." The knot of fear melted a touch as Katira talked.

"Really?" Issa's eyes widened a fraction. "From all this talk, I might have guessed more. Jarand said your power protected you, but you haven't started your formal training. Has it done that before?"

"Not that I know of." Katira touched the edge of the bandage. She hadn't been able to make much sense of that part either. "It took control. I don't remember much after that."

Issa's interest transformed into surprise. She exchanged a look with Papan. "Did you know this?"

"Yes. Saw the last moment of her using it before her power retreated. I'm not sure what it means."

Issa stopped on the landing of the second-floor corridor. "It's unusual, that's all. You best keep an eye on her."

"Wait, what is it?" Katira hated when people tried to hide information from her. Especially when it was about something she was involved in. Papan had promised to never do it again. She rounded on him. "What's unusual?"

He gripped the railing at the top of the stairs, needing time to catch his breath. "It's rare for the Khandashii to act on its own, but not unheard of. It might mean we need to train you differently. We'll see."

It wasn't a great answer, but it was better than nothing. At least he was trying. Issa, on the other hand, turned her attention to the corridor.

"Could you see where the hounds came from?" She touched the wall next to her. "Did they round the corner, or did they come out from somewhere else? Not sure what it would look like, might not have even been visible."

This far away from the bustle of the main hall and adjoining corridors meant less people to worry about. They could speak freely.

Katira walked down the corridor to the spot where she was scrubbing the floor. The bucket of water she had flung at the hound was still lying on its side. She tried to remember any detail that might help. "I heard them first. Sounded like they were by the door to Papan's apartment. When I looked up, no one was there. Then I saw the shadows shift." She hugged her arms closer around her, trying to be brave and push through the surge of fear making her hands shake. "I ran. I didn't make it far." She stopped at the point where she had fallen. Issa followed quietly behind.

"I should have come faster. Been here when it happened." Papan leaned his shoulder against the corner of the alcove that contained the door leading to their quarters. "If it wasn't for this stupid injury, I would have."

"This is no time to feel sorry for yourself, Jarand." The lines on Issa's arms glowed to life as she touched the wall. "You still saved her. Focus your energy on figuring out how they got in." A lacy net extended from her fingers and chased down the exposed stone of the hallway.

Katira stepped closer. She'd never seen power used like this. Where the net touched, the glyphs embedded into the walls awoke and glowed like a starry sky. She reached out her hand to touch it.

"You don't want to do that." Issa warned. "It stings something fierce."

Katira yanked her hand away and stepped closer to where Papan inspected the glyphs.

"Katira, is there anything else you can remember? Even the smallest detail might help," Issa asked as she walked the length of the wall.

"No. I wish there was. If anything comes to me, I'll make sure you or Papan knows."

Issa didn't look up from one particular spot. "Good girl." She pointed something out to Jarand. "There is only a touch of residue here. It might be from what *she* did. I'm not familiar with her power enough to be sure. Some of these glyphs could use with strengthening. But——" She straightened and shrugged her shoulders "I can't pin down much else. It's like you said in your report, something about it feels off." She scanned the tile, eyebrows furrowed. "What was done with the bodies?"

"Nothing." Papan poked at the floor with his cane. "When I returned to inspect the hall the first time, all traces of them, even down to the bloodstains, had vanished."

"Don't you think that strange? Things don't just disappear." Issa bent to inspect the floor more closely.

"They appeared from nowhere. I'm not ruling anything out at this point." Papan half-sat on one of the deep window casings. "Now that you've seen it, what do you think? Is this worth worrying about or not?"

The hard edge to his voice told Katira that he'd already decided.

He continued, "Convincing Lady Alystra to enlist the cooperation of the Order of Guardians is the only way we'll have enough manpower to watch over this whole place."

Issa relaxed her normally broom-handle straight bearing and ran a thumb over the shining steel of her sword's hilt. "She made her position clear, and I can see why she wants to keep this secret. But I'd feel better if we erred on the side of caution. She puts herself in more danger than necessary."

"Then you agree?"

"I'll see what I can do. She can be stubborn. After six hundred years, she's earned the right to be." Issa adjusted the scabbard on her belt. "Then again, I'm pretty stubborn myself and I'm still a few decades short of three hundred."

Talk of danger, the possibility of hounds appearing anywhere, and enlisting a whole battalion of warriors to protect Amul Dun made it sound as if they were going to war. Katira was tired of feeling helpless, tired of relying on other people to fight her battles for her. She was strong. She could learn. There was no reason for her to continue on not knowing how to defend herself.

Issa turned to leave and Papan headed back toward their quarters. Now was as good a time to ask as any.

"Teach me to fight," Katira blurted out before she talked herself out of it.

"What?" Both Papan and Issa froze.

She pressed her hands at her sides. "This power inside me might not be enough should they come for me again. I need to feel safe."

Papan answered first. "I'll have a guard assigned to you when I'm not around. You'll never be alone. Would that be enough?"

Katira glared at him. "You know that's not what I meant."

"It will take years before you've learned enough to defend yourself properly." His hand tightened around the head of the cane. "Teaching you now will only make you feel like you can take them on, instead of getting away where you'll be safe. A false sense of confidence could get you killed. I've seen it before."

Katira squared her shoulders, not willing to back down, not about this. "Then I better get started so I can develop some real confidence. Regardless of what I know, there will come a time where I have to face these things again. Teaching me will give me a chance. That's all I ask."

"I agree with her," Issa interjected. "She needs to learn how to defend herself, and if my suspicions are correct, the next few years might be rough ones. With proper training, she'll know her limits. She'll learn when she should stand and fight and when she should run. As a woman, it's even more important she learn that."

"Why did I know you'd take her side?" Papan sighed and rubbed at his forehead.

Issa shrugged. "I like her. She reminds me of myself."

"Fine." He turned and took hold of Katira by her shoulders. "I expect you to work hard and follow directions." His gaze flicked toward Issa before he continued. "And until I say otherwise, you will not try to take down one of these creatures alone. You will run. Understood?"

Katira's heart leaped up in her chest. She hadn't realized how much she wanted this and now it was being granted. She wrapped her arms around him. "Thank you. I won't disappoint you. I promise."

"I'll hold you to that." He returned the hug and patted her back before letting her go.

"If I may," Issa started, a cheeky grin crinkling one side of her face. "I'd like to be her teacher."

"Is it because you don't feel I can in my condition?"

She eyed his cane. "Do you wish me to be honest with you?"

"Never stopped you before."

"Yes, among other things." She took a deep breath and puffed it out. Her hands went to her hips. "You need to rebuild the strength and stamina that this last injury robbed from you. Your time would be better spent working in the training yard with one of our brothers. Also, women must fight differently than men, and you can't teach her that. I can."

"Fair enough. When do you want to start?" he asked.

The sudden turn in events made the Katira's thoughts spin and tumble. Not only was she going to train, but Issa, the head of Lady Alystra's personal guard, wanted to be her teacher.

Issa glanced back down the hall. "With things the way they are, as soon as possible."

CHAPTER SIX

The austere granite walls and bare slab floors of the Guardians' wing of Amul Dun brought back memories of a time when life was so much simpler. Jarand breathed in the smell of damp stone and hardworking bodies, letting the scent transport him back to his years when he served as a soldier and nothing more.

Returning now, so much older, after so many years, brought with it its own pang of nostalgia. He had changed since being here last. The cane clutched in his hand said as much. The attack earlier shook him far more than he let on to the High Lady, to Bremin, and to Katira. He was there, mere strides away, and because of his weakness Katira suffered.

Amul Dun Guardians outfitted in blue gambesons gave crisp salutes as he passed. He turned the corner and found the Captain's office open. Captain Edmont, a grizzled old campaigner, braced himself on his fists and leaned over his desk. Two men stood stiffly attention in front of him.

"I will not tolerate this kind of foolishness in my halls. Amul Dun Guardians do not pull pranks."

"Yes, sir," they replied in unison.

"You'll be spending the remainder of the week working in the laundry, and if that stain in my shirt doesn't come out, you both owe me a new one."

"Yes, sir."

"Now go, before I change my mind."

The two saluted and marched from the office.

Jarand tapped on the door frame with the head of his cane. "Captain Edmont, sir. Is this a bad time?"

The captain's craggy scarred face lit up. "Jarand, my boy! I was hoping you'd come visit." He burst out from the cramped space behind the desk and pulled Jarand into a back-slapping hug. "With all the chaos of this last month, I've been worried about you. Come, sit." He indicated a chair and poured them both a small glass of brandy.

"It's good to see you too." Jarand settled into the chair with a grimace. "Trouble in the ranks?"

"They thought it funny to balance an inkwell over my doorframe. Ruined my favorite shirt. I tell you, they don't make shirts like I like anymore. Last I checked, they don't even use the same technique."

"A lot can change in a century. We know that better than most. How are you these days?"

"Fit and fighting order." Captain Edmont slapped the taut muscles of his stomach. "Have a few new scars since the last time we talked. But it seems we all do. Why the cane?"

"You know how we used to say how a good healer can fix anything? I think I found the limit. I took a blade in Fortzala, and it damaged the nerves in my back. Firen and Cassim made it so I could walk again, but it hasn't been the same."

"That's a bloody shame, it is." He took a sip from his glass. "Do they say it might improve with time?"

"They want to be cautious with what they promise. Don't want to give me false hope." He set the cane behind the chair. There were other more important things he needed to talk about.

"Fools. All hope is false hope until proven wrong. They of all people should know that. It's better to live believing things will get better than otherwise. Nothing improves unless someone works for it."

This was the Captain that Jarand remembered, full of his own special brand of hard-earned abrasive wisdom. Jarand sipped from his own glass. "It's been too long since we've talked. I've missed this."

Captain Edmont looked into his brandy, suddenly somber. "I heard about Mirelle. So sorry. She was a good woman. She was good for you."

The dark root of grief deep within Jarand twisted. He tightened his hold around the glass. "We all have to go sometime."

"That's a trite statement, and you know it." Captain Edmont sat up and slapped the desk. "It wasn't her time. She was cut down in her prime. Anyone who tries to comfort you otherwise discredits her life. It's all right to be angry and upset about it, as long as you focus your anger into something productive."

The Captain's words struck Jarand hard. No one had been brave enough to put their foot down and speak their mind. Jarand was deeply grateful for it. This was what he'd been wanting someone to tell him; he just hadn't realized it. She had been murdered. It wasn't her time. Her death wasn't part of some bigger plan. It was a tragedy to lose such a bright star, especially when the night was now becoming the darkest.

"I can't tell you how good it is to hear you say that. I'm tired of well-wishers and people trying to comfort me. I need to surround myself with more people like you. Might be enough to whip me out of this fog I've fallen into." Thoughts of seeing Katira pale and bleeding this morning finally snapped something inside him.

Never again.

"Let me train with your men. Reclaim some of the strength I've lost. Being here with people I trust, people who will force me to work, is exactly what I need."

Captain Edmont set down his glass and studied Jarand over his steepled fingers. "Are you sure you are ready? We won't take it easy on you. You have a reputation around here."

Reputation be damned. He needed to be strong enough to protect Katira, and he had to start somewhere. "Waiting won't help anything. I need this."

The Captain shook his head with a smile. "You've always been one to push yourself. You know you're always welcome here." His gaze shifted to the cane. "That said, I forbid you to spar with the other Guardians until I have personally deemed you ready."

"Agreed."

"When would you like to start?"

Jarand steeled himself. He was ready for this, he just needed to convince his body he could take control. It was going to hurt. "Right now."

The captain's eyes widened momentarily before he nodded. "I didn't expect anything less from you." He stood from his chair and straightened his gambeson. "Come with me to the practice yard. I'd like to observe how this injury affects your movement and strength. You remember the six forms?"

"How could I forget? They are etched on my very bones." Jarand gripped his cane and followed the captain out the door. "You had a hand in that."

CHAPTER SEVEN

The elaborate mosaic tile adorning the floors of the main halls changed from intertwining vines to a simple border running alongside the wall as Katira and Issa made their way toward the halls where the Guardians worked and trained.

Issa guided Katira through a wide archway branching off from the tiled corridor to where the floors were smooth slabs of unpolished granite.

"These are the halls of the Guardians," Issa explained as they walked. Athletic men and women dressed in everything from shining ceremonial armor to simple tunics moved purposefully about their business. Several saluted the two women as they passed. Issa acknowledged them with a respectful nod.

"Here, we organize the main defense needs of the tower, train, and maintain our weapons. The end of this hall opens into the main training yard, and to either side are the private offices of the Captain of the Guard and his lieutenants." She indicated another door to her left. "That is the men's guard-room. Trust me, you don't want to go in there."

"Why not?"

"For starters, it smells like unwashed unders and sweat. You can imagine the rest. Guardswomen have their own guard-room." She turned down a narrow hallway and to an unmarked door. "This is the women's hall." She pushed open the door to show Katira a cozy dressing room. A line of iden-tical wardrobes marched along the far wall ending where a cheerful fire burned in a corner fireplace. In front of the fire, a woman in comfortable linens curled up in one of several deeply cushioned chairs with a book. She wore her hair in a snug knot on the back of her head.

"This isn't what I expected." Katira ran a finger along the smooth curves of the carving on the edge of the wardrobe nearest her. "I didn't know what to expect. This is nice."

"Men seem to believe living an austere life somehow makes them better fighters, something about not being distracted." Issa made a face, emphasizing how much she didn't believe it. "We, as women, believe discomfort is a distraction. There will be plenty of physical discomfort, true. But in every other respect, we take care of ourselves."

She picked up a pile of neatly folded clothes from the end of the table. "Your father, Stonemother bless the man, thought he'd be helpful and picked out some training clothes for you." She held up a yellowed cotton tunic, gave it a sniff, and wrin-kled her nose. "We also insist clothes be kept clean and well-mended. None of this, 'I worked hard to wear out this shirt training, therefore I can't wash or repair it,' business." She grimaced and dropped the whole pile into a wash bin. "Let's start over. Can't have you start out smelling like a sweaty man."

Issa opened a wardrobe and pulled out a blue silk shirt

similar to the one she wore and held it up to Katira with a nod. "I've been worried about your father. How is he?"

The change in conversation jarred Katira. She wasn't prepared to talk about this. After her brief discussion with Bremin, she felt better about things, but finding peace with their grief would still be a long road for both of them. Issa selected a pair of the loose trousers and set them on Katira's shoulder.

When she didn't immediately answer, Issa continued. "You know that he and I go back ages, right?"

"Never had the chance to think about it." Katira took the clothes. "I suppose since you are both Guardians, you'd have to have spent a good deal of time together."

"You can change behind there." Issa pointed to a screen in the corner of the room. "I was his first lieutenant in the war. I reckon we saved each other's lives dozens of times. You tend to bond to your Guardian brothers." She breathed out a long sigh. "You have to. Okay, come on out, let's see you."

Katira slipped into the shirt easily enough, but the ties on the pants confused her. She gripped the cloth in her hand and scooted out from behind the screen. "Sorry, this is all quite new to me."

"Nothing to apologize for. I'll show you." Issa tugged on the loose string on the pants, hugging the band tight around Katira's middle. She then wound the loose ends around the pants and tied them with a practiced hand before folding the top of the pants over everything. "You'll get the hang of it soon enough."

Katira turned to the mirror, trying to remember how the different ties worked for the next time she'd need to put them on. Issa let the silence sit between them, heavy with her unanswered question.

The weight of the silence finally pushed Katira to speak. "Mamar meant a lot to him. When they were together, there was this special connection I could never explain. Now that connection is gone, it's like he doesn't know what to do. I keep thinking he needs more time, but maybe that's not enough."

"It's not." Issa handed Katira a pair of soft soled leather shoes. "While nothing will fill the space Mirelle left, it would be wise for him to find something for him to give his attention to. Perhaps something that she loved. Do you think he'd be interested in gardening? Mirelle kept a lovely garden when she lived here."

The thought made Katira smile. It was hard to imagine Papan bending over a garden plot and gently tending to the plants there. But at the same time, she could see him perhaps enjoying it. He did like to work with his hands.

"Maybe." she pulled on the soft leather shoes. "Even if he doesn't, I would like that. Perhaps in the spring you could show me where her garden was?"

"Of course." Issa clapped invisible dust off of her hands. "You ready to learn?"

As soon as Katira answered, Issa swept her out the door and back into the corridor. Out in the open, Katira instantly felt out of place, like a cucumber trying to copy Issa's swanlike grace. Perhaps this was the first lesson. Walk with grace. Katira straightened her back and tried her best to mirror Issa's focused gaze, her purposeful walk. She might be a cucumber, but she would be a cucumber who was trying her best.

The wide corridor opened out into a sunny courtyard larger than Namragan's town square. Katira thought before that she had a good sense of the size of Amul Dun, but she was wrong again. The light snow that had fallen the evening before had been swept into tall piles that Katira suspected might have been there gathering since the first snow all those weeks ago.

Issa stopped her at the archway separating the training yard and the corridor. "Before entering, we bow to show our respect for learning and those who have gone before us." She demonstrated by facing the yard, cupping her fist at her chest, and giving a short sharp bow. Katira followed her example, all while reminding herself of all the many reasons learning to fight was still a good idea. Two of those reasons still ached under her bandages.

Out in the yard, Katira's gaze was drawn up to the imposing walls of the tower rising up impossibly high on three sides of the training yard. Balconies looking over the yard dotted the different floors at regular intervals.

The fourth side of the yard appeared as if someone had sliced the mountain away and left a smooth slab of layered rock.

Issa pointed to one of the many circles inscribed into the smooth tiles of the yard's floor. Each circle ringed a greater circle in the center of the training yard. "While you are here, this training circle will be your world. You are to keep your focus inside it. You will do as you are told quickly and to the best of your ability, understand?" Her tone reminded Katira of the many times Papan instructed her back home. It meant she wasn't to be second-guessed or argued with. He must have learned it here.

"Yes, Issa."

"Good. Stand in the center of the circle."

A flutter of movement at the corner of the yard caught her attention. Papan took a seat on one of the benches not covered in snow. He'd said something at breakfast that morning about not wanting to miss her first lesson. She'd hoped he'd gotten too busy. The last thing she wanted was for him to try to give her pointers later.

A sharp sting bit Katira's shoulder, bringing her attention back to Issa, who had just flicked her.

"Everything outside of this circle is now outside of your world. This teaches you to focus on your opponent and nothing else. When it comes to fighting an enemy, even the tiniest distraction could get you killed." Issa folded her arms behind her back. "First, you will demonstrate what you already know. With luck, some of the General's good sense has made its way into you. Ready position."

Katira thought about how she had seen her father fight, how she had seen the boys from the village scuffle with each other. She tried to mimic their wide stance and balled her hands into fists.

Issa stepped in gracefully and punched her lightly in the stomach without warning. The touch made Katira grunt and sent her hands flying back and away. Issa swung again, this time thumping under Katira's ribs hard enough to be felt, but not enough to hurt.

"Stop." Katira stepped back. "I'm not ready."

Issa followed her effortlessly, always within striking distance. "Why not? You are here to learn how to protect yourself. Why didn't you?"

"I didn't know that's what you wanted."

"You have to think for yourself here. This is your first lesson. Let's try it again."

Katira put her hands up, eager to please Issa, eager to prove she could do this. She watched for signs Issa might throw another punch. When it came, she jerked away and swung one of her arms to stop it. It was ugly and ungraceful, but the punch didn't land.

"Good." Issa used her toe to adjust Katira's stance, making it wider and correcting the angle of her foot. "A solid base makes a solid fighter. My first strike hit you here." She pointed to Katira's middle. "How would you defend yourself?"

Katira stepped out of the way, trying to remember to keep her feet wide.

"That's one way, but it takes lots of energy to move your whole body, not to mention time. Back to center."

Katira returned to the starting point and Issa balled her fist once more.

"This time strike my arm out of the way with your forearm. Considering the state of your arms, only use a light touch today. Cassim will be annoyed if I damage his hard work. We'll work up to harder strikes later." She swung her fist, this time moving deliberately slow.

Katira swung both of her arms down and tapped Issa's strike to the side. Issa's other hand darted up and gripped her by the neck, not hard enough to harm, but alarming nonetheless. Katira grabbed for the woman's wrist, not knowing what to do.

"Never use both arms. One blocks, the other is prepared to defend again."

The training session continued. Issa would throw a punch, Katira would block, Issa would correct. Over and over this pattern repeated until Katira could barely lift her arms. The intensity and focus Issa demanded was tiring, but it felt good.

Issa gave a short bow, signaling the lesson was over. "You've done well. Learning to fight alerts the senses and brings the body to a heightened state of awareness. Before we leave, we spend a few minutes calming our minds so we may go about our day in peace." Issa knelt, knees wide, toes together and gestured her to follow.

Katira knelt on the cold stone of the practice yard and tried to match how Issa folded her toes beneath her hips. It wasn't as easy as it looked.

"Rest your hands in your lap with the tips of your fingers together, palms up. Bring your attention to the flow of your breath. Clear your mind." Issa closed her eyes and breathed deeply.

Katira closed her eyes and did the same. Her mind spun in dizzy circles trying to remember all Issa had taught. Her whole body buzzed with adrenaline. She focused on her breath, feeling the coolness of when it entered her nose and the warmth when it flowed out. With each breath, her mind and body grew quieter, more serene. The fears and worries plaguing her since she came to Amul Dun, fears for her father, for Elan, for the life she had lost, shrank down until she could barely feel them. For a wonderful moment, her whole body felt light and free.

"When you are ready, return to your body by gently moving your fingers and toes," Issa instructed.

Katira heard the rustle of silks as Issa started moving.

"Open your eyes." Issa extended her hand and pulled Katira up to standing and into a backslapping hug. "You did wonderfully today. You may exit the circle."

Katira rubbed at her arms. Even with being gentle, there would be new bruises tomorrow alongside the still tender scars. She gave the instructed short bow, fist pressed into her closed hand. "Thank you for teaching me."

Issa returned the bow, neatly and with precision. "Thank you for allowing me to teach."

∼

From his vantage point in the corner of the practice yard, Jarand observed Katira's lesson with Issa, all while trying not to look too interested. He'd already distracted her a half dozen times just by being there, earning him several unladylike scowls. Each time her focus wavered, Issa flicked her shoulder with the tips of her fingers, eliciting a tiny yelp.

Centuries before, he had stood in this very yard doing precisely the same thing. His teacher, Master Iosephe, wore discipline like armor, hugging tightly around him like a vise where it both protected and weighed him down. It was a different time, when Amul Dun had different needs. Master Iosephe met those needs, and Jarand thrived under his strict rules and demanding practices.

Where Master Iosephe was demanding, Issa showed an unexpected level of compassion and understanding. Jarand was glad for it. Katira's only real learning had been under Mirelle's gentle hand. He knew she missed it. If training with Issa helped filled some that empty space, Katira would be better for it. But fighting was entirely new to her. It would take more time than she expected before she felt she was making any sort of progress. He prayed both of their patience would last.

Katira hadn't been thrilled when he mentioned he'd come watch that morning. But he wouldn't miss this for the world. He'd made a lame excuse that he'd not pay her any attention and instead he'd work on the project he'd brought with him. It wasn't completely a lie. She'd pay better attention to Issa if she knew he wasn't staring, and he'd still see plenty of the lesson while plotting out the design for one of his unfinished blades.

He unrolled the canvas of his engraving kit over his knee and selected a marking tool along with a sharp-pointed compass. With one ear trained on Katira, he drew in the delicate shapes and precise circles that he'd engrave later on his workbench. In the comfort of the training yard and the creative task at his fingertips, he allowed his mind to drift. For a few blessed minutes, the problems slipped away. They would still be there when he finished, but he soaked in the brief relief.

"I thought I might find you here." Bremin plopped down next to him on the centuries-old worn bench, causing it to wobble violently.

"Careful!" Jarand jerked the sharp point of the compass away from his leg. "Firen's seen enough of me lately. I'd hate making him fish this thing out of my thigh."

"Haven't you been doing that kind of work too long to worry about slipping?"

"That's a misconception. The more practiced you get, the less cautious you are. That's when the real accidents start." He tucked the compass back into its protective pocket.

Bremin shifted for a better look. "If Issa finds metal shavings in the practice yard, you might end up visiting the infirmary for a different reason. You know how she feels about that."

"She'd never." Jarand inspected the area around his feet to be sure, then carefully checked the thick canvas draped over his knee. "But best stay on her good side. Last time she was cross with me it took months before I earned her forgiveness."

"Was that when you hid a fish in her bedroll?" Bremin smirked.

"Not so loud." Jarand shushed him with a wave of his hand. "Best not to remind her." It was supposed to be a joke. How was he to know she wouldn't open the thing for a season?

Bremin tilted his head toward the unfinished knife. "Where have you been keeping this beauty?" He extended a hand. "May I?"

Jarand set the blade, handle first, into his waiting palm. "Forged it ages ago when Mirelle and I made a circuit to the Flame Tower. I'd still like to set up a forge out there one day. Maybe when all this craziness calms down."

Bremin tilted the blade so it caught the light of the morning sun as he studied the curves and the different colors hidden inside the thousands of tiny folds within the metal. "'One day' is code for something being too complicated to figure out right now. If that was something you truly wanted to do, I'm sure you'd find a way." He ran a finger over the figures Jarand had already engraved into the blade. "And if you do, promise to make me one of these. This is exceptional."

"I thought you liked the old one I made you and would never replace it." A playful mocking tone crept into Jarand's voice.

"I hadn't seen this one yet."

"Fine. One day, when Katira has been assigned to her Master and settled in her place here, then you can have the first blade that comes out of the new forge. I hope you're patient."

As if on cue, Katira misjudged a strike and landed on her rear end. "It might be a few years." Jarand firmly ignored how his gut squirmed at the thought of traveling anywhere without Mirelle. "It seems Lady Alystra is always on the lookout for someone willing to venture East."

"Do you think Katira's ready for a Master?" Bremin's too casual attitude made Jarand instantly suspicious. He was up to something.

"Yes, and no."

"I realize it's a big step. I'd want you in agreement with the timing." Bremin turned the blade over in his hand, studying the weight and balance on his fingertips.

"After yesterday, everything changed. I would have been happy waiting and giving her more time to be comfortable here. But having the Khandashii take over the way it did is dangerous, and not only for her. The sooner she's properly trained, the safer we'll all be."

Bremin handed the blade back, and Jarand tucked it back into the tidy kit. "Alystra and I discussed this at length after we talked to you yesterday. She agrees." He stopped to watch Katira for a moment before continuing. "She approached the Stonemother on Katira's behalf."

Even though he suspected this was coming, Jarand still stiffened at the news. He wasn't ready to hear this. Despite knowing it was right, it felt like she was being taken from him all over again. His heart seized at the thought. He rubbed a hand over his face, bracing himself to hear Lady Alystra's decision.

"It's you, Jarand. For some unfathomable reason, the Stonemother wants the two of you to remain together."

Jarand knew he was supposed to feel relieved, but it was a possibility he'd never considered. The idea struck him like a punch to the chest. Having her be assigned a Master was one thing, being her Master was something completely different.

"You're joking." Jarand struggled to work some moisture back into his mouth. "That's a terrible thing to joke about. I can't be her Master."

"Why not? You've been teaching her all her life. This is just another phase in her education."

Jarand's hands froze over the kit. "By the Stonemother's throne. You're serious."

"Like you said, this is not something I'd joke about."

"What about the apprentice bond? Doesn't that allow her to sense me?" A new flood of worries raged through. With a companion bond, the sharing of emotional cues, of danger, of injury, was a crucial part of keeping each other safe. It was intimate and personal, definitely not something that should be shared with a daughter.

"Relax, it's different. You're not companions. You are teacher and student. The apprentice bond facilitates that. It will give you the tools you need to keep her safe, but she won't have access to you, unless you want her to. It forces you to trust each other and communicate. She needs that more than anything." Bremin's voice dropped lower. "I know you wish to keep your personal suffering away from her, but from what she shared with me, that's hurting her more than you'd think. Regardless of how the bond works, you still need to take the time to comfort her and allow her to comfort you."

"You don't know what you're asking."

"I know this can't be easy. But, you've never shrank back from a challenge before, so why start now?" Bremin stood from the bench and rubbed his hands together to warm them. "This will be good for both of you."

"When?"

"Alystra can perform the ceremony first thing tomorrow morning. That will give you time to discuss this with Katira."

On the other side of the yard, the lesson had ended. Katira knelt in her circle. In that moment, she looked so small in his eyes, as if she were still a tiny child running around their humble cottage and hiding in Mirelle's skirts.

Starting tomorrow, he was the one who would have to force her to face her worse fears. For her sake, he hoped he was strong enough.

❧

The way Papan held his jaw and how he only answered her questions with single words made Katira worry she'd done something wrong. Whatever he and Bremin had talked about must have been serious, and from the glances and all the whispers, it had something to do with her. When morning dragged itself into afternoon without any change, her worry turned to something much worse, fear.

She had trusted Bremin. If she'd known he'd go straight to Papan and tell him about their conversation, she'd never have talked to him in the first place.

Isben, bless him for trying, was wrong. She should have trusted herself. Her instincts told her to let Papan sort through his grief on his own and she'd gone against them. She'd broken some unspoken promise to him, and his silence confirmed it. He must be upset with her, because why else would he be so quiet?

Back in their quarters, he'd tucked himself into his tiny study and shut the door. Occasionally, she'd hear the tap-tapping of his hammer, but mostly it was silence, and it was eating her alive.

She paced the smooth wooden planks of the floor, chewing on the edge of a fingernail. How dare he be mad at her for trying to help him? How dare Bremin break her trust?

By the time Papan reemerged from the study, she'd worked herself into a froth. Fear had a funny way of turning itself into anger if left to its own devices.

When he met her gaze, she found a flint-hard seriousness there. "Please, sit." His tone reminded Katira how unwell he was. Sleepless nights rasped in his voice and stained the hollows under his eyes purple. He gestured for her to join him by the fireplace. "We have a lot to talk about. I need you to listen and trust me."

"Trust you? Give me a good reason." She flicked at the skirts of her dress, still too agitated to join him by the fire.

Asking someone to trust them was like a healer saying something wasn't going to hurt; it meant something uncomfortable was coming. If anything, his efforts to calm her stirred her up even more.

"Why should I trust you? You still don't trust me." If words were daggers, he'd be dead. "I did what I thought was best. Can't you see that?"

"It's not that. Please, Katira. Stop making things worse." His head bowed low. He didn't want to fight with her, that much was clear.

"Then what is it?"

Papan watched her pace in front of the fire several more times before continuing. "Lady Alystra has decided who your Master is to be."

Katira tripped over her own toe and caught herself on the mantle, anger forgotten. "I'm not ready. I can't." She curled up into the armchair next to him and tucked her skirts around her legs. "I can't leave you yet. It's too soon."

"Shhh. Calm yourself." He took a slow breath. "It's me, Katira. I'm to be your Master."

She stared at him, unsure if she heard correctly. He couldn't be her Master. He was her father. "That doesn't make sense. You're a Guardian. I'm meant to be a Healer. I'm sure of it. Shouldn't I be apprenticed to a Healer?"

"It doesn't work that way. Generally, your first Master doesn't have the same focus you will. It's better if they don't really. Master Regulus—" he swallowed before continuing, "Master Regulus was my first Master, and he was a Seeker. He taught me what it meant to be a Stonebearer and taught me our values." He regarded her carefully. "Will you accept me as your first master here?"

Katira's mind spun in violent circles. "I don't know what that means."

"I'm meant to show you what it means to be a Stonebearer, teach you our history, guide you as you start understanding the power within you. In a way, you're lucky. I've taught you Stonebearer values your whole life. Never called them that, but that's what they were. Bravery, honesty, and hard work are all part of it. It will be easier for you because you've grown up learning the things a first master is meant to teach."

His soothing words calmed her and gave her hope. As her master, he would have to talk to her and work with her, something she had been craving for weeks. "When you put it like that, it sounds like how things were back home." The thought curled around her like a blanket, comforting and warm. "I'd be proud to be your apprentice."

"Glad to hear it. We'll meet with Lady Alystra tomorrow. There's a small ceremony to make it official. You'll be given your apprentice stone then." His brow wrinkled, as if he realized something painful.

"What is it?"

He touched the stone hanging around his neck. "A master and apprentice are bonded together. It helps me to keep you safe. It's similar to the bond I had with Mamar." He left the rest unsaid. Remembering her in moments like this brought him pain.

"Gaining me doesn't mean losing her. I promise."

"I know." His voice grew quiet. "I know."

"What is going to be done about the shadow hounds?" Katira changed the subject. She couldn't lose him to his grief again, not when there was so much she needed to know.

"Lady Alystra wishes to keep it secret for now. Between my investigation and Issa's verification, she feels we have the situation under control. As High Lady, she has access to a more complex system of warding around the tower and says it's still secure. Nothing should be able to get through."

"Wait." Mention of the additional warding sparked a memory of something Katira had seen in Master Regulus's notes. She crossed the room to the shelves built into the other wall. "You still haven't looked at these, have you?"

He shook his head. "Haven't had the heart to."

"The more I think about it, the more I'm sure that he was trying to tell us something important. Why else would he have worked so hard to get it all down?" Katira set the rolled stack on the small table nested between the two armchairs. "His handwriting is hard to read, but I know he mentioned shadow hounds. What if it was a warning?"

Papan untied the bundle and picked up the top page. "Regulus was an odd one in the best of times. Leave it to him to forget to mention the importance of this to anyone." He squinted as he read, lifting the page into the fading light of the afternoon sun streaming through the window.

"And here I thought all this was some kind of document meant to be added to the history." He continued to flip through the next few pages, growing more and more frantic with each one. "The High Lady needs to see these. Bremin too." He rolled up the bundle once more and reached for his cane. "Immediately. Come with me."

CHAPTER EIGHT

*W*hen they had delivered the pages the night before, Bremin had taken a moment to reassure Katira that most of her worries about Papan would be resolved when she formally became his student. The majority of Papan's responsibilities as General would be given to other Guardians in the tower so he could devote his time and attention to her.

Standing next to him as they waited at the doors of the audience chamber for the bonding ceremony to start, Katira had her doubts. Papan cared too much for Amul Dun to trust its safety to anyone else. Knowing him, he'd try to do both.

The rising sun spilled through the large stained-glass window in the eastern facing wall and painted the vast floor of the tower's main hall. A streak of blue streamed to Katira's left, the color of the Guardians. To the right, red, the color of the Healers, although they rarely wore it, preferring sterile white. The colors were fitting, blue for her father, red for her mother. Mamar would have loved to be here for this.

Familiar voices echoed from one of the four corridors leading out of the hall, making Katira's ears twitch. Issa's brightly polished breastplate caught the light from the stained-glass window and sent more colors running across walls and tall tapestries. Under the breastplate she wore a tidy yellow tunic trimmed in blue. An impressive sword hung from her hip. Cassim's usual apron was gone and his white healer's robe hung crooked. He struggled to straighten it as he crossed the wide floor.

"General. It's good to see you." Issa gave a respectful nod.

"You know you don't need to call me that."

"It's a formal gathering. Protocol should be followed."

Cassim broke into a smile and extended his hand for Katira to shake. "Like I said before, if you want to see me all you have to do is ask. No need for the dramatics." He nodded his head toward the audience chamber door. "Congratulations, by the way. This is exciting."

Issa arched an eyebrow at Cassim before setting a hand on Katira's shoulder. "Receiving your first Master is a big step in your journey. How are you feeling about all this?"

"Okay, I guess." Katira lied. A swarm of hornets had taken up residence in her head as too many conflicting thoughts fought for her attention. Everything was moving too fast.

The door opened, interrupting Issa before she could say anything else. A woman also draped in a tunic bearing the High Lady's colors of yellow trimmed in purple ushered them inside. Her timing couldn't have been better, in Katira's opinion. If Issa pressed her to say more, she worried she might say something embarrassing.

Behind them, the door shut with a decisive thud and the woman announced them. "High Lady Alystra, Master Advisor

Bremin, General Jarand Pathara and his daughter, Katira, are here to see you, accompanied by Guardian Issa Tarthan and Healer Cassim Parik."

There was no going back. The woman stayed at the door, arms crossed neatly behind her back, similar to how Issa stood when she taught. The chamber itself stretched long and deep and was large enough to hold Katira's entire home back in Namragan. The walls curved in on themselves shaping the room into a deep oval. The door they had passed through marked one far end. The High Lady and Bremin sat in two lavish high-backed chairs at the other. Slender pillars separated large ornate windows depicting different scenes along the sides of the room.

In the first window, bees and birds floated lazily over lush green trees and fields of wildflowers in a summer garden. Katira blinked. Stained glass windows that moved shouldn't have been possible. But if Katira understood anything about those who could use the power, it was that she shouldn't assume anything.

Papan limped his way down the center of the room, his cane clicking with each pair of steps on the tiled floor. The windows held no wonder for him. Katira imagined he had seen them many times. The seasons progressed as they made their way down the long chamber, passing through fall, winter, and, as they reached the High Lady, the triumphant return of spring decked in pastels and fluttering butterflies.

The High Lady stood to greet them as they approached. Her yellow ceremonial robe hung stiff and severe in the morning light. The colors of the other orders were worked into cunning panels that angled down her sides. To her side, a staff of office leaned in the crook of her ornate chair. Bremin had donned a deep purple doublet over his preferred buttoned shirt and had left the top open.

The corners of Lady Alystra's eyes tightened as she watched Papan make his way down the length of the room. Issa and Cassim made their way to the side of the gathering and stood at a respectful distance.

When Katira and Papan reached the raised dais, the High Lady held out her hands in welcome. "Greetings, Jarand and Katira. After all the trials you both have endured these past few weeks, I'm pleased to be able to offer something which will be good for both of you."

Papan made a formal bow, his hand pressed to his chest. "It is an honor to be chosen."

Katira fumbled for the right words to say. She didn't know what was expected of her. Finding nothing, she mimicked Papan's bow but stayed quiet.

"I imagine this brings the both of you a fair amount of relief." Lady Alystra continued. "Jarand, you've expressed reluctance about having Katira venture away from your protection, especially with all that's happened. Katira, you've had your own concerns and needs that haven't been properly met. Through this bond, both of your needs will be met. You need each other right now. The Stonemother knows this and has shown compassion." She descended the steps of the dais and faced Papan. As she did, her stern expression melted into a kindness Katira hadn't seen before.

"Did you have a chance to explain what this means to Katira?" she asked.

"Yes, my Lady."

"Good." She turned to Katira, now appearing more like a kindly grandmother than the cast-iron leader of the

Stonebearers. It put Katira at ease. "Do you agree to be apprenticed to your father?"

"Yes, my Lady," Katira said, hoping she sounded more confident than she felt.

"It is agreed, then." Lady Alystra stepped back, and her stern gaze returned. "Jarand, do you pledge to train up your daughter in our ways? Teach her our history? Instill in her the values which Master Regulus instilled in you all those years ago, and be her guide as she learns about the power she holds?"

Papan straightened. The worry creasing his forehead fell away. "Yes, my Lady."

She turned to Katira. "And you, Katira, would you have your father here as your first Master in the order?"

Katira squashed down the bubble of fear she always felt when speaking to the High Lady. "Yes, of course, my Lady."

A proud smile crept across Papan's face. For the first time in weeks, it felt real.

Bremin presented a small box to Lady Alystra. She opened it and lifted out a milky green pendant similar to the one Papan wore around his neck.

"Katira, this is your apprentice stone. With it, your father will keep you safe while he teaches you. Together, you will watch out for each other. Protect the other and choose carefully the way you work with each other."

Katira's breath caught. Papan had explained about the stone, but the idea of wearing it hadn't felt real until she saw it in the High Lady's hand. She pressed her hand over the place on her chest where the stone would lie. A whirlwind of emotions attacked her on a daily basis. Through this bond, she wouldn't be able to hide them anymore.

Papan would finally understand how Mamar's death had

left her broken and aching. Maybe, knowing that, he'd finally be able to share with her his own broken edges, and they would be able to grieve together.

On an unspoken cue, Papan fished out his stone and tied it into his palm using its own fine chain.

"Katira, hold out your hand." The High Lady instructed.

Katira did so, and Lady Alystra placed the small green stone in her palm. It was cool to the touch and heavier than she expected.

"Join your free hands together," she continued. "Jarand, open yourself to your power."

Katira wasn't sure what to expect, but it didn't take long to find out. A sudden heat prickled against where their hands touched. She took another steadying breath for what was to come.

"Katira, your father will now help you open yourself to your power. Breathe through the discomfort. Remember it only lasts a moment."

Papan gave her hand a tiny squeeze. A thread of warmth passed through his palm and into Katira's where it traveled up her arm. When it reached her center, it urged the spot of heat inside her to blossom and grow, slowly at first, but quickly gaining momentum until a roaring flame burst inside her. When the power had taken her before, she remembered how it burned. It seemed such a little thing when compared to the strength of her fear. This time, her body trembled with the intensity of it.

"Breathe, Katira," Lady Alystra guided. "This isn't your first time, and your body remembers. Trust it."

Katira forced a breath in through her nose and slowly let it out through her mouth. In. Out. The fire dimmed. In. Out. The burning faded to warmth. In. Out. Her awareness expanded. The connection to Papan, the one she wanted, the one she feared, inched opened slowly, like a heavy door.

In. Out. He was there before her. This time she was awake and aware enough to take it in. His worry, his resolution, and his pride flowed through her. They were no longer two separate people, but one and the same. They hung there in that moment, basking in each other's truth. There was no hiding here, no way to prevent either of them from seeing everything. Deep under all his layers, she sought out that dark network she'd seen for only a second when he'd joined with her before. It had grown.

She couldn't confront him about it, not during the ceremony. Here, in this moment, he needed to see her own sharp grief. He needed to understand how much the loss of Mamar hurt her. Worry had worn her raw. Had she been back home in Namragan and surrounded by those who cared for her, it might have been easier, but that too had been ripped away. Elan had been ripped away.

In that moment, the burden they'd both shouldered for the past few weeks fell away. All the worry about what the other would think, how they would respond, if they would understand, evaporated into nothingness. Papan met her gaze. There was a determination there to make things right.

Lady Alystra set her hand on top of Papan's and Katira's. "It's time for you to be joined and bound to your stones. Hold them tight in your hands and don't let go."

The warmth of the High Lady's power washed over Katira, carrying with it a wave of the High Lady's own emotions. The woman radiated duty and the weight of the responsibility of her position. At the same time, there was a gentler side to her, one that worried and cared and wanted the best for the people in her life. It was that touch of motherliness Katira had seen before.

The heat of her power raced from the stone in Katira's hand through her body to her father and his stone. This loop continued over and over, laying down a thread with each pass, joining them, joining their stones. The thread thickened and strengthened with each pass until there was a mighty rope binding them together.

As the last of the threads looped around them, the stone in Katira's hand grew uncomfortably warm. Lady Alystra had specifically instructed her to not let go, but the reflex itched at her fingers.

The stone grew hotter, blistering the skin of her palm. She gritted her teeth to keep from crying out.

A calming presence drew close. Papan was there in her mind, reaching for her, soothing her, bidding her to find comfort in him. She followed his lead, using the threads of their new connection to take his offered comfort. As she did, the burning faded, and Lady Alystra released her hold.

"Your stones are bound together now. As long as you have them with you, you will never be alone." Lady Alystra bid Katira to open her hand.

Katira hesitated, worried she would find the stone fused into her skin.

Lady Alystra gently opened Katira's tightly closed hand, one finger at a time. "It's all right. It was a test, no more. It wasn't real. I needed to see if you trusted your father enough to reach out to him when you needed him." She held Katira's hand in front of her, showing her that no harm had been done. "You passed."

Bremin approached and handed Papan a fine chain.

Papan took Katira's stone from her hand and threaded it

onto the chain with shaking fingers, then carefully placed it around her neck. "Never take it off, never let anyone take it from you."

"I won't. I promise." She tucked her stone beneath the front of her dress as she had seen so many other Stonebearers do with theirs. It clicked against Elan's locket. Part of her wished he could have been there to see the ceremony and be a part of her life still. She pressed a hand against both of them, a piece of her old life colliding against that of the new.

Then, a new want made itself known, that of needing Isben to be there with her.

Cassim, who had been quietly watching from the side of the room next to Issa, burst forward clapping and cheering. Issa grabbed his arm and tried to yank him back.

Papan laughed. "It's okay, Issa. This is something to be celebrated."

When Katira and Papan arrived back at their quarters, a steaming tray awaited them on the table and the fireplace burned brightly, making the room wonderfully warm compared to the rest of the tower. Katira touched the pale green stone around her neck. If she focused, she could pinpoint a vague sense of him through the new bond. This would take getting used to. As he set down his cane and sat at the table, she could tell he was unusually pleased with himself.

He motioned to the other chair. "Sit, eat. On a day like this, I thought you'd want something special."

She joined him at the table, tucking her skirts under her legs. After weeks of her fetching their meals, Papan had organized this breakfast without her knowing, which made it all the more special. Under a towel was a pile of soft fluffy biscuits, just like the kind Mama Thanes used to make back in Namragan. If Katira didn't know better, she would have sworn they were straight from her shop. She'd never seen them anywhere else. Next to the basket was a small pot of dark purple jelly. Katira lifted it and sniffed.

"Wildberry jelly! How on earth did you find this?" she asked as she broke open a warm biscuit and smothered it with butter and sweet jelly.

"The kitchens have been known to take special requests from time to time. I happened to have the recipe." He tapped on the side of his head.

"Since when have you had the smallest interest in baking?" As the question left her mouth, she felt a tiny shift in his emotions through their bond. "Wait, you're lying, aren't you?"

"Yes, I am." He tapped his stone and raised an eyebrow. "But, I do have friends here who know their way around a kitchen. I gave them a good description and they figured it out for me. Just for you." He snatched his own biscuit from the tray. "Don't get a big head about it."

The biscuit melted in her mouth, bringing with it so many memories of home. The soft crackle of the fire in the hearth, the smell of bitter herbs hanging from the rafters, her fingers stained purple from helping Mamar. Papan leaning back in his chair as he listened to them talk about their day. Those were memories that couldn't be repeated. Not there in Amul Dun, not with the same people.

Papan's mirth faded. He pinched his stone between his fingers, and the sense of brightness of his humor she sensed before turned muddy. "It will get easier, I promise. It's okay to be sad around me." He set down the biscuit and filled one of the mugs from the pitcher. "I imagine you have hundreds of questions. Where would you like to start?"

The memory of home faded. Of all the things she craved to know, one weighed heavier than the rest. She filled her mug with hot tea and cupped it in her hands. "What happened when I was a babe?" She didn't want to hurt him, but she had to know. "How did my parents die?"

Papan regarded her carefully. Katira sensed the echo of another immense loss, another hard memory.

"Never were one to start slow, were you?" He leaned forward, bracing himself on the table with crossed arms. "Before your mother and I settled in Namragan, we traveled from village to village all through the Northern Territory. Lady Alystra needed us to keep tabs on what was going on. Needed us to fight off whatever monsters slipped through from the mirror realm." His fingers holding the warm mug went white. "Stonebearers have always had enemies, some more dangerous than others. Word got out about who we really were. The wrong people learned of a family we'd befriended and took it upon themselves to punish them." As he spoke, sharp stabs of regret and shame flowed across the bond. "They barred them inside their home and set fire to the roof."

He paused to take a drink and his gaze turned to the window, as if he couldn't bear meeting Katira's eyes. "It was your parents' home. They fought to escape, but the old dry timber burned fast and hot. You weren't even a year old. Your mother wrapped you in water-soaked blankets and hid you beneath the floor in the root cellar."

Katira set her mug down on the table, food forgotten.

"The power hiding inside you called to us, voicing an urgent desperate need. At first, we didn't know what it was. All we knew is we had to move quickly. We rode hard and fast, nearly killing our horses. When we arrived, your home was burnt to the ground and your parents, our friends, were dead. We found you beneath the rubble, clinging to life."

She pressed her eyes closed, trying to process the torrent of different feelings as they flowed from him. The memory was bittersweet, the guilt and sadness of losing friends mixed with the relief of finding her alive. He missed them.

"What were my parents like?"

He took another drink. "They were good people. Honest, hardworking, and trusting. Too trusting. Had we never met them, they might still be alive." Another sharp stab of regret flowed through the bond. "But then, we would never have crossed paths with you until you were much older. Fate and destiny are strange that way."

A new feeling emerged when he spoke of her, hope. "What do you mean?"

"You had a spark of power within you, and that's a precious thing. The world isn't kind to young men and woman who have it. It felt right for Mirelle and me to raise you and keep you safe. We owed your parents that much. Had they survived, had they raised you, it might have taken decades, if not centuries, for our paths to cross. We would have met eventually. Stonebearers tend to watch out for each other."

Katira struggled to take in what he had shared. Even now, years later, the memory of the day he had saved her cut at him with razor sharp barbs. The surge of emotion quieted and changed into something new and unexpected as he continued: relief.

"Since the first day I held you in my arms, I feared the day I'd have to give you up to someone else to be trained. Being called as your Master was an unexpected kindness. I plan on being the best master you could ask for, but that means I can't take it easy on you."

Katira thought back to Namragan and hauling water and doing chores. She traced the edges of the calluses on her hands built up from years of hard work. "You've never taken it easy on me. You know that."

"I suppose I haven't." He took a bite of a biscuit and nudged another toward Katira. "Eat up. These are best when they are warm."

Katira buttered another. "What does it really mean to be your apprentice? I mean, I was apprenticing under Mamar to learn how to be a healer, but this feels so different."

He wiped the corners of his mouth. "Not as different as you'd think. For Mamar, you were expected to help clean the shop, collect herbs, prepare medicines, and learn from her as she worked. You'll do the same with me." He gestured to their rooms. "You'll continue to keep our rooms tidy because it teaches the importance of humility and hard work. You'll help me relay important messages and fetch items we'll need because it will help grow your confidence and make you resourceful. You will study from the books and scrolls here in the tower to understand your past." He tapped the stone hanging around her neck. "And you'll practice using your power with me, because that is your future."

Katira's uncertainty faded with each item he listed. She'd thrived working with Mamar. She loved the challenges the work presented, loved learning as much as she could to be the best apprentice possible. While working under Papan would be different, she imagined she'd find a sense of fulfillment there as well. At least with most of it. Thinking of working with the power made the hair on the back of her neck stand straight up.

"Okay. What will we do first?" she asked, hoping he'd choose something easy.

"Your first official duty as my apprentice should be important and significant." He pointed to the tray with a smile that was a fraction too wide. A wild flare of amusement flowed over the bond. "You'll clean up breakfast and take the tray back to the kitchens."

"Really?"

"Really."

CHAPTER NINE

*K*atira dipped her quill and wrote another line on the page before her. Papan had tasked her to write what she'd learned during their discussion that morning, something about helping her remember and giving her a way to look back on these days. While she worked, he'd carried several of the papers needing his attention to the fire to give her space. For years she'd prayed to get her questions answered, but having it happen in such a rush left her dizzy. She wrote another line before wiping the nib and setting it down.

Over the course of the morning, the raw edges of the rift between them knit shut as surely as if Cassim had healed it. As with any wound, the memory was tender. Had she been wiser, it wouldn't have happened in the first place. She'd have known what to say and been brave enough to ask.

The stone around her neck gave her glimpses of the truth. She'd been so wrong about everything. She'd assumed that he'd blamed her for what had happened, that he was angry.

The truth was, Papan was doing the best he could. He didn't hold any blame or resentment.

In that quiet moment, she extended her awareness to him again, wondering if he was at peace.

At first, all she sensed was the gnawing ache in his back. It was more persistent than when she first felt it that morning. Katira caught herself rubbing her own back, as if the ache were hers and not his. Her healer's training taught her how pain often worsened as the day progressed. Sensing the physical came easy; to sense his mind, she had to quiet her own fears. She calmed the swirl of emotion kicked up by her worry and refocused her attention. A vague unease trembled across the bond that she knew wasn't hers. She glanced toward where he sat by the fire. Nothing had changed. However, the unease grew until it screamed in her mind. Something was wrong.

The papers he intended to read slid off onto the floor. His hands trembled in his lap. Katira came closer. The pulse at his throat raced and his eyes twitched. He had fallen asleep. This was a nightmare.

She shook his shoulder. "Wake up."

In one darting snake-like motion, he seized her hand and twisted her arm behind her. His glazed eyes narrowed, and he mumbled something she couldn't make out.

"It's me." She pulled against his grip. "Wake up."

Papan shook his head and he blinked, confused to see her there. His grip loosened. "What is it? What's wrong?"

"Another nightmare. It seemed best to wake you."

He wiped the sleep from his eyes. "Thank you. Sorry I grabbed you. A reflex, I'm afraid. Did I hurt you?"

Katira rubbed her wrist and shook her head. "What was it about?"

"It's slipping away now. Can't quite grab the pieces." A

flutter of uncertainty touched the bond. He was hiding something. As soon as she noticed it, the bond shifted in a way she couldn't explain. It was as if he'd walled her off.

She nudged against this new boundary, suddenly worried again. "Was it about me?"

A knock sounded at the door. Katira ignored it, she needed to know.

"It was about me, wasn't it?"

His face darkened. "Yes."

Whoever was at the door knocked again, more insistent this time. Katira opened the door and found Bremin standing there, hand still raised.

He stepped inside without being invited and shut the door behind him.

Papan stood from his chair with a grunt and walked toward them. "What is it?"

"I've finished reading through Regulus's notes." He looked way too smug, like a cat that caught a mouse.

"And? Out with it." The line of Papan's jaw hardened. After a busy morning, he didn't have the patience for Bremin's games.

Bremin glanced down the hall. "Alystra needs us to meet immediately."

"That's not what I meant." Papan's hand tightened around the head of the cane. He lowered his voice. "What did you find?"

"It's not something I'm comfortable discussing in the open. Meet in Alystra's private office as soon as you can."

Before Papan could reply, Bremin gave a quick bow to excuse himself and hurried off down the hall. Papan closed the door, a look of confusion and disbelief on his face. "Did that really just happen, or am I still dreaming?"

"No, that was real." Katira shrugged into a woven shawl. "We best get going. You heard what he said."

Papan lifted his own coat from next to the door. "What makes you think you get to go?"

He couldn't do this. Not now, not when he promised to never push her away again. "Give me one good reason why I can't."

He opened his mouth to answer and raised an authoritative finger, then shut it and tucked his finger away again. "Fine. You can come. But if Lady Alystra wishes you to stay outside, that's her decision and you're not to argue. Promise?"

Katira hurried to help him into his coat. "I promise."

The High Lady's office shone with the polish one would expect from a queen. Even bustling with people, the thick patterned carpets and detailed tapestries muted the sounds of conversation and movement. The room reflected the same order and dignity that the High Lady embodied. Every book, each vase, each curious motherstone item nestled into its own appointed space.

Cassim and Issa clustered in quiet conversation next to the tall bookshelves in one corner. Nearby, Isben twiddled his thumbs alongside a gangly fellow with thick round lenses perched on his forehead, making him look like a four-eyed bug. His green robe marked him as a Bender.

Katira tucked herself behind Papan, who headed straight for the large desk in the center of the room. Her past experience with a Bender was far from pleasant, and she didn't want to attract this one's notice.

Master Regulus's pages rested in a tidy stack in the center of the desk, accompanied by a vase of yellow roses.

Bremin took note of their arrival with a nod and broke away from his conversation with a much older gentleman wearing a deep purple cloak. She'd seen him once before, hovering around the edges of Mamar's funeral and talking to Master Regulus. He wore the air of someone of importance, although Katira didn't know what that might be.

"Good. You're here." Bremin's gaze lingered on Katira longer than necessary. "I'll fetch Alystra and we can start." He then turned on his heel, crossed the office to a concealed door behind the desk, and disappeared through it.

"Looks like you're staying." Papan shrugged out of his coat. The fireplace across from the desk kept the room plenty warm. "I didn't have a chance to teach you the proper protocol for a meeting like this. You'll have to learn by watching and listening."

Katira rubbed at the prickling fear rising on the back of her neck. She hadn't thought any more about the meeting than wanting to be there, and now there was a protocol that needed to be followed? Maybe she should have stayed in their quarters. The gentleman in purple kept sneaking glances at her as if he wanted to say something. It made Katira even more uneasy.

She tried to catch Isben's eye and failed. The last two days had been so busy she hadn't had a chance to talk to him like she'd promised. He deserved an apology, and this was no time to give it to him. She hoped that perhaps afterward they could steal a moment, if only to let him know what was going on. She'd worried about him. With Master Regulus gone, who was watching over him? Isben never did look up, but Cassim caught her looking his way and gave a tiny wave with a single finger.

The concealed door opened again, allowing Bremin to pass through. He lifted a long staff from next to the door and rapped the floor twice. Cassim and Issa stopped their conversation mid-word and stood at attention, as did the older gentleman. The Bender, however, didn't seem to notice. He was too busy studying the draperies alongside the windows. Isben fumbled over his own foot briefly before straightening like the others.

"The High Lady Alystra," Bremin announced, and gave a short bow with his hand pressed to his chest.

Everyone in the room responded with a matching bow, holding the pose and waiting. Everyone except the Bender, who still hadn't noticed. Katira followed along, hoping no one could hear her heart thumping loudly in her chest.

Bremin cleared his throat loudly and shot a look at the Bender. "Master Aro, if you would?"

The Bender pivoted. "Sorry, so sorry. Didn't hear you," he mumbled. His face flashed pink as he joined them with his hand to his chest.

Lady Alystra entered, wearing her formal robes as she had at the bonding ceremony, and took her place behind the desk. She touched the edge of the stack of papers.

"Please be seated. We have a lot to discuss."

Isben finally caught sight of Katira as they found their seats and quickly moved so he could be next to her. He leaned in close. "Do you know what's going on?"

The room fell silent once more. Everyone waiting for the High Lady to continue.

There was so much to tell him. "Sort of. We'll talk later," she whispered back.

"Master Regulus made these notes in the weeks preceding his death," the High Lady began. "At first, we assumed he was making a last account of his life, a kind of reckoning between himself and the Stonemother. No one thought to give it a second look until yesterday."

Even with Papan's mental wall still in place, a tiny flash of grief pulsed through the bond. Mention of Master Regulus was bound to hurt. Papan had defended him when his Stonebearer brethren turned against him, had performed his last rites, and had held the man as he died. The memory was still too fresh.

Several of those present leaned closer to look at the document on the wide desk. The words swam together and tangled in knots. At the top of the page was the simple title *Khanrosh*.

Bremin tapped the page. "While under Wrothe's influence, Master Regulus extracted vital information about the mirror realm and about the demoness herself. It seems we've misunderstood both of their natures for far too long."

The gentleman in purple gave the tiniest gasp of alarm. No one noticed, no one except Katira, who would have missed it had she not caught him looking at her again.

"It's long been our quest to find a way to close off the mirror realm for good." Lady Alystra gave a nod of acknowledgment toward the man in purple. "Master Ternan, our Artifact Master and Head Historian, tasked Master Regulus to seek out an artifact containing an archive of ancient magic in the ruins at Khanrosh. Encountering Wrothe was an accident, but Regulus was loyal. He saw the potential to learn about the ancient magic from her instead. He sacrificed everything to obtain this information."

Papan shifted forward in his seat. "Many here still believe Master Regulus betrayed us. The rumors were damning, but they were false. He most certainly did not betray us. His loyalty ran deep, deeper than anyone I know. I would have him remembered as a hero."

Those in the room chorused their agreement, all except Master Ternan, who had gone strangely pale. Katira wondered if perhaps he'd fallen ill.

Master Aro twitched in his seat, hardly able to contain his interest. "I'll admit, I'm fascinated. If he's managed to crack the code which will allow us further access to research the mirror realm, then this is news indeed." His eyes narrowed as he studied those gathered. "Why isn't this something we are announcing to the tower as a whole? Why only this group? Why the secrecy?"

Lady Alystra's normally rigid authoritative posture softened, as if what she needed to say wilted her. She glanced to Katira. "There's no delicate way to put this. There was an attack in the tower itself a few days ago. The need to understand the barrier between us and the mirror realm is greater than ever."

Master Aro froze at the news as if he couldn't believe his own ears. "How? Our defenses are perfect. It's impossible."

Isben's head jerked up in surprise. He turned to Katira as if to ask her about it. She shook her head, this wasn't the time.

"Shadow hounds breached our defenses," Lady Alystra continued with admirable resolve. "We don't know how. It shouldn't have been possible with all our protections in place. After reviewing these notes, Bremin and I have concluded that there is a force in the mirror realm trying to cause havoc among us. We can't be sure if it's Wrothe, but if it is, we must be ready."

To Isben's right, smoldering anger radiated from Issa like a banked fire. "Captain Edmont must be told. The guard set on high alert. If that was a test, we will be seeing more breaches, and soon. Some directed at you. You can't expect to keep this threat under control with so little help." She held out her hand indicating those in the room. "My duty is to you first, Lady Alystra. Don't make me compromise that."

"It's complicated," Lady Alystra answered, speaking quieter than before. "There are politics involved."

"May I speak freely, my Lady?" Issa asked.

The High Lady pursed her lips slightly. "It seems you already have. Go ahead."

"Keeping a secret like this will only make the rumors more potent. We'll have a panic on our hands in a week, I'll stake my sword on it."

Papan gripped the head of his cane. "And if we tell them Wrothe orchestrated an attack inside of our own home, we'll guarantee it. We can't risk it."

"Trust me." Lady Alystra leaned forward on the desk and met Issa's gaze. "I've spent considerable time weighing both options. While it's easy to jump to the worst possible conclusion, it's possible this might have been a random act. It's still not clear how the barrier between the worlds work. I'll not put Amul Dun in an uproar until we are sure." She paused. Bremin drew closer and set his hand over hers on the desk. "After the events of the past few weeks, the Stonebearer Society as a whole needs to see our strength. If word gets out that Amul Dun itself has been compromised, it will throw the unity and solidarity we've worked centuries to establish between our separate societies back into chaos. I won't risk war over this, not again."

The rare display of emotion from the High Lady quieted everyone in the room. The heat of Issa's anger vanished.

"Let's return to the reason we've gathered." Bremin

expertly turned their attention to the stack of notes. "There are several points Regulus wanted to make in this document. The most important of these addresses the barrier between worlds. Regulus discovered a way to see the barrier and what it's composed of. He reasons that if we can see it, we can locate weak points and find a way to strengthen them."

Master Aro held up his fingers and carefully touched each one as if counting them. "That's why you need me, isn't it? You've got Master Ternan here as well, which makes me think you need some sort of device like we've seen in the artifact collection. That, or some manipulation with motherstone which hasn't been tried before. He could seek out the proper glyphs, a combination that will make it so anyone can see the barrier and work with it?"

Bremin's lips quirked into a half smile. "Precisely. There's not much to go on here, but I believe there's enough to experiment on what might be possible."

"Okay, then." Master Aro flexed his fingers, and several of them cracked. "That explains why you need me and Master Ternan then. Why are the rest here? Why do we need Guardians and a Healer? And who are these children? Why do you need two untested apprentices?"

Bremin's carefully maintained poise cracked under the weight of the Bender's questions. "Patience. We are not required to explain." He then opened a drawer and lifted out a much smaller stack of papers. "Here is a copy of the section of Master Regulus's notes pertaining to the work we need you and Master Ternan to do. I need both of you to study what he's written and see what you can make of it. You may use my office across the hall." He handed the stack to Master Ternan with a polite nod. "As soon as you've come up with some sort of plan, come find me."

Master Aro adjusted the thick lenses on his forehead in an indignant jerk. They were being excused, and he clearly still had questions he wanted answered. The door shut behind them leaving the room in silence.

"Was that absolutely necessary?" Lady Alystra asked Bremin as he returned to her side.

"In light of what I'm about to share, I felt it best that those two leave. It doesn't concern them." He rested his hip against the edge of the table.

"What I'm about to tell you does not leave this room. The only reason you get to know is because you five have been more deeply involved in this whole mess with Wroth than anyone." Bremin glanced to the High Lady. She motioned for him to continue.

"Wrothe is no demoness. On that, his writings are extremely clear."

"But how?" Papan nearly dropped his cane. "We all saw when she revealed herself, her alien features, the elongated face and horns. What else could she be?"

"He was inside her mind, and he said she's as human as any of us."

"But if she's human, she has use of some form of power. Would that make her a Stonebearer?" Cassim asked.

"I'm not sure what it makes her." Bremin stood and paced toward the window. "Master Regulus recognized the glyphs we witnessed her use at Khanrosh. He called them Dashiian magic. They're old, stretching back to the time of King Darius. They existed when he tamed the power and forged the first connection to motherstone. Over the centuries it's evolved into the Khandashii that we're all familiar with." He turned on his heel and crossed the room again, something Katira suspected he did when he was trying to figure out a puzzle, or unravel a clue. "We need to reconsider our assumption that the mirror realm is a place of monsters or of twisted things. If Wrothe is human, how did she get tangled up in all that? We're missing information."

"There has to be more. What else did he say?" Issa perched on the edge of her seat and watched Bremin's every move.

"He doesn't think Wrothe can be defeated while in this world. There's something tying her soul in the mirror realm. She can't die."

Katira flinched at the thought. Across the room Isben took a sharp breath. Everything could be killed. Everything died. They both knew that too well.

"Then how do we fight her?" The question escaped Katira's mouth before she could stop it.

"That's why we have to learn more about the barrier and the mirror realm." Lady Alystra finally spoke. "There might be more like Wrothe. She's proven she's a threat to all of us. If there are an army of people like her, we need to know. It is our solemn duty to protect the people of this world from the darkness, and we can't do that if we don't understand the risk."

"There's one last thing." Bremin stopped his pacing and stood to face them. "Master Regulus was certain there was a traitor in the tower. All the signs, all the clues he unearthed, point directly to Wrothe having at least one more connection to someone here, one she's had for hundreds of years."

Papan's forehead creased. "This device you've tasked Masters Ternan and Aro to create will draw that traitor out into the open. Force them to act. It puts everyone involved here at increased risk."

"It's a risk we have to take. That's why I needed all of you." Lady Alystra met the gaze of everyone in the room. "Who else could I trust more than the captain of my personal guard and the best general of my army?" She looked to Cassim. "When we find our traitor, I'll need a healer to see if his connection can be severed. You already understand the risk and what's at stake."

Isben raised a hand. "What about me and Katira? Why are we here?"

Lady Alystra softened. "Between your experience at Khanrosh, and your close connections to Master Regulus, Bremin and I feel it best we keep you both under close watch. If anything should happen, we want you surrounded with those who know the odds and can help you. From what I've heard, Wrothe is the vengeful chaotic type. She might target you because it's an easy way to distract us from figuring out her goal.

A cold chill marched up Katira's back. It was one thing to be a victim of chance; it was quite another to be a target.

"What happens now?" Papan asked. "There has to be more we can do."

"Stay vigilant. Watch for any signs of disruption to our protections here. Bremin will take charge of young Isben here while you, Jarand, have already taken charge of Katira. When Master Ternan and Master Aro come up with something useful, I'll have you summoned once again. Until then, this meeting is adjourned."

CHAPTER TEN

Katira's soft leather boots squeaked on the polished stone floors of the tower's lower service level. Fetching their lunch and the supplies Papan had requested was meant to be a quick errand, but Amul Dun's workshop was tucked deep into cavernous tunnels which ran in all directions beneath the main keep. She'd made a wrong turn somewhere. Where she expected to find the wide iron-strapped doors of the workshop, instead was yet another long corridor with far too many deep shadows for her taste.

Papan assured her that there were always plenty of people down here doing the same thing she was and she'd be safe. She was a grown woman, and he'd personally checked the lower corridors the day before. She wanted to believe him.

He wasn't there, alone, in a strange place with his heart trying its best to beat clear down to her shoes. After the discussion with Lady Alystra the day before, she couldn't help but jump at everything. By the time she found the workshop and returned back to their rooms, her hand had clenched so hard around her basket handle she had to pry it free.

Papan was in his usual chair by the fire with a book propped up on his knee. He didn't look up when she bumped the door shut with a hip, but she could feel his amusement. "Got lost, didn't you?"

She set the basket down on the table with a thump, causing one of the earthen mugs to tilt dangerously before it righted itself. "Whoever designed this place must have been a genius or insane. I haven't decided which." She slid a plate of chicken and roasted beets and turnips to his place at the table.

He limped over and helped himself to the pitcher, filling one of the mugs. "Did you ask anyone for help?"

"I only missed one turn. It was hardly necessary." Katira breathed in the scent of the herbed chicken and remembered how hungry she was. "Besides, I'm supposed to figure this out on my own, aren't I?"

"I never said that. I instructed you to go fetch a few things, nothing more. *You* decided that you weren't supposed to ask for help." He stabbed a small roasted beet with the tip of the knife. "Consider this an important lesson. Some rules are very clear, like the one about not fighting the hounds. But if you haven't been told something is specifically prohibited, and doing so will help you or someone else, as long as it isn't harmful, then by all means, go ahead and do it. It goes for when you are working with me; it goes for when you are working with anyone here." He popped the beet into his mouth.

"You are not expected to know all there is to know and are not required to go forward in the dark. Especially when it comes to working with the Khandashii. This power within us, it's frightening, it's powerful, and it's deadly. You will be required to trust your teachers and do things that frighten you, that you aren't prepared to do. But you can always ask if you need help or further clarification." He set down the knife and tore a chunk of bread from the basket. Katira was glad to see him eating well after weeks of watching him poke at his food.

"You aren't going to forget where the workshop is again, I imagine."

Katira laughed. That was the last thing she would forget in a long time. "No, I won't."

"You see? You learned something new already."

When they finished their meal, Papan set his plate aside.

"I owe you an apology. I should have started teaching you how to defend yourself ages ago. Had I known you were interested, I definitely would have." He wiped his neatly trimmed beard with the napkin.

"Don't apologize." With her own meal finished, she collected the empty plates into a stack. "Namragan was a peaceful place. Had you tried to teach me even a few months ago, I would have laughed at you." She finished clearing the table and carried the tray to the door.

"Leave it. You can take it when you go back later." He motioned for her to join him. "I've chosen your first lesson in the power. Do you think you're ready?"

Katira returned to the table, trying to ignore how even the idea of using the power, on purpose, made her tremble. "I have to start somewhere, I guess."

"Don't worry, we'll take it as slow as we need to. I want to teach you about shields. It's a perfect starting point to learn to use your power, not to mention useful."

Katira's stomach flipped itself into a tight knot. She pinched her stone between her fingers, brushing Elan's locket in the process. What would he think about all of this?

Papan unlooped the chain holding his stone from around his neck and placed the stone in his hand. "We'll start at the beginning. Simply put, the stone focuses your power and enables you to form glyphs. Glyphs allow us to instruct the power to do all sorts of different things."

He took the stone's fine chain and wound it around his hand in a motion so practiced and automatic Katira doubted he even thought about it. She tried to do the same with hers. It wasn't as easy as it looked. The chain kept slipping.

"When there's time, binding the stone like this frees both hands, should they be needed. In a pinch, you can simply grab hold of it. With training, both will work equally well. But in the beginning, I find binding helps with focus."

He unwound his chain and showed her one more time, guiding her through the different passes.

"As a Guardian, I am strongest in using glyphs meant to strengthen and to strike with force. Healers, like Mamar, are strongest in the glyphs that put broken things back together and purify." Once again, he unwound his chain and rewound it, showing the steps. "Travelers, like Lady Alystra, can move objects and people from place to place. Seekers, like Master Regulus, can find both objects and information. And Benders, like Master Aro, can alter the nature of an object and create things from others, as long as the elements are present."

Katira fumbled with the chain, trying to follow along. Her second attempt was better, but she couldn't see how to set the stone securely in place in the center of her palm the way Papan had. "Do you think I'm a Healer, like Mamar?"

"It's hard to tell. You do have a knack for it. In time, it will become clear where your talent lies. Until then, you must study from all the disciplines. All Stonebearers are capable of performing all the glyphs. However, if you don't have talent in that area, it drains off your strength faster and doesn't work as well."

Papan reached over the table and tucked the end of her chain between her fingers. "Are you ready?"

"Not sure." She closed her hand around her stone, liking how the binding made it feel secure.

"Set your hand in mine and pay attention as I open myself to the power. It will help you understand. The power is a living thing. It gives us strength, long life, immunity to disease, and the ability to form and use glyphs."

As he spoke, his mind grew peaceful and quiet. Katira closed her eyes to better focus. A warmth formed deep in his chest. He urged it to unwind through him. It wasn't a demand, but an invitation. The small point of warmth blossomed and grew, reminding Katira of the tendrils of a flowering vine. The heat grew to a fire, stretching and burning as it moved through him. The lines on his arms glowed to life, chasing up his fingertips and up the sides of his neck.

"Does it always burn like that?"

"Yes. I'd love to say you get used to it, but you really don't. When you need it most, it doesn't matter."

A ribbon of power flowed from his stone and formed into a solid floating disk the size of his outstretched hand. "The glyph for a simple shield is possibly the easiest you will learn. It's a circle. You hold the idea of a circle in your mind and picture where it needs to be, and ask the power to fill it." He added more energy and the shield grew larger. "Some say it's not a proper glyph because the glyph is the shield itself. The argument is interesting, but not important."

He let the first shield dissolve."Because it's so simple, most Stonebearers don't give shields much thought, or consider the different ways they can be used." Another shield formed over his open palm, larger this time. "Guardians master all the different uses of shields because they are often the difference between life and death."

Katira extended a hand to touch the shield.

"You don't want to do that." He stopped and reconsidered for a moment. "Actually, perhaps the best way to help you understand is to let you."

Katira pulled her hand back. He wouldn't say that unless something bad might happen. "Perhaps I don't want to now."

"I think I'm going to insist. It won't cause any lasting damage, and it's important to understand."

She locked her hands together in a ball beneath the table, suddenly uneasy. "What will happen?"

"You're going to feel what someone else's raw energy feels like. Once you understand, then in the future if you ever are struck by it, you'll know what it is and be able to recover more quickly. Nothing is more crippling than uncertainty."

"Have you done this?" She unlocked the hand not holding her stone and returned it to the table's edge.

"Hundreds of times."

"How many of them were on purpose?"

He let the shield he was holding fade and formed another one, this time closer to where she was sitting. "Only once."

The hovering disk floated too close for comfort. She could smell its dry metallic odor and feel its heat.

"I'm afraid."

"Good. You should be. Fear will protect you, make you move faster, give you focus, and keep you safe. Now, move your hand as if you are going to slap the shield. You want to go quickly."

Katira raised her hand, willing herself to be brave and wishing she had a better idea of what might happen. The only person she hated more than anything, and wouldn't pause to slap silly, was that troll, Surasio. Even dead he still haunted her nightmares. She pictured him there with his greasy strands of hair hanging in his face let her hand fly.

The second she made contact with the shield, streams of lightning wrapping around her arm and chased over her body, grabbing and seizing each muscle as they passed. The force of it threw her off the chair and sent her twitching to the floor.

Papan hurried from his seat and knelt in front of her. If he was speaking, she couldn't hear it.

The fiery pain disappeared to nothingness. In its place, a sickening memory churned to the surface. She'd experienced similar pain at the hands of Surasio and then Wrothe when they'd bound her in that horrible Death Oath. Any misdeed on her part and they could activate it and send her screaming to the ground. The second they lifted it, the pain vanished leaving no trace. While she knew what Papan did was far different, her body remembered the horror it had endured. Bile rose up in her throat.

He helped her to her feet, not letting go of her shoulder until she was safely seated.

"That was awful."

"I didn't think you'd hit it so hard." He took the hand she'd used to strike the shield and rubbed at the bright pink welt. "Do I dare ask what you were thinking of? It wasn't me was it?"

The thought of striking him like that was so absurd it was funny. Thoughts of Surasio and Wrothe fell away and her mind cleared and calmed.

"No, never you. It was Surasio. I've never hated anyone more than him."

He stopped rubbing her hand and returned to his seat. "He's gone now, but I doubt that changes how you feel. It's okay to hold onto that hate for a while. He hurt you when you were defenseless. Let that motivate you to work harder, use it to help you grow stronger." He rubbed a hand over his face. "Do you understand why it was so important to try it, even when it summoned up that memory?"

"If it happens again, I'll be ready." She shoved down the image of Surasio clenching his fist, the hate she saw in his eyes when he wanted to hurt her. "I didn't think the memory would be that strong."

"And you'll carry it for a long while, longer than you might imagine. It will haunt you when you least expect. Wake you in the middle of the night." His gaze drifted somewhere far away. "I know. I have my own collection of horrible memories that refuse to let go."

For a long moment they sat in silence. A cold afternoon breeze crept through the window they'd cracked open for fresh air and teased the papers on the table.

Katira finally broke the silence. "A wise man once told me 'you can't change what's already happened, you can only prepare for what's next.'"

Papan roused out of his silent contemplation. "Did I tell you that? It's good advice."

"You told me lots of things. Never really gave them much thought. They make more sense now."

He shifted in his chair, trying to get more comfortable. "The lesson behind all this is, should someone use a shield against you, or should you feel the urge to use one against someone else, you know exactly what to expect. The faster you can learn to recover from the shock, the better. It gives your enemy less chance to strike again."

He adjusted the chain around his hand, centering the stone in his palm. "I'd still like you to try to wake your power today, if you feel up to it."

While touching Papan's shield dredged up a foul memory, the prospect of learning to use the power held only fascination. She'd seen all the good it could do, the way it could heal, the way it could protect, and she wanted to better understand it.

She touched her own stone. "I'm not sure what to do."

"Trust yourself. Your power has been with you from the beginning. Find the warmth within yourself and allow it to fill you." His calm confidence strengthened her.

Katira turned her focus within herself. Between the bonding ceremony, and when Papan had cleansed her from the venom, she'd become familiar with the place her power hid. She clamped down her focus and pressed her eyes shut, trying to make that warmth come alive again.

"You can't force it," he guided. "You must open yourself to it. Try to relax."

She released her pent-up breath and bid it wake again. This time she imagined that point of warmth as a vessel she was permitting to tip and pour. It moved so slowly she wasn't sure anything was happening until the first tiny hot streaks seeped out.

Encouraged at the small success, she pressed at the vessel, tipping it further, allowing more to flow into her. The small trickle grew to a stream of liquid heat surging through her veins and nerves. Unlike the shield, this pain didn't scare her, but it was far from welcome. The handful of times she'd experienced it had always been at the mercy of someone else, or the Khandashii itself, she'd never invited it to fill her like this before. She curled inward, pressing her arms and chin to her chest as if the motion could contain it somehow, could hold her steady. In the midst of the uncertainty and fear, a deep peace settled over her, as if the power itself was a balm. She found strength in that peace.

"Don't let go. You've almost got it," Papan urged. "The burn settles once you are filled."

The vessel poured out in an unending torrent, filling every cell, every capillary until Katira's whole frame pulsed with it. Sweat beaded on her neck and face. She grabbed the edge of the table with her empty hand as the fire inside her eased back, pulsing and ready. Silvery glowing lines chased up her hand and under her cuff. She had done it.

"Good. Very good. It gets easier and faster with time and practice. Don't try to do it alone until I say you are ready. It can be unpredictable at times."

Katira agreed with a nod, unsure if she could trust her voice while keeping her hold on the energy flowing through her.

Papan watched on, carefully observing her as if measuring her readiness. "Keep that steady focus and hold out your stone. You're going to make a shield like I showed you."

The bright lines on her arms wavered as her focus snapped away. Mention of the shield made her flinch. She pushed those thoughts away and sought out the unexpected peace she'd found in the power.

"When you're ready, imagine a perfect circle hovering over your palm. Keep it small, about the size of an apple. Allow the power to fill the circle." He held out his own hand and a small shield formed.

Holding the power was one thing; asking it to do something was another. Her hold slipped again as she worried if she could do it. No, that line of thinking led to failure. She needed to find the same confidence she felt in Papan, had seen in Mamar so many times. Calm. Peace. She could do it.

A stream of energy flowed from her stone and danced into the air before her. She fixed the image of a circle in her mind and marveled as the glowing ribbon flowed into the shape. For a brief moment, a perfect tiny shield hung over her hand. She looked up at Papan, eager to see if he was proud of her, excited that her very first glyph worked as easily as it had.

As soon as she looked away, the shape melted and her power retracted back to her in a stinging snap.

"Damn it."

"That was excellent. Try again; you got distracted. It's an easy glyph, but you can't let your mind slip." He raised an eyebrow at her. "And watch your mouth. I'm pretty sure I didn't teach you that."

"Sorry. Bad habit." She'd picked up a few curses during her time with Surasio and they tended to fly out when she was frustrated. She expected to see disappointment when she dared meet Papan's gaze, but instead he had a hint of a smile on his lips.

"Form the circle. You already know you can do it. It will be easier this time."

She tried again, determined to make the shield stay. The energy flowed, swifter this time, and formed the circle.

"There, you've got it. Hold it there." He returned to the basket and pulled out the sachet he had her collect from the workshop, inside of which were dozens of small glass marbles. He selected a handful. "Whatever happens, maintain the shield where it is. Don't move it, don't drop it. I'm going to toss these marbles at it."

"And what will happen?"

"You'll see. Nothing bad, I promise."

He tossed the first marble. When it struck, it bounced off and fell to the surface of the table. "Good, keep your focus." He tossed another, harder this time. This one clicked away as it bounced across the room.

The shield wavered, Katira tried to force it back into shape. Instead, it collapsed, and the next stone bounced off of her hand. The suddenness of it surprised her and she released her hold on the power. It shrank away back into its vessel.

"What happened? It wouldn't stay."

"Simple shields can't be held for very long. It has something to do with the energy growing stagnant." He placed several more marbles in front of him. "Thankfully they are fast to form, so having one fail only means to make another."

"I want to try again."

"Are you sure?" He considered the request for a long moment. "We can rest a while if you need to."

Tasting this small success made her want more. The tiny ache of fatigue building up behind her eyes wasn't enough to stop her. "I want to go again. Can I try to make it bigger?"

"The bigger it is, the more energy it takes to create and the more focus it requires to hold. Usually, a simple shield is used to deflect things coming at you, which means you can selectively block what needs to be blocked. There are better versions of the shielding glyph suited for larger shields. I'll teach them to you in time. For now, you need to master the basics." He selected a few more marbles and placed them in his hand. "Are you ready to try making a series of shields one after another?"

"It couldn't be any harder than forming one, I suppose."

"That's my girl. Go ahead and open yourself to the power again."

At first, Katira tensed, her instinct telling her that something that powerful must be forced to comply. When nothing happened, she remembered that she was supposed to be calm, that this was an invitation. Several minutes passed before she could manage to get the vessel to tip once more. All the while, Papan watched on patiently, saying nothing and showing remarkable restraint to not offer advice.

"There. That was harder than before."

"You were agitated. Finding calm can be hard." There was the glint of a challenge in his eye. "If you're ready, I have a game. I'll toss these marbles at you and you will create shields to deflect them." Without warning he flicked one straight at her. She stumbled back trying to summon the circle and invite the power. She wasn't fast enough. The marble bounced off of her shoulder.

"No fair, I wasn't ready."

"Your enemies will not play fair." He flicked another.

She fought to form the shield in time. It collapsed into ribbons as the marble sailed past. "But I just barely learned this. I need time."

"Focus. Do you think your enemies will think about that when they move in for the kill?" Another.

This time the shield formed, but a moment too late. "Stop it, you're scaring me."

"Good." He flicked another. "Keep trying."

Katira formed a shield in time and was so pleased she let her focus slip. He flicked another and another and they both clicked to the floor before she could react.

"Don't celebrate until the task is over." He paused to gather another handful.

With each flick, her calm wavered. The razor-sharp focus each shield required took more and more effort. Papan pushed harder still, the marbles kept flying at her. She was succeeding more than failing, but it wasn't enough. He kept going.

"Please, stop." The dull ache of fatigue pressed deeper and demanded her attention.

"Not yet. Keep going." He picked up another handful, this time sending two at a time. She was so tired, but she didn't want to fail. She formed two shields, one for each marble. They formed and dissolved the second the marble hit and fell to the table.

He continued, flicking three at a time, then four.

"Slow down, I can't ..."

"Yes, you can." He flicked another group of four.

Panic started to set in, Katira couldn't stop, couldn't see a way to safely end the exercise. The marbles didn't stop.

"Push past your fear, push past what you think your limit is." Five pebbles flew.

"I can't." The shields stopped forming properly. They were no longer smooth discs, but bursts of energy, ragged and fast. Some stopped their target; some barely formed before dissolving. Her desperation peaked. The power surged away from her control, leaving her in that same eerie calm she experienced when the hounds attacked.

He tossed another five. Katira floated somewhere just outside of herself, watching on as the power flowed from her fingers in ribbons. Each shield made contact, but she wasn't doing it.

"Keep going, one more."

He tossed one final handful. Six marbles flew into the air. The ribbons split into a multi-faceted blast. Each burst stopped a single marble mid-air and dropped it to the table.

Papan braced his hands on the table, breathless. "You did it. You actually did it."

With the test over, Katira needed to release the power. It flared against her, showing that while she might be tired, it still had enough strength left. The lines on her arms pulsed with it. She balled her fists against the intrusion. If she had to be calm to use it, then maybe if she forced that calm away, it would have to recede back into its vessel.

Papan glanced up at her. "You can let go now. We're done for today."

Katira couldn't speak, and despite her efforts, the power stayed put.

"Katira?" The amused grin fell from his face. "What's wrong?"

She shook her head. *Help me.*

His reaction was instantaneous. With one breath his own power flowed back, ready for him to use. He grabbed both of her wrists and let it flow through her, his presence warm and welcome. Just as he'd encouraged her power to open before, this time he gathered it up and urged it to sleep. Bit by bit, it finally withdrew.

Katira fell back into her chair and let her head flop back. All she wanted to do was close her eyes.

"No, no, no. Stay with me for a moment." He stayed connected, his warm and comfort there. "It fades, like a dream. Don't give in to it."

Sure to his word, the eerie calm fogging her mind eased with each passing breath.

"Why?" she finally asked.

"I had to know how much you could take, if you would give up when it got hard."

"You know I don't give up." Without the power she felt

strangely hollow. "I'm your daughter, do you expect anything less?"

"Of course not." The glow of his markings faded away, and he unwound his stone from his palm. "But we need to figure out how to keep the power from taking control. It's a living thing, and like any living thing, it can be tamed."

CHAPTER ELEVEN

The next afternoon Papan escorted her to the infirmary to study healing under Master Firen. Stepping into the orderly space was like stepping into her memories of work with Mamar and was both familiar and welcome. The smell of cleaning alcohol and floral laundry soap filled the air. It would be good for her to spend time here learning, just as training with the Guardians was good for Papan.

One worry gave her pause. This was the last place she had seen her mother alive. She waited for the pang of grief to strike as she walked past the empty bed. To her relief, it never came. The cleanliness, the precise folds of the blankets, the bright sunlight flooding through the windows, all brought with them memories of good things, of working in Mamar's shop, of being productive, of helping people. Being here felt right.

Cassim hummed to himself as he arranged supplies on a shelf. He no longer wore the long white robe that she had seen him in earlier, but a tidy white tunic with leather ties at the neck over loose trousers. He smiled when he saw her.

"Ah, perfect. You're right on time."

"Hello Cassim. Look, I'm not being dramatic today," she joked. Master Firen was nowhere to be seen. A blue shirted Guardian lay in one of the beds with his leg splinted and resting on pillows. In his lap was a book, but he wasn't reading it. He was studying her.

"Well that's good." He chuckled. "Come with me, we'll work in my office." Cassim gestured for her to follow as he made his way down the wide aisle between the two rows of beds.

As she walked, the Guardian's eyes followed. "I thought I was working with Master Firen today."

"He's been called out for the afternoon. Official Amul Dun business. You'll have to make do with me today." He pushed open a small door at the end of the long room. "I apologize in advance."

Cassim's office, if that's what it could be called, was nothing like the rest of the infirmary. Instead of orderly clean lines and pristine white linens, there were jumbled shelves stuffed with everything from books to piles of dried herbs. On a stand in the corner, a large black raven basked in the afternoon sun coming through the window.

"You're disappointed." Cassim side-stepped his way past a pile of books and papers balanced on the corner of his desk.

While Katira was looking forward to learning under the same man Mamar had studied under, Master Firen was still a stranger to her. On the other hand, Cassim was a friend.

"I'm really not. If anything, this is better." She lifted a stack of papers that had accumulated on the chair in front of

Cassim's desk. "I'm happy to be somewhere I feel I belong. Where do you want these?"

"A spot on the floor is fine." He made his way over to the raven and scratched the feathers at its neck. "This is Onyx. I've had her since she was a baby. She fell off the roof in the main hall and broke her wing. We've been together ever since." The raven made a sound deep in her throat that sounded almost like a purr.

"Is she friendly?"

"Once you get to know her, she's very sweet. It takes her a while to get used to new people." He offered Onyx a peanut from his pocket that she carefully took with her pointed beak. "Now that the introductions have been taken care of, let me take a look at your arms." He joined her at the messy desk, sitting in the chair on the other side. "How does it feel?"

"It's fine. It still itches off and on, but not nearly as bad as a few days ago."

Cassim pushed a stack of papers out of the way. She rolled up her sleeves for him.

Although Katira knew there wasn't much to see, she still looked at her healed skin in wonder. She'd treated bites from wild animal attacks back in Namragan with stitches and poultices. They'd never looked this good after a few days. They rarely looked this good after a month.

She touched the fresh pink crescents left by the hound's teeth. "Will you teach me how to do this?"

"In time." He tugged her sleeve back straight and checked a note anchored to the desk by the skull of a large animal Katira couldn't identify. "First things first, you need to learn how to delve. Master Firen's instructions." He nodded to himself, agreeing with what was written. "Good place to start anyway. Most students need to spend months, if not years, learning how all the pieces of the body work together. You've already done that, so you get to skip to the interesting stuff. Not that the study of physiology isn't interesting..." He trailed off and patted the front of his tunic and then fished out the stone hanging around his neck.

"I suppose the best way to teach you about it is to show you. You mind if I use your arm again?"

Katira hesitated briefly. For a moment, the memory of Wrothe demanding her to hold out her hand and then cruelly testing her barged into her mind. While she knew it made no sense to be scared, the fear was very real. After a few calming breaths, she set her arms down on the desk. Cassim could be trusted, and she could be brave.

"There's one glyph used in delving, 'see'. It kind of looks like an eye." As he spoke, he held out his hand and a ribbon of power flowed upward. Two lines curved and joined at their ends, making the shape of an almond. A spiraled circle hovered inside. "The spiral is actually part of another glyph, 'focus' but it's never used on its own. It's what makes it possible to guide the glyph once it's released." The glyph shrank into a bright light and hovered over Katira's now bare arm. "I usually set a hand on the patient and allow the glyph to form inside. It's faster. However, as you are learning, you'll want to form it where you can clearly see it."

Katira nodded her understanding. The light winked out.

"Let's talk through a scenario. Tell me, what's the first thing a healer must do when approaching someone who needs their help? Say there's been an accident, like a rockslide."

Easy question. Mamar had instructed her on this many times. "Assess the most critical needs first. If they are unresponsive, check for breathing and a heartbeat."

"Good. Then what?"

She had to think for a moment, but the answer was there. "Then serious bleeding, followed by spinal injury." She paused when one of Cassim's eyes narrowed and reconsidered her answer. "No, if they must be moved then spinal injuries come first."

"There you go." He reformed the glyph, pausing at each step so she could see. When it winked into the bright point once more, he guided it down into Katira's arm without warning, making her jump. "That's the other reason why I normally don't show it. It freaks people out." The familiar warmth of the glyph stayed under the surface of the skin.

"Without the aid of the power, all of that must be done by what you can see and feel. It's easy to miss things and also cause your patient pain, especially when you are seeking out possible fractures." The light started to move, but not nearly as fast as he'd done it before. "With the power, you can scan the whole body in seconds and pinpoint anywhere there might be a problem without moving the patient." The light zipped up Katira's arm and away. She felt its warmth flowing through her, then returning back to Cassim. The lines on his arms faded.

She tucked her arms between her knees. "So, am I healthy?"

"Yep. Although you're a bit more drained than I expected. Did you work with the power today?"

"Papan showed me how to make simple shields." Katira's thoughts returned to how she'd lost control. Would that happen again if Cassim pushed her? Would he be able to bring her back?

"That must have been some lesson."

"I'm not sure what he wanted, but it felt like a test. He kept throwing marbles for me to block."

Cassim paused as he unwound his stone from his palm, his interest spiked. "I swear, Guardians are so weird. Always trying to push the limits. Everything is a contest to them. How many could you do?"

"Six."

His eyes bulged, as if he couldn't believe what he heard. "Six! You know that's really unusual, right? Most Stonebearers can only do two, sometimes three. Trained Guardians can do more, but it takes them years to work up to it." He finished tucking his stone away and continue to mutter to himself. "Six! I never got past two myself."

"He didn't tell me any of that. Not sure why not." A knot of unease tightened in her stomach. "Don't tell anyone, please."

"No, I won't. It's rude to ask really, but we're friends." He held out his hands in an apology. "On that note, I know it's only you and me here, but you need to get used to calling your father by his title around other people. It'll be Master Jarand to you, because you're his apprentice. No doubt you've heard him called General a few times as well. Most around here, including myself, use that title because we were with him during the war years. He's not fond of it, never has been. But it's an honor he's earned."

Onyx squawked and bobbed her head in her corner, as if agreeing.

"Shush. I'm working," Cassim scolded.

Onyx clicked her beak and bobbed her head again.

"Fine, you can come over. But you have to behave." He set another peanut on the desk. "It's like having a kid, I'm told. Where were we?"

"You were trying to explain delving. What exactly does the glyph let you see?"

Onyx hopped onto the edge of a nearby shelf and shuffled her way to the desk using her claws and beak for balance. When she arrived, she climbed up onto Cassim's shoulder and nuzzled his hair.

"It's not exactly seeing, really. If anything, it's closer to what happens when you touch someone while you're both holding the power, except this only shows the physical, not the emotional. You can feel what's out of place, what hurts, what's struggling, what's empty. A big part of learning to be a Stonebearer Healer is identifying what those feelings mean and how to fix them. The other big part is doing the fixing." He absentmindedly scratched the feathers of the large bird's chest. "Would you like to try?"

After being tested by Papan, Katira wasn't sure she was ready to work with the power again. It was all too fast. She'd only barely figured out how to access her power a few hours ago. Now Cassim wanted her to try something else entirely new. What if she did something wrong? What if she lost control again? What if she hurt him on accident? There were too many questions.

"This is a lot different than creating a shield. I'm nervous. You understand, right?"

"Yes, and no. It's okay to be scared when faced with something new. But the longer you avoid trying, the more frightening doing it will be until you're paralyzed. I really think you should try once." He rolled up his sleeve and set his arm in front of her. "It's easier than it rightfully should be. Would you like to see the glyph again?"

Katira shook her head. "I think I got it. You sure I'm okay doing this to you?"

"Stop hesitating and get out your stone." He huffed, not

STONEBEARER'S APPRENTICE | 121

unkindly. "Open yourself to the power. I know all of this is still really new, so take the time you need."

His assurances paired with her curiosity finally convinced her to go ahead. She wound the chain of her stone around her palm as Papan had showed her, securing it with a tug before seeking the quiet submission that permitted the vessel of power to tip and fill her.

Cassim watched on with interest. Her mind and body remembered the steps, albeit slowly. The vessel tipped with intention this time and poured power into her, filling her until her whole body was white hot with it. The discomfort would pass, but her hands still balled into fists. Her jaw clamped shut and her breath caught in her teeth.

After a long moment, the power finally settled into its calming thrum. "Okay, I'm ready."

"You're doing fantastic. First, how do you feel?"

The question was so typical for Cassim that Katira smiled and shook her head. "Good enough now. Getting through that, not so much. Papan–" she stopped herself when she saw Cassim's raised eyebrow, "I mean Master Jarand says it will get easier with time and experience."

"And he's mostly right. It's never supposed to be easy or without cost. If it was, it would be that much harder to use responsibly."

There was a knock at the door. Cassim pursed his lips at the intrusion.

"It's open," he called, not bothering to get up.

Issa stepped into the cramped confines of the office. Instead of the padded gambeson she usually wore when working over in the High Lady's wing, she wore the fine blue silk shirt she'd worn for training. Onyx flapped her wings and cawed.

"Oh, shush, you." Issa shot the bird a glare. "I'm supposed to train Katira this afternoon. When will you be finished?" Her eyes scanned the stacks of papers and sighed. "I thought you were going to tidy things up before teaching today." From her tone, this was an ongoing discussion the two of them had had several times.

"I did tidy up. There's some space on the desk to work. And..." He motioned behind where Issa was standing. "I took care of the stuff behind the door."

While they talked, Katira allowed her power to retreat back into its vessel. She needed to know that she could put it back to sleep when she needed to, and it was a relief when it did.

Issa rubbed at her forehead, not willing to enter into an argument. "You two finish what you needed to?"

"I was supposed to have an hour. You're early."

"Well, how much longer do you need? I can wait."

"A few more minutes. Katira is to try delving."

"Really? Isn't that a bit advanced?" Issa shut the door behind her and eyed both of them.

"Not with her background, it isn't." He returned his attention to Katira. "Go ahead. One good try. Ignore her."

While Katira had almost come to terms with trying a new glyph alone with Cassim, doing it in front of Issa made her doubt herself. Should she fail, Cassim would be understanding and patient. Issa on the other hand, was far more demanding.

Under Cassim's watchful eye, Katira went through the steps to open herself to the power once more. She brought the eye-shaped glyph into focus in her mind and hoped the ribbons of power obeyed. A single ribbon danced from her stone into the air and formed the shape.

"Good. To activate it, send a small bubble of energy toward it. Stay focused," Cassim spoke in a calm, even voice.

She imagined a spark of energy extending up from her palm to the glyph. As soon as the thought took hold, the glyph winked into a bright spot of light hovering in the air, waiting for her.

"Excellent. Guide the light to my arm."

Before Katira could follow the direction, Onyx jumped off of Cassim's shoulder and down to the desk. Katira's floating light flickered out. The vessel of power drew the power back to itself and the lines on her arms faded.

"Sorry. I thought I had it." She clenched her hand around her stone. Stupid bird.

Cassim scooted Onyx to one side. She scolded him in a series of throaty chirps and growls and then proudly marched back up to her perch on his shoulder. "Really? Is that how it's going to be, Onyx?" The bird clicked its beak and started preening his hair. Cassim turned back to Katira. "No need to apologize. Between these two girls in here—"

"Women." Issa corrected him.

"Right, women. It got a bit distracting. We'll keep working on it. All this comes down to practice, endless practice. You'll get it." He waved her off.

Katira thanked him and left with Issa. The idea of practice wasn't new in the least. Both Papan and Mamar had taught her about the importance of working at something until it felt right, this was the same. If anything, she knew how to work.

After such a busy day, Katira sank into her chair in front of the fire. Nothing sounded better than a quiet evening curled under a blanket and reading a book. Papan sighed as he eased into his chair next to her. His limp was worse that evening and he'd barely touched his dinner, both signs that his back was really bothering him.

Katira fought back the urge to mother him. After what she'd learned through their bond, she knew it wasn't welcome. A quiet evening and a good night's rest would do both of them wonders.

Not an hour had passed when a timid knock came at the door. Katira wanted to ignore it. If they were knocking that quietly, then perhaps it wasn't important. She burrowed deeper into her blanket and pulled her book closer. Papan had nodded off in his chair, head resting against the tall back rest, blanket pulled up under his chin.

The knock came again, a fraction more insistent than before. Papan stirred at the sound.

Katira pushed off her blanket. "I'll get it. You stay here."

Before she reached the door, Bremin let himself in with Isben trailing behind him.

"Jarand," Bremin said. "A word."

"You used to knock."

"I did."

Papan neatly folded his blanket and set it on the arm of the chair before standing. "It's late. This better be important."

The way his shoulders drooped and his head hung low, Katira didn't need their bond to know he was exhausted.

Isben stayed near the door as if unsure he should enter without permission. Katira waved him in. "What's this about?"

"Not sure. I'm guessing something with the pages, but I could be wrong."

"Did those two masters figure anything out yet?"

Isben shook his head. "Don't think so. They've been

driving Bremin crazy all day with their arguing."

"It's important for you." Katira overheard Bremin tell Papan. "Will you come?"

At that, she turned back to her father, ready to give him an excuse if he needed one.

"It's fine, Katira." He plucked his coat from the hook by the door and eyed his sword resting in its stand. He hadn't worn it since returning to Amul Dun because its weight pulled the muscles around his injury the wrong way. He laid a hand on the scabbard for a moment before leaving it and shrugging into his coat. "When Bremin or the High Lady calls, you go. No questions."

"Do you want me to stay here? Or come with you?" The thought of being alone at night, even in their quarters, made her shiver.

Isben stepped in before Papan could answer. "You could come to the library with me." Spots of color blossomed on his cheeks. "I'm not needed for the rest of the evening. I can stay with you until your father finishes. It's close to where he'll be anyway."

Katira looked to Papan for his approval. The brief moment she'd shared with Isben the day before wasn't enough. It had been far too long since she'd spent an evening with him. She missed his company.

"He's got a point." Bremin tapped his chin. "It would be better if they both stayed somewhere public, and the library will still have a few Seekers wandering the stacks. It's a much safer option than forcing them to spend the evening alone in their respective quarters." Katira swore she saw a twinkle in the man's eye. "It's all right with me."

"It's a plan then." Papan patted Katira's shoulder. "I'll come find you when I finish."

CHAPTER TWELVE

The last time Katira had been in the library was the day after Master Regulus's death. She'd promised herself she'd make a greater effort to be there for Isben, but with all that had happened, she'd been a really rotten friend. Perhaps she'd be able to make it up to him.

Isben pulled open the tall carved doors and ushered them inside. In the evenings, yellow glass-like spheres dotted the slumbering line of tables, each casting a puddle of warm light. The towering bookshelves stood to either side of the tables, reminding Katira of silent sentinels.

Isben took a sphere from the nearest table and led her back to their tiny alcove where one of the many power-fed braziers poured warmth into the small space. Isben had planned their being there even before he'd asked her to join him.

Katira tucked herself into the bench in her usual spot, and Isben slid in with her. Memories of Master Regulus aside, this was one of the few places in the tower she loved because it meant spending time with Isben.

"Hey." She laced her fingers in his. "Now we can have a proper conversation. How have you been?"

His gaze dropped to where their hands joined and the smile he'd been wearing faded. "Today was better than the last few days. Master Bremin made sure to keep me busy with different teachers. The distraction helps me keep my mind off of what I could have done different."

"You can't blame yourself for what happened. You did what you thought was right." Katira stroked his hand and wished she could ease his guilt with her words alone.

"What about you? Surely you have regrets."

Katira had already walked down this path many times. "Of course I do. I should have been there, been with her in her last minutes. Maybe if I'd spoken up about the herbcraft I thought would help her, it might have saved her." Time had softened the sharpness of each regret, but not blunted them entirely. "What's done is done. We both have to live with our decisions."

The quiet of the library drifted around them as they soaked in the moment. Sometimes silence was best.

Minutes passed before Isben finally spoke. "What's it like being apprenticed to Master Jarand? Is that weird?"

"I haven't decided yet." She touched the stone at her throat. "I guess he's been teaching me my whole life. But, I'm paying much better attention now. This new life is slowly starting to make sense."

"Any news from home?" What he was really asking was if Elan had written in the weeks since he'd left.

"No. I'm not expecting any either." When she'd said her goodbyes to Elan and told him they couldn't ever be together, it tore away part of her heart. Whether he knew it or not, he took it with him. She loved Elan deeply and he loved her as well. They would have been very happy together secluded away in Namragan without a care more than if their chickens laid enough eggs or if a freeze would come too soon.

She studied the darkened window on the other side of the alcove. During the day it looked out on the steep sides of the mountains on the other side of the valley. In the dark all she could see was her reflection. "Part of me still imagines I'm home and I'll wake up in my own bed. I miss Namragan and the market and the forest outside my window." She closed her eyes and thought back to the sound of iron on the anvil and the sharp scent of herbs, Elan sitting on the low wall outside the cottage and laughing. She wondered what he was doing right now. It was late; was he already sleeping or looking out at the endless stars?

"Can I ask you a personal question?"

He shrugged. "I don't see why not."

"Did you leave someone behind? I mean, before you left your home and everything. Was there... someone?"

"You miss him, don't you?"

Katira slid down onto the bench, putting distance between her, the window, and the reminder of home. "I keep thinking about him. Wondering what he's doing. Hoping he's well. Winter is hard up north. I shouldn't worry about him, but I do." She touched the locket resting close to her heart. "You didn't answer my question."

He wrung his hands over the power-fueled brazier. "No, there wasn't anyone more than my family. I still miss them. I worry about them every day. Things weren't good when I was forced to leave. No one looks kindly on those who protect wielders where I'm from."

"Do you think they might have been harmed because of

you?" Katira regretted the question as soon as she said it. "I'm so sorry. I shouldn't have asked that."

His hands stilled. "It's okay. Back in the beginning, I sent letters. Anything to reassure them I was okay, that things worked out. I never heard back. Not sure if they even got them. It's been a few years since then." He gave a comforting smile that helped her feel better. "This is home now. One day it will feel like your home as well."

"I'm not sure about that." She looked up at the towering bookshelves looming over her. All the books in Namragan wouldn't have filled a single shelf here.

"I've had a few years to get used to it. I still remember when I first came here. It's normal to feel unsettled, over-whelmed. Let yourself adjust. Take your time." He snorted out through his nose. "That's one thing we have plenty of, as wielders, time."

While Isben meant it to be funny, it struck Katira wrong. "I bet my mother thought that as well, and Master Regulus. Just because wielders have uncommonly long lives doesn't mean life won't be ripped from them when they least expect it."

He grew serious once more and tried to meet her eye. "It's not normally like this. In the few years I've been around, things have been amazingly dull. Stonebearers spend their days in study and practice. This business with Wrothe is new. It's frightened the whole tower."

As he talked, Katira's attention shifted. Somewhere deep within the tall shelves she heard a faint tapping. As much as she wanted to push the growing horror behind her and ignore it, she knew what that sound meant. She fished her stone out from beneath her shirt, not daring to look away.

"What is it? You've gone as white as parchment." Isben turned toward where she was looking.

"You hear it? That tapping?" She bound her stone into her palm.

He stilled himself and listened. The sound stopped. "What do you think it is?"

"I heard it before the attack a few days ago. Heard it back at Khanrosh when the hounds came. I think they're here." She scrambled up onto the table. Isben joined her and silently unwound his own stone from around his neck and bound it to his palm. The tapping came closer and with it, a low growl.

Katira lifted the sphere of light above her head, pushing away the nearest shadows.

"This is where you become my hero. You know how to fight, right?" Katira asked as she tried to remember how to unlock her power. The vessel refused to tip, feeling instead as if it was hidden in a deep cloak of fear. She tried to breathe past it, tried to calm herself. The shadows dared to creep closer. One glance at those razor-sharp teeth and all she could think of was getting away.

"Fight? Not really. But I've got a few tricks up my sleeve." He sucked in a pained breath as the marks on his arms glowed to life.

"Really? You didn't just make that joke right now." Katira tried to tip her vessel again, but it stayed stubbornly upright.

"Well, what about you?" He yelped as a shadow lunged forward and then darted back. "Your father is one of the most renowned Guardians alive. He must have taught you something."

"Yeah. When to run, and the pointy end goes in the bad guy." She reached for her power again. It had saved her before, why couldn't she summon it now? "Got anything pointy?"

He gestured toward the portable writing desk on the

corner of the table. "A quill probably won't do much. How do you feel about running?"

"There's more than a dozen dark shadowy aisles between us and the door. I don't like those odds." She gripped the stone in her palm. If Papan could sense her, he'd feel her building terror and know something was wrong.

"Oh, and being eaten in our favorite alcove is better?"

"Fine. We move, but not through the aisles. To the next alcove. We can defend ourselves from there if we have to. Ready?"

"Almost." A glyph was forming over Isben's palm. "Go on my signal." A second glyph joined it and it winked into life. Bright white light burst through the darkness, sending the hounds back yelping. "Go now!"

He grabbed her arm and bolted for the next alcove. Before they made it, one of the hounds lunged forward, snapping at Katira's heels. She struck it with the glass sphere, surprised that it made contact. It shook its head and backed away snarling. There were more than before. She dug deeper, again seeking her inner calm that allowed the vessel to tip.

"Careful!" Isben pulled her onto the next table. "You break that and we'll be left in the dark." He formed another small glyph and a white shot of light zipped at an approaching hounds face. It shook its head, but didn't fall back.

Isben muttered something to himself as he formed another ball of light at his fingertips. It sounded suspiciously like Master Regulus's old mantra, 'to do nothing is death.' Hearing it now made Katira smile and shake her head.

More skittering scratching sounds surrounded them. Katira didn't dare count. Isben flung more glyphs into the mass of writhing shadows, desperately trying to push them back. She pushed at her vessel of power, a last desperate effort before the wall of teeth and shadow collided with them. It wouldn't move.

The wall lunged up, snarling and biting. Teeth wrapped around Katira's arm, her leg, pulling her from the table to the ground. She screamed and flailed, her kicks passing through their dark mist-like bodies. Isben's lines flared brighter as he punched and kicked at one latched onto his arm. Another dove for his ankle, sending him reeling and falling. The glow of his power winked out.

The teeth came faster, snatching and ripping at anything they could get a hold of. No matter how hard Katira struggled, nothing pushed them off. Nothing could stop them. She stopped fighting and curled into herself, trying to protect her neck and stomach. Her mind emptied leaving her with a crystal clarity of thought that dulled the knifing pain of each tearing mouth.

In that strange peace, the vessel holding her power shattered. Heat burst through her, bounding along the familiar pathways like an explosion. Full of fire and fury, the power took control. A wave of energy formed around her, breaking the hold of the hound's needle-toothed jaws. She would not die lying down, not today. A torrent of power leapt from her fingers, catching the closest hounds and turning it to ash.

A string of curses ran from Isben's mouth as he struggled on the floor. One hound snapped at his flailing arms, grabbing hold and shaking its head. No one else would get hurt because of her, not when she could help it. Glyphs formed and arched through the air, striking the one holding him and knocking it away before a different glyph obliterated it. There were more. They weren't finished.

Power raged through Katira in sweeping torrents, raw and ragged. She couldn't feel where the hounds had pierced her, couldn't feel anything but the heat. Another hound bounded out of the darkness, leaping at her face. It fell like the others. Silence fell. Isben sat on the floor dazed, eyes glassy, clutching his bleeding arms to his chest, though his power still flared weakly, trying to defend her.

Katira started to shake. It was too much. She needed to let go, needed the power to retreat back inside her. There was something else she was forgetting. Her mind was too overwhelmed to make sense of what she was seeing, what she was doing.

Shouts rang from inside the library. Doors slammed. Someone had come. Another shadow broke free from the darkness, this one bigger than the rest, a wolf. Katira lifted her stone to face it, it felt too heavy. Without thought, a glyph formed and released, striking it.

Nothing happened.

The light broke around the wolf without touching it. It came closer, its claws grating against the floor.

One more strike. She couldn't make it this far and fail. Not now, not when help had come. Glyphs swam into being, combined together, and shot again. Power laced tendrils of light wrapped around the wolf in a sphere, as if something was protecting it. Her glyph cracked into it, forcing its way through. The sphere shattered.

The wolf leapt at her, faster than she could react, and locked its jaws around her middle. Each dagger-like tooth drove into her skin, piercing and cutting deep as the weight the wolf knocked her backwards. As she fell, a streak of light burst toward her from the corner of the alcove. It caught the wolf in the side, the force of the blast ripping its teeth free and throwing the monster back into the shadows.

Katira sank to the floor as Issa leapt into action, sweeping the area for more threats, checking down the long aisles between the shelves. Her sword danced in bright arcs around her, streams of power streaking from the tip as she cut down the remaining hounds.

As quickly as it came, Katira's power retreated, leaving her hollow and shivering.

Isben crawled over to her, clutching his bleeding arm to his chest. "Hold on, it's okay." He laced his hand into hers as the world faded into darkness.

CHAPTER THIRTEEN

"You useless fool!" Wrothe screamed. "I need to see her dead. I need to see her blood on the ground. Need to feel her heart stop beating. And you couldn't help me hold a tiny window for another moment?" She gripped him by the back of his collar and forced him to his knees with inhuman strength. "Why do you vex me so?"

"Forgive me, Mistress. I had a moment of weakness," Ternan begged. He'd never tell her it had been on purpose. The girl deserved a chance.

She grabbed his hair and yanked his head backward, exposing the pulse points of his throat. The heat of her breath grazed his neck. If she let her anger rage unchecked, there was a chance she might accidentally kill him. He hoped she did. Without him, she had no way to breach Amul Dun. She would be helpless again.

Ternan found himself nodding vigorously at the thought while he whimpered a string of incoherent apologies.

The warm flow of her influence poured over him, unexpected and jarring. He expected punishment, even torture, as she had done so many times in the past. He flinched away from her outstretched hand; it brought him so much suffering for far less failures. Instead, she patted his head the same way he had seen her stroke her beloved wolf.

She knelt and wiped away his tears. "I don't like failure." Wrothe sucked on the tip of her sharpened nail before pressing its point against his breastbone, sending a thrill of pain through him.

"We don't know if we've failed," he said. "The last hound had her. She was weak. That boy was too far away."

"No. She still lives. I'd feel Jarand's despair if she had died. That seed I planted in him is already bearing fruit." She twisted the nail. "I should have listened to you. She's too strong to be killed by hounds now." She leaned closer, Ternan could see traces of insanity in her dark eyes. "You must do it for me."

The words struck him hard. In all their years, she'd never asked him to venture outside what his oaths allowed. True, he'd helped her do horrible things and aided her in her quest to escape the mirror realm. But now she was asking him to murder a young girl. He needed to distract her from the thought. Make her forget. Even if it made her angry. He knew the perfect thing.

"You let Regulus learn too much. He saw glimpses of your mind, of the mirror realm. Enough that he figured some things out. And worse, he wrote it all down before he died. It wasn't much, but it's enough for them to find a way to put an end to you for good."

"Fools, all of them. It doesn't matter. I'm smarter." Her dark eyes drilled deep into him. "Kill the girl so I can take the man."

"Why? You've already broken your oaths. I won't break

mine. They know you're here now, know you're a threat. You can't win using your pets, not anymore. The Stonebearers here are too strong for you. Go back to your world, leave us in peace. You've lost."

She pressed her nail deeper. Ternan gripped at the low table behind him.

"Never," she whispered. "It's you who's lost. I will continue to punish your line. I will have Jarand for my own. He will replace you." She drew in a deep breath before letting it out in a laugh that lodged deep in her throat. "If you refuse to kill the girl, then you leave me with little choice. I'll take her as my new host body. She's young and strong. Jarand would do anything for her, we already know that."

"You can't. Please, don't." The thought of Wrothe corrupting Katira, ripping the girl's mind apart, using her body like a puppet like she had to so many others, made him shudder. "There's another way. Regulus also wrote about the barrier between our worlds. I'm working with a talented Bender as we speak. The goal is to make it impossible for you or anything to cross. But manipulated correctly, I believe it will make it possible to finally make a door between the worlds. Allow you to return. That's what you wanted from the beginning, isn't it?"

She withdrew the nail and it slid free of his skin. He sagged in relief. With this distraction, maybe she'd leave the girl alone.

"Can you keep the possibility of a door secret from them? Only you and I would know?"

"Of course, mistress."

The familiar hunger reappeared in her eyes. She was forming a plan. "How long until it's ready?"

"A few days. You'll know. You'll feel the changes. Come for me then."

She turned and walked away. "I will."

The dreamspace world library folded in on itself around him. The streamers of power holding him there withdrew and let him go. The real version of his office returned. He slid to the floor in front of his desk and cradled his head in his hands. If she returned to this world, they might finally be able to put an end to her.

CHAPTER FOURTEEN

*J*arand entered Bremin's office and shut the door
behind him. "I still would prefer to read the pages
on my own time. This is a bother to you."

Bremin rounded on him with unexpected anger. "Had you
read them, or at least looked at them when they'd been given
to you, we might have prevented that attack." He slapped the
desk. "Don't tell me you didn't think of that."

Jarand flinched back at the unexpected confrontation. "Of
course I did. Katira suffered because of it. I've agonized over it
every second since it happened. It was a failure on my part. I
know that. It was your failure too."

Bremin's head whipped up. "What?"

"You knew as well as I did that he was writing them. As
Master Advisor, you had every right to take them after his
death. We both failed." Jarand gripped his cane. Accusations
served no purpose; they needed to focus on the future. "We
have a chance to make it right. Did Master Ternan and Master
Aro come up with anything?"

Bremin rolled his eyes. "They've been squabbling like children since the moment they started studying the pages. I feel like a cranky mother hen having to keep her chicks in line."

"Where are they?"

"Sent them off the same time I came to get you. They've figured out what our next steps are to be. That was the goal."

Jarand's back tightened and he leaned on his cane. He was tired, and Bremin wasn't making his intentions clear nearly fast enough. "What do you need me for?"

Bremin tapped Regulus's notes. "Despite your reluctance, you need to read these. He was writing them with you in mind. There are several sentiments within the text that were meant for only you to see."

"Sounds like him." Jarand worked his way across the room toward the desk. The limp he tried his best to hide was now obvious. "He felt that he let me down personally, that it was directly his fault for what happened to Mirelle. I gave him my complete forgiveness before the end, but I don't think he ever forgave himself. Avoiding reading them was easier than facing that again."

"With the current state of Amul Dun, I need you to understand the full extent of our problem." Bremin indicated a comfortable armchair and footrest next to the fire. A large mug of ale rested on the table beside another bright stone sphere. "I hate making you do this, so I figured I'd try to at least make it comfortable."

"This either makes you a horrible or wonderful friend. I'm not sure which." Jarand lowered himself into the chair which had warmed with the fire. The heat felt like heaven on his aching back.

"Let's hope wonderful." He set the pages into Jarand's lap. "I won't be far if you need anything."

Jarand took a sip of the ale and picked up the first page. At first the spidery scrawl refused to form into words. Lines of text ran all over the page, uneven and often trailing up the edges. In years past, Master Regulus always insisted on a scribe; this was why.

The words came into focus, and Jarand began reading. Before the end of the first page, Master Regulus began a detailed description of how Wrothe had torn his mind and anchored herself to him.

Jarand pressed his eyes shut. The memory of the man's death was still too raw. Reading an account of the torture he had suffered at that monster's hand tugged at the raw aching point deep inside. He wanted to be repulsed, wanted to find yet another reason not to read further. Instead, he found himself desperate to know what happened to his master.

When Wrothe took Master Regulus, she joined herself to his mind as well as his power. She invaded his thoughts, grabbed hold of important information and used it to her own ends. She stole everything he knew, from the weapons he had created, to the whereabouts of the Stonebearers hidden away in the cities. And as one of the top Seekers, Master Regulus knew far more than most.

The writing continued. Through the connection Wrothe had established, he found he could use it to his advantage. When she was distracted, he slipped into her vast store of knowledge. She punished him cruelly when she found him, but because he was her anchor, she could not kill him.

He did it over and over, each time, dipping deeper into her mind, each time coming back with a tiny sliver of information about her past, about the mirror realm, about their weak-nesses. He stored every piece of information away. When he was finally free, he dedicated his last days to putting it to paper.

Jarand's breath hitched. He hadn't realized how much pain these pages cost his master. He continued reading. Several pages in, a scrawled message written in the margin of the page caught his attention.

"Jarand, when you read this I will be gone. Don't feel guilty. I got myself into this mess. You withstood Wrothe's pull and put her back where she belongs. You rescued me from her cruelty. I only wish I could have been stronger against her. She wants you, don't give into her, no matter what. Please forgive yourself, this had to be."

The words soothed him like one of Mirelle's balms. Master Regulus told him the same thing the day he died, but Jarand wasn't ready to hear it. He was now. His daughter was in danger, and these pages contained the clues to make her safe. Bremin mentioned other, more pressing things in the pages, information on Wrothe's true nature, a way to stop the attacks.

Regulus's difficult scrawling hand made the process slow. Jarand stood, stretched, and fed the fire before returning to the pages, this time grabbing the woven blanket Bremin had left draped over the back of the chair. He drank the remainder of the ale and resumed reading.

As he settled back into the chair, a strange twinge of pain wrapped around his calf followed by another. With the promise of finding answers in the pages, he wanted to shrug it off. Blind fear screamed in the back of his mind, in the place he felt Katira.

The pain wasn't his.

He set down the pages and gripped his stone and his mind filled with her spikes of panic and desperation. Something sharp and jagged clamped down on her arm.

He rushed to the door, cane in hand, nearly knocking over Bremin in the process.

"An attack. Katira. I need Guardians, now!" Jarand barked orders and expected to be obeyed. In a time like this, every second counted.

Bremin dropped the book he'd been reading and bolted to the door.

Jarand centered himself on the bond between them. Katira's mind had turned to the desperate quiet that comes when nothing else but survival mattered. It was a feeling he knew all too well.

Bremin sprinted down the hall toward Lady Alystra's quarters to raise the alarm. Jarand hobbled as best he could toward Katira, ignoring the spike of pain slamming into him with every step. He urged himself to go faster. Katira had been lucky before, her power took control, eliminated the hounds.

The hall behind him filled with rushed heavy footsteps and the sound of metal on metal.

Issa dashed past gripping her sword. "What's going on?"

"Save her, Issa. I can't."

The Guardian's eyes widened, and she redoubled her speed.

When Jarand reached the library, he fell back into his training. He circled the room, stone in hand, wishing he had worn a blade. Even a belt knife would be enough to force distance between himself and one of the hounds. The cavernous library had dozens of dark alcoves for a hound to hide in; he had to be sure. Each noise pricked at his ears, each scratch of an armored boot on the tile, each brush of a hand over one of the library's tables.

As he drew closer, ash and charred piles of bone littered the floor. Katira lay curled up on the floor. Issa knelt next to her and talked to her in a low soothing voice. A few paces away, the Guardian who had been outside Lady Alystra's apartments knelt next to Isben, who sat propped up against a wall clutching his arm. Wet bloody stains marked his clothes.

"She needs you, Jarand." Issa said as she stood to face him. "I've summoned Cassim. He'll be here soon."

Guilt stuck in his throat like broken glass, cutting at each attempt to swallow it down. He'd promised her he'd do everything possible to keep something like this from happening again, and he'd failed. He lowered himself to the floor next to her, opened his power, and joined with her. If there was any time she needed his comfort, it was now.

Hurried footsteps on tile announced more people coming. Bremin burst into the alcove with Lady Alystra following close behind.

"Tell me what happened," she ordered.

"Hounds again. More than last time. Not sure who struck the killing blows, but Katira did some of it." Jarand wanted to be strong, but feeling Katira shuddering and twitching under his hand, feeling the void of shock through their bond, broke him. "You said you'd strengthen the wards. How is this possible?" He couldn't keep the anger from his voice. The one person he cared about was suffering again. He had failed her. Amul Dun had failed her.

"Calm yourself." Bremin stepped between the two of them, creating a barrier as if he worried Jarand might get violent. "Being upset won't change what's happened."

"I made promises that keep being broken. I have a right to be upset. Hasn't she suffered enough?" He brushed the hair from Katira's face, wishing he could do more.

Lady Alystra stepped around Bremin and knelt next to Jarand. "I made you a promise and I couldn't keep it." She lowered her head. "You must forgive me. You have every right to be angry. Please focus that anger on the problem. Your daughter is being targeted. We can't ignore that. For the time being, she is not to leave your sight. I can think of no one else better equipped to protect her than you."

The High Lady's humility took Jarand by surprise. He had expected a reprimand for raising his voice to her.

"All of Amul Dun needs to know about this danger," he urged. Surely she'd have to agree now. "Those who live here have the right to protect themselves. You've said it yourself, we are stronger when we work together. Katira might be the one being targeted, but that doesn't mean Wrothe won't try something new."

Lady Alystra swept her eyes over the scene, her brow wrinkling at the sight of the two young apprentices being tended to. "We will inform the heads of the orders. They will decide the best way to communicate this threat to those they serve."

"That's not enough, and you know it."

The library doors opened again. Cassim ran straight to Issa, his fear for her clear on his face. It didn't take him long to see why he'd been summoned, or who needed him most. He picked his way around a smoking pile of ash to Katira's side.

"It's what I'm prepared to do for now. No general pronouncements. Keep Amul Dun strong. I assign you to inform the Captain of the Guard of this threat and I expect you to tell him of my concerns to keep this quiet."

Jarand placed his fist over his heart. He was loyal, but she was wrong. "As you command, My Lady."

Darkness. Shadows darting in and out of the edge of sight.

Teeth, fangs, claws. Broken pillars. Wrothe. Falling. Katira clutched the broken stone blade, readying herself to strike and at the same time knowing this was the past. No matter what she did, she would fail. Wrothe triggered the oath. The burning web tightened, cutting into her arms and her legs.

A sound.

Soft, gentle, comforting.

"Shh... it's alright. I'm here. You're safe now." A cool hand brushed her hair from her face. The ruins were weeks ago. Papan straightened the blanket.

Katira couldn't shake the confusion filling her head. "Where are we?" She touched the new bandage on her arm and felt the stiff ache of other wrappings concealed beneath her bed clothes. "What happened?"

"What do you remember?" Papan opened the shutters and bright light flooded in, filling her comfortable room. Deep creases marred his forehead.

Katira pressed her eyes shut, waiting for her sluggish thoughts to materialize into something useful. She was in the library. She wasn't alone. Hounds materialized out of nowhere. "Isben?"

"Both of you needed a bit of patching up. He's fine." He selected a plain woolen gray dress from the wardrobe and draped it over the chair. "What else do you remember?"

More fragments of memory returned and linked together. The events of the night before became clearer. "It was like before. I heard their nails against the tile. A shadow shifted in the darkness between the shelves."

Watching Papan select clothes for her was oddly comforting. She peeled back the blankets and sat on the edge of the bed. The cold morning air made her shiver in a way that told her she wasn't well.

"You don't need to get up. You're not training this morning. Cassim's orders. He'd have you stay in bed all day. Knowing you, that's not going to happen. These are for when you feel ready." He laid out a pair of thick socks. "What else can you tell me?"

"I tried to make a shield, something to keep them back." She hugged her arms around herself. "I couldn't wake the power, not until one of them bit me, then it woke itself."

"Go on."

The ache under the wrappings around her middle triggered another set of memories. "One of them was larger, the last one. Something was different about it. My power couldn't touch it at first."

Papan stopped searching through the wardrobe. "What do you mean?"

"Something stopped it, sucked it in. Reminded me of a shield now that I think about it." She touched at her waist, tracing the line of tender points where those teeth had dug in. "I couldn't stop it. If it weren't for Issa, this might have been much worse. It had me."

He joined her on the edge of the bed, shoulders slumped. "It's my fault. I underestimated our enemy. It won't happen again. It can't." His voice cracked as his emotions got the best of him.

"I promised you if they came for me again, I'd run." The words tumbled out, trying to soothe away the guilt wrapping around him, trying to take some of the blame. "We tried. We didn't get far before we were cornered. I didn't know where they were coming from."

He wrapped a comforting arm around her and pulled her close. "You did what you needed to do to survive. Don't think I'm upset. I'm not."

With him this close, it was easy for Katira to feel the truth in his words. There was no anger toward her there, no blame. Instead, he radiated with a determination to keep her safe, to keep his home safe. She leaned into him, taking comfort in his presence. The strain from fighting and the ache of being injured crept back. She let her eyes close.

He stroked her hair as she slipped back asleep.

When she woke again, hours later, bright sunlight poured in through the window. She flexed her hands, carefully testing the muscles and connective tissue Cassim healed. The ache from before was mostly gone. Her stomach growled with a ravenous hunger.

She pulled on the clothes laid out by Papan and went out to the living room. A covered tray of food rested on the table. When she saw it, she immediately felt guilty. As apprentice, she was meant to get the breakfast tray and ready the room for the morning's lesson. One day in and she'd already failed.

"Stop beating yourself up." Papan said from his chair by the fire. "Part of my job as your master is to take care of you as well. How are you feeling?"

Katira's face went hot. She forgot he could tell things through the apprentice bond. "Better. Thank you."

"Eat up." He joined her at the table and lifted the cloth, revealing a simple meal of porridge and dried fruits. "When you're finished, Bremin wants us to meet with him."

CHAPTER FIFTEEN

*P*apan led the way to the abandoned western
observation tower. The glowing sphere in his hand
pushed past the gloom of the seldom used dusty passage. This
far back in the tower, fragile winter afternoon sunlight fought
to reach the few scattered windows. Katira stayed close to him,
glad for the extra light, glad to not be alone. Even still, the
halls and ceiling pressed in, as if at any moment the whole
tower might tumble down through the arched ribs of the
ceiling.

The itching need to leave, to escape, welled up within her.

"You're tense. Everything okay?" Papan asked.

They passed the last dim puddle of light from the final
window and walked into the gloom.

Katira ran her finger over the edge of her stone. "Talk to
me about something."

"What?"

"Distract me. Dark hallways make me nervous."

"What do you want me to talk about?" He rested his hand

on the long belt knife in its well-worn leather sheath at his waist. She remembered watching him carefully hone and polish it during long quiet evenings when she was growing up.

Katira's mind spun, eager to find anything to fill the silence. "When did you take up blacksmithing?"

He tapped his fingers on the sheath as if trying to remember. "When Mamar and I were assigned our first protectorate to watch over, an opportunity to learn it came up, so I grabbed it. Finding work and learning a trade makes a good disguise, keeps people from suspecting who we really are. That was about 190 years ago." The mention of Mamar made him pause, and a hint of longing and grief touched the bond. He didn't wall it off this time. "I looked younger then. When the local iron smith's apprentice got married and moved away, I offered to step in. He taught me everything a decent town's blacksmith should know. I made farming tools, chain, hinges, horseshoes for the town farrier, and simple knives. I was good at it too. After about a decade it started to feel too easy. I needed a greater challenge."

The tight knot in Katira's chest started to loosen. "Keep going, that's helping."

"We left as the first whispers of rumor start to spread. Townspeople grew suspicious of us. It was time to move on. We traveled from town to town, ten years here, fifteen there. Mamar set up shop as a healer, me as a blacksmith. Both of us continued to learn and master our trades, all while secretly defending the towns we were near against dark things." He shifted his grip on his cane with a grunt. "Even before everything changed, most people weren't comfortable with having a Stonebearer in their midst. They felt threatened by us, scared because they didn't understand what we could do. It was only a matter of time before something cracked."

"Are you talking about the war?"

Papan's face hardened as if even the word stung. "Everything changed overnight. The idea that the power was evil, was unnatural, swept through the whole world like a plague. Militias and strike forces assembled everywhere the belief took hold. They wanted us exterminated." He pressed his fingers to his chest over where the stone hid. "Lady Alystra gathered all of us, organized proper defenses, did what was necessary to protect our strongholds. I had seniority and experience; I ascended the ranks quickly."

"And you became a General."

"Yes. Because in the end, that's what I was." He stopped at the base of a flight of stairs, breathless from the long walk. Voices echoed down from above. "Here we are. Give me a minute and we'll go up and join them."

A new, terrible thought dawned on her. "Did you kill anyone?"

Beads of sweat gathered on the bridge of his nose and glittered in the light of the glowing sphere. "Yes." The word fell from his lips, heavy and full of memory. "Hated each time my hand was forced. Still hate the thought of it." He set his foot on the first stair of the spiral staircase.

Katira shrank back from the cloying darkness of the narrow stairwell. She'd been forced down one like it at the ruins, and the memories from that place still gave her nightmares. Papan pushed ahead, ascending the stairs one labored step at a time. If she stayed below, she'd be stuck alone. She hurried to climb with him. The voices from above grew louder. Papan's breathing grew shorter and labored.

The door at the first landing was so old, it appeared to be crumbling from the edges in. At the next landing, the door and walls around it were charred and black. They continued to climb.

At the third landing, the welcome sight of daylight filtered in through narrow windows. They were higher than she'd imagined. The tops of the different wings of the tower spread from the central hub of the main hall. Beyond, the outer wall separated them from the encroaching forest.

They climbed another three flights. There, the top of the stairs opened into a small room no more than six paces wide. Windows made up of hundreds of tiny panes filled each of the four walls, making the room seem much larger and opening it to an impressive view of the entire valley below. Katira stepped closer and was rewarded with an extreme desire to huddle on the floor. Her stomach seized at the dizzying height. A chill wind rattled the panes and crept in, making her wish she'd brought a cloak.

Standing tall in the center of the room was a chair that looked as if it had been grown from the very walls and floor. Green streaks of motherstone climbed the arms and tall back like a creeping vine.

Lady Alystra and Bremin stood in a tight knot, locked in conversation with Master Ternan and Master Aro around a narrow table that looked as if it might crumble at any second. Two simple stools were tucked underneath and out of the way. In the other corner, Issa and Cassim waited alongside an impatient Isben. With them all in there, the room was full to bursting.

"Good, General. You made it. Now we can begin." Lady Alystra acknowledged him with a nod of her head. She rested her hand on the ancient stone chair. "This is the relic we will alter to help us better see and work with the barrier. From the clues Master Regulus left us, Masters Ternan and Aro have pieced together a way to manipulate the energies with the hope that once we can more clearly see what we are working with, we can find a way to strengthen it and prevent those horrors from slipping through."

Isben quietly maneuvered around Cassim to stand next to Katira. "Are you okay?" he whispered into her ear.

Katira let her hand brush against his and was pleased when he took the hint and curled his fingers around hers. "I'm okay now. You?"

Bremin stepped forward, his hands tucked neatly behind his back. "The security of Amul Dun comes first. Jarand already informed Captain Edmont of the situation and warned him that there might be more unwelcome intruders before we finish. He will do what's necessary to secure the inhabited areas of the tower." He fixed his eyes on Papan. "Jarand, your responsibility is to ensure the security of this room and the relic it holds. Issa has already agreed to be your second. Create a plan and present it to me as soon as it's complete. From the moment work begins up here, this area will become a target for our enemy. We must be prepared."

Papan agreed, pressing his fist to his chest and giving a short formal bow.

Bremin stepped back and nodded to Master Aro, whose attention was fixed on an item in his hand Katira couldn't see. Cassim tapped the man's shoulder.

Master Aro yelped and fumbled the item, nearly letting it fall through his fingers. "Sorry, excuse me. Wasn't paying attention. Did you need something?"

"Take a moment to explain what you and Master Ternan need to do." Bremin prompted. "Just like you explained it to me earlier."

The ungainly man took a hesitant step forward. His eyes

darted around the room, and he had to swallow several times before speaking.

"You see, erm, our understanding of the barrier between worlds is flawed at best. Our wards and protections have worked in the past because they stopped monsters already in the world. There are set points out in the world where monsters can cross the barrier, none of which are located anywhere close to the tower. The only way a shadow hound could get inside the tower is because one of these points has formed inside the walls, or the barrier itself has weakened to the point where they can pass through anywhere at will. Let's hope it hasn't come to that."

He shuffled his feet and rubbed the item in his hand. Lady Alystra gave him an encouraging nod to keep going. "With what we learned from Master Regulus's notes, we believe it's possible to see the barrier itself over large distances and find these points or weaknesses." He turned to the large stone chair. "The Occulus Seat is already glyph bound to allow its user to see long distances, as it was originally used to watch for invading forces. When we created the newer warning net system, it was no longer needed."

"Is it necessary to have this thing clear at the top of a blasted tower?" Cassim interrupted. From the sweat staining his tunic, he didn't like the climb up all those stairs either.

Katira caught sight of a tiny smile crossing Papan's face; he was thinking the same thing.

"Ignore him." Issa elbowed Cassim. "Please continue, Master Aro."

Master Aro crooked his head to the side, not quite under-standing what Cassim meant. "Of course, it has to be up here. This is where the chair is. The pathways of motherstone are already laid."

Master Ternan cleared his throat. "What he means, Cassim, is it would take far too long to relocate the chair and start in a new location. We need this working as soon as possible. Like the High Lady said, the security of Amul Dun depends on how quickly we can assess and strengthen the barrier."

The healer's shoulders sagged, and he muttered something under his breath. Issa patted him on the back.

"Show them what you showed us, Aro." Lady Alystra said. "They need to see what you've learned so far."

Master Aro opened his hand to reveal a palm-length rod of smooth pale green motherstone. His markings at his wrists and along the backs of his hands began to glow. "This testing rod holds a series of fixed glyphs Ternan and I have been manipulating to see if it's even possible to make the barrier visible. It took ages, but we stumbled on a combination that worked." A thin ribbon of power flowed from his fingertip and touched the rod.

Katira involuntarily stepped back. If breaking the barrier meant hounds could come through, then by using this thing, they risked an attack without even knowing it. Isben squeezed her hand. If anything happened, they would face it together.

The rod came to life, glowing and casting more tiny ribbons into the air in front of Master Aro. These ribbons formed intricate symbols that laced in and through each other, far more complex than the simple glyphs Katira had been taught. Dozens of tiny stars shot from the pattern and assembled themselves in a flat plane hovering in front of Master Aro. These stars burst into tinier and tinier points until something new started to form.

Master Aro watched on, as intent and curious as ever. "These are the threads of the barrier itself," he said, indicating the blanket-like mesh. Each thread shone with its own distinct color and pattern and wove around the thousands of other threads, constantly moving and pulsing with life. "From what we can tell, it moves and reacts like a living thing. If it is indeed alive, we can make it stronger, heal it." He touched one of the threads and it twitched away from his fingers. "That's where we'll need your expertise, Cassim."

If Cassim looked flustered before, he looked like a hooked fish now. His mouth snapped open and shut in disbelief.

When he finally brought himself to speak, it was a worried protest. "This is really a job for Master Firen. I work with people, not pulsating carpets. I don't even know where to start."

"Regardless of what you think, you're the best choice for the job." Lady Alystra said. "You've had the most success working with those harmed by Wrothe. You've fought against the hounds. Most importantly, you already know what danger Amul Dun is in and I can trust you not to spread rumors. I can't say the same about Master Firen."

Papan tightened his hand around the head of the cane. A tightly controlled anger radiated on his side of the bond. "Yesterday, you promised me that the heads of the orders would be informed about this threat at our doors. That includes Master Firen. What was he told?"

"Watch your tone, Jarand," Bremin warned. "He knows shadow hounds were spotted within the tower and of the possibility of there being more. That's the extent of what he needs to know. We've never been able to trust him with secrets. This is no exception. He can protect the infirmary well enough knowing only that."

"I agree with them." Cassim added. "The man can't keep a secret for the life of him."

Master Aro fiddled with the motherstone rod in his hands before speaking up. "As I was saying, we think the barrier here at Amul Dun can be examined and strengthened to the point nothing can pass through. But first, the glyph sequences we've developed need to be integrated into the Occulus Seat." He squinted as he studied the light shining in through the windows. "That will take the remainder of the day today and perhaps some of tomorrow."

"Then we have a plan." Lady Alystra tugged her sleeves straight. "Jarand and Issa, coordinate a guard detail that will ensure there's always one of you up here when these two are working. Cassim, you won't be needed until this first phase is complete, so you are free to go. As for our young apprentices here—" She suppressed a sigh, as if hating what she needed to say. "This place was supposed to be a safe home for you. For all of us. Until we find a way to prevent those monsters from coming through, you must always be paired with someone who can protect you. No exceptions."

"Yes, High Lady," both Katira and Isben said in unison.

"To work. You all know what you need to do." Lady Alystra clapped her hands.

The stillness in the room broke as everyone set into motion, jostling around each other to get where they needed to be.

Isben turned to face Katira, hands fluttering like butterflies eager to touch her face. "You had me so scared last night. By the Stonemother's throne itself, those things kept coming after you. I thought they'd killed you."

"I really am okay." She took hold of his hands and stilled them in hers. "Help came in time, thankfully. What about you? Where did it get you?"

He pinched at the snug bandage at his wrist and made a

face. "Just my arm. It's pretty tender. The stupid hound really dug in. Took Cassim ages to finish patching it up. I can't complain. I was able to walk away from it. When Lady Alystra Traveled out of the library with you and your father, I feared the worst."

"She did? I don't remember that." Katira glanced over to the High Lady who was speaking with Master Ternan. Beneath that stern commanding exterior, the woman did truly care about her people. "I feel fine now. A little tired, that's all."

Papan finished his conversation with Issa and approached the two of them. "I'll be taking first watch up here. Isben, Bremin's heading down, it's time for you to go with him. Katira, there's no use wasting time sitting around. For the next while you will be studying with me during my watch."

Bremin cleared his throat from where he stood at the top of the stairs. Isben gave Katira's hand one more squeeze before leaving. She would have felt better if he had stayed. Papan could have easily taught them together. With everyone gone, the muttering and paper shifting of Master Ternan and Master Aro grated on Katira's nerves.

"What about them?" Katira flicked her gaze to the two Stonebearers bent over the table. She always felt uneasy around Master Ternan. The thought of working with the power in the same room with him made her feel sick.

Papan glanced over to the table and sighed. He didn't like the idea either. "Knowing them, they've already forgotten we're here. We can use this to our advantage. You need to be comfortable working with the power regardless of the environment or who is around. It's not ideal, I know. We must do our best with what the situation will allow."

～

Katira snatched one of the pair of rickety stools out from under the table where the eccentric pair of masters continued to work. Master Ternan had already claimed the other stool and busied himself drawing arrays of symbols and glyphs onto a large paper while Master Aro paced the length of the room. Now and again, he'd stop and study the glyphs already scattered on the table's surface and adjust them. With each new completed glyph Master Ternan finished, Master Aro took it and carefully inspected it before laying it into the pattern.

From the looks of it, Master Aro wasn't one who could work sitting down. Katira tucked the stool into the nook behind the jutting wall of the stairwell for Papan before settling herself on the floor and tucking her skirts around her legs to ward off the chill. It didn't do much. Cold crept its way through the thick wool skirt and she shivered anyway.

Papan settled himself on the stool with a relieved sigh. "We need to talk about why you struggled to use the power last night."

Another breeze teased in from between the panes of the drafty windows. Katira stuck her hands into the warmth under her arms. "The calm wouldn't come. I was too scared and couldn't focus properly. I knew what those things could do to me."

He rested his elbows on his knees. "None of that is your fault. You need more time, more practice. Back when I was an apprentice, my first months were spent learning only that. Frustrated me to no end then." He smiled and shook his head at the memory. "Looking back, I think Master Regulus was a far more patient teacher than I could ever hope to be."

Katira tried to remember what Mamar used to tell her when she became frustrated during her lessons.

"You're not him," she started. It felt right. "We don't have time to do it his way. When this crisis is over, we can slow down, fill in the gaps of what we missed. But for right now, you must teach me what I need to learn to survive."

"I wish it were that easy." He wrung his hands together in front of him. "The power is as dangerous as any hound. More so, even. It takes years of working with it before you can tell how much is safe to use and how much you have in reserve. There isn't any alternative than to keep practicing." His hands stilled and he looked her straight in the eyes. "Using too much will kill you."

"That's what happened last night, isn't it? You worried I might have got too close to my limit."

He didn't need to say anything; the way his forehead pinched together told her plenty.

"Then it's best I start understanding this." She glanced to where the two men continued to piece together papers on the table. Papan was right; they were so engrossed in their work that they probably wouldn't notice if the room was on fire, let alone if she practiced. She drew the small apprentice stone from her neck and bound it to her hand. "Why couldn't I use the power when I wanted to?"

The sudden change jarred Papan back into the moment. "Right." He withdrew his own stone but didn't bind it. "It's like you said. Your fear of being attacked made it too difficult to focus. Without calm and focus, the Khandashii cannot be summoned."

"What about later? When it took control?" She stroked the smooth lump of motherstone against her palm. Its solid presence helped ground her.

"That's different. Not many born with the power are tested like you've been, especially not so young. Most will never experience it. I know I never have. The Khandashii itself was protecting you. No one knows exactly how, but it can sense when its host is in mortal danger and isn't able to defend itself. It's the only explanation for when it's manifested itself these last two days. It's not the first time." He scratched at his beard. "It saved you when you were a baby as well."

They both fell quiet. Papan locked in memory and Katira locked in thought. The whistling gusts outside grew stronger, and the observation tower creaked and gently rocked back and forth. If she were to master her focus, would that mean the power would no longer come to her aid when she needed it most?

It was a risk she was willing to take. If she was going to be of use to anyone, if she was going to ever be able to protect herself, she had to learn and practice until using the power came as natural as breathing. Mamar taught her how to study. Papan taught her to be responsible and work hard. There was no time to waste. First things first.

"How do you find focus when you're afraid?" she asked.

The knot in Papan's forehead relaxed. "It's not really something you can learn. You need time, that's all. You can't force it. The more you work with the power, the easier it is to use it regardless of the situation. Most take years to reach that point, some take decades."

"That's not helpful. I need to be able to use it now, regardless of how scared I am. You said it yourself, I'm in danger here." She gingerly touched the tender scars on her arms. "Help me learn this so I can't fail again."

"You're supposed to be taking it easy today." He grunted his frustration and his gaze dropped to the tidy bandage around her arm. "Knowing you, you won't be satisfied if we just talk, will you?"

In the weeks after the battle at Khanrosh and before they'd

been bonded, all Katira wanted was for him to lower his walls and talk to her. It struck her as darkly ironic he now offered it freely and she wanted something else. "Can't we do a bit of both?"

He unlaced his fingers and pulled a short fat candle from his pocket. "Suppose we can," he said with a resigned smile. "But, I insist on keeping things simple. Today, you will learn to light a candle. Nothing more."

Another draft from the windows worked its way down Katira's neck, and she shivered. Knowing how to make a fire quickly would be a welcome skill.

Papan stuck the candle on the edge of the windowsill and removed his stone from around his neck. "Funny enough, I think this glyph has saved my life more than any other glyphs combined. I can't tell you how many times I've been stuck out in the wild when the weather's turned nasty. Being able to create fire without flint or dry tinder comes in handy."

He bound his stone to his hand. Katira felt the echoed hot rush of power as his markings glowed to life. A glyph formed over his extended palm and hovered for a moment before winking into a bright spark. He guided the spark to touch the candle's wick where it caught and started burning.

"Considering your current needs, this is the perfect glyph for you to practice today. With each attempt I'll require you to start from nothing. You'll go through the process of opening yourself to the power, focusing to form a simple precise glyph, then closing it once more." He licked his thumb and pinched out the flame.

"That's it?" Katira knew she should be grateful. After what had happened, Papan had every right to force her to rest and wait a few days before resuming their teaching. The places where the hounds had bitten her ached and itched as they continued to heal. The vessel of energy within her felt hollow compared to the day before.

Still, this was her chance to learn as much as she could, and they were wasting time by practicing lighting a candle. "But I could learn so much more," she protested. "Couldn't you teach me two or three glyphs today?"

Papan raised an eyebrow.

"No, forget I asked. This is perfect." She turned her attention to the candle. "Show me the glyph again."

He held out the hand where his stone was bound into the palm. A glyph resembling a starburst with six sharply angled points appeared. It hung in the air between them for the space of a breath before shrinking down and lighting the candle once more.

"The Khandashii is a form of energy, and energy creates heat. As you've noticed, the power burns when you open yourself to it. The lines marking the skin of mature wielders comes from that heat slowly altering the body along the pathways it travels." He held out his arm showing the series of branching white lines there.

Katira leaned forward and traced one with a finger. "So, the lines are caused by scarring? I thought it was something else."

He nodded and continued. "With the simple shield, we formed a circle to channel raw power into a specific shape. Lighting a candle is very similar in that it still uses raw power. The simple fire glyph focuses raw power into a sharp point hot enough to create a spark. Once formed, you guide the spark to the wick. Fairly simple, but, like all work with the power, it requires a controlled stream of focus."

He pinched out the candle once more. "Once you're ready, start by forming the glyph above your hand."

Katira glanced toward the two masters still working at the table. She could do this with them there. It was a skill, just like anything else. She pictured the vessel within her and willed it to pour out and fill her. It stayed put, not even wavering a fraction. She balled her fist and tried again. If it didn't move willingly, she would simply try harder.

"Stop." Papan instructed. "Your ability to use the Khandashii is a partnership, and you must surrender to it. Try again."

She relaxed her hands and allowed her breathing to grow calm and steady. This time when she pictured the vessel, she also imagined how it was cradled firmly in place with strong rope. It wasn't a matter of only tipping the vessel. She also needed to allow the rope to loosen and fall away. When she tried again, the vessel gently tipped, and the familiar heat raced through her.

She formed the pattern Papan showed her, taking care to include six sharp points. Once it was ready, she allowed it to spring to action, forming the bright spark.

"Good," he encouraged. "Keep your focus."

As soon as he had said the words, her attention shot toward him and the spark flew at his face. It popped against a tiny shield he formed faster than she could see.

Her power shrank back into the safety of its vessel. "Sorry! I didn't mean to."

"It's all right." He chuckled to himself. "Same thing happened to me when I was training with Master Regulus. Lit his hair on fire. I was ready. Again, focus is so important. The more you practice, the easier it will be to maintain control of your glyph. Try again."

Katira envisioned the vessel and its rope once more. It came easier this time, faster. She formed the glyph and watched the spark form. Papan gave a nod of approval and gestured to the candle. She willed the spark to move. It jumped and wiggled as she guided it until it touched the wick. A tendril of smoke, then a small flame appeared.

"Well done. You can let go of the spark." He continued to coach.

They continued on through the morning. With each attempt, lighting the candle came easier and faster, the spark moving smoother and with more control. By the end of the morning, her confidence surged.

CHAPTER SIXTEEN

*N*oise in the stairwell brought Papan to his feet. Katira pinched out the candle and gripped the stone bound in her hand. After all the warnings of a potential attack, she wanted to be ready. Something metal bounced down the stairs followed by a string of muttered curses. A sharp reprimand followed. Katira relaxed her hand. Isben and Issa had returned.

The great bell in the center of the tower tolled, sounding far away. Issa rounded the top of the stairs carrying a small table with a small power-fueled brazier like the ones down in the library precariously balanced on top. Before she could set it down, Master Aro straightened from his work, pulled a piece of paper from one of the dozens of pockets dotting his clothes, and pushed it at her without a word. It earned him a well-deserved glare. He blanched and tucked the paper back in its pocket.

Issa set the table over in the nook where Katira and Papan had spent the morning working, then lifted the brazier and placed it in the center of the room in front of the imposing chair.

"You manage to get the things we discussed?" Papan asked.

Issa cocked her head toward the stair. "He insisted on carrying most of it. Stubborn one, that."

Isben huffed up the last few stairs, bristling with supplies. He carried a large basket piled high with odds and ends. Katira spied the corner of a thick warm blanket poking out. A pair of simple wooden chairs with curved armrests were strapped to his back.

Master Aro shifted from foot to foot, clearly eager to give Issa the paper.

Issa made a point of ignoring him and instead motioned Isben to set his load on the table. "Anything of interest happen while I was gone?"

"Not really." Papan snatched out a cup and bottle from the basket and poured himself a drink of water. "They're still organizing the glyphs, haven't even touched it yet."

"Any sign of hounds?" She lowered her voice, but Katira still heard.

"Thankfully, no, and no unusual activity against the ward I set either." He took a long drink. "This can't last."

Master Aro continued to stand and awkwardly shuffle, waiting for Issa's attention.

Issa took a breath and slowly let it out before turning. "Okay, I'm ready now. What is it?"

The lanky Bender rummaged through his pockets and pulled out the rumpled list once more. "Supplies. If you take this list to the main workshop, they'll know what it means."

Issa scanned the list and furrowed her brow before handing it to Papan. "The General is finishing his shift and will be heading down. You won't object to him seeing that this is taken care of." It wasn't a question.

Master Aro shook his head. "The sooner I can get these materials, the sooner we can begin integrating the new glyphs into the Occulus Seat."

Papan took the list. "Understood."

Another set of footsteps echoed up the stairs, these ones lighter, almost soundless.

"That's Bremin," Papan said. "I'd recognize his steps anywhere."

Sure enough, Bremin rounded the last bend of the spiral stair, satchel slung over his shoulder and a basket under his other arm.

"It had to be the highest part of the entire keep, didn't it?" He took a moment to catch his breath as he set down the basket on one of the chairs.

"It's, well, it's in the plans, and..." Master Aro trailed off at the sight of Bremin's utterly unamused face.

Master Ternan looked up from the glyph he'd been carefully sketching. "It was a rhetorical question, Aro. It's not personal. They don't like climbing the stairs, that's all." He turned his attention to Bremin. "Have you considered my idea?"

"That's why I'm here." Bremin slid a short stack of papers from his satchel and laid them out on the smaller table. "The High Lady and I discussed it and agree that inducing a dream state in the user might be the key that allows us to see the extent of the barrier. I've drawn out a few options of glyphs that might make this possible."

"Wait, what?" Papan asked. He didn't wait for Bremin to explain himself before launching into his attack. "That's a completely foolish idea. It would leave the user defenseless."

Isben handed a cup filled with water to Katira. "This might take a while. Lady Alystra had the same argument."

"Hear me out." Bremin held up a hand to halt any further objections. "The barrier isn't just a flat wall between the worlds. It's more like a twist in realities. The mirror realm and our world exist in the same plane. If we limit our ability to only what we can see, we might miss something vital. That's why Master Ternan feels invoking a dream state would make it possible for whoever is sitting in the chair to intuitively understand the barrier better."

"Why wasn't either of us consulted about this change?" An angry growl crept into Papan's voice.

"It doesn't affect your duties." Bremin rested his fists on top of the papers he brought. "You'd need to watch over whoever used the chair, regardless of what state of consciousness they are in."

Issa thumbed the pommel of her sword. "I'm with Jarand on this. The whole business of manipulating the barrier already has me on edge. This idea introduces elements we can't begin to imagine, let alone control."

Master Aro pushed his way to the table and bent over the new notes, grunting here and there as he thought. He flipped a page and studied a series of sketched glyphs. He pointed at a block of compact text. "I don't remember discussing this."

Bremin looked closer, squinting at the words. "Oh, that's important. You must create a way for someone else to pull the user from the dream state safely. I won't risk someone having their mind accidentally torn should there be an emergency."

Papan stiffened and glanced at the stone chair. "What do you mean? What kind of emergency?"

Bremin replaced the page neatly back into the stack. "If my theory is correct, and it usually is, healing the barrier will require one of us using the chair to both find and heal weaknesses in the barrier. Both of these things will require the use of the power. We're not sure how aware the user will be of their own power in the dream state."

Isben approached the table, giving voice to the question no one wanted to ask. "Is there a way to prevent this device from draining a wielder dry? If not used carefully, this thing could kill."

Bremin's gaze shifted to the chair itself. "It's a real danger and needs to be addressed. For now, we will need to proceed with utmost caution, knowing that this is a possibility. No one can be allowed to use it without someone else keeping watch over them, preferably a bonded companion. Even with every foreseeable safety in place, there's no way we can predict everything that might happen."

Master Aro fidgeted with his cuffs. "I'm confident we'll find a way to make it work and make it safe. It won't be easy, but I've never turned my back on a challenge." He grinned to himself. "I suppose that's why you wanted me. I have the most experience working with motherstone of any of the Benders, and the scars to prove it."

Katira leaned into Isben. "Does he really? Or is he joking? I can't tell."

"I don't think he knows how to joke. Most Benders are a little strange like this. I think it comes from having to have that intense focus to work on a particle level, to be able to move and shift things around that can't be seen."

"And that makes them..." She didn't finish the thought. It wasn't very polite.

"Crazy," Isben said. "Well, that's not quite the right word. Let's just say it's like they are from another world."

Master Aro cleared his throat and glared at the two

apprentices before continuing. "The supplies I've requested are to reinforce the structure of the seat itself. If something goes catastrophically wrong, the last thing we need is for the relic to fracture, ignite, or explode."

"Right." Papan held out the list. "Bremin, if these are needed quickly, it's best if you take care of it."

Bremin took the list and studied it with a nod. "None of these should present a problem."

"Issa, I turn the watch over to you." Papan gave an informal salute before gripping the railing and working his way down the stairs. "Come, Katira. Master Firen has agreed to teach you for the next few hours. He really doesn't like to be kept waiting."

So much had happened since Katira's first lesson with Cassim the day before that it felt as if more time had passed. Walking into the infirmary summoned up fractured memories of the night before. Papan, setting her on one of the crisp white beds. Master Firen's stork-like face bent over her, talking quietly, as his long slender fingers mended where the hounds tore her skin. Lady Alystra, standing at the foot of the bed. Then, nothing.

There was no trace of her being there now. All the beds were neatly made up. All the supplies and linens stood in neat lines on their shelves. Master Firen's office door yawned open, waiting for her to step inside.

Unlike Cassim's office, which was filled with a jumble of odds and ends, Master Firen's office matched the clean, bright order of the rest of the infirmary. The shelves lining one wall were filled from floor to ceiling with neatly stacked and filed books and scrolls. No doubt the Master Healer could find the precise item he needed instantly. Mamar was the same way. All the items in her healer's shop had a place.

From the little time Katira spent with him, she was sure his mind worked in precisely the same way. Each thought and idea precisely cataloged, awaiting the time when it was needed. As much as he was a Healer, he had the orderly mind of a librarian. He closed the book he'd been reading with a quiet snap and returned it to its spot on the shelf.

"Welcome, Katira. I'm glad you are here." He gestured to a sturdy wooden chair in front of the pristine desk. "Have a seat."

Katira settled into the chair, being careful not to make a sound and break the peaceful silence. Master Firen studied her between his long steepled fingers. "It seems we only have been able to meet under stressful circumstances. I'm glad I can remedy that today. Tell me, how is everything?"

The question was too broad for Katira to answer it easily. What did he mean? How was her stay at the tower? How were her injuries healing from the night before? How was she coping with so many changes? A simple answer was best.

"As good as can be expected, I suppose," she answered.

He held out his hand across the desk, palm up. "May I?"

His friendly manner put her at ease. She set her hand into his. Thanks to Cassim, she knew what he was doing now. The delving glyph was nothing to be afraid of. The markings at his wrist pulsed to life, and she felt the familiar warm flow of the power wash through her and fade.

"I thought I told Jarand that you were supposed to take it easy today," he said. There was the quirk of a smile in the corner of his mouth. "He had you working with the power, didn't he?"

"Don't blame him. I pressed until he gave in. Even then, he only let me light a candle."

"No need to explain. There's no use in being upset at what can't be changed. However, I'll have to be careful with you today. A little extra caution, no need to worry." He drew a sheet of paper from a drawer in the desk and set it down along with a stoppered bottle of ink and a fine quill. "To begin, please draw the glyphs you've learned so far."

Katira picked up the quill and dipped it in the ink before sketching the handful of glyphs she'd been taught. First there was the simple shield, then delve, then the one for simple fire. She wished she knew more. After witnessing the complex work of Masters Aro and Ternan at the relic, she knew a wealth of glyphs existed beyond her understanding. She set down the quill.

Master Firen glanced over the paper with a nod. "Excellent. With these you can perform some very basic life saving techniques." He laid his hands on the table, his stone already bound into his hand, palms facing up. The lines on his arms began to glow and a soft sigh passed through his lips. "Healing is a fairly simple art. A healer identifies what is broken and knits it back together the way it ought to be. You may or may not have noticed, but Stonebearers don't get sick. This is because of the Khandashii itself."

"What about Mamar? The fever meant she was sick, didn't it?"

"Smart girl. Your mother was suffering from a reaction to the toxins on the weapon that wounded her. While she had symptoms of illness like I'm sure you saw back where you came from, it wasn't caused by being exposed to another sick person."

Back in Namragan, people sometimes fell ill in droves and

needed medicine. Even then, Katira had never seen Mamar get sick, or Papan for that matter. When she didn't know any better, she'd attributed it to Mamar's cleanliness and the healing herbs that hung around the cottage. This made more sense.

"Because of the power, wielders never get sick." Master Firen continued to explain. "Common colds, fevers, plagues, and illnesses born by contagion can't take root in us. The power itself burns it away before it can begin to grow. You've already learned about venoms because of your experience with the dark hounds. While the Khandashii will eventually burn away venoms, toxins, and poisons as well, usually the process is too slow. That's why the inflicted wielder must burn it away themselves or have someone help them."

Katira touched one of the older scars on her arm from Khanrosh. It was the first time she'd ever been bitten. Issa had helped her then.

"That leads us to physical injuries. Just because we can't get sick doesn't mean we can't get hurt." He gestured to her new set of bandages to make his point. "The Khandashii will keep a wielder alive far beyond what a normal person can survive. It lends us strength, it heals us faster, it protects us. But it also means that wielders endure far more before finally succumbing than normal people do. It's a blessing and a curse.

"Because of this, most of a healer's training revolves around putting the pieces back together and knowing what goes where. I have a feeling Mirelle already taught you much more than most of my students will ever learn about the body." He opened his hands wide. "Should you become a Healer, you would do very well here." He turned and selected a shallow porcelain dish and filled it with water from a nearby pitcher. He then set a smooth board between them on the desk. "Tell me, how do you stop a significant bleed?"

An easy question. Mamar's teachings covered this in detail. "Apply firm pressure at the site. If the bleeding doesn't stop, apply pressure also at the pulse point between the wound and the heart. After that, a tourniquet can be used as a last resort."

"Superb. What is the recommended treatment afterward to avoid infection?"

Katira knew this as well. "Apply an antiseptic ointment, or diluted alcohol. If that's not available, the heated blade of a knife will do in an emergency."

"I'm pleased Mirelle taught you as much as she did. You are absolutely right. Today, I'd like to teach you a different way to stop bleeding using power. It's a bit crude, but it gets the job done quickly, sterilizes the site, and is something all Stonebearers should know." He dipped his finger in the water and made a line on the wood. "Pretend this is a cut in someone's arm. The idea is to use the simple fire glyph and carefully seal off the bleeding vessels using heat. While it is preferred to knit tissue back together using more sophisticated glyphs, as it speeds recovery and minimizes scarring, most Stonebearers outside of the healing order can't manage it. With this, they can at least get serious wounds under control until they can get help."

The simple fire glyph formed over his open palm and he guided it along the top of the water where it sizzled and turned to vapor. "The goal is to vaporize the water without lighting the wood on fire. If this were a real wound, you'd look to see where the blood was flowing from and seal off the individual vessels."

When the last of the water disappeared, he allowed the spark of light to fade. The wood beneath showed no mark of the intense heat. "Your turn. Go ahead and open yourself to the power, but don't form the glyph just yet. I'd like to check something first."

Katira bound her small apprentice stone into her palm. After all the practice from earlier in the day, she expected her power to open smoothly. She was wrong. The vessel remained stuck in place. The unease of working with Master Firen held the ropes firmly and they refused to loosen.

"Give me a moment, I'm still getting used to this."

"Take your time."

She bid the Khandashii within her to wake once again and urged the ropes holding it back to grow slack. Master Firen watched on with interest, as if making mental notes on what he saw. She closed her eyes and pictured Papan there with her, and her unease faded. The vessel finally tipped, and the familiar white-hot heat of the power flowed through her. She tried hard to not flinch and worked to keep her breath slow and even as Papan taught her until it faded.

"Do you always close your eyes?" He sounded every bit like a healer working to diagnose a patient.

"No. I just needed the extra focus. Usually I'm with Papan."

He looked down his long pointy nose at her. "Use his proper title. The little formalities are expected around here."

"Sorry." She fumbled to remember his correct title. It still felt awkward in her mouth. "Master Jarand."

"Better." He cracked the joints of his fingers and leaned back. "You open remarkably well for the short amount of time you've been in formal training. Some can't do it at all for months, sometimes longer. You will have to work on not closing your eyes in the future."

"Why is it so much harder when I'm not with," she stumbled over the name again, but corrected herself, "Master Jarand?"

"Use of the Khandashii requires a certain amount of submission from its user. It's not under your control; you are asking it to do what is needed and it complies. When you are around someone you aren't comfortable with, it's harder to find that submission, that ease of being. Part of your training will be to overcome that as well. Working with different people around the tower helps." He scooted the plank of wood closer to her and traced another line of water onto its surface. "Your turn."

Katira set the hand with the bound stone onto the surface of the desk and fixed the simple fire glyph into her mind. Thanks to the practice from that morning, the six-pointed star formed easily. But when she urged it to shrink into the spark, it flared and sputtered before winking out with a puff of white smoke. She clenched her hands into fists.

Master Firen held up a hand. "Fight the urge to tense when things go wrong, it only makes things more difficult."

Katira loosened her fingers and took a breath. The fire glyph came to life once more, and this time she was rewarded with a bright spot of heat floating above her hands.

"Very good." Master Firen encouraged. "Now, guide it to the line of water. Let it flow over the top of the surface. Above all, stay relaxed."

Katira nodded and lowered the focused hot spot to the water. As soon as it touched, the water hissed and a black spot formed beneath.

"Your spark is far too hot. Try imagining the point as yellow instead of white. It should bring down the temperature a touch." He dripped another line of water onto the wood.

She formed the spark again and did her best to make it

appear yellow instead of that intense white. This time she was pleased that the water sizzled the same way as Master Firen's did.

"Good. Guide it along the water. The goal is to dry it all in one smooth pass."

Katira guided the spark like she had when lighting the candle. The way the water hissed and popped distracted her and made her line jump as her focus struggled to stay put. It took ages, but she finally was able to dry the line of water. A series of dark burns marred the wood in jagged lines.

Master Firen gave her a reassuring smile. "Allow the power to recede and take a short rest."

She was glad he was pleased with her effort. Had it been a real patient, she would have caused more harm than good.

He slid the wood toward him and studied the pattern of the burns. "Not bad for your first successful finish. Now, all you need is repetition. For the remainder of your time today, you will practice opening yourself to the power, forming the glyph, guiding it over the water, and allowing the power to recede. I'll stay in the room and watch over your progress but will be working on my own research so you can focus a bit easier."

Katira nodded her understanding and continued to work at smoothly drying the water. By the time Issa came to fetch her, she had succeeded in doing it twice. The effort left her hands shaking with fatigue.

Master Firen picked up the wood and studied her most recent attempts with a pleased grunt. "You've done very well for today." He slid the wood back into its place on the shelf and folded his arms over his chest. "I look forward to teaching you again."

CHAPTER SEVENTEEN

By the time Katira figured out the ties on the slick loose-fitting pants and entered the training yard, shadows already chased across the smooth slabs of floor. The last rays of sun reflected off the small panes of windows dotting the top floor of the west wing of the tower. Cool bluish light from a pair of glowing orbs flanking the entryway eased away the oncoming night. Several other orbs dotted the walls. As the depths of winter approached, the days continued to grow shorter.

A chill wind swirled down from above. Katira gave a respectful bow as she crossed the threshold and a shiver raced from the top of her head straight down her back. Only a handful of Guardians dotted the yard at this time of evening, some working in pairs, others practicing on their own. She'd overheard Papan mention to Issa that they'd increased the standing guard around the tower. It was the least they could do to prevent someone else from being hurt by a monster passing through the barrier.

Issa worked in the same practice circle they had used the day before. The warrior woman flowed like water in the space as she practiced the precise strikes and blocks and kicks in such a way that it looked more like a dance. It reminded Katira of the few times when she'd seen her father fight, how smoothly he moved, how each motion was measured and precise, each breath perfectly timed. Issa's face remained serene, as if the motions brought her peace.

"Wow," a familiar voice said from behind her. Isben. "I've never had the chance to watch her practice forms before. She's amazing, isn't she?" He also wore a set of training clothes, although his were a sturdy canvas instead of the slick silks she and Issa wore.

Katira turned to face him, surprised he'd be here of all places. "What are you doing here?"

"In light of all that's happened, Master Bremin thought it a good idea if I spent some time training with the Guardians. What about you?"

"I asked to learn how to fight. Issa offered to teach me."

Isben let out a low whistle. "You know, she ranks among the top five Guardians still living, right? That's quite an honor."

Katira continued to watch as Issa flowed from one stance to another, the motion holding her in a trance. "I never really thought about it."

Isben started walking toward Issa. "You know who else is in that top five?"

"I have a feeling I already know." Katira followed behind him, her stomach suddenly tight.

"Your father. Which is why this injury of his is such a concern. No one likes being reminded that even as mighty Stonebearers, things can go wrong."

They watched as Issa finished her series of movements before turning to face them. Her breath steamed in the cold. "Good. Right on time." She nodded to each of them. "In light of the events of last night, today's lesson will not involve contact of any kind. You're both still healing and I'd rather not get an earful from Master Firen."

Katira opened her mouth to protest. While the injuries under their snug wraps still itched and burned, especially the one in her side, she had promised Papan she would work hard.

Issa turned an unblinking stare on Katira as if daring her to challenge her order. Katira immediately thought better of it and snapped her mouth back shut, remembering another promise she'd made. She'd said she'd do exactly as instructed.

Issa gave an approving nod. She pointed to where the centerline of the circle intersected with the curved edge. "Katira, this will be your center." She then led Isben to the matching point on the opposite side. "And Isben, this will be yours."

With her hands grasped behind her back, Issa walked along the outer curve of the circle until she stood in front of them, completing the triangle. "When working in a group, you must maintain awareness of where the other is to keep from accidentally striking each other."

"What about the cold? It's freezing out here." Isben's teeth chattered as he spoke. He hugged his arms around himself and bounced from foot to foot.

"You'll warm up soon enough. Don't worry."

Katira took her position, standing tall, feet firmly together, hands at her sides, as Issa had taught her. It was much colder that evening compared to when they worked before. She tried to ignore how her fingertips were beginning to lose feeling. As soon as they started moving and working, the effort would warm them both up.

"Do your best to follow along." Issa told Isben before turning her back to them and taking a wide stance.

Katira copied Issa's slow deliberate strikes, falling into the familiar patterns she'd learned the day before, one arm sweeping in, then the other, all the while imagining blocking the punches from an imaginary enemy. Compared to Issa, she still felt like an ungainly cucumber, her arms swinging out in too large of arcs while her feet kept catching on each other. At least she hadn't fallen yet.

Isben, on the other hand, fared much better. Where she struggled with her balance, he followed Issa's different motions with ease. Here and there, Issa stopped and quietly corrected his footing or demonstrate a hand position, but not nearly as much as she had to do for Katira.

The familiar burn of exertion worked up Katira's limbs. With each pantomimed block and punch, her mind spun, restless and uneasy. In the shadow-striped darkness of the yard, her thoughts grabbed hold of the fear the attack of the night before. A hound could easily hide in the darkness surrounding them. She struggled to follow Issa's lead as her attention darted from corner to corner. A wave of dizziness caught her off guard and she stumbled.

Issa paused with one arm extended downward as if deflecting a low kick. "These last few days have been tiring for us all. Use this time to clear your minds. Find stillness and peace in the motions. Lose yourself."

Katira thought back to when they entered the training yard and watched as Issa practiced her forms. Was that what she was doing? Trying to find a small island of peace in the stormy sea that was Amul Dun? This place had been her home for far longer than it had for either Katira or Isben, so these recent changes would be far more upsetting for her than it was for them.

Then again, she'd lived for so long, maybe this was just another challenge to face, another problem to solve. Katira tried to quiet her mind and pull her awareness back to the moment. Papan had taught her the same thing when they were both trying to cope with Mamar's loss. Firen did it as well when teaching about working with the power. Now, Issa taught it as a part of training. The message remained the same: find calm where you are and in what you are doing.

Another memory floated to the surface as Katira continued to flow through the motions, one from years ago when life was peaceful back in Namragan. Mamar was grinding the last ingredient for one of her medicines, one that took days of careful stirring and measuring and precise timing over the heat. Katira tended to the fire, adjusting the coals to maintain the required temperature for the medicine to cook properly. The ingredients in the small iron pot atop the clay burner started to bubble, signaling the precise moment when the next ingredient needed to be added.

Just then, there was a sharp cry of pain from the forge behind the cottage. Papan rushed in through the rear door of the cottage, ushering Gonal, his smithing apprentice, through the kitchen and to Mamar's workspace and to one of the sturdy wooden chairs. The boy clutched his arm to his chest. Bright arterial blood flowed around his fingers.

Katira watched on, expecting Mamar to be upset about the medicine which would be ruined, and days of their work lost. But Mamar's calm didn't budge. She set down the pestle, removed the iron pot from the heat, and hurried to gather bandaging, all while issuing orders to both Papan and Katira.

Later, in the quiet of evening over a cup of tea, Mamar explained that the medicine could be remade. Caring for the living was more important. Had she become upset or angry, the medicine would still be ruined, but worse, she wouldn't have been able to care for Gonal properly.

It was the same now. Without that calm, Katira couldn't use the power, couldn't fight, couldn't do what was needed. That was why she couldn't summon her power when she needed it in the library. She couldn't maintain her calm and therefore couldn't help Isben keep the hounds away from them both using the shield glyph Papan had taught her. It wouldn't have been much, but it might have made a difference.

Mamar's words from that memory struck her, as if she was still there trying to teach her. "Remember, Katira, without calm, the work can't be done."

After so long of pushing away the pain of Mamar's loss, this memory tore at the fragile wall Katira had built inside herself. The calm she'd tried so hard to hold onto while following Issa's moves shattered. She let her arms fall. Her shoulders shook from grief. She tried to push her mother's memory back behind the wall where it didn't hurt, where she could stay in her comfortable numbness and forget all that had happened. It dug in its heels and didn't let go.

Her view of the training yard was swept away in the tears that followed.

Isben set his hand on her shoulder. "Hey. What's wrong?"

She couldn't speak, not while each breath came out in shuddering sobs. Instead, she let him wrap her in his arms and cradle her head against his chest. They'd done this before. On the night her mother died, Isben had been there for her when she needed it, had comforted her. And now here he was, comforting her again. She felt the warmth of his power open to her, a gentle heat against her cheek and where his hands held her secure.

It was an invitation. This way she didn't need to speak; he would simply know. She let the vessel of her power tip and fill her. The focus that came with anguish made it easy, made the burn welcome.

A wave of his presence washed through her, bringing with it relief, drawing away the sting. She let him in, let him see and feel what was troubling her. In return, he shared with her how much he cared for her, how he wanted to help her. With his help, the tears dried and the shaking stilled.

"It's too much." Isben spoke softly into her ear as he held her. "You've pushed too hard without giving yourself time to heal."

Katira nodded. His words rang true and she needed to hear them.

He exchanged a few words with Issa that Katira heard muffled through his shirt before leading her from the yard and back into the tower.

The next morning, Katira shouldered the basket holding breakfast for both her and Papan as well as the supplies he'd tucked in there for their morning's lesson. He'd been careful with her that morning, taking her lead, waiting for her to choose the moment she was ready to talk about what had upset her so much the night before. She hadn't been able to yet, not when she didn't understand herself why she broke down crying. It was unlike her, and the intensity of it caught her off guard. Strangely, she felt much better for it. Perhaps Isben was right, and she needed that moment of release.

When they reached the top of the stairs, Master Ternan and Master Aro were already bent over the worktable studying the array of papers. Master Aro muttered about something and pointed at one of the drawn glyphs. Master Ternan pursed his lips and scowled. The room was so cold their breath came out in puffs of vapor

"No, that's not necessary. We've already done that here." Master Aro stabbed at another paper with a finger.

The two continued to argue back and forth as Katira set down the basket and began setting out the different parcels of food on the table as well as a warm jug of sweetened tea. The heat felt good against her hands.

"I thought they couldn't be up here without a guard in place." Katira asked Papan in a whisper.

"They're not. Not like I can stop them though." A thread of irritation flowed through the apprentice bond as Papan bent over the small brazier. "There's enough stubbornness between the two of them to wear down tempered steel. I'll remind them again, not like it'll do anything." He sighed. "Might have to lock them out when Issa and I aren't here."

He sent a pulse of energy into the side of the brazier, and the patterns woven through the stone and metal began to softly glow. "You realize you two would be much more comfortable if you lit this before you started."

Master Aro looked up as if startled. "Oh, General. Do you mind lighting the brazier? It's awfully cold up here this morning."

Papan's irritation faded into amusement. Not only had the two masters failed to light the brazier to warm the small drafty room, they'd not even noticed when they were no longer alone. After all of her own different reminders about needing focus to do the work, Katira wasn't surprised. But with the possibility of danger lurking in every shadow, it struck her as odd that the two men wouldn't be more vigilant.

Breakfast was a simple affair: bread, cheese, and several brilliant red fall apples. The masters joined them at table, but to Katira's relief they were content to quickly eat and drink their fill and return to their work.

As soon as they were done and the plates tucked back into the basket, Katira caught Papan regarding her in that way that meant he wanted to talk about something serious. She held tighter to her warm mug.

He took his usual seat across from her and leaned in, resting on his elbows. " I want you to know that I understand what happened last night. There's no need to be ashamed."

Even thinking about how hard the memory hit her made Katira's eyes sting. "I'm not. I mean, why should I be?"

"You forget, I have some idea of what you're feeling." He touched where his stone hung from its chain. "Don't lie. It won't help anything."

"I just..." She swallowed, unsure of what to even say. "I wanted to be strong for you."

He reached out his hand and she took it, letting the touch of his coarse skin comfort her. "You are so strong. I know you are. But that doesn't mean you aren't allowed to hurt sometimes."

Katira settled into the soothing rhythm of working with Papan in the mornings, then with Master Firen or Cassim, then Issa. With each passing day, the two masters came that much closer to finishing the relic, that much closer to putting an end to the looming threat of shadow hounds breaking through again.

Each day without an attack should have brought Katira a sense of peace, but instead, it only increased the tension of waiting. They would come, it was only a matter of when, not if. When they did, they would target her again.

It wasn't until the fourth day that something felt different. The small room buzzed with an unmistakable energy as Master Aro set to work on the chair itself, carefully easing in the complicated series of glyphs that he and Master Ternan had prepared for this moment. It made it impossible for Katira to focus on the glyphs she was supposed to be learning.

Papan tapped the paper, drawing Katira's attention back to him and the paper on the table. She dipped the quill back into the ink and resumed copying the new glyphs she had learned that morning. The energy in the room shifted again, this time violently. Master Ternan clicked his tongue, displeased. Master Aro tottered to the nearby chair and fell into it, rubbing his temples.

Katira found herself watching once again, wanting to know what had gone wrong, wanting to know if Master Aro was all right.

"Perhaps it's best if we finish this later." Papan closed the book he'd been trying to read with a snap, also distracted by the two Masters. "From what Bremin says, they're nearly done. In fact..." He listened at the top of the stairwell. The quiet tap of footsteps bounced off the stone walls. "Yes, that's him on the stairs, and he's not alone."

Katira cleaned the tip of her quill and stoppered the inkwell before setting them both in the tidy writing case. The two sets of footsteps grew louder, and she caught herself smiling. The second set of footsteps belonged to Isben. He'd been spending his mornings studying theory with Bremin just as she studied with Papan. The one difference was Bremin couldn't show him the actual glyphs. For some reason that no one understood, whenever Bremin used the power it rendered him unconscious.

The bell tolled noon.

As Bremin reached the top of the stairs, more footsteps echoed from behind him. "Gentlemen," he addressed the two masters, "Is it ready?"

Master Aro stammered, trying to answer but tripping over his tongue.

"Yes." Master Ternan stepped forward. "It is finished. We were just refining a few small things while waiting for your arrival."

Isben scooted around Bremin and made his way over to Katira. "Isn't this exciting?" he asked. "Bremin says it's been over a century since a device on this scale has been created. If it works, we will be part of history."

"Not sure." Katira studied him. He looked eager, too eager. "What do you mean, if it works? Why wouldn't it?"

Cassim emerged from the top of the stairwell mopping his forehead with a handkerchief and clinging to the handrail. He gave a respectful nod to those gathered before flopping into the nearest available chair and fanning himself.

Isben shrugged. "There are always risks when working with motherstone. Especially when it's something really complicated. But Master Aro's skill is unparalleled by anyone at Amul Dun. I'm sure he's been careful."

Another set of footsteps on the stair signaled the arrival of Lady Alystra, followed by Issa.

"So, what happens now? Is someone going to try it?" Katira asked.

"Setting glyphs requires a massive amount of energy, and Lady Alystra is believed to be the strongest wielder at Amul

Dun. Master Ternan felt it appropriate if she did the honors, historic occasion and all." He scratched at the hair at the back of his neck. "Then someone will use it for the first time."

"Do you know who? Has someone volunteered?" That familiar thread of anxiety wormed its way around Katira's throat. She suspected she already knew.

"I'm sure he was planning to tell you. With what happened last night and all, he must not have felt it was the right time."

Katira sighed. Of course Papan would be the one to volunteer. It was fitting really. Of everyone living, he was the one most closely involved with Wrothe. Having him be the first to add his strength to the barrier was almost poetic.

Still, the thought of something going wrong with the chair and hurting him was more than she could stand. "Why can't Master Aro test it?"

"He tested the smaller parts as they went." Isben glanced to Master Aro who continued to feed thin strings of glyphs into part of the armrest. "Lady Alystra agrees. Both masters thought it best for a Guardian to be the first to enter the space between worlds. They're not sure what he will find there."

Lady Alystra approached the front of the chair, running her fingers over the finely polished edges and symbols worked into the back. "Fine work, both of you. You should be proud." She patted the armrest. "If this works, we will have a powerful tool to keep out the monsters who threaten our home. It will be one large step toward learning how to keep them out of our world."

"Thank you, my Lady." Master Aro gave a small bow from his waist. "When you are ready, we can proceed to setting the glyphs."

She nodded and stood to the side of the chair opposite Master Aro. "I'm ready."

The room fell into an expectant hush. No one dared move as the markings on both of their arms glowed to life and elaborate rings of glyphs formed around them. Master Aro's ring grew until it encircled both them and the chair. Lady Alystra's ring twisted into a helix that hovered between them before snapping into a channel of light connecting her to the motherstone of the armrest.

In the few days Katira had been learning about using glyphs, never had she imagined they could look like this.

"Aro, when she is fully linked, begin the transfer," Master Ternan instructed. "If we've done things correctly, the motherstone in the chair will do the rest." He then addressed Lady Alystra. "My Lady, you will allow your power to flow as each set of glyphs solidifies and becomes part of the chair. Do not remove your hand until the glow fades."

The knot in Katira's stomach pulled taut. The unease she felt when she caught Master Ternan watching her before, returned. She chided herself for doubting him. The man had graciously given his time and expertise to help transform the chair it to fit their needs. What was it about him that bothered her so much?

Master Aro's ring rotated until it was standing on its edge before it collapsed into dozens of ribbons of light, each weaving an elaborate braid between Lady Alystra and the chair.

The veins of motherstone in the chair began to glow, starting at the point where the High Lady's hand rested and chasing through the stone in detailed patterns that mimicked the lines of the Khandashii chasing up both Master Aro and the High Lady's arms. A bright point of light gathered at the peak of the chair before rushing up and through the roof to the beacon above.

Bremin stepped closer, stone gripped in his hand and lines shining bright. Despite that mask of calm he always wore, Katira spied the traces of his own unease creasing the corners of his eyes. With his connection open, he'd sense if there was anything wrong long before anyone else, including Alystra herself.

Long moments passed where no one dared move. Those moments turned to minutes and each of those minutes dragged along as the room throbbed with energy. The translucent motherstone pulsed with the High Lady's energy. Deep within the chair, power churned and spun.

Lady Alystra whimpered, her knuckles went white on the hand gripping the armrest. Her body stiffened. "It's too much. It needs too much."

Bremin hurried to her side and set his hand on her neck. "It's draining her. It shouldn't take this much power to lock the glyphs into place." The fear in his eyes flashed to anger. "Master Aro, what's happening?"

The gaunt Bender hadn't moved from his place on the other side of the chair. Compared to the fear Katira saw in Bremin, Master Aro's face spoke of an unimaginable terror. He didn't acknowledge the question. Instead, more glyphs formed and spun in front of him.

"What are you doing, man?" Bremin demanded.

Isben stepped forward, eyes narrowed as he studied the swirling dance of glyphs. "Don't distract him! He's making it so someone else can take her place."

"Are you certain?" Bremin asked. His lines lit up, readying himself. It was a bold move. If he ended up using even a fraction of his power, he'd end up in convulsions the second he let go. Judging from the amount the relic was taking from Lady Alystra, taking her place would put him in a coma if it didn't kill him outright.

Isben shifted on his feet. Katira prayed he was right. He'd shown talent with bending and had spent time learning with them as part of his training. Maybe he could see things in the glyphs that Bremin couldn't.

"Yes." Isben nodded, resolute. "But it can't be you. Lady Alystra needs you. It has to be someone else."

Katira's heart began to pound. Something inside her, the powerful presence of the Khandashii which saved her before, the intelligence hiding within the power, pushed at her, telling her that she needed to be the one.

Her gaze swept around the room. It couldn't be her. It didn't make sense. There were so many there that were more experienced than she was, and it wasn't her place. It all was happening too fast.

The High Lady began to shake. Her knees gave out.

"Does it matter where the power comes from?" Katira shouted over the growing panic.

Cassim lurched to his feet, suddenly alert now that he might be needed.

Master Aro shook his head. "No, it shouldn't." His eyes widened when he realized what Katira meant to do.

She didn't give him time to protest. She darted inside the circling glyphs and set her hand next to Lady Alystra's.

Papan reached for her. "Katira!"

Cassim held him back. "The link is already forming. Stopping her might harm them both."

A roar filled Katira's ears as her power surged and connected with the chair. Bremin pulled the High Lady away to safety. Katira's power flew away like a flaxen fishing line chasing a brook trout, moving fast, faster than she expected.

Through her connection to the relic, she saw the vast network of glyphs the two masters had worked days to assemble. There were hundreds, if not thousands, of them, arranged in lacy nets. Those which the High Lady had already fixed in place appeared as if etched into the heart of the stone. Hundreds remained. Master Aro's braided connection fanned out, seeking, charging, and setting those glyphs which drifted in place like leaves on a lake.

The braid set several at time, but even then the process seemed too slow. She'd only just started to understand how much of the power she could use safely at a time. This, this might be too much. She had to finish, had to see this through. She could be strong. She could hold on.

Papan stood close. She smelled his familiar leather and oak and held tight to knowing whatever happened, he was there. Hundreds of glyphs, reduced to dozens, to a handful. Her vision swam as the last two settled, joining the now completed network of glyphs. The last glyph faded, and the chair went to sleep once more. A pair of hands caught her as she released the power and her knees melted out from under her. Voices filled the air around her.

"Check her. She might have drained herself too far." Cassim's voice sounded far away.

A hand pressed over her heart. She couldn't focus on who, and it didn't seem like it mattered. Sleep curled around her like a warm blanket.

"Damn you! Why couldn't you let someone else?" Papan cursed. He reached for her through their bond, urging her to return. A warm familiar flow washed through her. She gasped for breath, and the fading beat of her heart grew stronger.

"Katira, can you hear me?"

She blinked. Above her, Papan cradled her head and

shoulders. They were both on the floor. Across the small room, Master Aro sat clutching his head next to the chair.

"Why did you do that?" Papan scolded, his arms trembled around her. "You could have died."

"It wasn't me. Another force, maybe it was the power, maybe it was something else, compelled me to."

"Whatever it was, it was a stupid risk. You're not prepared to handle that much power." He tried to sound stern and failed. With all that had happened, this was too much for him to take. "There are worse things than dying. It could have torn your mind and left you trapped inside your body, unable to speak or move."

"That didn't happen. I'm okay." The first pangs of a massive headache pressed against her temples. "The High Lady was in danger, and I needed to help. I thought I was strong enough."

His head dropped to his chest and closed his eyes. "You weren't. It took more than you could safely give there at the end." He didn't finish. He didn't need to. Katira knew what he was going to say. 'I had to bring you back.'

It wasn't fair for him. She should have ignored that call, ignored that driving compulsion to step in. She should have let someone else answer. Why did it call her? Why not Issa? Surely the warrior was strong enough to complete the sealing of the glyphs.

Deep down, she already knew. Had it been anyone else, the pull would have been too great. Anyone else would have been killed immediately. Something about her power was different, even if no one understood what.

She freed herself from where Papan cradled her on the floor, the motion making her head hurt even worse. "Is everyone else okay?"

"Okay enough."

On the opposite side of the small room, Bremin helped Lady Alystra into one of the rickety old chairs and stayed close to her as if he worried she might faint.

"Here, you're shivering." Isben took one of the blankets from the basket in the corner of the room and tucked it around her.

Katira pulled the blanket close. Isben scooted next to her and wrapped an arm around her shoulders.

"Did it work?" Katira asked. The Occulus Seat no longer glowed or pulsed with light. "Please tell me that worked."

"Must have." Isben answered. "I don't think I've ever seen Master Ternan smile before."

"Good." Katira rested her head against his neck. "If I ever try to do something stupid like that again, promise me you'll stop me. Sit on me if you have to."

Isben gave a quiet laugh. "Not sure I could ever stop you, even if I wanted to. But I'll try."

CHAPTER EIGHTEEN

"*I*'m telling you Jarand, you have to rein her in." Lady Alystra paced in front of the wide window in her private study, hands gesturing wildly as she spoke.

"And I'm telling you, I don't think she had any control over it." Jarand kept a tight hold of his anger, needing to find the calm, clear mind he'd been teaching Katira. As long as he didn't have answers for what went wrong while they were setting the glyphs, that calm would elude him. "She said she felt compelled, like the power itself was pushing her."

"I don't care if it was a moon grizzly pushing her, what she did was irresponsible. The relic might have been destroyed, and then where would we be?"

Bremin, who had taken his usual chair next to the desk sat deep in thought. If there were pieces to this puzzle they hadn't found yet, he would be the first to hunt them down.

"Master Aro disagrees." Bremin said. "According to him, if Katira hadn't stepped in when she did not only would all their work have been destroyed, but Alystra would have been killed. You know the man, he isn't one to exaggerate."

"Then I suppose I should be thankful." Lady Alystra stopped at the corner of the desk and leaned her weight on it with her eyes pressed shut.

Concern creased Bremin's forehead. "You need to sit down. I'll get some tea."

She waved him off. "I can't think sitting down. Not with something like this." When the moment passed, she resumed her pacing. "She's always been different, Jarand. The power she holds is unique. I haven't felt anything like it in all my years as High Lady. She's showing all the signs of being an Innate."

Jarand had only seen the term in dusty tomes deep in the library. An Innate was someone the power itself used for its own purposes. Some called them oracles, but that wasn't right. They couldn't tell the future, but their actions often influenced the outcome of future cataclysmic events.

"You can't mean that. There hasn't been an Innate reported for hundreds of years." A new fear inched down Jarand's spine. If Katira was an Innate, there was something coming, something big, and she would be drawn into it as surely as a magnet to steel.

"All the same, we need to keep a closer eye on her. If she is an Innate, she is a danger to everyone at Amul Dun." Lady Alystra finally met Jarand's gaze and he saw how she struggled with what she needed to say next. "The safest option for all of us, including her, is exile until her moment comes."

"You'd turn her away?" Jarand couldn't believe it had come to this. It was so absurd it didn't feel real. "If anything, she needs more support and protection from us than ever before. I promised Mirelle I'd do everything I could to take care of Katira. Don't make me break that promise."

"The last known Innate who survived long enough for history to record his name was King Darius, himself." Bremin angled his head toward one of the hanging tapestries that flanked the fireplace, one that depicted King Darius, holding his stone and wreathed with different glyphs. "It was how he learned how to tame the power, how he was able to teach others to use it safely. Some historians believe the power itself guided him, that the time was right for those with the power to learn how to use it."

"King Darius was killed by his own power." Jarand's mouth went dry. "Katira might share his fate. You can't send her away."

"I'm not unmerciful. I know how hard this all is." Lady Alystra softened her tone, sounding more like the friend Jarand needed instead of his High Lady. "We don't even know for sure if this is what's happening. I refuse to turn a blind eye to the possibility, for your sake as much as hers. We'll keep a watchful eye until we know more."

"As her Master, I ask you to keep this from her until she's ready to know. No child should have to worry about this. Let the burden fall on me, I can bear it for her. I can keep her safe, even if it's from herself." Even as he spoke, the weight of this new secret settled like a cannon ball in his gut. "It's best for everyone if she learns to use the power assuming she's no different than anyone else."

A look of pain crossed over Lady Alystra's features, as if mourning something lost. "These last few years have changed you."

She was right. He had changed, but in a rightful needed way. "Katira is more than my charge. She is my daughter as much as any flesh and blood. Raising a child from infancy, giving up so much for something so small and helpless, makes you braver than any war, stronger than any captain of the guard. Or any General, for that matter."

Lady Alystra sighed and finally took her seat next to Bremin. "I would have a dozen like you. Brave Stonebearers willing to sacrifice so much for what's right."

"Thank you, my Lady." Jarand pressed his fist to his heart, excused himself from study, and carefully started building a mental wall around this new secret he'd have to keep from Katira, brick by brick.

Nearly a day had passed since the incident with the chair, and Katira's head still throbbed. Papan had warned her it might hurt for a few days. What he didn't say was that the ache would be bad enough to make her vomit up breakfast. This was the price of overdrawing her power to rescue Lady Alystra. She'd do it again if she had to. But hopefully not in the near future.

Up in the small room, the late morning light streaming through the hundreds of windowpanes held no warmth. The sky outside shone a piercing blue to the east, but to the west, towering banks of dark clouds marched forward in an unrelenting line. Wind already whistled around and rocked the thin tower. Outside, a winter storm was coming.

Inside, the storm had already arrived. Despite what had happened the day before, the Occulus Seat still had to be tested to see if Master Ternan and Master Aro's efforts were successful.

Nine Stonebearers and apprentices tucked themselves into the different corners of the small room. When Issa glanced Katira's way, it was with a strange mix of expressions that might have been intended to appear reassuring, but instead only served to remind her that what she'd done the day before was stupid. She'd better not try anything like that today.

When Master Ternan glanced at her, he made a face resembling that of a dried fish, all wrinkled brow with an open wrinkled mouth. Katira couldn't tell if it was guilt or indigestion. He'd had everything to do with designing the glyphs they'd set into the chair the day before. Maybe what had happened was his fault?

Cassim broke away from his conversation with Issa and made his way toward her, adjusting his long white robe as he walked. At last, one friendly face.

"I was meaning to get this to you sooner. With everything going on, I barely remembered to grab it before coming up here." He pressed a tiny vial into her hand.

"What is it?"

"Sovereign cure for that headache you're probably enjoying right now. One of the few herbcraft medicines I know. Take the whole vial before things get started. You'll be glad you did."

More footsteps on the stairs signaled Lady Alystra and Bremin's arrival. The Masters, who up until that point had been sitting at their worktable muttering to each other, stood and both respectfully bowed, followed by Issa and Papan. Cassim nudged Isben's arm, signaling him to stop intently studying the chair's armrest. He made a clumsy bow and hurried out of the way and next to Katira.

Katira bowed, thumbed open the small vial, and quickly poured the liquid into her mouth, grimacing at the bitter taste, before tucking the vial away in her skirt pocket. It tasted of white willow bark along with something she couldn't recognize.

She hoped the medicine didn't make it harder to focus. With the headache, she doubted she could access the power right now, even if she needed to. If the medicine worked, but made her head fuzzy, she'd still be no help at all should anything happen.

If there was a force, or a malicious traitor trying to stop them from fiddling with the barrier, this would be the time for them to strike. Papan wore his long-bladed knife on his hip and Issa wore her sword and no less than four knives strapped to her belt. They both stayed silent and watchful. It did nothing to help Katira's imagination which continued to summon up the idea that dozens of hounds were waiting to break through and eat them all.

Lady Alystra and Bremin took their places on either side of the impressive stone chair.

"I've been assured that everything is in place to test the Occulus Seat," Lady Alystra started, allowing her gaze to rest on the two masters. She didn't look pleased. "Masters Ternan, Aro, and Cassim have checked the different glyphs bound to it and have determined that it is ready. That said, I'm asking you all to be alert and ready for anything." She paused and for the briefest moment her gaze dropped to her hands before returning to those gathered. "We all have suffered because of the weakness in the barrier between worlds. It's time we make that weakness strong."

"Hear, hear," Bremin called out, clapping his hands. Several others followed.

Lady Alystra's attention turned to Papan. "Master Jarand has suffered the most, so it's only fitting he be the first to see the fruits of the information Master Regulus worked so hard to procure for us. It is our job to ensure that he comes out of this test unscathed."

Papan stepped forward. Even knowing this was the plan, Katira's heart thudded painfully in her chest. Despite all his reassurances, she wouldn't relax until the test was over.

Finally, Lady Alystra turned to Katira. "It will be your duty to monitor your bond to him while he is in the chair. He might not be able to speak. You'll be the first to know if anything goes wrong. Do you understand?"

Katira nodded and wrapped her fingers around her stone. "Yes, my Lady."

"Good." She motioned Papan to approach the chair. "Everyone else, keep alert. There's no saying what might happen. Let's hope it's nothing."

Papan squeezed Katira's hand and leaned in close. "Nothing is going to happen."

She squeezed back, unwilling to let him go. "I'll believe that when this is over."

"I trust you. Keep good watch." He let go and took his place in the Occulus Seat.

Isben closed the gap formed by Papan's leaving. "Remember. He's not alone, just like you're not alone." He let his hand brush against hers. "I'm here with you." Their fingers linked.

She didn't reply, because there were no words that could be said. She was both too full and too empty. At least her head had stopped pounding. She'd have to thank Cassim when they finished. In front of them all, Papan sat straight-backed and serious on the chair. She'd seen that face before, that steely calm mask he wore when duty pressed on him. Through their bond, she felt thorny prickles of fear marching around his heart.

Master Ternan came closer to give his instructions. "When you are ready, General, place your hand on the sphere at the end of the armrest and open yourself to the power. Feed a small stream into it and the chair will do the rest. To exit, return to the Occulus Seat and repeat the process, feeding in a stream of power in the dreamspace sphere. See what you can learn in one hour."

Papan nodded and set his arms and hands in position. As the lines on his arms started to glow, he fixed his eyes on Katira one last time and sent a wave of reassurance through the bond. Then, all sensation from him turned dull and distant, as if he suddenly moved somewhere far away. His eyes fell closed.

Master Aro turned a large hourglass on the table and a slow thread of sand began to fall. The motherstone of the chair awoke and began to pulse as it had the day before. Light gathered at the top of the chair, directly behind Papan's head, then shot up through the column in the ceiling and out to the upper portion of the beacon.

Katira watched, carefully observing his face while monitoring every awareness that echoed through her. He was calm. The underlying fear disappeared. The chair used his energy in a steady stream, slow enough that should he stay there for several hours, or even a day, there would be no risk of him running out too quickly. Keeping watch over him was her one job, and she wouldn't let him down.

On Katira's other side, Issa stood at attention. She stood with her weight on the balls of her feet, ready and waiting for some disaster to happen. She would not let him down either.

The sand in the hourglass continued its slow steady fall. Its soft hiss the only sound in the small room besides the howl of the wind and the rattle of loose windowpanes.

When half of the sand had fallen Bremin leaned in close to Lady Alystra. "How long do we allow the test to continue?" he asked in a low voice.

"Until the hourglass empties, or if Katira senses a problem. I won't cut this short, not when it's this important."

Katira kept her vigil, catching the sideways glances of those with her as if they were checking if she was still paying attention. There was nothing to say; she could feel no change, sense no form of distress. If anything, her father was more relaxed while in the relic than she'd ever experienced since they'd been bonded. She didn't want to assume anything, but it seemed as if he was enjoying himself.

The last grains of sand fell into the bottom on the hourglass and Lady Alystra stepped forward. "Master Ternan, how do we signal to him that it's time to come back?"

Master Ternan narrowed his brows and his fish mouth twisted as if he hadn't thought about ever removing someone from the chair. Master Aro flinched at the question. Katira was there when they had been ordered to design the relic to do just that.

Lady Alystra's tone changed from one of calm control, to one of exasperation. "I made it very clear how I felt about this. There must be a way to wake him."

"There is, I assure you. Give me a moment." Master Ternan leafed through the stack of papers that had collected on the table, madly seeking an answer for the High Lady. Master Aro floundered and stammered over his words in a staccato of syllables.

Bremin came close to Master Aro's face, so the man couldn't see anything else. "Focus. Can he be roused safely?"

The lean man nodded vigorously, his thick glasses bouncing on his forehead. "By all means. He should be able to bring himself out when he is ready."

Bremin continued, forcing Master Aro to keep his attention fixed on him. "And how will he know when it's time?"

"I don't know."

Bremin exchanged a worried glance with Lady Alystra. "Can he hear me?"

"There is no reason he shouldn't be able to." Master Ternan finally added, looking up from one of the papers. "Ah, here it is. We designed it to be like walking into a dream, so to rouse him, all you need to do is wake him up."

Bremin shook Papan by the shoulder. "Jarand! It's time."

Papan didn't stir, didn't make any response. There was no change in the bond.

Bremin gave another firmer shake and called again before looking to Katira. "Can you sense anything on your end? Do you think he is trapped?"

Katira focused once more. Papan wasn't feeling any panic, or any frustration. "He isn't feeling anything. It's like he's too deeply asleep to feel anything."

Lady Alystra leaned closer to Papan and studied his silent, still face. "Master Ternan, what happens if we remove his hand from the sphere?"

"His mind is woven into the stone of the chair. Removing him forcefully could separate the two. I don't recommend it."

Bremin tapped his lip. "What if someone were to touch the sphere and join him?" Bremin asked.

"In theory, it should work." Master Ternan said. "Whoever goes needs to stay focused on leaving. Otherwise they risk falling into a too deep of dream state as well."

"I'll do it." Isben volunteered.

An icy stab of fear pierced Katira. "No, not you. Someone else should do it, someone with more experience," she protested.

"I've already decided, and unless the Lady forbids it, I will help him. I've spent quite a bit of time with the Benders lately, and I understand how the glyphs are supposed to work, perhaps even better than Master Jarand does." He glanced around the room. "Plus, if something goes wrong, there's no better team than those already assembled to try something else."

Issa gripped the hilt of her heavy sword, not to use it, but as something to hold on to. "Do you believe you can do it?"

"At least let me try." He looked straight at Katira. He was asking her permission first, even if it wasn't her decision. When Katira couldn't answer, he turned to the High Lady, who gave a tight-lipped nod.

Katira reached for his arm, but it slipped through her grasp. "Please be careful."

"I promise." He set his hand on the sphere, the thin ribbon of power already surging across his fingertips. His eyes fell closed as he joined Papan in the stone.

Katira's hands curled into fists around the fabric of her dress, and she marched over to Lady Alystra. Issa gripped her elbow to stop her.

"How long do we wait?" Katira demanded. "When do we decide that this was all a horrible mistake and the two people I care about most are helplessly trapped with no hope of escape?"

Bremin raised his hands the same way one would calm a skittish horse. "Easy, Katira, give Isben a few minutes before jumping to conclusions. He's got a good head on his shoulders, and you still have a job to do." He turned her back around so she was facing the chair once more. "Keep watch. You're our only link to what's going on."

Katira relaxed her grip and brought her hand back to her stone. Her anger couldn't get the best of her, not now. Bremin was right, of course he was right.

She sensed no change, even with Isben inside. "When do we decide when enough time has passed?" her voice trembled, and she hated it.

Bremin shook his head. He didn't know either. He turned the hourglass once more. Another five, then ten, minutes passed. Katira couldn't stand the wait, but didn't dare make another outburst.

Papan twitched and lifted his head. He looked around the room blinking as if confused. Isben released his grip on the sphere and pulled Papan's hand free, setting it in his lap.

Katira hurried to her father and shook him. "Can you hear me? Do you know where you are? Do you know who I am?"

"I'm all right, Katira. I'm back." He wiped at his eyes. "It's different from what I expected. How long was I in?"

Bremin studied the hourglass. "An hour and a quarter. If it wasn't for Isben here, you might have spent the rest of the night in there."

"Really?" Papan stretched his neck. "It felt like no time at all."

Bremin turned to the notes, eyes narrowed and lips tight against his teeth as he flipped from page to page. "Master Aro, care to explain why the High Lady's instructions weren't strictly followed? Or perhaps you have a good explanation, Master Ternan?"

Master Ternan furrowed his brow and started muttering something.

"He believed it would take too long to incorporate into the plan," Master Aro interjected. "He thought it best to finish the chair and figure out that part later, that getting to this point as fast as possible was far more important." The comment earned him a scowl from Master Ternan. "I'll have it known that we didn't agree on this. He was rather adamant that we focus on the primary goal first. Since he is my senior, we did it his way."

"It doesn't need one, really." Master Ternan finally found enough words to defend himself. His face had gone several shades darker. "It's easy for the user to remove themselves, when they are ready, of course."

"You're wrong, and this was a direct order, not an option." Lady Alystra said, her voice cold and hard as iron. "Between this and what happened yesterday, it might be time to retire you from your position on the council. There are several qualified Seekers eager to take your place."

"No." Master Ternan knew a threat when he heard one. "That's not necessary. You must show some understanding. Work like this hasn't been done in centuries, and there are bound to be a few missteps before we find our way."

She lowered her voice to an angry hiss. "Your *misstep* nearly killed me yesterday. For all we know, it could have severed the General's mind from his body today. Don't tell me to show understanding until you yourself figure out how serious your mistakes are."

The High Lady fell silent and let Bremin finish what needed to be said. "Master Aro, should Master Ternan show another lapse of judgment, come straight to me. As it stands, we can't put the Occulus Seat into use until this oversight has been corrected. Can we trust you to get this done?"

Master Aro went pale, then slightly greenish with the sudden responsibility. "Yes, of course."

A look of disbelief crossed Master Ternan's face. With a huff, he stomped out of the room and down the stairs.

"Oh dear. He's going to be a real delight to work with later," Master Aro said. It was as if he'd deflated. His whole body shrank into itself as he watched Master Ternan leave. As soon as the man was gone, he sniffed, drew himself back up, and returned to the matter at hand. "As this was the first test, can I talk to the General about his experience? We still don't know if it any of the other bits worked."

"Jarand? You ready to share?" Bremin asked.

Jarand rubbed at the bridge of his nose and nodded. "The first goal was to make the barrier visible. It's hard to describe, but yes, you can see in in there. It's strange though, not what I was expecting. The dreamspace, or whatever you call it, has no color to it."

Issa entered the circle, nudging Katira aside so she could join the conversation. Katira moved to let her in, but stayed close so she could hear.

"Did you attempt to strengthen the barrier?" Issa asked.

"Wasn't quite sure how to do it, I tried a few things. Used the same glyphs we'd use when warding physical walls here in the tower. Not sure if it did much. I couldn't tell if the barrier changed at all. If I go in again, there are a few other things I'd like to try."

"Interesting." Master Aro tapped a sheet of paper. "Perhaps you could write up the patterns you used. I might have a few suggestions."

"Where did you focus your efforts?" Issa asked.

"Critical areas first. The High Lady's quarters, this room, the main hall, and the principal corridors."

"Do you think that will stop them?" Bremin asked.

"I can't be sure. I think it will help. Once the chair is deemed safe, I'd like to spend the next few days getting a good feel for what it is capable of and how robust the barrier needs to be to shut the creatures out. Until then, we will still need to use caution." Papan gripped his cane and stood, stretching his back with a wince.

While they were talking logistics, Isben drew close to Katira. "Is there a plan, then?" he whispered.

"I guess. What was it like in there?" Curiosity got the best of her; she had to ask.

"Bizarre. It really is like a dream, but you've got control. Feels more real too. Maybe one day they'll let you try it."

"Maybe. Might be a long time before Papan feels comfortable with that. I'd like to see it."

The discussion at the table was winding down, which meant both Katira and Isben would soon need to return to their studies.

"We continue taking shifts up here, then?" Issa asked.

"Looks like it," Papan answered. "Keep to the same schedule. Hopefully in a few days, we'll have a better idea about how to use this relic to protect Amul Dun." Papan watched from the corner of his eye as Bremin took Master Aro aside. "I'm sure Lady Alystra wouldn't mind having you back personally protecting her rather than being stuck up here."

"Stonemother knows I wouldn't mind either. It's the most tedious kind of boring." Issa gave a casual salute. "See you in a few hours."

Katira paused at the last narrow window in the spiraling staircase and took in the light. She hated these stairs, hated the memories they brought back from her time in the dungeons at Khanrosh, hated the feelings of helplessness they always summoned. She had grown so much stronger since then, she'd learned so much, and still the thought of descending into the darkness made her hands tremble.

Below, on the landing, Papan formed a light over his palm

to guide their way. Despite his reassurances, using the chair had left him more tired than he was willing to admit. When they returned to their quarters, she intended to ask him about it.

Footsteps sounded higher on the stairs moments before Bremin came into view. A stack of pages was stuffed under his arm as if he'd gathered them quickly. "Good, I was hoping to catch you two before going after Master Ternan." He passed Katira and stopped on the landing with Papan, taking a moment to organize the sheets of paper and tucking them into his satchel.

"You left Lady Alystra up there with Master Aro. You sure that was wise?" Papan extended an arm to Katira, inviting her to join them as they descended.

"Technically Issa is up there too, although she's smart enough not to get involved in that conversation. It's Ternan who has me worried. He's always been perfectly dependable before. This lapse of judgment is concerning."

Katira followed Bremin's lead down the narrow winding stairs, glad to have him for company. The man had a knack for making people comfortable, and she liked having him around. Besides, listening to him talk with Papan took her mind off of the wild shadows dancing across the walls.

"How are you liking training so far? Issa tells me you are doing well with her." Bremin's question caught Katira off guard. She didn't expect to be part of their conversation.

"It's different than I thought it would be. She's a very good teacher."

"Good to hear. And Master Firen? Have you liked working with him?"

Katira opened her mouth to answer when she heard the

scratching. The sound froze her feet where they stood. "Did you hear that?"

Bremin stopped and cocked his head to listen. "Hear what?"

"They're back. I swore I heard a hound." She flared her power awake. The vessel tipped easily this time after the hundreds of times she had practiced. Power leapt to her ready fingers. She expected the cold hand of fear to creep up and grab her by the throat as it had before. Instead, all she felt was a grim acceptance. She heard Issa's teachings ringing through her head. She was far more prepared this time.

Papan swung back, eyes wide. His hand darted to the hip carrying the long dagger. "What is it?"

Katira didn't need to answer. Claws on tile stone scurried from a deeply shadowed corner to their left.

The echo of Papan opening himself to his own power flashed a wave of heat through Katira. "Stay ready, they could be anywhere. Katira, keep back, be ready to shield yourself."

"Show yourselves, cowards!" Bremin yelled.

Papan yanked Bremin back behind him. "Don't provoke them."

A snarling hound leapt out of the shadows, teeth snapping, hair on end. Papan formed glyphs lightning fast, one after another. They winked together and formed a ball of swirling light which slammed into the hound's flank, flinging it into the wall. The hall filled with the smell of burning hair.

Bremin placed himself squarely between the hounds and Katira. "I'll provoke them all I want if it gets them to show themselves. You can't fight what you can't see."

Another snarl came from the shadows.

Papan bound his stone to his palm and drew his blade.

"And I'd rather fight them on my own terms, if you don't mind."

The blade flashed to life in Papan's hands. Lines of power glowed a bright cutting blue along its edge.

Katira stepped back into the shelter of the stairs behind her. She had seen Papan intense and ready to kill only a handful of times before. It still frightened her.

The hound leapt forward once more, charred patches marring its coat. Papan whipped into action, his motions smooth and sure. His blade caught the hound square in the chest and sent it boneless to the floor. He swung around seeking out the next hound that dared to show itself. An anxious moment passed in which there was no sound, no click of nails, no snarls. "I don't like this. It should be here. Why isn't it attacking?"

"There were more, I'm sure of it." Bremin gripped a shorter dagger by the tip of the blade, ready to throw it. He hadn't opened himself to his power, and he wouldn't, either, unless he was forced to. The risk was too great.

Another skitter of claws sounded, this time from behind Katira. Bremin's eyes widened. "Alystra's up there." He bolted back up the stairs, shoving Katira out of the way.

Papan planted his cane on the stairs. "Issa! Incoming!" he shouted.

"Do you think she heard?" Katira started mounting the stairs. They had to be warned.

"Stop where you are." He hooked her ankle with the crooked end of the cane. "What happened to you promising to run from these things?"

"They're in danger. And—"

Papan cut her off. "And Issa will take care of it, or Lady

Alystra herself. Besides, you're in no shape to even try. You think that headache is bad now?"

Issa's shout echoed down from the top of the stairs sounding distant but clear enough to make out. "Was it just the one?"

"I think so. Stay alert." Despite reassuring Katira that Issa would take care of it, Papan's markings still glowed as he climbed back up the stairs.

When Katira reached the small room, the Bender was muttering and crawling around the base of the Occulus Seat.

Issa stared at him, her hands on her hips. A shadow hound lay in two pieces off to the side of the room. "Would you believe he didn't even look up?" she said to Bremin.

"Yes, I would."

Lady Alystra stood ready, lines on the sides of her neck still glowing. "Is the room clear now?"

"Should be." Issa said.

Bremin pinched the bridge of his nose. "How have you survived this long, Aro?"

With a groan, Papan heaved himself up the final stair. The climb left him pale and breathless. "Everyone all right?"

Master Aro adjusted the thick glasses on his nose and sniffed. "What kind of question is that?"

"Never mind. It's not important."

The man hadn't noticed any of what had just occurred. He glanced up at the High Lady as if to ask something and saw her lines still glowing.

He frowned and waved a dismissive hand. "That won't be necessary until I find where the glyphs need to be changed, my Lady."

"We're fine." Bremin answered Papan.

"Good." Papan fought to catch his breath and rolled onto

his back on the floor. "Why a tower? Why not in the main courtyard? Or even a spare office?"

"It has to be high." Master Aro chimed in without turning. "Why are you all back up here? Bremin, you're supposed to be delivering those notes to Master Ternan. Stonemother knows he needs them."

Katira shook her head. Isben was right; the man didn't really exist on the same plane as the rest of them.

"It's nothing for you to worry about." Papan studied Master Aro from his place on the floor. "It seems the problem has been resolved."

Master Aro pressed his lips together, his face went a shade darker. "No, it hasn't," he stammered. "The chair isn't safe, and you aren't helping where you're supposed to."

"Mind your tone," Bremin warned. "Remember who you are talking to."

Master Aro crossed his arms over his chest and almost rolled his eyes. He stopped himself short when he saw the unamused glare on Lady Alystra's face.

"What do you think this means, Bremin?" Papan asked. "Katira wasn't the target."

"No. She wasn't. If anything, it was directed at you first, then Alystra." Bremin tapped his lip. "That test got our enemy's attention, scared them perhaps. Threatened people do unpredictable things. We'll need to stay on our toes. I have a feeling it might get worse before it gets better."

Issa gave a curt nod and carefully checked her blade before sliding it back into its scabbard. "Looks like things just got a lot more interesting," she said with a grin.

"For you perhaps." Lady Alystra shook her head and headed to the top of the stairs. She pointed to Master Aro.

"Promise to keep him alive until we can sort things out with Master Ternan?"

"Yes, my Lady." Issa pressed her fist to her chest and bowed.

"Keep me alive?" Master Aro asked, finally paying attention. "What on earth just happened?"

CHAPTER NINETEEN

*T*he tear between worlds snapped shut as the last hound died, mere inches from taking Lady Alystra by the throat. Ternan fell back, panting from the effort of helping Wrothe rip holes in the newly reinforced barrier. He wasn't strong enough for this.

Wrothe wasn't done with him. The dull grays and blacks of the dreamspace shifted around them she dragged him to another place in the tower.

She'd wanted so much more, needed so much more. Anger radiated through her in crashing waves. Her patience had worn out; she was in no state to think or plan. The hound attack on Jarand and the High Lady was out of rage, not strategy. Wrothe was furious the relic hadn't worked as expected. The glyphs she'd had him sneak into the relic were supposed to give her access to anyone in the dreamspace. This was supposed to be her chance to anchor herself to Jarand as he stepped unwittingly closer to her world.

Ternan would have to pay the price, even though it was

her failing, her glyphs, and her meddling that didn't work. He had tried to counsel her, teach her about what needed to be done, but her pride kept her from listening.

The punishment came faster than expected. Her great wolf knocked him to the floor and pinned him there with its great paws planted firmly on his chest, claws digging into the already raw flesh there. It licked its chops, waiting for her command. It looked thin. Hungry.

Wrothe stood over him and stroked the fur between the great wolf's ears. "Can I tell you how much it annoys me that I can't torture you to death when you fail?" Her voice maintained an unsettling calm. "I've never been in this situation before. Fear is such a big motivator."

Ternan worked the moisture back into his mouth, desperate to find the right words to please her. "Every time I fail, I learn more. I know now what works, and what does not. I've been careful. Surgical. Precise." He gasped to draw a breath under the weight of the mighty wolf on his chest. "Isn't that what you wanted? A tool to serve you? I am that tool. Tools serve best when they are taken care of."

Wrothe didn't answer. Her gaze passed over the elaborate stained-glass windows of the dreamspace audience chamber. This room represented power, control, respect, everything she wanted. She left his side and approached the throne on the raised dais, hesitating a moment before pressing her hands against the arms of the tall chair and then sinking into it.

"I am taking care of you. Look at where your efforts with me have gotten you." She gestured to the gilded room. "You've earned respect among those here at Amul Dun. You are the head of your order. You've made it hard to tempt you with more. I've already given you everything you've ever wanted."

Ternan tugged at the great wolf's paw, trying to shift it. It didn't budge. "You're a horrible person, you know that?"

"What's your point?" She leaned her head back and studied the paintings which adorned the ceiling, each portraying a different scene of triumph. "Those who try to change the world for the better are often seen as monsters by those who place themselves in the crossfire. Those same monsters are heralded as saviors when peace is restored. Those who fight against change, fight regardless of the reason. People are stubborn that way. It's better for them to die than to suffer for the rest of their lives."

"Could you get the wolf off me? I already know I'm your slave. This demonstration doesn't impress me."

Wrothe tapped her leg and the wolf slunk back to her, its massive tail twitching back and forth as it went. Ternan took a much-needed breath and dragged himself back to standing. He refused to negotiate with the her while lying flat on his back.

He rubbed at the sore points on his chest. "Your impatience does you a great disservice. If you'd allowed me to alter the relic the way I wanted, Jarand would have been yours today."

"I hate it when my pets get too familiar with me." She set her hand on the wolf's head and scratched it with her long fingernails. "What happened to those days when you groveled at my feet?"

"I got old." He straightened his coat. "It got old."

"Yes, I'm disappointed. More of my lovely hounds were killed and I have nothing to show for it." She stood from the throne-like chair and approached him, a single sharp nail extended. "Perhaps I could give you another scar, hiding with the rest of them. Another stitch in the tapestry of my artwork."

Ternan flinched away from the probing nail, grateful she hadn't chosen to restrain him as she had in the past. His wrists and shoulders weren't as young as they used to be. Being tied up left him sore for days.

"That's not necessary. Plans are already in place for you to trap your prize. Jarand will test the Occulus Seat once I've deemed it safe to use again. The changes I will make to the chair will work this time. You can take him face-to-face if you wish, watch as his eyes go dark, pin him down until he stops fighting."

"You promised that before." Wrothe balled her hands into fists. "Why must you frustrate me?" Chains snaked out from the corners of the room and coiled up around Ternan's leg. A threat. "How will it be different this time?"

"Creating any device with motherstone is challenging. Master Aro is a smart one. We can't attack the user of the chair directly, it's too obvious. But I can create a door for you. He won't be looking for it." Ternan forced his clenched fists to relax. His stomach turned at the thought of her taking Jarand this way. It wasn't fair. He'd be defenseless. If she hadn't already planted her glyphs in him at Khanrosh, already started the process, he would have worked harder to keep her away. Ternan hoped that by sacrificing Jarand, it would buy him more time. He would find a way to protect the others. At least for a while.

Wrothe seized him by the throat. "You're plotting something. I can always tell. It hurts you when I win, I know." The tips of her nails dug into his skin. "Let me take that pain away from you."

"Please. I've already agreed. This isn't necessary." He didn't want her to take away his pain. He wanted to keep it so that he would not descend into deeper depravity and worse sins.

She tugged at the inside of his mind. The cloud of pain and panic lifted like the sun coming through clouds. He fought to pull those clouds back. He couldn't forget that what she was forcing him to do was wrong.

She pushed harder, filling him with the sunshine of contentment. "Stop your inane plotting and you can always feel this way."

The warmth filled him. The ease, the peace. Something nagged at the tiniest back of his brain. He swatted it away and stretched out in the sunshine of Wrothe's influence. His mistress needed to enslave that bothersome Jarand to be happy. He wanted her to be happy, as happy as he was. He'd do anything she asked. It would be simple. Wrothe would get what she wanted and more.

The audience chamber faded, folding back into itself as it disappeared. The dust and paper strewn desk rematerialized beneath Ternan's hands. He grinned to himself, eager to please Wrothe, happy to be so useful. With a freshly dipped pen he set about engineering the glyphs he'd need.

CHAPTER TWENTY

*D*own in the training yard, Katira took her position on the outer edge of the circle. Isben was already standing in his spot and moving through one of the sequences Issa taught them a few days prior. She liked having him there, liked learning alongside with him, liked knowing she wasn't the only one who didn't know what to do sometimes. With the two Masters back to making alterations to the Occulus Seat, their schedule returned to normal once more.

The day's practice followed the same pattern as usual. Issa began with leading them both through a series of warm up exercises, then moved onto teaching technique. They were alone in the yard, and the space echoed with the rhythmic sound of their feet striking the ground in unison.

As much as Katira tried to find peace in the practice, her thoughts turned back to Papan and his meeting with Lady Alystra several days earlier, after the setting of the glyphs. Ever since then, he practically radiated unease. At first she thought it was because he was still upset, but when it didn't pass she began to worry it might be something else entirely. Whatever he'd discussed with the High Lady bothered him enough that he couldn't let it go.

She sensed him coming down to the training yard long before she could see him. When he finally rounded the last corner and stepped into the puddle of bluish light, Katira stopped following Issa's motions entirely.

Issa thumped her arm lightly for allowing her attention to wander. "Stay focused. If it was urgent, he'd come over right away."

Katira returned to following Issa, feeling twice as graceless as before knowing he was watching her. Finally, after several long minutes, he crossed the yard. He wore the simple linen shirt and trousers he favored while in the tower, not the loose-fitting clothing she'd seen him wear when practicing in the yard. He hadn't come to train.

"Rest position," Issa ordered as she turned to face him.

Both Katira and Isben had worked with Issa long enough that the rest position came automatically. Katira brought her feet shoulder width apart, joined her hands behind her back, and tried to listen in on their conversation.

Papan shouldn't be there at that time of day. He was supposed to be up in the observation tower until the next bell sounded. Issa furrowed her brow as she listened and answered him with a shake of her head. This back and forth continued until Issa shrugged and walked away. Whatever he wanted, he had talked her into it despite her misgivings.

Katira overheard something about having to close the tower early because the two masters had gotten into some spat. Made sense.

Issa returned carrying a tall stack of boards which she proceeded to place at regular intervals against the back wall of the yard.

"At ease." Papan commanded.

Katira allowed her arms to fall at her sides and shook out the stiffness in her shoulders.

"In light of our current situation, we need to accelerate this part of your training. Today Issa and I will instruct the two of you in the use of a few basic defensive glyphs. Isben, you've learned a few of these, so this will be a good review."

Katira tried to keep her face calm and passive. She'd seen what some of the defensive glyphs could do, and as a healer, the thought of using them against anything living made her a little sick.

"Don't worry. We'll take it slow." He gestured to the empty yard. "I've requested that no one enter the yard while we work, to help avoid distractions."

"Are these glyphs that dangerous?" Katira asked.

"No and yes. The first few you learn are fairly harmless, and we'll start with easier ones until you feel comfortable. But yes, learning this is inherently dangerous. Not all my scars are from blades." He patted her on the shoulder and led her to the other side of the yard.

Issa set several boards into a notch in the wall of the training yard cut from the mountain side, then returned to join them.

"First, watch." Papan bound his stone to his palm. "The first method I'll show you is using the circular shield you are already familiar with, and modifying it." A ribbon of power flowed from his palm and assembled itself into a small glowing shield.

"You change the size the same way as with a shield, by fixing the size and shape you want in your mind. For this, the shape should look like a cork from a bottle." The glyph shrank down and grew brighter as if hovered in front of him.

"To release it into your target, envision the cork traveling through the space and striking the target. The greater your focus, the more accurate you'll be." His shot streaked across the yard and struck the board with a hollow thunk.

"Just like a shield, this skill uses focused raw energy. It will hit and hurt your enemy the same way touching a shield does. It's useful if your goal is to disarm, but not kill." Papan lowered his hands to his sides. "Your turn."

Katira stepped back involuntarily. When he had had her work with shields, he had pushed her too hard and the power had seized her and wouldn't let go. This was the type of lesson where it would too easy for him to push like that again.

Isben stepped forward. "May I?"

Papan agreed with a nod and indicated where he should stand. Isben released several shots that arched across the yard and struck several of the targets.

Then it was her turn. She stepped to the spot where Isben had been standing. It seemed simple enough.

"You've got this," Isben told her as they changed places. Katira hoped he was right.

Both Issa and Papan fixed their eyes on her, pinning her to the spot.

"Remember the steps?" Issa asked.

"Yes. Form a shield, shrink it down, send it to the target." She bound her stone into her palm and drew a breath, holding it for a moment to steady her nerves.

"Good. Open to the power and form the shield. We'll move one step at a time."

The opening fought her. Too many eyes watching. Even if one of those sets of eyes was Papan, the other two were Issa, who she'd never successfully opened in front of before, and Isben, who definitely distracted her. It took several tries before the vessel reluctantly tipped.

A circle of raw power formed between Katira's outstretched hands and hovered there ready and waiting.

Papan took position back and behind her shoulder. "Maintain your focus. Condense it down to a small point."

Katira followed his lead. The point shrank down to the cork sized missile he'd described. The edges wavered and shook as she fought to maintain the idea of the size in her mind. From the corner of her eye she caught sight of Issa binding her stone into her hand and her markings glowing to life.

Katira's attention shifted and the missile squirmed away from her control like a slippery fish. She tried to get it back, tried to force it to reform from the splintering pieces. Instead, it broke apart and shot out in all directions. Part of it struck Katira's shoulder with a zinging snap. Another struck a shield which sprung from Papan's hand.

"Tell me what happened," he asked, although his tone said he already knew. Making her explain it would help her learn.

Katira rubbed at the sore spot on her shoulder. "I lost focus. Issa moved."

"Try again. Hold your focus until after you've made your shot."

Katira formed the glyph once more and didn't wait for her father's instruction to shrink it down. She willed the missile to leave her hands and fly toward the target. No sooner had she thought it, the missile moved in a blur, faster than sight, and slammed into the board.

It exploded.

Fragments flew in all directions.

Katira ducked her head under her arm. The shimmery sheen of a shield flashed around her where Papan had flung it.

The line of practice dummies at the back of the hall toppled over, as well as several archery targets.

Isben ducked for cover behind Issa, who had formed her own shield.

Papan brushed the debris from his shirt. "This is why I had the yard cleared. Nothing like an unexpected surprise to get the heart pumping, eh?" At least he was still smiling, so Katira couldn't be in too much trouble.

Issa, on the other hand, surveyed the toppled equipment in dismay. Papan seemed way too amused at her first try.

"What?" Katira asked. "What's so funny?"

"It's really nothing." Papan answered with a laugh. "It's not about you."

"Your father and I had a bet, that's all." Issa scrubbed her hands through her short blond hair. "He thought you might blow up the board, I didn't." She righted one of the downed dummies. "I reckon I owe you an armor polishing then."

Papan continued to chuckle to himself. "And you can't have one of your men do it either. It's been a while, so it really could use it."

Issa tossed a chunk of splintered wood at him with a smirk.

He turned back to Katira to explain. "Usually a first try results in a weak bolt that doesn't even touch the target. Occasionally, a student will overcompensate and blow the target to smithereens." He bent to pick up the thumb-sized piece of wood Issa tossed at him. "Seems you are one of the rare ones. But with you, that's becoming the normal. Isn't it?"

Katira blushed. This attention was not what she wanted.

She just wanted to learn. Being embarrassed didn't help. She let the power fade out and become dormant once again. "It seems I have too good of a teacher."

"Probably not that. Although Issa is excellent, I agree." He scooped up his cane from where it had fallen. "Nothing to get worked up about. We face each challenge as its presented. It's easier to help a weak student build their strength and confidence. It's a bit trickier to help a strong student tone it down. You'll get it."

He turned his attention back to Isben as he casually stepped out from behind Issa and pretending he hadn't just tried to use her as a shield.

"Your turn again."

Isben gave a nod and took his position. Katira envied the smooth control when he opened, how he gave no hint of discomfort when the burn of power washed through him. One day she hoped she could do the same.

Issa studied each shot before returning to Jarand's side. "He's got good mastery of this. I think he's ready to learn the cutting glyph."

Papan watched as Isben sent two more missiles in clean lines across the yard, each striking the new target with a satisfying thud. "I agree. Take him to the other side of the yard. I'll keep working with Katira here."

Katira felt a pang as Isben left. While his presence was distracting, she liked having him close. With him learning beside her, it meant the focus on her was that much less intense.

"Ok, Katira. Try again. This time, shoot the missile slower. Instead of a streak of light, imagine it's an arrow flying."

"I think I can do that." Katira invited the power to fill her once more and ignored how Papan's power flared to life behind her.

The circle formed between her hands, and she quickly dropped it to the size of a thumb tip. It hovered brightly before her, ready and waiting. She fixed the idea of an arrow flying with its graceful arc and its solid hit. As she prepared to release, Isben's first bright missile using the new glyph sped across the yard like a shooting star, drawing her attention and her missile with it.

Issa's shield flashed into place a moment before the missile smashed into it. "Really, girl?" The shimmer vanished and Issa shook her hand. "Do you know how much that stings?"

"She didn't mean it. Isben's shot distracted her right as she formed her missile." Papan explained.

Katira's hands fell to her sides. "Sorry. That was entirely my fault. Let me try again."

"Stay focused." He directed her back toward the pair of targets in front of them. "One more misfire, and I'll have to train you up in the mountains where you can't accidently shoot someone."

"I thought the mountains were impassable in this snow."

"We'll wear boots." Papan chuckled. "That said, I'd rather stay here. Try again. This time at the target."

The chiding was all Katira needed to double her efforts and try again. She had to prove to herself that she could keep focused when it mattered.

The missile formed above her hand, sailed through the air, and struck the target with a firm thwack.

"There you go. Well done." Papan clapped.

Katira couldn't help but be pleased. With this skill she could keep the shadow hounds away from her and stop them before they grabbed hold of her with their razor-sharp teeth. Her heart pounded at the thrill.

"Keep going," Papan encouraged. "Do it until you can form and release it in one step."

Katira set her sights on the first target again and formed and released two more missiles, trying to go faster, trying to match what she had seen her father do. They struck their targets, but not as hard as before.

When she re-centered herself to try again, the circle snapped shut in her face with a crack.

"Slow down a touch. Make sure each step is there," Papan guided, still patient, still pleased.

She didn't want to slow down. She wanted, no, needed to be good at this. Failing here meant failing when it mattered, and she refused for that to happen again. She slowed enough to be sure the missile was formed properly before letting it go. With each try, her shots became easier and more precise.

"You can stop now. I think you've got it." Papan instructed.

Katira panted with the effort. "Please, not yet."

"No." He set a hand on her shoulder. "You need to stop. Using raw power like this drains you far faster than using glyphs."

She shrugged him off. The targets transformed in her mind into snarling hounds. She had to defend herself. Another missile formed over her hand. She split it in two and let it sail, striking the two targets with precision. The shadows in the corners of the training yard surged, she wasn't sure if what she was seeing was real, but she wasn't going to let them near her again.

"Katira, stop!" Papan yelled, his hand now squeezing her shoulder like a vise.

His yell transformed into something else. He was in danger

too. She formed more missiles, desperate to keep the approaching shadows away from her, from Papan, from all the people who were killed by Wrothe. The power surged beneath her skin, pulsing and ready. The twin shots turned into three, then four at a time. Anything to protect the people she loved.

"Issa!" Papan shouted. "Get Isben out of here, then stand ready." The hand on her shoulder clung tight. The familiar warmth of Papan's power flowed into her.

The flurry of movement from the side of the yard caught Katira's attention. She sent more missiles sailing, not looking, not thinking. Everything was a threat; everything was coming for her.

Papan wasn't trying to help, he was trying to stop her. Couldn't he see? They were being attacked again. Katira couldn't stop, not until the threat was gone. Her power snapped to that eerie calm, trapping her inside a safe bubble of space just outside herself. A different type of shield burst around her, forcing Papan to step back.

Issa sprinted back across the yard, the lines on her arms and neck glowing fiercely. She deflected Katira's missiles with quick sure pulses of power all while leaping and turning out of harm's way.

"She's lost control. On my signal, bind and block her." Papan ordered, his own lines shining bright and a new series of glyphs spinning off his fingertips.

A deeper, more intense surge of power gathered deep inside Katira, something far more dangerous than a simple missile. It stretched and gathered at her fingertips.

"Now!" he yelled.

A blast of power slammed into Katira and wrapped around her, holding her fast. Within the blow, dozens of ribbons burst free, knotting themselves around her vessel and stuffing her power back into it.

Papan grabbed her neck. A single sharp stab of his power sent her boneless to the ground and her world went dark once more.

CHAPTER TWENTY-ONE

*K*atira curled into the warm armchair in front of
the fire and burrowed under the thick quilt.
Ever since what happened in the training yard, she'd been not
allowed to even touch the power. That was two days ago. She
caught the edge of a handful of whispered conversations as
different people came and went from their apartment.

There was mention of leaving, of another safe place that
might be more suited for the two of them. Papan was against
that idea. After what she did, Katira wanted to disappear,
maybe that was best. Maybe she was too dangerous to be
around others in the tower.

Isben visited when he could, usually when Bremin needed
to speak with Papan. Some visits they talked, but mostly Katira
let him hold her and stroke her hair. When he was there,
words were unnecessary. She needed him to hold on to as her
world fell apart once again. The visits always ended when
Bremin had to leave, and that was always too soon.

Papan promised that if she was careful, maybe she could

start again tomorrow. She wasn't sure if she wanted to. The thought of summoning the power, knowing what it was capable of, made her sick.

The fire cracked and an ember jumped onto the hearth. Katira watched as its light stayed strong for only a few moments before dying. The apartment was empty now save for Papan, who had hidden himself into his small study. A thick tome, *Anatomical Studies by Master Reaves Baccurate*, rested on her lap open to a diagram of the muscles of the arm. Master Firen loaned it to her to study, saying she might need the distraction. While it was quite possibly the best anatomy book she'd ever studied, she found herself nodding off to the lullaby of the crackling fire and deep shushing wind of a winter storm howling outside the window.

A sound within the storm knocked her from sleep and sent the book banging to the floor. She hurried to her feet, wrapping her stone around her hand and scanning the corners of the room.

Papan stuck his head out the door of the study. "What is it?"

"A growl. Something's here." She turned slowly once again, listening for any scratch, any tap, anything out of the ordinary.

Papan did the same, his head tilting as he listened. His lines glowed to life and he set a hand against the wall. Glowing lines like a spider web raced along the stone blocks and circled the room before returning to him. "It's okay. Nothing here. Must have been a dream."

She unwound her stone from her hand and willed her heart to stop pounding. "Must have been."

A soft, familiar knock came at the door. Bremin let himself in and closed the door behind him. He wore his usual buttoned shirt with the purple band on the short collar and a practical woolen coat to ward off the chill of the tower's hallways.

"Well, they've done it." He shrugged out of the coat and hung it on the stand near the door. "The Occulus Seat is ready."

Papan still held one of his engraving tools in his hand. "What about testing? I thought I would be notified," he asked as he returned it to the desk in his small study.

Bremin shook his head and pulled up a chair at the table. "Wasn't necessary. This was a minor thing. Master Ternan tested it himself during Issa's shift and was successful. I was up there this evening. I'll admit, the timing mechanism Master Aro came up with is brilliant. The man has a rare talent."

Katira collected the book from off the floor and placed it on the small side table near her armchair. Mention of Master Ternan using the chair made her uneasy.

"What happens now?" Katira asked as she poured herself a cup of tea and hoped it would soothe her nerves.

For nearly a week, the promise of this relic being able to secure Amul Dun against shadow creatures had kept her hoping for its completion. Now it was ready, a whole new set of fears sprung up. Everything about it and what it was supposed to do was still a mystery. Despite Bremin's reassurance that it was safe, Katira couldn't bring herself to believe it.

"Alystra's first priority is to learn how shadow creatures are getting into Amul Dun." He turned his attention back to Papan. "She wants you in the chair first thing in the morning to start your investigation. If you can strengthen the tower against any further attack, then you are to do so. Our home must be secure."

"No. Not him. Not again." The teacup rattled in Katira's

hand and she set it down before she dropped it. "Papan, please. I don't want you in there."

"Easy." Papan met her gaze, concern wrinkling his brow. "Nothing happened last time. I came out unharmed."

"I know. It doesn't make sense. But even the thought of it scares me." She joined them at the table. "Why can't it be someone else?"

Papan thought for a moment. "Could Issa do it?" he asked Bremin. "She and I are equals and, if anything, she's got a better feel for the tower than I do right now. She's more than capable to begin the investigation." He tapped the table with a finger as if considering another possibility. "Now that I think about it, you should be the one to go in. You understand more about what this barrier might be and have a much better head on your shoulders for uncovering truths. Definitely better than both Issa and I."

"And I would do it in a heartbeat, if it were possible." Bremin said. "I'm dying to know more about how this dream-space works, if only to be able to seek out its weaknesses and strengths." He touched the stone hanging under his shirt. "Alystra forbids me to even try. The way it uses the power would probably put me in a coma."

Papan leaned on the table, suddenly serious. "Damn it. She's right. Even if it didn't, chances are you'd still faint and forget everything you'd seen. We can't risk it. We need you on the outside to analyze whatever data is gathered." He traced his finger along the grain of the wood. "For Katira's sake, I'd prefer it be Issa tomorrow. Can that be arranged?"

Bremin pursed his lips. "Master Ternan specifically asked for you to try again. Something about since you'd already been in, you'd know better how well their changes were implemented. Issa wouldn't have that insight. It has to be you."

Katira gripped the edge of the table so hard her fingers went white with the strain.

Papan eased her one hand free, then the other. "Worrying now won't help anything. The decision is made. The best we can do now is be ready for it."

"That's easier said than done."

Despite Papan's advice, a persistent gnawing worry curled itself inside Katira's head. Even with all the assurances, all the safeguards they put in place, she couldn't shake the feeling that a new evil awaited them come morning.

The next morning, the energy surrounding the Occulus Seat pulsed against Katira's skin, doing nothing to soothe her anxiety or growing impatience. She found Isben standing a step behind Master Aro, watching intently as the man worked green tinged glyphs over a tiny portion of the armrest. The glyphs settled, drawing the rough, unfinished surface to a glossy shine that matched the stone next to it.

Close by, Bremin bent over the table alongside Master Ternan, pointing at sections of a page and asking questions.

When the Bender finished, his power faded away. He pushed his odd thick glasses up on his forehead, making his greasy hair stand up. Dark circles hung under his eyes. It looked as if he hadn't slept for several nights.

When Cassim saw Katira exit the stairwell, he made his way over to her. "Hey, you doing better today?"

"Good enough, considering all of this." She gestured to Papan. "I can't believe they want him to go in again. It feels like a bad idea."

"If it were up to me to pick, which it never would, I'd have chosen him. You forget, he's got a long history here. This feels like something he would do for the sake of Amul Dun."

As Cassim spoke, he got a distant look in his eyes, as if reliving some memory. He knew stories about Papan that she had never heard. He'd been through things with him that she couldn't imagine. Perhaps she was being foolish about all this. Her fears probably sounded childish to these legends who had lived lifetimes already.

"Is Issa coming?" If Papan was in the chair, Katira felt better if the warrior woman was there.

"She'll be up with the High Lady any minute."

A gust of wind made the whole room sway enough that Katira's stomach flipped over. The hints of the storm humming at her window the night before had grown into a blizzard.

The High Lady rounded the last curve of the stairwell. "Bremin, report. Are we really ready this time?"

Bremin took her hand as she ascended the last stair. "I've reviewed all your concerns, and mine as well. We're are ready as we'll ever be."

Those assembled gave the expected bow as she entered.

"I see no reason to draw this out." Lady Alystra took her place by the wide working table. "Jarand, are you ready to try again?"

"Yes, my lady." Papan approached the chair and placed himself in it. Master Ternan quickly explained the new timing feature they'd crafted into the armrest alongside the larger motherstone sphere. From where Katira stood, it looked like an hourglass no larger than her palm.

Papan rotated the small hourglass once before placing his hand on the sphere. He glanced toward Katira one last time. "You know what to do. I'm counting on you." Then he fed a ribbon of energy into the motherstone. Once again, his eyes went blank and his body relaxed in a slow sigh.

Katira couldn't stand idly by. She took one of the chairs from the table they'd so often worked at and placed it at Papan's knee to wait. The faint sendings across the bond took on the same dreamlike peace as before.

That is, until they didn't.

Half of the sand had fallen through the glass when the first flutter of unease echoed through their bond. The change was subtle, hard to define. It reminded her of the uncertainty he'd experienced when he'd been called to Lady Alystra's office and wasn't sure why.

Isben pulled up the other chair close to her. "What is it?" he asked in a whisper.

"Not sure, a change. That's all."

Bremin caught them whispering and stepped closer. "Anything to be concerned about?"

Katira studied the stream of emotions trickling in. The unease subsided, and in its place grew a stone-cold focus and the steady flow of his power surged briefly. "I don't think so. He's using the power. Maybe he found a weak point and is fixing it?"

"Maybe." Bremin glanced at the hourglass, only a quarter of the sand remained. "Keep close tabs on him. It's not much longer."

Papan's controlled focus remained. He had to be fixing something, what other explanation could there be?

Isben slipped his hand around hers. "You've got this. He said he'd be trying a few new things. Trust him to make the right decisions."

Katira's hand trembled inside of his. She promised Papan

she'd keep a good watch over him. Fearing the unknown wouldn't help anyone.

A spark of a different fear crossed the bond, so small Katira nearly missed it as it mixed in with her own. Then another, larger spike shook her. She'd only felt fear like this when he was in the middle of a nightmare. It shouldn't be happening here.

"He's in trouble. Something's happening." Katira pulled out of Isben's grasp and leapt to her feet. She eyed the sphere where her father's hand rested. "How do we get him out?"

Master Ternan tapped a smooth raised dome the size of a thumb tip next to the hourglass. "You can signal him by feeding a small amount of power here."

"I don't want to signal him. I want to wake him." Katira wanted to pull at her hair. Why did Master Ternan frustrate her so much?

"He still has to do that on his own. It's the only way he can come out safely." Master Ternan sounded irritated that she didn't understand.

"Signal him." Bremin gestured to the chair, lines of worry etched his face. "He might need reminding he can leave."

Isben reached for the spot, but Katira beat him to it, the power leaping to her command. The second she touched it, a deep tone sounded within the chair.

"Anything?" Bremin asked.

Katira tried to tease apart what she was feeling. Papan's power surged over and over in bursts, and that icy grip of fear still gripped him hard. The chime had changed nothing. She shook her head. Her power surged, eager to do something, anything. "I'm going in with him."

"No." Bremin gripped her wrist before she could touch the sphere. "Let Jarand fight this. He's a trained Guardian."

"What if he can't?"

Bremin's grip faltered and his gaze twitched to Papan sitting in the chair.

Then came the pain. It started at his old wound and shot straight into his skull.

"It's hurting him!"

Lady Alystra leapt to her feet and started giving orders. "Issa, go in. Bring him out. Cassim, keep watch. Master Ternan and Aro, you better be ready to forcefully remove the two of them on Cassim's word."

Issa stood poised and ready. The second Lady Alystra gave the word, she sprang into action. Ribbons of her power flowed into the sphere, and as her hand made contact she stiffened, the chair's grasp freezing her in place.

Bremin released Katira's outstretched hand, and it brushed past the sphere on accident. The same power that wrapped itself around Issa grabbed of her and pulled her in faster than she could scream.

The small room faded as if the colors had all washed down the drain. Katira found herself in a world dominated by shades of gray. Isben stood frozen in this altered world, his eyes fixed on her, his hand reaching out to stop her, a protest stuck to his lips. When she blinked, he shifted into another frozen position, as if he were arguing with Bremin.

Issa stared at her, mouth open with shock. "You can't be in here. You have to leave. Now."

"I didn't mean to. It was an accident." Katira protested.

"Doesn't matter. Get out of here, I've got to find Jarand, and quickly."

Another sharp pain radiated across the apprentice bond. This time Katira could feel it as clearly as if Papan was standing next to her. She winced at the intensity of it. "Let me help you. I can find him."

Issa gripped the hilt of her sword as she considered this new option. In the end it was a strategic choice. "If he's in trouble, I can't lose time searching. Take me to him, then promise to leave."

"Don't let go." Katira held out her hand. "We have to hurry."

She anchored herself to that tiny beacon within the bond that knew where he was and willed herself to move closer. The dreamspace moved around them in a blur as she flitted through the massive tower with each of her racing thoughts, passing down the long spiral stairs, then the dark abandoned hallway, then the great hall.

She found him in the audience chamber, and he wasn't alone.

The air before him was split open like a ripe plum, bursting and oozing trails of light down the center of the chamber. Thick dark ribbons of power flowed from the opening, wrapping around him and pinning his arms to his sides. He held fast to the long knife in one hand. Bright blue glyphs still raced up its edge.

The sight shook Katira and a cry burst from her lips before she could stop it. "Papan!"

His head whipped around, eyes stricken and tight. "Get out of here!" His voice was coarse and strained. "You can't fight her, not here."

Not her, not Wrothe. The thought of that awful woman made Katira tremble. She couldn't be here in the dreamspace; they'd sent her back to whatever hell she'd crawled out of.

"I'm here, Jarand," Issa yelled over the noise. "Tell me what I need to do."

"Cut me free." He gasped as the dark ribbon pulled tighter. "Don't let these things touch you."

Wrothe's shrill laugh sliced through the air. Through the narrow split, Katira saw her. Her hands were aflame with the power, her hair wild, and she grinned as if she'd already won.

"Stay back. This isn't your fight." Issa pushed Katira further away from the chaos as she leapt into action. She dodged the seeking ribbons, cutting apart those that drew too close and with a smooth sweep of her blade, sliced through the one holding Papan. He toppled onto his hands and knees, gasping for air. Issa stood between him and Wrothe's power, cutting down anything that dared come close as he gained his feet.

He assumed a fighting stance and held out the knife he'd grown used to wearing around the tower. He eyed Issa's sword for a moment and a wry smile crept over his face. A moment later, his knife transformed into the long glowing sword he favored. Katira blinked, not knowing that was a possibility in the dreamspace. "I've got this," he yelled over the noise. "Take Katira out of here. I'll be out the second this breach is closed."

"Not doing that." Issa gritted her teeth as she swung again. A burst of light shot from her palm, pushing back a new ribbon trying to slip out of the tear. "We force her back, together."

Katira had promised to stay clear of the danger, but as she watched, it was clear that no matter how hard they fought, Wrothe had more power here. For every strand of power they forced back, another slipped through. They couldn't heal the split while fighting off those cursed ribbons, but she could.

She skirted the fight, drawing closer to see how the fabric of the barrier had been ripped. If this was like a living thing, then perhaps it was as simple as joining the damaged parts back together. At last, she could do something instead of feeling helpless. The vessel of her power tipped, filling her quickly. She formed the few glyphs Master Firen had shown her for knitting muscle back together and threaded them into the side of the split.

"What are you doing? Get back!" Papan yelled. His brief distraction allowed one of the ribbons to snag his ankle. Issa cut it away.

"I think I can close it. It'll keep those things from coming out," she yelled back. The threads of her glyph stretched out and snagged the fabric of the barrier along the way. Several ribbons twisted their way toward her.

Issa dashed in, cutting them back and away from Katira. "You promised. Get back or I'll force you back."

Katira didn't stop the threads of her glyph, didn't let her focus waver, and didn't answer. All it would take is one good pull and the cut in the barrier would close, just like stitching a wound.

As Issa reached out to grab her, Katira collected all the threads and heaved them back. The opening shrank.

"Issa, stop!" Papan called. "It's working. Keep them off her."

Katira heaved again. The broken threads at either end of the tear merged back together under her guidance and the opening shrank.

Issa paused to take in the sudden change before returning to the fight, this time preventing the dark ribbons from reaching Katira. "I don't know how you're doing that, but keep going," she encouraged.

Wrothe fought against it, wildly trying to rip the split back open, her face contorting in rage. Papan shot missile after missile to keep new ribbons from coming all while slashing at the ones that got too close. Paired with Issa, and aided by the rapidly shrinking opening, the last of the dark ribbons disappeared.

With a final yank, Katira's glyph forced the split closed, cutting off Wrothe's shrieks and plunging the room back into a startling silence.

Papan's labored breathing sounded too loud in the quiet. "We need to leave." He swayed a fraction. Issa sought out the cane which had been abandoned on the floor and returned it to him. "There are at least half a dozen weak points just like that one here in the dreamspace."

Katira's power quieted, leaving her ears ringing and her mind fuzzy. "Then we patch them up, like this one. We can't leave them for someone else to get caught."

"No. This was an act of sabotage. The weak points weren't here last time. We knew there was someone in Amul Dun that might harbor a connection to Wrothe. This proves it. What's worse, I think I know who it is." A fierce headache echoed through the bond, one like what Katira experienced after she'd overdrawn. He'd pulled too hard trying to free himself.

Issa swore quietly. "Besides you, only Master Ternan has used it. This is enough evidence to build a case, but we best let Lady Alystra deal with it. She's the only one who can order an interrogation against him."

"She won't like it. When news gets out, and it will, it will splinter Amul Dun's strength down even further. There's no way around it." Papan turned to leave. "We need to get out of here. If another one of those things opens, we're dead."

"I'll hurry ahead. The sooner one of us wakes up, the better." She touched the stone bound to her palm. "Cassim's sick with worry."

"Wait," he called, catching her as she turned to leave.

"What will you tell them? If Master Ternan suspects that we know, it will be that much more dangerous for all of us until he's brought down."

"I wasn't going to tell them anything." Issa's voice changed from one of unamused disbelief, to that of firm resolution. "I have half a mind to tackle the man and bind his power away from him the second I get out of here. Lady Alystra can decide what to do with him after he's secured."

Papan smiled at that. "Be careful. He's old."

Without another word, Issa hurried from the audience chamber. The dreamspace folded around her as she flickered out of sight.

Katira's hand still shook as she reached for Papan, needing reassurance that he was okay. Wrothe had had a hold of him, and there was no telling the damage she might have done. The echoes and traces of him through the bond had gone strangely quiet again.

"What did she do to you?"

"Tried to suck me dry, get into my mind." He took an unsteady step toward the door. "Break me."

As he spoke, the tight hold on what he was allowing her to sense shifted for a moment, giving Katira a glimpse. Wrothe had hurt him in a way she couldn't begin to understand, and worse, she didn't know how to help him.

Ternan stayed quiet in the corner of the room and watched as Jarand entered the dreamspace once more. This was it. After hundreds of years of being cruelly manipulated, he'd be free.

Jarand had always been strong. He was a man of firm convictions and strategic action. If anyone could withstand her, it was him. Even if she did sink her anchors into him, it would take weeks, maybe months before she could force his hand.

Waiting made him anxious. The longer it took, the greater the risk of failure. And if she failed today, there was no telling what insanity he'd face when she came for him. For the moment, things were calm, but it wouldn't last.

He regretted what would happen with the girl. Katira would be forced to experience a fraction of what her father would endure. Even not knowing what it meant, it would be a terrible ordeal for her.

He honed his focus, watching for traces of her satisfaction through their bond to know if she was succeeding. And she was. Curse her, she was.

Until she wasn't.

In a single moment, she transformed from triumphant to terrible.

The burn of her came faster and hotter than he could stand. He coughed and flecks of blood spotted his hand. The dark stone burrowed deeper into his chest. Something had gone wrong. Her anger bordered on an insane rage he'd only experienced a handful of times.

Wrothe pulled hard once more, weakening his knees and making his hands tremble. If he didn't leave the space, she'd cause him to pitch unconscious to the floor right there in front of everyone.

He slipped from the room and stumbled down the spiraling stairs. At the base of the stair, he crawled into the dark recess tucked behind the circular wall and hoped his body remained hidden until she finished with him. With a sigh, he toppled face first into the thick dust as she yanked his consciousness away.

He awoke in the dreamspace chained hand and foot to the corners of a narrow torturer's table. Wrothe gripped the edge of the table, restraining herself from striking him. Dark threads of power, augmented by what she stole from Jarand, arched off her and sizzled the air. Metal tools heated in a flaming brazier too close for comfort. The heat seared the sweat from his skin.

She pulled a long set of tongs from the fire and studied how it glowed in the greyness of the dreamspace.

"You failed me again."

"Everything I promised worked exactly as it was supposed to. The girl entering was an accident. I swear it. I had no part in that." Ternan pleaded. He could smell his hair burning.

Wrothe shook her head. "You must think me a fool." She clamped the red-hot tongs around the smallest finger of his left hand.

An animalistic scream ripped from his lips. His body jerked involuntarily against the restraints, and all conscious thought fled. He was pain. His world shrank down to knowing nothing more than the searing horror as the metal melted the joint and charred the bones. The iron clicked shut and the finger fell away.

Wrothe replaced the tongs into the fire. "When I free you, you will use the Occulus Seat to create a portal directly from my world to Alystra's chambers. This is the price you will pay for your failure. You will watch as I personally murder your beloved High Lady."

Ternan tried to speak. His throat, raw from screaming, refused to make a sound. This was the one thing she promised never to do. In return for his cooperation, she vowed that no matter what, she would never harm the High Lady. He wildly shook his head, the back of his skull thudding against the thick wood of the table.

"You think I'm going against my word. I'm really not. You've always known my mind, my ambition. My promise to you was always a lie, but you were too stupid and weak to admit it to yourself." She pulled free a different set of glowing tongs and set them against his ring finger. "You will do as I ask."

"No. Never," he managed to whisper.

Another wave of pain washed over him. He forced himself to breathe through his nose, to focus on the passage of breath as it entered and exited. Anything other than the rush of panic threatening to take over as she removed another finger.

Spots of white crowded the edges of his vision. It was too much. Pain overwhelmed his senses. Soon he'd fall into blessed blackness and whatever she did to him wouldn't matter.

The tongs were thrust back into the flames and Wrothe grabbed his face. Her power surged through him, pulling him back from the edge. "I miss when you were young and strong. You lasted longer."

"Burn them all off." He struggled to get her hand off him. "I won't do it. I'll never form another glyph for you ever again if she dies."

Her fingers tightened in his hair and her power threaded into his mind. Dreaded comfort filled him, the kind that made him pliant and willing. "You realize, if you don't agree, I'll turn you into a puppet and then you will be the one to plunge a blade into her heart."

Ternan's mind was caught in a hopeless loop. If he let Wrothe do it, Lady Alystra would die by the hand of a powerful enemy. It would be a noble death, one they'd write stories about, and her fame would grow all the larger for it.

But, if he were the one to do it, the High Lady would die knowing he'd betrayed her for all those years. It was the worst possible way to die. A brush of Wrothe's compulsion tightened on his mind, a threat.

In the end, she left him no choice. "I'll do it."

"Louder. Tell me exactly what I want you to do. Make me believe."

He coughed, cleared his throat, and drew a deeper breath. "I'll use the Occulus Seat and open a portal that will allow you into the real world. " His mind reeled against the words. This was agony, this was torture. "I'll let you destroy her." He couldn't bear to say her name.

"That's a good boy." She patted his cheek and wiped away tears from his face.

The brazier, the heat, the chains all disappeared. A layer of dust rolled under his palms. His hand burned and he clutched at it surprised to find the fingers intact. She made it so real. In the past, she had forced him to keep his scars.

He had a horrible task in front of him, and too many obstacles in his way.

CHAPTER TWENTY-TWO

*W*hen Katira exited the dreamspace, the sudden noise and color assaulted her senses. She pressed her eyes closed against it. Isben was so close to her, she could smell the washing soap used on his shirt.

"Come on, talk to me. Are you okay?" he asked. One of his hands slid up to cradle her cheek.

She pushed away his hand and stood to scan the room. "It was a trap." Master Ternan was nowhere to be seen.

"What do you mean?" He kept a hand on her shoulder as if worried she might collapse.

"Where is he?"

"What are you talking about? What's going on?"

"She was in there. She had him. The dreamspace had been intentionally weakened to let her break through."

"Is that why Issa took the High Lady to safety?"

"She did? Good." Katira searched the room again, needing a minute to find her center. Next to her, Papan and Bremin were locked in an intense exchange. New protections needed to be put in place immediately. Cassim tried to squeeze his way in, but Papan waved him off. Healing was something that would have to happen later. If at all.

Isben shook her, trying to get her attention. "Who did this?"

"Master Ternan. He's the traitor. Issa said she'd secure him. Where is he?"

"Not up here. He left in a hurry while you were stuck inside."

Papan grabbed his cane and started giving orders. "Master Aro, you and Isben stay here. Do everything in your power to keep Master Ternan from reaching the chair. Katira, you come with me to mobilize the Guardians. Bremin, get your hands on a few Seekers. Find Master Ternan before he has the chance to do any more harm."

"What about me?" Cassim asked. "What do I do?"

"Go tell Master Firen what's happening. All of it. We might be on the brink of an attack on Amul Dun. He needs to be prepared."

Katira hurried after Papan as he hobbled down the spiral stair. Bremin held his silence as he followed behind. It wouldn't last. She'd caught the quick glance the two men exchanged. To Bremin's credit, he made it halfway down the long dark abandoned corridor before quickening his pace to walk alongside Papan.

"What aren't you telling me? What really happened in there?" Even in the emptiness of the hall, he spoke in a controlled whisper.

Papan didn't slow. "Someone wants me dead. Or worse." He paused as they turned the corner, checking if anyone was there. "Wrothe was waiting for me."

Bremin's step faltered. He studied Papan, taking a good

look at him. "You don't look well. You should have let Cassim take a look at you."

Papan stopped and leaned on his cane. The color had drained from his face. "I don't have time for that. Not with this kind of threat. Rally the Seekers, root out Master Ternan and get him into custody. There's no way of knowing how badly the barrier into Amul Dun has been compromised. Her creatures might descend any minute."

A surge of dread pierced Katira through. They weren't moving fast enough. She bound her stone to her palm. If any of those horrid creatures came for her, she'd be ready. She had to be. Papan wasn't in any state to protect them both.

They found Captain Edmont in the training yard, working on forms with a handful of Guardians. The second he spotted them approach he broke from the group, nodding for a tall man with dark cropped hair and wide shoulders to lead the class.

For a moment a smile crossed his face, then he got a better look. "What in the blessed Stonemother's name happened to you?"

Papan wore a hard mask of authority that Katira had only seen when things were dire. It scared her.

"Mobilize the Guardians immediately. Amul Dun's been compromised. Expect an attack."

Katira expected the Captain to be startled or at least surprised at the turn of events. If he was, he didn't show it. He immediately turned and issued orders without question. The men who were training quickly moved into action.

Papan's knuckles on his cane went white. He swayed again, blinking and shaking his head.

Katira stepped in closer, worried he might fall into a dead faint here in the middle of the yard. He didn't need or want that kind of attention. Not right now. She gripped his hand and squeezed it to get his attention. "You need to sit down before you fall down."

He shook his head. "Not yet. We need to return to the High Lady and see if Bremin's managed to snag Master Ternan." He wiped at his forehead with a sleeve. "I can rest there."

Before Katira could object, he was already on the move.

By the time they reached the vaulted main hall, sweat dripped down Papan's rugged face. At least he no longer forced himself to move faster than he had strength for. Some of his color returned.

A shout of dismay sounded from deep inside the hall that housed the High Lady's private office and quarters. Papan reached for where used to wear his sword, his hands closing on the knife on his belt instead. Two Guardians hurried past.

Katira gathered up her skirt to run where they had gone.

Papan seized her by the arm. "If Guardians can't handle it, you have no reason to be there."

She struggled against him. "Someone may be hurt. By the time someone comes up from the infirmary it may be too late."

"Don't be so dramatic."

She knew he was trying to sound calm, but his own emotions betrayed him. By the time they rounded the corner and saw the doors to Lady Alystra's office chambers flung open, he was moving in a lopsided dead run. A wide-eyed messenger ran past them, barely dodging Papan as he rushed down the hall.

Inside the doors of the office, three shadow dogs smoked on the ground. The acrid smell of Stonebearer lightning filled the air. One of Lady Alystra's guardswoman moved methodically along the walls checking for signs of a breach.

Issa's familiar blond hair caught Katira's attention. She knelt on one knee near the door leading to Lady Alystra's private chambers, face red and pinched.

Katira didn't dare look at the crumpled woman lying in the doorway or the blood that stained her dress, didn't dare see Bremin clutching her to his chest, or hear the muffled talk of those rushing around her, for fear of making it real. Lady Alystra couldn't be dead, not now, not when they had come so far and learned so much.

They were too late.

Or were they? Lady Alystra's slippered foot flexed.

Katira broke free of her father and ran to her side.

Bremin spoke too quietly, his face was too pale. He was in shock. "It's okay, Katira. Firen should be here any second." He rested his head against the top of Alystra's and gently rocked her. "She's a tough bird, she'll make it through." Bright lines chased down Bremin's arms. His hands glowed against the High Lady's skin.

"What about you?" Katira watched on as the threads of his power eased into her. "This puts you in danger."

"It's okay. She needs my help for a few minutes, that's all." His voice held the detached emotionless quality of one submitting to the power.

Katira studied the leader of the Stonebearers, noting the lines of her face, the strength of her jaw. This woman held the power for centuries, witnessed the changing of an era, and survived the great wars. It wasn't fair for her journey to end here.

Bremin had been there for her through it all. He escorted her through her most dangerous missions, sought out important information, and made it so Stonebearers could thrive in secret. To lose the High Lady now was to risk losing everything they had worked for.

Katira could not let that happen, not when she could help. Master Firen and Cassim had already taught her so much. She opened herself to her fledgling power, ignoring the burn, ignoring the pain. Bremin watched on and did not stop her.

She slipped her fingers over the High Lady's hand where it rested on her stomach. Cassim taught her how to delve, and unlike some of his other teachings it came to her so naturally he hardly had anything to teach. The High Lady's body became an extension of Katira's own. Every bruise, every cut, every bite, Katira could feel as if it had happened to her.

None of it explained why the woman lay dying. There had to be something else, something not caused by a shadow dog. Katira redoubled her efforts, carefully checking each vital point until she found the horrible truth. Someone had stabbed the High Lady under the ribcage with a long thin blade.

This was no random Shadow attack.

This was an assassination.

Whoever stabbed her was aiming for the heart. Had it pierced even an inch deeper she would have already passed. Even so, the space around her heart was filling with blood, making it harder and harder for the heart to beat.

The High Lady could not wait for Master Firen. Soon the pressure would stop her heart entirely and it would be that much more difficult to get it started again. Katira's panic of uncertainty faded, replaced with a driving need. To do nothing meant death and she wasn't going to let the High Lady die.

The deep intelligence within the power stirred in response. It would save the High Lady, and Katira would serve as a conduit. She submitted to the unnatural calm and let it guide her. This was necessary. This was good. Glyphs formed and worked in unison to make damaged vessels whole. It relieved the pressure on her heart, sealing up the space around it, and pushing the blood back where it belonged.

All the while, Bremin's steady presence and the warmth of his power trickled in, supplementing Katira's efforts and strengthening the High Lady. Connected this way, Katira could feel the raw edge of his fear soften with each vessel she sealed up.

Long minutes passed. The High Lady's heartbeat grew stronger with each glyph, with each healing touch. The dusky blue around her lips began to fade. It was done, the woman would live.

The unnatural stiffness in Bremin's back softened and a tear of relief glimmered beneath his closed eyes. His hand went to the side of Alystra's face and he smiled as he kissed the top of her head.

A hand pressed on Katira's shoulder.

Master Firen's eyes darted around trying to figure out any explanation that fit what he saw. His eyes caught on the blood staining the High Lady's dress. "What's the meaning of this? What happened?" He pulled her hand away and replaced it with his own. "Never mind, I best check for myself."

Katira's power thrummed beneath her skin, holding her in that odd calm. Before, when it had taken control, it fought her to let go. This time, it felt as if there was an understanding between them. It retreated back into the vessel like a fine silk sliding over skin.

Cassim stood close behind, his brow furrowed so tightly that his eyebrows disappeared. He wrung his hands in the fabric of his white apron. It had all happened so quickly that Katira doubted he had the chance to explain anything to the Master Healer.

The room fell into an unnatural quiet as they waited.

Katira worried she might have missed something, or done something wrong. Without the calm of the power, a new avalanche of fears pummeled her.

A long minute passed, then two. Papan lowered himself carefully next to Bremin to wait.

At long last, Master Firen withdrew his hands and his power faded. "Bremin, she's safe. But you already knew that. You can let go now. Jarand will stay with you."

Bremin pulled her close once more and gave her a gentle kiss before allowing the other Healers who had come with Master Firen to carefully lift the High Lady out of his arms. As soon as his power faded, he stiffened, and his eyes rolled back. Papan caught him and carefully lowered him to his lap so he wouldn't strike his head on the marble when the convulsions took him.

"Watch over him." Master Firen instructed. "He'll have lots of questions when he wakes up." He then turned his attention to the small crowd that had gathered. "Is there a Traveler who can assist me back to the infirmary? This is precious cargo."

A narrow-faced man waiting nearby nodded and stepped closer, as well as the High Lady's personal guards with the dark short cropped hair.

Before Master Firen readied himself to leave with the High Lady, he turned his attention to Katira. While his tone remained quiet and gentle, his words cut like knives. "What you did was stepping far beyond your boundaries as a new apprentice. You could have killed her. I will discuss this at length with you when things have calmed down."

～

From her spot on the floor, Katira watched as Firen and the

High Lady disappeared into a bright star that winked out as quickly as it appeared. Cassim drew himself closer to Issa who hadn't moved. Her hands were shaking.

When she finally found her voice, there was anger there. "How could this have happened?"

"We tried." Papan finally said softly. "Neither of us expected her to strike this quickly."

Papan undid the button at Bremin's throat, allowing him to breathe easier as the tremors took him. Katira had only seen the man like this once before, after the battle with Wrothe at Khanrosh. He hadn't woken up for two days after his efforts there and never did regain the memory. He wouldn't remember this either. Perhaps it was for the best.

Issa leaned into Cassim, and he wrapped his arms around her.

"It all happened so fast. Three of those awful hounds spilled straight into the room. Distracted me. It only took seconds. She was down before I could even turn around." She choked on the words.

Cassim held her closer. "No one is blaming you. Especially not us."

"I'm the head of her personal guard. This is my responsibility. I failed and she nearly died. No one has to blame me." She held her hands out in exasperation. "I blame me."

Jarand shifted, adjusting the angle of Bremin's upper body to be more comfortable. His tremors had already calmed. "How long do you think he'll be out?"

Cassim wasn't close enough to touch Bremin's hand, so he caught hold of the man's ankle instead to perform a quick delving. "Not long. It doesn't take much power to keep a heart going, especially when it comes from a companion. He didn't spend hardly any."

As if on cue, Bremin twitched and his hands flexed. One of them would have to tell him.

Cassim wrung the corner of his apron in his hands. One of the more unpleasant duties of a healer was to share bad news. Bremin jerked awake and flailed to sit up. One hand gripped the fabric of Papan's shirt; the other reached for his stone. His eyes darted around the room, seeing where he was, who was with him, and finally the blood on the floor.

"What happened?" He searched the room again, frantic. "Where is she?"

Cassim held out his hands in a calming gesture. "It's all right, Bremin. She's going to be fine."

"What do you mean?" He clenched the stone in his hand tighter. Some of his initial panic faded, only to be replaced with horror. "Tell me everything."

Papan shared what happened, carefully outlining facts and allowing Bremin to make connections of his own. As the story unfolded, his normally schooled face changed from outrage, to worry, to gratitude.

"Last I remember, Master Ternan hadn't been found yet. He's still a risk." Bremin leveraged himself to his feet, leaning on the nearby door frame to steady himself. "Issa, you better hurry back up there. Master Aro and Isben are both brave and resourceful, but we don't know what Master Ternan's capable of. Take Cassim with you, just in case."

Issa gave a nod and helped Cassim to his feet.

"What about us?" Papan used the corner of Lady Alystra's sturdy desk to help himself up.

"Best you go up there as well. For the safety of Amul Dun, those weaknesses you found need to be sealed as soon as possible." He furrowed his brow. "Are you well enough to go back in?"

The way Papan leaned on his cane made him look like he'd aged fifty years in the course of the last hour. "Well enough. Issa will be up there. Between the two of us, we'll figure something out."

He turned to Bremin, his voice dropped low and quiet. "Go to her, Bremin. She needs you. We'll handle this and report back as soon as we're able."

The room was empty and quiet after Bremin left. Papan sank into one of the chairs facing the High Lady's desk and rubbed his face. The mask he'd stubbornly kept on in front of Issa and the others crumbled. For the first time since leaving the relic, he let his defenses fall away. All that fear, all the anger he'd been holding back, coursed out of him and balled up into his clenched fists.

Before Katira could do anything to comfort him, he forced back a semblance of composure.

"We best hurry. Bremin is rarely wrong."

The mask returned, cracked at the edges, but there none the less. Katira hated it. Hated that he had to pretend, that he had to put duty over his own needs. Wrothe had done something to him; she could sense it in the uneasy darkness lurking behind his every thought. This was something far more than his own grief or fear playing havoc with his mind. Sooner or later, he'd have to face it or risk it consuming him.

When they drew closer to the top of the stairs, Katira strained her ears to hear anything unusual. It wouldn't help anyone if she burst straight into the jaws of one of those horrible hounds. The room above was too quiet for her liking. A dread chill crept up her spine.

When she finally rounded the last corner, Katira couldn't make sense of what she saw. Master Ternan sat straight backed in the Occulus Seat, eyes blank, lines pulsing in rhythm with the relic itself. Cassim crouched low behind the brazier in the center of the room, close to Master Aro, who was curled up on the floor. Steps away, next to the study table, Isben looked like a rag doll abandoned by his owner. Issa knelt next to him, her hands glowing near his head. Katira's insides seized.

She rushed to his side. Blood pooled over the floor and soaked into his hair. Mamar's voice from ages ago echoed in her head, instructions on what to do. *Check the heart, check for breathing, if you suspect damage to the neck check for breaks, stop the bleed.* The list tumbled through her head. She set shaking fingers against the groove to the side of his throat. A fluttering fast pulse raced under her fingers.

Through all this, Issa hadn't moved.

"What are you doing?" Katira asked.

"It's okay. I'm keeping him calm until Cassim finishes with Aro. We think he hit his head pretty hard when he fell, so it's best if he doesn't move around too much."

Katira wrapped her stone around her hand. "Perhaps I can help?"

"I don't think so, young lady." Cassim didn't look up from his work. "You got lucky with the High Lady, because wounds from blades are fairly straightforward. A head injury is far more complicated. Don't touch."

"But what if…?"

"Unless he stops breathing, which he won't, he can wait." Papan crested the top of the stairs, red-faced and out of breath. "What in the Stonemother's name happened here?"

Issa shifted, being careful not to jostle Isben's head. "We found the three of them like this. Judging from the state of the blood and how the edges have dried, they were hit close to same time as Lady Alystra."

He stepped closer to where Isben lay splayed on the floor and rested a hand on Katira's shoulder. "Will they be okay?"

"In time. I'm glad we got here when we did. Master Aro stopped breathing while Cassim was delving him."

During their exchange, Katira had been watching Issa, trying to figure out exactly what she was doing. Could it be as simple as joining? It made sense. When joined, two people could sense each other. Isben had done it for her a few times to help calm her.

"Is that something I could do?" Katira pointed to Issa's hands. "Then you and Papan can talk easier?"

"Only if you can be calm. If you're upset, you won't help him."

Katira took a breath and let it out. The events of the day had been upsetting, but in that moment, she could be calm if that's what Isben needed. "I can do that."

Issa shifted to one side and showed how she was supporting his head. "Hold the power, then hold him. Do nothing else besides stay calm. Do not try to heal him. Promise."

Katira nodded her agreement before taking Issa's place and cradling Isben's head in her hands. Her power came smoothly, and she welcomed the rush of heat. The connection to Isben opened.

She was met with a ragged mess of fear and pain. He was on the edge of waking. As soon as he sensed she was there, the fear shrank back. She sent him thoughts of comfort, of long nights talking in secluded corners, and of walks in the summer air. It was enough. The fear disappeared, and the pain became manageable.

Papan approached Master Ternan, who was sitting stiffly

in the chair. "What about him? Was he like this when you got here?"

"I signaled him to wake." Issa answered. "Of the three, he better have answers for us."

Katira had been too preoccupied with Isben. She hadn't given time to piece together what might have happened. As she studied the room, the story told itself. Isben and Master Aro had both been struck with a glyph that knocked them out cold. Master Ternan showed no signs of injury or being in a struggle.

"Why would he do this? What did they do to him?" The question flew out before she could think.

Papan lowered his head. "He shouldn't have. It's against the code for one Stonebearer to strike another. It's not in his nature either. Whatever is compelling him to act must have a really strong hold on him. I can't see any other explanation. It has to be Wrothe."

Ever since Katira first saw Master Ternan, she'd felt uneasy about him. This had to be why. If he was involved with Wrothe, then he had part in the shadow hound attacks against her. No wonder he couldn't stop looking at her back when this all started. It must have come as a huge surprise when she survived.

"The High Lady's attacker passed through shadow like smoke. I didn't see much, but it wasn't him." Issa's voice remained deadly calm. "Wrothe is changing, adapting. Keeping us off balance. If he is linked to her, he must be contained. With the right incentives, we might be able to get him to talk. Explain himself, explain what kind of threats we are facing."

Cassim let his power fade and his hands fell to his sides.

Master Aro hadn't moved, but from the little Katira could see, the color had returned to his face.

"Will he be all right?" Papan asked.

"Should be. I'd like to have Master Firen check him over, just to be sure." Cassim sought out Katira's gaze. "How's he doing? "

Under Katira's fingers, Isben tensed the muscles of his neck. "He's close to waking. The sooner you can care for him, the better."

"I'll see to him right away then." He scooted over to Isben, not bothering to stand up. "Issa, if you could sit with Master Aro, he should be coming around pretty soon."

As if on cue, the man stirred with a moan and opened his eyes. "What happened?"

"Move slowly. I imagine you still have a horrible headache." Issa told him as she came closer and helped him sit up. "We were hoping you could tell us what you remembered."

Aro nodded and closed his eyes. "It was Ternan. Came up the stairs after you all left, like the General warned us about. Struck faster than I expected, with no warning. He threw a glyph, something big, tangled the whole room in it. I don't remember anything else." He grimaced and reached for his head. "Ow."

"Do you remembering him hitting you?" Issa asked.

"Thankfully no. I think the glyph knocked us both out."

He glanced around, squinting against the light. "The kid, he okay?"

"We'll know in a few minutes." Issa helped Master Aro to his feet and guided him to a nearby chair before draping a blanket around his shoulders.

Cassim continued to work quietly. Glowing glyphs streamed from his hands and sweat gathered around his neck with the effort. Katira couldn't tell if things were going well or not. She'd never really watched Cassim work on anything other than simple cuts. This was far more complicated.

It was only after Master Aro was situated that he noticed Master Ternan sitting stiffly in the Occulus Seat. "He's not supposed to be using that. What is he doing?" The anger in his voice was unmistakable.

"We were hoping you would know." Issa said. "I've signaled him to come out. Shouldn't be long now."

Master Aro's face reddened in indignation, his hands tightened on the edge of the blanket. "I told him not to go in after what happened with the General. It's not safe for him."

"I think he knows," Issa muttered.

Katira tried to keep her focus on staying calm for Isben, but watching Master Aro grow angry like that unsettled her. The man rarely showed anything more than his usual disconnection to the real world and sometimes annoyance.

Cassim tapped her shoulder. "Your duty is helping Isben. Keep your focus on him."

Papan signaled them with a hand. "Ternan's coming out."

"Good." Issa crossed her arms over her chest. "He's got a lot of explaining to do."

Master Ternan's head slumped forward and he flexed his fingers on the armrest. When he finally opened his eyes, he startled to see both Issa and Papan staring him down. For a tense second the three of them studied each other.

Master Ternan broke the silence first. "Oh, good. You came back faster than I thought. I assume Issa is here to help seal up those troublesome weak spots."

She shook her head, her well-contained rage teetered on the brink of breaking through. "Something happened up here and you're the only one not on the floor. Explain yourself."

It was only then that Master Ternan glanced around the small room. "Oh dear. Oh dear." To his credit, he seemed genuinely surprised. "It's coming back to me now. A breach opened behind the chair and a dark shadow jumped out, too fast. Struck them before I could act. I forced it back through the breach. Sealed it up."

The unease Katira always felt around Master Ternan flared up into something much stronger—hatred. The man was lying. He'd done this and was making up a story to get out of it. She wanted to grab him by the shoulders and shake him until the truth fell out.

Isben twitched in her hands. She'd lost her calm and it scared him. Worry flowed from him in waves and with it came fear. Katira didn't want this for him. He deserved better. She took a slow breath and let her calm return.

"I know it's hard." Cassim said so only she could hear. "Stay calm for him a few minutes more. He should wake up soon and then you can close your connection." The glowing lines faded from his hands and arms as he finished.

Master Ternan's gaze darted from Master Aro to where Cassim continued to work on Isben. "I worried another breach might happen. I jumped into the chair to see if I could stop it." He slouched forward, leaning his elbows on his knees. "We must make the dreamspace secure immediately or else we've made it easier for those monsters to come through into the real world."

Issa's hands curled into fists behind her back. "Do you swear on your life and stone that this is the truth?"

"I swear it." He nodded solemnly.

"Bind him." Issa ordered. Papan cast the glyph he'd been holding, and it wrapped around the man.

Master Ternan sputtered with surprise. "What's the

meaning of this. One of those monsters slipped through. Why would I lie?" To his credit, he seemed genuinely confused. It had to be an act.

"Save it for the interrogation." Issa answered. The man didn't deserve answers.

"What about the boy? Will he be okay?" Master Ternan's concern knotted his forehead.

Katira fought the urge to shout at him. All this was his fault, and he knew it. She forced her attention to stay rigidly fixed on Isben. She couldn't lose her calm again.

"We don't know yet." Issa's eyes narrowed. "Tell me one thing, did you find another breach while you were in the dreamspace?"

"One, down in the High Lady's office. I sealed it up and then the chair chimed for me to leave." His lies grew bolder.

Issa's fist tightened. Katira had the impression she wanted to wrap her fingers around the old man's throat. "What made you think to check there?"

Master Ternan shied back. "I had to be sure the High Lady was safe. If they were bold enough to attack us up here, what's to stop them from attacking her directly?"

Katira couldn't contain herself. Every time he spoke, she could sense the deceit streaming off of him like a foul smell. "He's lying. Can't you see it? All these answers, they've come too easily."

Papan stepped closer, leaning in so he could speak in her ear. "Quiet," he whispered. "Issa's gathering information. Getting him to talk. Forcing him to dig his own grave as he starts to contradict himself against what we have learned already."

She pressed her lips shut. Now she felt stupid for the outburst. She could have ruined everything had she continued.

"Don't fret about it." He patted her shoulder. "If anything, what you said might get him to say more than he planned. Make him even more defensive."

Issa kept asking questions, and Katira could see the genius behind what leads she chose to follow and which ones she ignored.

Isben groaned and stirred in Katira's hands. She let her power retreat back into its hiding place as Cassim helped him to sit up slowly.

Katira stayed close. "Hey, you okay?"

He touched the back of his head gingerly and blanched when his fingers came back wet. "I've been better."

Cassim brushed his knees off as he stood. "Let's get these two down to the infirmary. I'd like to keep my eye on them for a while."

"What about him?" Katira asked Papan so no one else could hear. The thin glowing ribbon of the binding he held on Master Ternan wavered.

"Issa, are you finished?" he asked, holding up his end of the ribbon.

She nodded. "I have what I need. Until I can talk to Lady Alystra, he needs to be kept bound and under watch. Are you up to that?"

Katira knew he wasn't. Whatever had happened between him and Wrothe had left him dangerously drained. Issa had to see it. She'd been there when all of that happened. Then again, Issa liked to push limits, both her own and those of others.

"It would be better to assign a fresh Guardian to him. Neither of us is in a good position to hold the binding."

"I was hoping you'd say that." She relaxed the fist she'd been holding and massaged her fingers. "One of my lieutenants can handle it. As for me, the High Lady's security detail needs to be reorganized and her study formally investigated." She looked Papan over and a trace of worry touched her eyes. "As for you, please let Firen look you over."

"I'll be fine. Just need a little time to recover, that's all."

CHAPTER TWENTY-THREE

*K*atira followed Papan back to their quarters and a thousand questions peppered her brain, none of which she felt comfortable talking about in the halls. When they reached their quarters, she couldn't hold them back any longer.

She busied herself with stacking kindling and relighting the fire. "What's going to happen now?"

"Don't bother with the fire, we won't be here long." Papan lowered himself into his favorite chair, leaned his head back, and closed his eyes for a moment.

She set down the flint. Even after learning to light a fire using the power, this came to her easier. "You said you would rest."

"I am resting. Just need a few minutes to reset. A lot happened." He cracked an eye open and spotted her still kneeling in front of the unlit fire. "Same for you. Take a few minutes here in the quiet before we get back to work."

She curled into the chair next to him and pulled her knees to her chest. "What will happen with Master Ternan?"

Papan rubbed at the bridge of his nose. "Stonebearers' oaths are strong, so it's very rare for them to be broken. Master Ternan's seniority and his position as head of his order complicates everything. He's proven his loyalty countless times over the years. It doesn't make sense for him to hurt anyone, especially using that kind of violence."

Katira twiddled the stone hanging around her neck and her fingers brushed against Elan's locket. Thankfully, he was somewhere far away from all this mess. She imagined him standing over the tanning vats with a large paddle in hand, or bent over a workbench stamping a pattern into newly cured leather. Whatever he was doing, she hoped he was happy. Having that tiny reminder that good people were living a normal life while hers was in turmoil made things easier.

"Do you think Isben will be okay?"

"Cassim believes he will. Heads bleed plenty, it looked far worse than it was."

"But he was knocked out cold. Back home, Mamar taught me how anytime that happens there has been a serious injury to the brain. There's always lasting damage. Confusion. Persistent pain. Memory loss. Fatigue." She tried to continue the list, but with each fact her worry for Isben grew out of control.

"Easy, easy. Enough." He stopped her. "I know how difficult a head injury can be, because I've had several. You forget, Stonebearer Healers can use the power to alleviate pressure from any bleeding inside the head. Mamar could do it too." He lifted the hair behind his ear revealing a scar the length of a finger. "Fell off a roof, hit the stone foundation when I landed. Townspeople thought I was dead for sure. It took a while for Mamar to put me back together. I saw double for nearly a week. But I came out all right. Cassim will do the same for Isben."

Katira itched to hurry to the infirmary, needing to see for herself if Isben was okay. "What do we do now?"

Papan ran his hand through his hair. "As soon as Lady Alystra is well enough, we present what we've learned to her. She must be the first to weigh the evidence against Ternan."

"And then what?"

"There will be a meeting of the High Council where the heads of each of the orders will decide the best course of action. After that, a trial. Give Master Ternan a chance to defend himself."

He fished his cane off of the floor. It hadn't been nearly enough time for him to have recovered at all. Katira mind hadn't slowed even a fraction from the events of the past hours.

"You're exhausted. I'm exhausted. When will you take the rest you need?"

"Soon. I promise. But first, I must go speak to the Captain of the Guardians, to find a few more companionships who can help me seal up the breaches in the barrier." He stopped halfway between the chair and the door when he realized she wasn't following him. "The safety of Amul Dun comes first. With Master Ternan in custody, our chances of sealing Wrothe off are better than they've ever been."

"Promise me one thing." She tucked her stone back under her dress and stood to join him.

"And what's that?"

"Don't go back into the dreamspace, not until this business with Master Ternan is settled."

"I promise. I would have to be an idiot to tempt Wrothe like that. She's got some kind of vendetta against me, I swear it." He walked to the door and set a hand on the handle. "As much as I'd prefer you to stay with me, I think there's somewhere else you'd like to be." There was a twinkle in his eye.

"Do you mind?"

"It's okay." His tone softened. "Knowing you, you won't rest until you see that Isben is fine with your own eyes. With Lady Alystra in the infirmary, there will be plenty of Guardians keeping watch there."

Bright winter afternoon sun spilled in through the windows lining the hallways leading to the infirmary. A handful of people moved through the space carrying their trays and messages as if nothing had happened. Katira wanted to shake them. Didn't they know they had nearly lost their precious leader? Didn't they understand that Amul Dun was under a malicious attack?

Then again, Katira was pretending that everything thing was fine as well. She followed Papan's lead, keeping her face passive and emotionless as they wound their way through the corridors.

Perhaps they, like her, were all pretending as a way to cope. She hoped it worked better for them than it did for her. Hiding away her fears had a way of making them grow and press against her insides until she thought she would burst. She craved for someone to wrap their arms around her and hold her close, if only to keep her from breaking apart.

When they reached the infirmary, Papan gave a crisp nod to the Guardians at either side of the door before opening it and ushering Katira inside. "Stay here until I come back for you. I won't be long," he told her through the open door.

Before she could reply, he turned and walked away, allowing the door to close on its own behind him.

With all the hurt she'd seen that day, Katira half expected to find healers rushing around and piles of bloodied clothing kicked out of the way. Instead, the infirmary felt too quiet for all that had happened.

The familiar smells of clean laundry and antiseptic tinctures filled her nose, and the sight of shelves lined with tidy stacks of linens and bandages calmed her fears.

She found Isben resting in one of the beds on the left. A white swath of bandage wrapped around his head made his hair stick up like a pile of straw. He laid back with his eyes shut. Katira didn't recognize the man in the bed next to him for a moment. Gone were the thick glasses and the layers of coats, gone were the constantly busy fingers. Master Aro looked as young as Isben resting like this, although Katira knew he was much older, possibly by hundreds of years.

To the right, closest to Master Firen's private office, another bed was filled. Bremin sat in a chair and leaned against the bed, his hand woven into Lady Alystra's. Katira had never seen him tired before. He looked utterly exhausted. He glanced at her as she crossed the space before closing his eyes again and resting his head against his other hand.

A clatter of noise sounded from the back of the infirmary. Cassim cursed as he scrambled to pick up the pile of items he was carrying.

"By the Stonemother's throne, that's just perfect." Cassim muttered as he crawled on his hands and knees to fetch something that rolled under the last bed in the row.

Katira bent down to grab it from the other side. It was a small rod like the one Master Aro had used to make the barrier visible, and it was broken in two.

Cassim spied her under the bed and quickly stood, straightening his robes. "Hello, Katira. I thought you might come."

Katira handed over the pieces of the now useless glyph rod and motioned to Isben and Master Aro. "How are they?"

"Thankfully, sleeping it off. Head healing is tricky. The patient needs lots of rest. Master Firen says they'll make a full recovery in a few days." He adjusted the stacked tray of items and continued down the aisle between beds toward Master Firen's office.

"And the High Lady?" Asking scared Katira. If her attempt to save the woman caused lasting damage, she wouldn't be able to forgive herself.

"She's doing surprisingly well for taking a blade near the heart. Firen wants her to rest for a few days, preferably here. But we'll see. She's hard to keep down. I wager she'll walk herself out before the end of the day." He opened the door to Master Firen's office and slid the tray onto the Head Healer's immaculate desk.

"Here are the things you asked for."

"Thank you, Cassim." Master Firen began sorting through the items. "You may go."

Katira turned to follow Cassim out. With luck, maybe she'd avoid that lecture he'd warned her about.

"You, on the other hand, need to stay," Master Firen said. "We must discuss this morning."

Or, maybe not.

Katira stumbled over her foot and caught herself on the door frame. A cold chill gripped at her neck. "I can explain."

"Not necessary. You did what you felt was needed and you made a difference. A critical one. That's not why I wanted to talk to you." He picked up the broken glyph rod. "Dropped it, didn't he?"

Katira nodded, but was too anxious about what he might say to smile.

"No matter, I can fix it." He set it aside and his face grew serious. "I need you to understand that what you did was dangerous."

"I know." Katira wrung her hands together. "I could have done more harm than good. I'm sorry."

"It's not that. You let the power take control in a way that could have hurt her, yes, but also you. It's not common, but there is always the risk it will drain more than you have to give." He paused. "Katira, it can kill you."

"Papan…" She quickly corrected herself. "I mean, Master Jarand has been careful to make sure I understand that." She tried to reassure him, he seemed so concerned. "I know the power is dangerous."

"I'm afraid it's more than that. When the power controls you, it won't stop if your reserves are running out. It will keep on pulling until there's nothing left." He swallowed as if remembering something hard. "Promise me you will stay in control, stick to the glyphs you've learned, keep careful track of your reserves. I'd hate to have anything happen to you."

The sentiment took Katira by surprise. While Master Firen had always been kind in his strict sort of way, she never realized how much he cared.

"I'll do my best to not let it happen again. I promise."

He picked up the broken rod segment again and ran it through his fingers. "People are harder to fix than things. Please be careful."

Katira slipped out of the office. Her need to be held and be reassured that everything would be okay grew stronger. She gravitated toward Isben. Even if he couldn't hold her, being near him helped her feel better.

He'd woken since she arrived and stared out the nearby window. He looked up when she approached, and the smile on his face washed over her like sunshine on a cold day.

She shifted a chair closer to the side of his bed. "Hey, you want someone to talk to?"

"Absolutely. Distract me from this awful headache." He reached out a hand to her. "Even in here I can tell something's happened. No one will talk to me."

Katira braced herself, knowing what she had to share would not be welcome news. "Something passed through the barrier, and tried to assassinate Lady Alystra. Almost succeeded. It frightened Bremin and Issa terribly. Papan too."

His hand trembled under her touch as each layer of news settled. "By the Stonemother's throne. That's why she's here?"

Katira nodded and stroked the back of his hand. "I suppose you already know about Master Ternan. They've got him locked up and awaiting judgment for what he did."

"Good. He's crazy." Isben leaned back into the pillows and closed his eyes. It had only been a few hours since they found him bleeding on the floor. The healing was intact, but there hadn't been time for those connections to become strong again. He needed something that Cassim couldn't give him, comfort.

Tipping the vessel of power was so easy when she was with him; she craved his closeness, that connection. As the warmth raced through her and brushed against their joined hands, she immediately sensed how overwhelmed he was, his fear something else was going to come out of a wall and come after him. Nothing was safe.

He blinked as the lines on her arms came to life. "What, what are you doing?"

"Shhh," Katira urged. "Just be for a moment."

He closed his eyes and his shoulders relaxed. "I'm sorry."

"For what?"

"I should have stopped him, kept him from hurting Master Aro. I wasn't ready. Didn't expect it." He was babbling.

Katira set a finger on his lips. Back when she first came to Amul Dun, when everything thing was new and raw and she was hurting from the loss of Mamar, he had joined with her like this and soothed her. She wanted to do the same for him. Right now, he needed to know he was safe and that she cared for him so much that it hurt.

"Do you really feel like that?" he asked.

"I have for a while. With everything going on, I wanted to let you know before anything else happened."

He smiled and leaned his head back. A moment later, the smile vanished. He swallowed convulsively with a grimace.

Katira had seen this before. "Nausea?"

He nodded and pressed a hand against his eyes. "It's awful. Cassim says it will fade in a few hours. He better be right."

A book rested on the bedstand. Katira picked it up in hopes of helping him take his mind off the discomfort. "This one of yours?"

"No. Cassim fetched it for me and said he would read to me later. I've read the other ones in the collection, fascinating stuff."

Katira squinted to make out the dark faded ink on the cover. The title itself was unremarkable, *History of the Khandashii Volume Four*, but the name of the author rang through Katira's mind like an immense bell. Master Ternan.

She opened the book and scanned the table of contents.

While both Papan and Issa were sure he shared some form of connection with Wrothe, they had no idea how long he'd harbored it, or where he might have gained it from. Perhaps he had left some sort of clue in his writings.

Isben watched through the corner of his eye, curious about her sudden interest. "What is it?"

"How much do you know about Master Ternan?" she asked.

"Just what I've uncovered in his books. He's forever old. He was around at the time of King Darius, and he's one of the only ones left from that era." He covered his eyes again with a quiet moan.

Katira had pushed him too hard; the spike in his discomfort came from her trying to talk to him long before he was well enough.

"I should let you rest."

"There's more, isn't there?"

"Of course, there's more. But my talking to you has made your headache that much worse." She thumbed open the book to where a slim strip of paper served as a bookmark. "Perhaps it would be better if I read to you instead. Then you could simply lie back and listen?"

"You've got at least one more question burning inside your head to get out. Ask it first. Then—" A tiny smile crossed his lips. "It would be lovely if you read to me."

"Are you sure?"

"Don't waste your one question on that."

"Okay, right." Katira leafed through the book. If she could ask him one question, she needed to make it count. "What was the earliest point where Wrothe could have corrupted Master Ternan?"

"Ouch. That's a big question." He cracked open one eye,

then the other. "The easiest would have been when she first came into our world from the mirror realm. Caused all sorts of chaos then, that's how she ended up in the disk prison. He documented the whole thing in volume two." He picked at the corner of the blanket and rolled it down off his chest. "But I think it had to have been earlier than that."

"Why?"

"Nope. I said only one question. You better let me sleep. I'm injured." He closed his eyes and let his mouth flop open.

"You can't possibly tell me that and expect me to just leave it." Katira caught sight of another sly smile.

"We had a deal."

Katira resisted the urge to slap him on the shoulder. "You're making jokes. You must be feeling better."

"A little." He stopped pretend-sleeping and gingerly sat up again. "It seems like Wrothe is using him because of something to do with the barrier. My guess is she can't open it all the way without him. The barrier hasn't changed. She would have needed him to help to breach it the first time. I think they've shared a connection for far longer than anyone expected. Possibly since the days of Darius himself."

Katira stood and started to pace. "But why haven't we seen far more of her meddling? If she's been around for ages and connected to him for ages, then there should be a long history of fighting her."

"No more. Really. I wasn't completely joking." His hand went back to his head and his eyes screwed shut again. "We'll talk more later. I'd still like you to read, if that's okay?"

"Sure. I'd love to."

CHAPTER TWENTY-FOUR

*I*t wasn't long before Papan returned to the infirmary. He leaned heavier on his cane, walked slower. The echo of that ever-persistent ache in his back had blossomed into hot knifing pain that shot down his leg. The closer he came, the more clearly Katira could sense it, and she rubbed the same spot on her back in sympathy.

He stopped to whisper a few quiet words to Bremin as he made his way through the long aisle of beds. Cassim, who had been working at the far end of the room, put down the linens he was folding and approached and gestured to his office.

Isben had fallen asleep and snored softly into his pillow. Katira shut the book and followed Papan into Cassim's office.

Inside, Onyx worked at a dried sunflower head over by the window. She squawked as they entered and bobbed her head until Cassim let her climb up on his shoulder.

Bremin pulled the door shut behind him. "Tell me everything."

Papan settled into the only empty chair not filled with

books and papers, and rested his cane between his knees. "Master Ternan was still in the Occulus Seat when we got up there. From the looks of it, he was in there at the time of Lady Alystra's attack. He also struck down both Master Aro and Isben to get there. Aro's willing to testify if needed."

Bremin did nothing to make himself comfortable, instead choosing to lean against the doorframe of the closed office door. "Is he being guarded now?"

"Issa is seeing to it personally." Papan dropped the tone he used for his report. "I take it Alystra hasn't been told the extent of what has happened, or anything about Master Ternan yet."

Bremin shook his head. "Didn't have a chance. I'd rather wait until I know she's strong enough. Knowing her, she'll return to her duties the second she learns of it."

"Does she have to know? Can we do any of this without her leave and let her rest?" For what the High Lady had endured, Katira couldn't stand the thought of doing anything that would jeopardize the healing process.

"No. I wish we could." Bremin's shoulders sank. "I'm oath-bound to report any act of treason immediately. Once she's been informed of the situation, it's up to her whether she'll sanction testing to see if Master Ternan is indeed linked to Wrothe." He opened the door. "Cassim, if she agrees, can you administer the test?"

Cassim jerked up his head and dropped the seed he'd been offering Onyx. "Yes, but why me? Why not Master Firen?"

"Because I trust you to be discreet. We've discussed this." Bremin rubbed at the back of his neck. "You three stay here. The sooner we can put this to rest, the better."

∾

It wasn't long before Bremin returned, face grim. "Alystra sanctions the testing."

A wave of relief washed around the room, but no one felt it more than Katira. She'd suffered more than anyone, save perhaps Papan, because of Master Ternan's betrayal. If the test confirmed that he was guilty, all her worry would be justified. It was one step closer to putting a stop to the madness.

Cassim tapped on the windowsill and Onyx hopped back onto her perch there. "Best get it over with then."

"Wait, there's more," Bremin added. "She insists we do everything in our power to preserve his image. We deal with this quietly. If he's compromised, he'll remain under watch until the council can decide how to proceed. If we've learned anything from what happened to Master Regulus, it's that everyone is a victim here."

Papan glanced out the door. "How is she?" he asked quietly.

"Weaker than I've ever seen her before. Tired. She's recovering, but slowly." Bremin's head lowered, his gaze falling to his boots. "Having one of the Five accused of treason isn't helping. She trusted him. For her sake, things need to stay quiet for a while."

"Assure her that everything possible has been put in place to make sure of it." Papan's no-nonsense tone of voice returned. This was his duty at Amul Dun, and he would do it well. "I've made arrangements to begin repair of the barrier. Guardians have been strategically posted around the tower where the most likely targets might be."

"Good man. Let's hope it's enough."

He didn't need to say more. They all feared the same thing. Even with all the precautions they'd taken, there was still the risk of Wrothe surprising them. And a surprise from her was bound to be terrible.

Katira trailed behind the small group as it left the infirmary, crossed the main hall, and climbed one of the wide flights of stairs leading to the west wing of the keep. She wanted them to move faster, wanted to sprint to the Head Historian's office and make sure he was indeed still there.

All along the way they passed Guardians at their posts, backs erect and fingers tight around their staffs and swords. More torches had been lit, keeping the growing shadows of the afternoon at bay.

Instead of standing at attention, Issa leaned against the wall outside Master Ternan's office examining the edge of one of her many knives.

"For a moment, I'd thought you'd forgotten about me. What's going on?"

Cassim motioned to the door. "I'm to test him, see if I can find a connection between him and Wrothe, or anything else in the mirror realm."

Issa glanced to Bremin who's lips were pressed into a tight line. "Has this been approved?"

"By the High Lady herself," he answered. "Anything happen since you took him into custody?"

She tucked the knife back into its leather sheath on her thigh. A thin glowing line of power extended from her wrist down under the door.

"No. He's been quiet. I thought he'd fight me more about staying bound for a while, but he's been too docile about it. It's making me anxious."

"I thought you were going to find someone else to guard him." Papan said.

"I will. I wanted to take the first shift, make sure I knew

what I was asking before I assigned someone else." Her brow furrowed and she stood up straight. Her full attention turned to the thin line of power that connected her to the glyph preventing Master Ternan from using his power. "Wait. Something's happening."

Papan reached for the handle. The lines running down his arm flashing to life. "Is it Wrothe?"

"Can't tell, but it's trouble."

A strangled cry echoed out from behind the door.

Issa didn't waste a second. With Papan at her side, they burst into the room together.

Master Ternan lay in a heap in the center of the room. His hands clawed the smooth wood of the floor, his heels drummed and kicked at the air. A dark glow shone from the lines on his arms, the same as they'd seen once on Master Regulus. Issa stopped short inside the door, one hand gripping the hilt of her sword, the other bracing against the wall. There was no one to fight.

"I thought you had him bound. How is he doing this?" Bremin pushed past her for a closer look.

"It isn't him." Issa answered. "My binding is in place. Whatever this is feels like a rancid oil being forced through him. If I were to guess, I'd say he's being used."

Papan took one look and shook his head. "I didn't want to believe it. Master Regulus's power was corrupted the same way. It's Wrothe. She's trying to use him."

A thin dark tendril formed in Master Ternan's extended hand and darted toward Bremin's foot. He jumped back and out of reach. "Whatever you do, don't let that touch you. Judging from what I've seen so far, it can't be good."

Cassim stayed a safe distance as he studied the man. "If this isn't his power, then it has to be coming from somewhere.

Can anyone spot another thread anywhere?" He squinted and leaned forward as he searched for something that would explain what they were seeing.

Katira stepped closer, trying to see if she might be able to spot anything unusual. Papan held her back with an arm. "Don't. If it is Wrothe, she will stop at nothing to hurt you."

Cassim rubbed the back of his neck and straightened. "Issa, you're still connected to him. You might be able to pinpoint where her flow is coming from."

"That's the thing, it's coming from behind him straight into the core of his power. There's only floor there, how is that possible?"

Bremin dodged clear of the sweeping tendril once more and moved further back. "It's the dreamspace. I can think of no other explanation. If she'd already linked herself to him, then it would be that much easier for her to make this connection."

"Then to break it, we need to create a warding around him that prevents her from getting to him." Papan set a hand on the wall, and a bright pattern of glyphs appeared, just as they had done when he and Issa were investigating the hallway. "The tower's protections are still in place. She's smart enough not to touch those. Issa, is there a way you can cut her off? Keep her from reaching him?"

Issa nodded. "Move back." Her markings flared brighter, and multiple glyphs gathered and formed into a pattern.

Even with Papan trying to make himself a shield in front of Katira, she wasn't going to leave anything to chance. She let the power fill her, and this time it spilled eagerly.

Issa released the series of glyphs she'd formed, and a shield like nothing Katira had seen before snapped into place around the struggling Stonebearer. Master Ternan's kicks slowed and his body calmed. He moaned and curled up onto his side and coughed.

Cassim edged in closer. "Is it safe now?"

"Safe enough. But, be quick." Issa shifted to the side to let him in.

Cassim set to work. He placed a hand on the Master Seeker's neck and worked his glyphs in a gentle flow. Master Ternan didn't move to stop him. Instead, he stared at the floor, eyes glassy, breaths coming in short bursts. He looked as if he were in shock.

"Master Ternan?" Cassim touched his shoulder. "Can you hear me?"

He groaned and hugged his arms tighter. "What have you done?"

"I'm keeping her from reaching you." Issa gripped her stone harder, her features serious. The shield bent in on one side as if an invisible force was trying to pierce through. "I don't think she's very happy about it."

"She's never very happy." Master Ternan pushed himself off of the floor. "You can't do this. When she breaks through, her rage will be stronger than ever. She'll use me as her tool to kill you all." A hint of panic crept into his voice.

"Calm yourself." Bremin said. "We're trying to help you." He studied the room before turning to Papan and Issa. "People come to this office day in and day out. He needs to be somewhere more secure, more private."

"The cells down in the dungeon seem a bit much, but they would get the job done." Papan said.

Issa shook her head in disagreement. "No, still too visible. Is there anywhere else?"

With Wrothe's influence subdued, Katira let her power slide away and took a moment to consider the room they were in. A blocky desk stacked high with books and scrolls took up most of the space by the window. Bookshelves crammed full of everything from papers to boxes fought for space. "Are his personal quarters far?"

Bremin's face brightened. "That should work. No one would think twice about him being shut in there for a day or so."

Cassim removed his hands from Master Ternan and wiped his forehead. "She's done quite a number on him. I'd prefer he be somewhere with a bed."

"It's decided then. He stays in his quarters." Issa slipped a hand under Master Ternan's arm and helped him to his feet. The shield shifted with him, hugging close to him like a second set of clothes.

Papan helped Issa guide Master Ternan down the larger hall, then onto a smaller branching hall that led to his equally cluttered quarters. Once inside, Master Ternan fell on to the bed in a heap. The sharp lines of his face relaxed. He looked strangely at peace.

"While he's isolated from her, I was hoping he could answer a question or two." Bremin lifted a stack of books from a chair near the bed and set them on the floor. "Cassim, do you think he's in any state to talk?"

The large Healer shrugged. "No reason he shouldn't be able to. I'd only ask you to limit it to the few most important questions so he can rest."

Bremin sat on the edge of the chair and leaned so his eyes were level with Master Ternan's face. He set a hand on his shoulder and shook him gently. "Tell us what was happening when we found you."

The old man opened one eye halfway. His mouth moved

and he struggled to speak, struggled to make any sound at all. His eyes grew desperate.

Bremin's voice stayed calm and quiet. The control it required was admirable. "Does she have some sort of binding on you so you can't reveal her?"

The old master snapped alert, his once glassy eyes now clear and focused. He stared at Bremin without blinking.

"It's true then. She does have a hold on you." Bremin continued speaking softly. "She has been using you for a while, hasn't she?"

The man maintained his steady stare, telling Bremin with his eyes that the answer was yes. A tear formed in the corner of his eye.

"This morning, did you help her open the barrier into Alystra's office?"

Master Ternan's hands began to shake. He pulled at his hair.

"You never wanted her hurt. I can see that." Bremin's voice grew hoarse with emotion. "What about Isben and Master Aro?"

Master Ternan pressed his eyes shut, his face creased tight with anguish.

"Enough, Bremin." Cassim said. "He's already suffering."

Bremin held up a hand. "One last question. If we keep her away from you, can she open the barrier here in the keep?"

Master Ternan's face changed to one of determination. He shook his head.

Papan sagged against the wall with relief when he heard the answer. Katira felt the same way. "We can't shield him indefinitely. One misstep, one too strong burst of power from Wrothe, and she will seize control of him again. The council must be assembled, and a trial held as soon as possible."

"Agreed." Bremin tugged his shirt straight as he headed for the door. He took one more look at Master Ternan. Katira couldn't decide if it was with pity or disappointment. "Stay here, keep him safe."

Issa held out her hand where her connection to her shield was fastened. "I'll help Bremin rally the council. Speed things up if I can." The ribbons of power streaming from her stone wove themselves into a clean orderly line.

Papan collected them up and grimaced as he joined them with his own power. "Don't be too long."

Without another word, Bremin, Issa, and Cassim hurried out of the room leaving them alone.

Katira watched on as the shield pulsed with her father's now familiar power. It hummed against her temples, sweet, strong, and reassuring.

"Did you mean it?" she asked. "Do you think you can protect him until the council can reach a decision?"

"I wouldn't lie to Bremin." He slid into the chair Bremin had emptied with a relieved sigh. "He knows me too well."

Katira sought out another chair and finding none, lowered herself to sit on the floor next to him.

Soft snores came from the bed. Master Ternan had already fallen asleep.

"You didn't tell me everything about what Wrothe did to you this morning. You're more tired than I've seen you in weeks."

His head bent forward, and he leaned his weight onto his elbows. "It's not fair. You shouldn't have to worry about me like you do."

"You're all I have." She pulled his hand between hers and took comfort in the strength she found there. "Of course I'm going to worry about you."

The shield warped under another invisible attack. Papan narrowed his eyes and the webbing drew tighter, strangling Wrothe's attempt to slip through.

Deep inside the bond, Katira could sense a tremor of fatigue scratching through him.

"Would it be okay if I joined with you?" She traced the glowing lines on his wrist and waited for him to respond. "After all that's happened, I need to know you're all right."

He regarded her for a long moment before agreeing with a small nod. She leaned her head against his forearm. The power came quietly this time, the flash of burn hardly noticeable. With the events of the day throwing both of them off balance, she expected to find his mind unsettled and racing. Instead, it was weary. There, present behind every heartbeat, was the constant ache of missing Mamar. Carefully banked under each measured breath was the fiery rage over what had happened to Lady Alystra. His worry for her flowed steady as the blood in his veins. If Katira was to judge, it was what troubled him the most. Threaded through it all were the dark root like threads of dread she had seen earlier. They had grown thicker and stronger since the last time they joined.

She allowed her thoughts and own worries to flow to him, letting him know that despite all that had happened, she was still okay and could hang on a bit longer. He soothed her fears of what might have happened with Lady Alystra if she failed.

With their connection open, she urged him to draw from her reserve of power. If he was going to maintain this shield, he needed it far more than she did. Wrothe had left him so hollow that for a brief second, she worried he would draw too quickly, like a man dying of thirst when he finds water. But this was her father, and even in desperate moments he still carried that rock-hard unfaltering control. He drew carefully and slowly while keeping a careful watch.

The first hour passed slowly. Katira tried to meditate the way he had showed her, anything to relieve the constant worry of what might happen next. Wrothe prodded at the shield often enough that it required constant vigilance.

Another hour. Wrothe's prodding came more often and with greater force.

The evening bell tolled long and deep through the keep.

"It shouldn't take this long." Papan said. The strain of holding the shield around the sleeping master for that long showed. "We should know something by now."

If no one came, Wrothe would eventually break through and claim control of Master Ternan once more. By then, Papan would have given his everything to keep the shield intact. He wouldn't be strong enough to fight.

Katira hated leaving him alone where that demon of a woman could reach him. It dredged up all the memories from Khanrosh when he was fighting for his life with that cursed dagger in his back. Even with all she had learned, she knew she couldn't fight Wrothe, not on her own.

"If I go for help, how long can you withstand her?" Katira asked.

"What?" His grip on her hand tightened. "What are you talking about?"

"I have to get help, another Guardian, Issa, anyone. I have to do something. We can't stay here. We both know what she's capable of if she gets through."

His eyes were bloodshot, and sweat soaked through the collar of his shirt. Understanding what she meant came slowly, too slowly for her comfort. "I'll hold out as long as I can."

Katira raced through the halls, narrowly dodging a dumpy man in dark green robes. His annoyed shouts about proper decorum followed her until she turned down the wide stairwell. She rounded the last corner and careened into the great expanse of the main hall.

The space held an unusual silence, one that Katira hesitated to break. No small groups of Stonebearers dotted the marbled colonnade locked in discussion. No rapid staccato of footsteps punctuated the air as messengers and servants rushed about. Those gathered in the hall stood in silence, all waiting for the council to adjourn.

Issa stood guard outside the door to the audience chamber. She would know what to do. Katira crossed the wide mosaic tiled floor toward her. The closer she came, the tighter her worry wound up like a spring needing to be released.

A familiar curly haired young man pushed off from one of the plush couches along the wall and approached her. He looked much better than when she'd seen him hours before. The color had returned to his face and she saw no trace of unsteadiness in his walk. He moved cautiously, as if trying not to jostle his head too much.

Her first instinct was to scold Isben for disobeying Master Firen's orders to stay in bed, but when she saw the sheer relief on his face it dissolved away.

He caught her and pulled her into his arms, pressing his face into her hair. Something had scared him. "I can't tell you how relieved I am to see you. Are you okay? What's going on?"

Katira shook her head. Trying to tell him what was going on with her father was too much and it brought tears to her eyes and tightened her throat.

Isben stroked her back. "It's okay. Shhh."

"No." She said when she could finally speak again. "No, it's not. Papan is in danger. I came to get help before it's too late."

Isben loosened his hold so he could face her. "I heard Bremin was assembling the council. Is that what this is about?"

A chill raced down Katira's back. "It's like what happened with Master Regulus all over again. But this time we know what's happening. They are to decide what has to be done."

Isben's hands tightened around hers. The corners of his eyes twisted at the mention of his master. He still carried the guilt of the man's death close to his heart, despite the assurances that there was nothing he could have done. "Do you think they can cut him free?"

"I don't know. Whatever they do, they need to do quickly. Each minute they delay, she gets stronger." She tugged on his hand. "Come with me."

Issa watched as they came closer, making no move to leave her post.

"What's happened, girl?" She asked quietly, her voice and face full of concern. "Where is Jarand?"

"No one came. He won't last much longer holding her back. You have to help him."

Issa's face contorted in anger and frustration. "It took ages to get the council gathered. They've been debating for too long. I feared it might come down to this. Curses." She took a moment to calm herself before continuing. "How much longer can he last?"

"Not long, minutes really." Katira shivered. She would not cry, not now. "I should have come sooner."

Issa looked toward the stairs that lead back to Master Ternan's quarters. "Then we must assume Wrothe can take control of Master Ternan again and the barrier could be breached at any minute. Lady Alystra and all available order heads and their seconds are in that room. It will be a prime target. They must be warned."

She tugged a ring off her finger and handed it to Isben. "Take this to my lieutenant; she's standing guard in the hallway leading to Lady Alystra's office. She's to report to Master Ternan's quarters immediately to assist the General."

Isben took the ring and stood in mute disbelief for a few seconds before hurrying away with a salute.

Distantly, through Katira's bond to Papan, there was another push of power to cut Wrothe off. He was still fighting. At least she had that small comfort.

Issa's power flared to life. She checked her sword in its sheath and before Katira could ready herself, flung open the doors.

"Guardians, secure the chamber!" Issa shouted as she rounded the hall to take her position near the High Lady.

Bremin jumped to his feet. "What's the meaning of this?"

"Jarand can't hold her back. We must prepare for anything."

The room burst into chaos as the members of the council shouted over each other and struggled to leave the table. Some already had their stones bound and ready, their lines glowing up their arms.

Katira gripped her stone, relieved she could still feel him. However, the strain was overwhelming. He was fighting a battle he could not win. Minute by minute, his presence through the stone grew dimmer. Would she know the moment Wrothe took him? Would she feel it happen?

Bremin pounded a fist on the table. "Council! Control yourselves. We won't be taken so easily. If it's a fight they want, it's a fight they'll get." He wrapped his stone into his palm. "Protect the High Lady at all costs."

An aching surge echoed through the apprentice bond unlike anything Katira had ever felt before. Wrothe's power had seized Papan and dug into him, searching out his power to drain away, all while pressing against the wall he'd flung up to protect his mind. The intensity of it buckled Katira's knees. She pressed her hands to her head, blinded at the overwhelm.

Frantic hands shook her shoulders. "What is it?" Cassim asked.

"She has him." Katira grabbed at Cassim and used him to leverage herself to her feet. "By the Stonemother herself, she's breaking him. I have to go."

Cassim held her fast. "No. If you go, she'll get you to. We have to fight smart. Work together."

Katira twisted her arm, trying to free it. "You don't understand. She's already done something to him. There's no time. We have to help him."

Within the noise, someone screamed. A bolt of Stonebearer lightning streaked through the air. A wall of darkness uncoiled from the darkening shadows in the corners of the chamber. The attack had begun.

Another shove of dark power pushed against the shield that Jarand struggled to maintain around Master Ternan. Wrothe was growing desperate. Her attempts to reach the Seeker became less predictable, more dangerous. He was glad Katira had left. A child should never be asked to protect their parent. The farther she stayed away, the safer she'd be. Help would come.

He wrapped himself around that hope as he retreated to the place inside him that allowed him to be aware and alert but not spend precious energy on anything other than the task at hand. His world shrank down to maintaining the shield.

Master Ternan stayed slumped in the bed, curled into himself as expecting her to strike at any moment.

Two probing forces pressed in against the shield at once, then three. Jarand fed more power into the shield, focusing all his efforts on preventing Wrothe from reaching her target.

"I'm sorry, Jarand." The old man sighed. His face was wet with tears. "I'm so, so sorry. I never wanted any of this. Never thought Regulus would die. Never imagined my weakness would take your companion from you."

Ternan's talk of Mirelle drew Jarand's attention like iron filings to a magnet. Jarand pushed the words away. He couldn't break his focus, not now, not when it took all his attention to repel Wrothe.

A force broke through, piercing the shield like a needle. Jarand shot it back and sealed the puncture just as another broke through. The shield grew more fragile. He couldn't maintain it. He made a desperate choice. He let the shield fall.

Dozens of Wrothe's tendrils flowed in from the dream-space, each searching and grasping for their prize. Jarand formed one wide sweeping cut after another. Even with his best effort, several already wrapped around Ternan and his lines began to glow darkly. The man groaned as if in pain.

"Fight it, Ternan! Don't let her use you!" he shouted. Anything to keep the man from doing something stupid.

"Get away from here!" Ternan cried out as his eyes started to roll back. "I can't hold her."

Before Jarand could back away, a series of dark glyphs sprang to life at Master Ternan's fingertips. They formed and leapt at Jarand, wrapping tightly around his chest and seizing him by the legs. He shot at both, hoping to cut himself free. Instead, they squeezed harder before flinging him backward against the wall. His head struck with a crack.

The glyphs kept forming, more binding flows wound around his limbs, around his chest, over his face, far more than he could push away. He couldn't see, could barely breathe. They pulled him to the floor and blocked his sight. He held his stone in his fist, reminding himself he would continue to fight against her. Even still, a dread sense of panic wrapped around him as the first one passed ghost-like through his chest.

Wrothe's presence filled him like a foul oil sliding against his insides. It made him sick. Her voice came in breathless distant whispers, growing ever closer. The tendril wrapping around Jarand's throat and head tightened. Something inside him shifted and began to grow. The numbing grief he carefully kept at bay rose up and crashed over him in a great wave, tumbling him its wake.

"Hello, Jarand. Did you miss me?" She was there, her presence filling his mind. Even without words, he knew what she wanted as clearly as he had thought it himself. Master Ternan was no longer a suitable connection to the real world. She wanted him instead.

She had the power to break him. It would be easy for her to snap his mind and turn him into her slave. With the weight of the power she'd stolen from Master Ternan, she was strong enough in that moment to do it.

"You poor thing." Her voice filled him up again. "Look at all that pain. You're suffering. I can take it away. It would be so easy. Allow me to join with you, bond myself to you, and you'd never feel like this again."

"Why don't you just break me then?" he growled back. "Take what you want. Why the game?"

"Don't be stupid. The bond I want with you requires your cooperation. This isn't just a mindless taking, it's a partnership."

"Never. Leave me alone." Another violent spike of pain and grief smothered him. He couldn't breathe.

"I have something you want. Something you've craved for a long time." The phrase tickled unpleasantly inside his mind.

"There's nothing I want from you." He blindly loosed a cutting glyph, hoping to distract her.

She snarled. The flow seizing his throat tightened and stars danced behind his eyelids. The sharp edges of the world grew fuzzy. As she loosened her hold, she showed him the peace she offered. If he took Master Ternan's place, she would make the ragged edges of his heart be whole and the endless ache he carried around with him would fade into comfort.

Her warm influence, the very same he had experienced at the ruins when he was bleeding and dying, poured over him. With no strength left to fight it, he had to make a strategic choice. He let himself sink into the peace she offered. It would give him time to let his mind rest and heal before she tried to strike again. As long as she wasn't tampering with anything else, it might be the only chance he had to find his center once again.

At the edge of his awareness, Katira's worry throbbed through the bond along with a sense of purpose. She was still working toward a solution.

Wrothe's next strike didn't come. Her extended silence should have triggered his suspicion. He swatted the irritation away as if it was nothing more than a pesky fly. While floating in the peace she offered, he would quickly gain back what he had lost fighting her. He sank into the peace a fraction deeper. Layers of pain peeled away, and for the first time in months, his back didn't hurt. The ache from Mirelle's loss didn't cut as deep. The regrets and horrors from the wars, the ones that still haunted his nightmares, eased back a fraction. Her influence coated over those old wounds like a thick salve. He was new again, eager again, unbreakable again. Strength and power he hadn't felt in years returned. It felt good.

Good enough that Katira's spike of fear and surprise didn't register at first. It wasn't until the echo of her drawing on her power raced through him that he remembered where he was. He fought against his bonds, but they held firm.

Footsteps approached down the narrow corridor. The darkness pressing over his mouth prevented him from calling out. The footsteps drew closer. In one clean cut, Wrothe's influence fell away like smoke. The pain it had lifted from him tumbled back with all its crushing weight.

The sharp sting of a slap erupted on his cheek. He grabbed the offending hand and found Issa's first lieutenant hovering over him. "Where's Master Ternan?" she demanded.

Jarand pushed up to sitting and scanned the room. It was empty except for the two of them. While Wrothe had distracted him, the Head Seeker must have left, and if Wrothe was controlling him, there was only one place he could have gone.

The observation tower and the Occulus Seat.

CHAPTER TWENTY-FIVE

ore than a dozen hounds spilled into the audience chamber. The pair of Guardians flanking the door swept forward, bolts of light flying from their fingers. The smell of sizzling hot metal and burnt hair filled the air.

Cassim pulled Katira down into the protection of the heavy table. He'd already opened himself to his power.

"I have to get you out of here," he yelled over the noise. "This in no place for an apprentice."

She cupped her hands around her mouth. "We have to get to the Occulus Seat."

"What?" Cassim's eyes grew larger. "No, I meant away from the danger."

"We have to heal the tear. It can't be done from this side." A bright missile missed its mark and exploded too close. Katira flung her arms around her head. "It's the only way to stop this attack."

When she looked up again, Cassim had formed a shield around him. The effort left him breathless.

"Why us? Why not anyone else?"

Katira pulled her feet under her, getting ready to run. "Because I've done it before."

"That's a terrible reason," Cassim complained.

A hound darted around the table, hunting for prey. When it saw the two of them, it snarled and rushed forward.

"Oh dear." Cassim swung his shield forward, stopping the hound short.

Issa darted in, swinging her sword and dispatching the hound with ruthless efficiency. Cassim released his shield.

She stood with her back to them, watching for any other hound to dare come her way. When it was safe, she turned and shouted. "Get to the tower, grab another Guardian if you can. Seal this off."

Another shadow saw its chance and darted forward, its snapping jaws rushing for Issa's face. She spun around, catching it midair and slicing it apart. "Go now! I'll come as soon as this area is secure."

Issa's tone left no room for debate. The sooner the tear was closed, the better for everyone. Cassim formed another shield and held it steady. He reached his hand toward Katira. "The faster we go, the better this works. Stay close."

As soon as Katira had grabbed Cassim's hand, he charged forward, using the shield as a battering ram against any hounds that dared to get too close. In moments, he had them out the door and into the main hall.

"And now we run." The shield flickered away and Cassim took a moment to catch his breath. "I hate running."

"What about grabbing a Guardian?" Katira asked.

One of the hounds spilled out into the hall behind them.

In seconds, a blue coated Guardian hurried after it, glowing sword swinging.

"Leave them to fight here where they're needed." Cassim called out as he jogged toward the corridor leading to the observation tower.

Katira ran after him. "But Issa said…"

"I know what she said. This is what I'm saying." He turned down the next corridor and the sounds of fighting dwindled. "The sooner we shut that tear, the better. We can't waste time trying to explain."

Katira heard a new set of footsteps behind them. Isben was running to catch up.

"What are you doing?" he asked between gasps.

Katira didn't stop. When every second could mean a life saved, she wasn't going to waste a single one.

"Opening. In the barrier," she managed to say between her own labored breaths. "Got to close it." This was not the time to be arguing.

"Then I'm coming with you." Isben folded forward to grab his knees and suck in air before running after her again. "Go on ahead, I'll be there as soon as I can."

"Okay." Knowing he was there, knowing he would stay by her side, eased the wild pressure off of Katira's heart. Together, there was a chance all this would turn out.

As she reached the foot of the stairs another need struck her, this one far more worrying. If the barrier had been split that wide, Master Ternan must have managed to get back up to the Occulus Seat. Papan would never have let that happen willingly. She pressed her fingers against her stone. He had to be alive.

A steady persistent thrum of his determination answered. Small mercies.

She passed Cassim in the stairwell and hurried up to the Occulus Seat. Once again, Master Ternan sat in the chair, stiff backed and tense. His fingers trembled over the sphere. With a quick glance, she searched the room, making sure no hounds lurked in the shadows.

All the doubts of the past few days surged into her mind. She shouldn't be doing this. Another Stonebearer should be here using their experience and strength to seal off the breach, not her. But every moment that tear in the barrier stayed open, was another moment those fighting down in the main hall stayed in danger.

The old master whimpered. He was suffering. She could wait no longer. She seized the armrest and powered the glyph to let her enter. The room faded, its color sucked away, and the false world came into view. Cassim and Isben would be there soon enough, she wasn't alone.

Duty first; seal the barrier shut. She fixed her mind back on the main hall and the audience chamber and willed herself to return. Each time she blinked, she rushed closer. Along the way she caught sight of Cassim as he passed the last landing. Blink.

Isben mounted the first of the stairs, frozen in place.
Blink.
Another corridor, closer now to her goal.
Blink.
Shadow hounds dotted the main hall, their teeth bared. With each blink the scene shifted forward, creatures burning, people moving. She wove through the space to the audience chamber.

Inside, Issa froze in a lunge. Dark blood smeared down one of her arms and across the side of her face. Two of the councilmembers stood on the table, power held at the ready. With each blink, the scene flashed forward.

A shuddering breath drew her attention in the silence. Master Ternan stood in the middle of the audience chamber with his hands extended and power surging around him. Strange, angular, angry-looking glyphs flew from his fingers. The power whispered and crackled as it held open a portal leading from the dreamspace to the real world. Close behind him, another portal hung open in shreds as if it had been shredded. For the first time, Katira caught a glimpse of the inverted reality of Wrothe's world. Wrothe could break into the dreamspace should she be desperate enough, but it appeared she needed Ternan to make an opening to the real world.

Regardless how they were made, they had to be shut or there'd be nothing keeping those monsters from crossing through into the tower. To do that, Katira had to cut Master Ternan free. Without him, Wrothe couldn't keep the portals open.

She allowed herself to find that submission needed to access the power. Another blink, another shift. A shadow hound stalked Issa from behind. Katira shouted to warn her. The noise was buried within the rush of sound coming from the ragged edges of the portals. The warrior woman couldn't hear her.

Katira's vessel tipped, and heat rushed through the familiar pathways, lighting up the lines on her arms. She needed to move faster.

Another blink. The shadow hound's jaws crunched down on Issa's sword arm. Master Ternan grunted in his bonds and sagged to his knees. Somewhere on the other side of the portal to the mirror realm, Katira heard Wrothe laughing. On the far end of the hall, Bremin placed himself between a hound and the High Lady, glowing dagger held at the ready. Blood stained his shirt where they had already broken through. The High Lady herself stood with one hand braced against a pillar, the other outstretched with her stone.

An anger ignited deep inside Katira. These were good people and they were suffering. The fire of her anger burned away the last of her worries, her doubts, and her fears.

She couldn't lose control, not now. The simple cutting glyph formed in her hand. With a huge push, Katira blasted it out in a torrent of light, slicing Wrothe's ribbons away from Master Ternan. With him freed, Katira's attention shifted to pushing Wrothe's flows back. She formed a series of shields and missiles, each nudging the different flows back and away from the two cuts in the barrier.

The flows slipped through her glyphs like eels. The harder she worked to push them back, the more insistent they became. Despite her best efforts, there was no way she could tie the edges back together while fighting Wrothe's flows.

A tremor of panic shook her outstretched hands. She was strong enough, but not skilled enough to both fight the flows and close the barrier at the same time. If she was going to succeed, she'd have to let go. She loosened her grip on her control and let it slide through her fingers.

The unmistakable deadly calm descended, fueled by her vast need and fear as if it was waiting for her. The flows from her hands split into dozens of bright streamers and surged out. Half wove their way into the edges of the torn barrier, the other half bound themselves around Wrothe's ribbons, slowly inching the last of them back and away. With a huge pull, the opening shrank.

Fatigue struck her like a massive gong, shaking her bones

and sending her to her knees. Master Firen was right, the power paid no heed to how much she could supply. It wouldn't be long before the portals shut; she could hold on a little longer. With each shove and pull, the opening squeezed tighter. The filaments of the barrier itself merged back together.

She blinked, and Issa struck down one of the final remaining hounds. With a final tug, the last of the tear disappeared.

Bright spots flashed across Katira's vision. She fell onto all fours, blinking away the dizziness and swallowing down the wave of nausea. Her power pulsed against her temples, eager and awake. She held tight to it, worried that if she tucked it away she'd be too drained to keep going.

She blinked and the scene shifted again. Issa leaned against the massive council table, injured arm clutched to her stomach. Lady Alystra sat on the floor next to the pillar, cradling Bremin where he'd collapsed. Master Firen and several of his order hurried around the room, delving and healing the worse of the injured there.

Katira wheeled around. Master Ternan was nowhere to be seen.

Even bolstered up with the power, Katira's feet grew heavier with each step as she traveled through the dreamspace. Master Ternan had to still be in there, Wrothe couldn't possibly be done with her plan, not after an attack like that. With total control of the old master, she could break her way into any part of the tower at will.

Katira leaned against cold gray stone of one of the archways leading out of the main hall. What was she doing? Even if she found the man, there was no way she could close up another opening. If Wrothe was going to be stopped, someone else would have to do it.

She set her mind to return to the observation tower and the real world. With luck, Issa was there and ready. Darkness crowded around the edges of her sight, joining the stars she couldn't blink away. Different parts of Amul Dun flickered past as she walked toward her destination, but not fast enough. She didn't dare think what might happen if she passed out before reaching the Occulus Seat.

Her stone warmed against her palm. The gentle flow of Isben's power pushed its way through along with his worry and hope and need to protect her as he joined with her. She clung to his presence and took in what he offered. Her head cleared and the darkness pushed back a touch. It was enough to see her through. With his help, she made it back to the small room, the Occulus Seat, and back to him.

When she arrived, she found Master Ternan bracing himself on the sturdy worktable. In the dreamspace it was easy to spot dark tendril wrapping up his leg, piercing his chest, and connecting him to Wrothe.

Isben stood frozen and grey next to the chair and to her, his hand laced with hers. Her own still grey form appeared stiff and unnatural where the relic held her hostage. Seeing herself like that gave Katira the chills. Issa had arrived and was locked in a very serious conversation with Cassim as he worked on her wounded arm.

Katira drew herself closer to Master Ternan, careful not to brush against the dark ribbon of power. Glyphs streamed from the stone in his outstretched hand. Whatever madness Wrothe was working through him, it had to be stopped. If she managed to cut into the barrier here, there was no telling what chaos she'd let loose.

He moved slowly, each glyph forming in a stutter. Katira wanted to believe he was fighting Wrothe's influence or the cut would have already been made. It was either that, or the old man was as exhausted as she was. Regardless, she was grateful. It bought her much needed time.

Behind him, just as it had been down in the audience chamber, the air shimmered where Wrothe was fighting to break through.

A single cutting glyph would cut Ternan free once more and prevent that glyph from being released. The cut into the real world wouldn't form. Even if Wrothe managed to make it into the dreamspace, without Ternan she would be powerless to go any further. Her plan would be stopped.

"Master Ternan, I know you can hear me. I'm going to get you out of here."

He didn't respond. Another glyph fell from his fingers into place.

"Leave the dreamspace as soon as I cut you free. Help is waiting on the other side." She took his free hand, hoping to rouse him. She needed his cooperation, or the plan would fail. "Nod if you understand."

Still nothing. His cut in the barrier started to form. Katira couldn't wait any longer. With the small infusion from Isben she had just enough power to form a single cutting glyph. The deadly calm from before had faded, she found her control and focus. A bright spinning wheel formed over her hand. She guided it through the ribbon holding him hostage.

Master Ternan's eyes cleared and the large pattern of glyphs he'd been holding shattered. The cut sparked and hissed as it fought to heal itself.

She gripped him by the shoulders and shoved him back toward his own ghostly form sitting in the chair. "Get out of here. We'll do all we can to keep her from you."

The historians mouth worked wordlessly for a moment before what she said took hold. He nodded and set his hand on the sphere. As soon as Katira saw his glyph to exit, she formed her own and followed him.

The colors of the small room surged back, overwhelming the grays of the dreamspace. Isben stood close, the warmth of his hand in hers a reassurance that despite pushing far past her limits, she'd be okay. In front of her, Master Ternan stirred and rubbed his eyes.

Before the last of the gray faded, one of Wrothe's dark ribbons seized Katira and yanked her mind back into the dreamspace.

Katira held tighter to the sphere on the Occulus Seat, refocusing her need to leave and threading in another glyph. It had to work. She couldn't let Wrothe keep her in against her will. Even with Isben's help, she was no match for the woman.

Wrothe tore open the barrier separating the mirror realm from the dreamspace where Katira was now trapped. Great black streamers of Wrothe's power whipped around the room, seizing Katira in an instant. They wrapped higher and higher around her body as they strained to reach her heart.

"Give in," Wrothe commanded.

The ribbon pressed harder. Katira fought against it.

"Let me take you, make you into my vessel." Wrothe loomed over her, dark hair falling in sheets around the crimson red of her dress. Dark power swirled around her in a storm. Katira's own power strained to fight it.

If Katira let go of her control now, she'd never gain it back. That intelligence within the power had a goal, and

Wrothe was an obstacle to reaching it. It would burn Katira from the inside out to destroy the woman.

Dark power swirled around Wrothe faster, forming a flurry of glyphs that locked into a much larger sequence. This was more than an attack, this was a bending. Wrothe intended on breaking her mind and taking her body as her own.

Katira would rather die. She scrambled back, yanking against the ribbon holding her fast, and trying to get away from the swirling ominous glyph. The wild glint in the woman's eye shone with success. If that glyph were to touch Katira, all would be lost.

The power surged stronger, thrumming against Katira's temples, eager for her to let go. Just as she started to loosen her grip for the last time, Papan appeared in the chair where Master Ternan had just been.

With a flash, Wrothe's glyph sprang into action, sending dozens of sharp streamers toward her. Katira braced for them to pierce her, for the demon to take her.

Papan grabbed her arm and yanked her back. The lines on his arms blazed with power, and he threw a shield between the glyph and them. It solidified just in time for the glyph to slam into the surface and shatter. He curled around her, protecting her with his own body.

"Get out of here," he said between labored pants. "I'll deal with her."

"Hello, Jarand." Wrothe voice changed back to honey sweet. The room fell into an uneasy silence. "I was hoping you'd come."

Papan pushed Katira back toward the Occulus Seat and turned to face Wrothe. "Go now, that's an order."

"You can't do this alone. Not with her," Katira protested.

He looked her in the eyes, his gaze pained with the decision he'd already made. "Leave me here. This is my fight."

Katira knew that look. He would not be budged. She would leave, but that didn't mean she was done. With both Cassim and Issa at her side, they would do what it took to ensure he came out of the dreamspace alive.

The dark storm of power swirling around Wrothe grew to a deafening roar. More glyphs sprang to her fingertips, linking and growing into another complex attack.

Glyphs sprang from Papan's outstretched hand. A huge flash and crack of noise split the air. "Go, Katira! Go now and don't come back."

She set her hand on the sphere and threaded in her power, all while anxiously watching for any sign he would succeed. Another flash of power filled the space before the grays of the dreamspace and sight of him blew away like smoke.

"She's coming out," Isben said wrapping his arms around her, catching her as the stiff hold of the relic released its grip. "Easy. Take it slow."

The crippling pain of having drawn too much shot through Katira's head, making her stomach turn violently. Another warm presence leaned closer on her other side and Cassim's familiar hand wrapped around hers as her whole body trembled from shock.

"Get her lying down somewhere," Cassim instructed. "Issa, find a blanket or something."

Isben lifted her as if she were nothing and carefully lowered her down to the floor while Issa fetched the blanket from the basket of supplies in the corner of the room and wrapped it around her.

"By the Stonemother's throne itself, Katira! Why on earth

did you think it was a good idea to go in there alone?" Issa scolded her softly, lines of worry etched the sides of her face.

Isben lifted her head and shoulders into his lap. He wrapped a protective arm around her to calm the trembling that racked her whole frame. All the voices around her came and went in loud bursts that resonated through her head like trumpets.

"Not the time, Issa," Cassim reminded her quietly. "She's been through a lot. Give her a minute."

Katira shook her head. "He doesn't have a minute." She swallowed down the nausea threatening to empty her stomach. "Is Master Ternan shielded? Wrothe can't be allowed access to him again."

Issa gave a curt nod and gestured to the thin line of power connected to her wrist. "Did it the second he came out." She held tightly to where her sword arm was bound to her chest. "What is Jarand facing in there?"

Katira pressed her stone between her fingers, carefully reading the muted signals from within the dreamspace. "Wrothe. She can break into the dreamspace at will. He was going to force her back, close the tear, then get out."

Issa swore and kicked the wall protecting the stairwell. "We could barely do that when we worked together. There's no way he can do that on his own." She then whipped around and studied Papan in the chair. "That's it. I'm going in."

Master Ternan stirred from where they'd let him crumple on the floor and looked up, grim faced. "There's one more thing you can do."

"What's that?" Cassim asked

"Take my stone from me. It'll distract her, give the General the upper hand for a moment. It would make it so if she..."

His gaze shifted to Papan in the chair and he struggled to speak.

Katira had seen this before. "You can't say her plans even now, can you?"

He let his head fall. "Take it. Quickly. I'm not worthy of it anymore."

Issa shuddered. "No, we don't have the authority to do that. It's cruel. Only the High Lady can remove a Stone."

Master Ternan turned to the Healer. "Cassim, please. I don't want to be burdened with it any longer."

"We're long past considering the rules anymore." Cassim left Katira's side and approached him. "If this will stop Wrothe's attack, I'm willing." He looped his fingers around the cord at Master Ternan's neck. The old Seeker nodded, letting him know it was for the best.

Cassim tugged at the cord, but his stone did not come free. He tugged again.

Master Ternan's face wrinkled with pain. "You'll have to cut it out."

Cassim's hands froze around the cord and he exchanged an uneasy glance with Issa. He made quick work of unbuttoning the man's shirt and gagged when he saw what was holding his stone back.

Katira needed to see it for herself. She pushed Isben's hands away and forced herself up to sitting. A fresh stab of pain pierced her skull. Isben kept a warm hand on her back, supporting her.

Master Ternan's stone had buried itself into his skin. Instead of being pale green, it shone a deep red, almost black, just as Master Regulus's had. Dark lines extended from the stone, spiderwebbing up the old man's thin skin.

Issa set the hilt of her heavy belt knife into healer's hand. "Just do it. Don't think too hard about it."

Grim faced, Cassim took the knife. Katira prayed it was as sharp as it looked. Back under Mamar's tutelage, she'd helped drain pockets of infection. The knives they used were smaller and specialized to the task, but the process was the same. Open up the wound, remove the diseased material. For the old man's sake, it would be best if Cassim moved quickly with a sure hand.

With a steadying breath, he carefully inserted the tip of the knife along the edge of the man's stone. Dark blood welled up from the cut. Master Ternan cried out, then fell back, quiet and still.

Issa's eyes nearly leapt from her head. "By the Stonemother's throne, did that kill him?"

Cassim felt at the man's neck. "No, it's a faint. Better for him, I suppose." He pushed the shirt aside and started cutting once more.

The shield around Master Ternan flexed. Issa's gaze instantly shifted back to the Occulus Seat. "What's happening with Jarand?"

Katira studied the bond. The intensity of the fight had faded and was replaced with the focus he found when set to a difficult task. But, he was tiring quickly. "He's still trying to stop her."

Issa nudged Cassim as the shield flexed again. "I know you're being careful, but could you speed it up a bit?" Part of the shield strained to stay together as something from the other side pried at it.

"Don't rush me. This is a person, not a rabbit. It would be easier if I could use the power, but I don't dare." He slid the sharp blade under the man's stone, all while making a face like he wanted to throw up. With a yank, the stone came free. "Where do I put this?"

"Far away from him," Issa said, holding out an open handkerchief. Cassim dropped the stone into it before setting to work knitting the wound closed.

"I'd feel better if it wasn't even in the keep." He didn't look up from the glyphs flowing from his fingers. "It's been tainted. Who knows what she will be able to do through it still?"

Issa wrapped up the stone with a grimace and set it on the far end of the worktable. The shield around Master Ternan stopped flexing.

"Katira, any change?" Issa asked.

"I think…" She closed her eyes, not wanting to miss any trace of what might be happening on the other side. "I think that might have done it. He's stopped what he was doing."

"Cassim, check him." Issa directed with a jerk of her head. "He's smart enough to not drain out, but stupid enough to sacrifice himself. I'd rather know which."

"I'd know if he was in trouble." Katira pulled the blanket closer. "I'd tell you."

"All the same. He's my friend. It's the least I can do to be sure." Issa finally found one of the chairs over by the smaller table and sat into it sideways, laying her unbound arm over the armrest.

Cassim heaved himself up from off the floor. "You can technically do this too."

"But you're so much better at it." Issa bit at the edge of a fingernail. "I've been wanting someone to look at him ever since we patched that breach this morning. He can't refuse now."

"When it's not an emergency I'm supposed to ask for

consent." Cassim rolled back Papan's sleeve and set a hand against his arm.

"And Jarand is supposed to take care of himself." She quirked a half smile. "Remember when he tried to hide when he got shot by an arrow? Went two days before finally falling off his horse."

"I'm doing it already." Cassim rolled his eyes. "Stop talking so I can pay attention."

The room grew too quiet as they all waited. Isben leaned in close to Katira and spoke so Cassim couldn't hear him. "Are you feeling any better?"

Between worrying about Papan and removing Master Ternan's stone from him, Katira hadn't thought about her own condition more than trying to ignore the headache which was trying to dig its way out of her head with a spoon.

She held out a hand. It was steadier than before, but that wasn't saying much. The dizziness threatening to throw her out of her seat had shrunk down. Isben urged her to lean back against him and rest. Until Cassim finished, or Papan awoke, she needed a moment to process all that had happened.

When Cassim finished, he didn't look happy. He joined Issa over by the smaller table and spoke quietly into her ear.

"What about his stone?" Issa asked loud enough for Katira to hear. "Is it..."

"No." He shook his head. "It hasn't been touched yet."

Katira straightened. "What is it? What did you find?"

"It's hard to say." Cassim started, but struggled on the words.

"He found something." Issa continued instead. "He thinks it might be where Wrothe has tampered with him. Unlike those with compulsion, this is affecting his heart, not his mind."

Cassim found his tongue once more. "I haven't seen anything like it. We'll have to watch him. All I know is it wasn't there at Khanrosh or detected in the week after when we worked on the damage to his back."

She knew what he was talking about. She'd been worried about Papan ever since she first saw them weeks ago. A series of black roots grew around Papan's heart, pressing and piercing as they went. At first she thought they were a figment of her imagination, her mind's way of trying to explain why he struggled so much with Mamar's death. Having Cassim find the same thing meant they were real.

Katira hands trembled in her lap. She should have pushed harder to find out what they were when she first spotted them. "It was there when we were bonded. Ever since he's been in contact with Wrothe, it's grown larger."

Cassim fell silent as Papan sighed and shifted in the chair. As he came around, he scanned the room, a habit left over from years of living as a Guardian.

He reached for Katira and she placed her hand in his, giving him the reassurance he needed. She had scared him. He needed to know she was okay.

Master Ternan sat propped up against one of the walls, legs splayed out and shirt hanging open to reveal the large, fresh pink scar where his stone should have been.

"What happened to him?" Papan asked.

"He asked us to remove it. He believed it might keep her from using him." Cassim was about to run a hand over his face when he saw it was still stained with blood.

Papan's eyebrows shot up. "You did what?"

"His stone was black, Jarand, just like Regulus's." Issa explained. Unlike Cassim, she kept her cool.

"Where is it now?"

Issa pointed to the folded handkerchief on the table. "Inside that. I don't recommend touching it."

Touching only the corners of the cloth, Papan unfolded the bundle and examined what was inside. "This needs to be added to the evidence gathered against him. Did the council decide on how to proceed?"

"There will be a trial. Should Wrothe dare reveal herself, they'll attempt to free his mind from her bindings while the strength of the tower is gathered." Cassim looked relieved when Papan folded the stone securely back into the handkerchief. "Thankfully they got that far before all hell broke loose down there."

"What's going to happen with Master Ternan until then?" Katira asked.

"He'll be kept under constant guard." Issa helped the old master to his feet with her good arm.

"When will they hold the trial?" Isben asked.

"As soon as conceivably possible. For the good of Amul Dun, it's best to get this resolved." Issa made her way down the stairs, carefully escorting Master Ternan.

Cassim lingered behind. "I wouldn't be a good friend if I didn't ask, but are you quite all right, Jarand? You've been through a lot." He made a gesture toward the Occulus Seat that was meant to be casual, but came across hurried and anxious.

"I know you delved me while I was in there." Papan scooped up his cane from where he dropped it. "Is there something wrong?"

"That's just it, I'm not sure. I found something. It's like a darkness gathered around the center of your power. Never seen anything like it before. So, I'll ask you again." Cassim grew more serious. "Are you quite all right?"

Papan's face sagged with exhaustion. "I don't want to have this conversation right now. Like you said. It's been a long day. A lot has happened." He stood to leave.

"Please, Jarand. Stuff like this can be dangerous." Cassim placed himself between Papan and the exit. "Tell me I shouldn't be worried. Tell me this isn't harmful to anyone, including yourself."

"I'm not a danger to anyone. Trust me on that." Papan set a hand on the healer's shoulder. "When this is all over, I'll let you poke and prod to your heart's delight. But not before. The safety of Amul Dun comes first and always."

Cassim deflated under Papan's touch, clearly worried, but unable to do anything more. Katira believed her father. He would never intentionally be a danger to anyone else. But as long as that thing was still inside him, there were more doubts than answers.

For the moment, Katira found herself drifting back to Isben. She let his soothing touch distract her from her worries, and from the ache in her head. Even if all went well, the next few days promised challenges that she wasn't ready to face.

CHAPTER TWENTY-SIX

The iron-strapped doors of the Judgment Hall loomed too large at the end of the hall. Katira followed two steps behind Papan, her gray ceremonial apprentice robes hanging stiff and heavy from her shoulders. Papan told her they were meant to be uncomfortable, to remind the wearer of their duty. For the first time in months, he wore his sword over his own ceremonial robes.

Inside the Hall, glowing light from orbs embedded in the walls glinted off Papan's shining breast plate. Whatever happened in that room in the next hours would determine Master Ternan's fate. Judging by what happened to Master Regulus when Wrothe was severed from him, the chances of the Head Seeker coming out unscathed were slim, even if he was found innocent.

Knots of Stonebearers were scattered around the room, each wearing their own set of ceremonial robes in the color of their order. High overhead, morning sun pierced through stained glass windows ringing the great arched dome. At the four points of the compass, the window's pattern formed large glyphs symbolizing the four key Stonebearer values; honor, valor, duty, and wisdom.

In the center of the room, an empty chair and narrow pedestal awaited Master Ternan and his treacherous stone.

When Isben saw Katira, he hurried over to her. His ceremonial robes hung too short on his frame and were wrinkled as if they'd been pulled out of a crate that morning. He no longer wore the bandage around his head.

"They want us to sit over there." He motioned to where Cassim tugged at the neck of his robe. Next to him, Issa shifted on the balls of her feet as she scanned the room. It had been only two days since hounds had flooded the audience chamber, so a gathering like this was bound to make her uneasy. Her arm was still bound tightly across her chest over her own ceremonial armor.

Isben led them around the seats ringing the circular room along the low wall separating those being judged from those who watched.

Papan approached Issa and tapped her bound arm. "Will you be personally guarding the High Seat?"

"Yes. She needs someone she can trust at her side. I won't fail her." Her measured gaze studied Papan, as if making an assessment. Strain hid at the corners of her eyes. "It'll do everyone good to put this matter to rest."

Isben slid his hand into Katira's. Despite his outward calm, his fingers trembled.

He lowered his head and spoke softly into her ear. "Nothing about this feels right. I can't shake the feeling something horrible is going to happen."

Being in the judgement hall felt too similar to when they faced Wrothe in the great hall in Khanrosh. What was worse, they both knew too well what Wrothe was capable of.

Katira wrapped her other hand around his to stop it from shaking. "It has to be done. Guilty or not, Wrothe's influence must be cut from him for good. Only then will he be able to share the information he's collected about both her and the mirror realm over the centuries. Papan thinks he might have the key to closing the barrier between worlds for good. It's the only way to secure our world against hers."

Papan turned to Isben and Katira, his face that mask of responsibility Katira hating seeing. "A trial like this is bound to get ugly. I don't imagine Wrothe cooperating without a fight. If things get out of control, you are both to get far away from here."

Isben's solemn nod of agreement came too quickly.

Katira couldn't make that promise. "No. After all that has happened, I have to see this finished. You must let me stay."

Papan's jaw tightened. "Don't make me choose between my duty to Amul Dun and my duty to you." He'd walled her off from sensing him again, but she didn't need the bond to know he was scared. "Please, Katira. This way I can guarantee your safety as well as do my part to put an end to it all."

The words of their bonding ceremony rang through her mind. While he shouldered the greater responsibility of the bond, she had been charged to watch over and care for him.

"It's just..." The worry of something happening to him summoned up a surge of unexpected grief from the loss of Mamar. "I wasn't there when Mamar died. I never had the chance to tell her goodbye. If you send me away and something happens, I'll never forgive myself."

His forehead wrinkled and he pulled her into his arms like he used to do when she was little. "We are surrounded by the strength of Amul Dun. Nothing like that will happen. It might be that nothing happens at all, then all this worry will be for nothing."

"All the same, promise me you won't take any stupid risks."

He squeezed her tighter before letting go. "I hope it doesn't come to that."

He turned back to Isben, as serious as Katira had ever seen him. "I don't care how you do it, but if I give you the word, I'm counting on you to get her out of here."

"Yes, Master Jarand." Isben gave her hand a reassuring squeeze.

Katira opened her mouth to protest. It wasn't fair to pit Isben against her. She wanted to fight harder against her father's decision, but the discussion was over. Instead, she would have to cling to the hope of the trial being thoroughly uneventful.

Papan gave a curt nod and turned back to Issa, no doubt needing to coordinate plans and anticipate any defensive measures that would need to be taken.

Isben turned to face her. "You can't fight this. Let him protect you. You are all he has left."

Katira blinked back a tear that threatened to form. A torrent of emotion coiled up in her throat. "You were there when Cassim confronted him about the strange darkness inside him. It was Wrothe who planted it there, I'm sure of it. She's got a plan for him. I won't let her turn him into her slave."

His gaze met hers. "You can't stop her alone. You know that. He's got a roomful of people here to help him fight against her, should it come to that. I trust them. You need to trust them as well."

The Guardian at the door announced the High Lady's entrance in a loud, clear voice. The room fell silent, cutting off any chance Katira had to discuss things further with Isben. Issa excused herself and made her way to the dais to take her position next to the High Lady's seat.

The gathered crowd stood and bowed in respect as Lady Alystra made her stately march across the center of the room. While she still held her head high, one hand wound tight into the folds of her yellow robe, while the other clung to her staff of office. For the first time since Katira had known her, she looked old.

Bremin followed two steps behind. His purple ceremonial robes were a stark contrast to his preferred simple shirts and trousers.

When she reached the raised platform at the far end of the room, she faced the crowd and banged her staff of office on the floor twice. "All have gathered," she announced. "Prepare the room."

Four Guardians entered in a stately march, each step precise, each turn crisp. They took their places around the circle of the open floor. Captain Edmont entered behind them, securing the fifth position directly opposite the High Lady's platform and in front of the door. In unison, they opened themselves to their power and the lines on their arms glowed to life. Each formed a shielding glyph and merged it with the next until a great cage was formed around the lone chair and pedestal.

Captain Edmont turned and saluted the High Lady. "The room is prepared."

She nodded and banged the floor twice more. "Bring him in."

The great doors swung open and the assembled group watched on as a pair of Guardians escorted Master Ternan to the center of the room. He walked willingly with his head bowed low as if too tired to hold it up. When he reached the offered chair, he slumped into it, hands hanging limply at his sides. They bound him in chains, securing his elbows behind him to the high wooden back of the chair, before doing the same with his feet. Captain Edmont himself set the small rectangular box containing Master Ternan's stone onto the pedestal. A glimmer of a protective ward shone around its edges.

Lady Alystra banged her staff one final time and the crowd returned to their seats.

She remained standing. "We who hold the sacred trust have gathered on behalf of Master Ternan who has become entangled with Wrothe, a known enemy of our society. Our purpose in gathering is to determine his guilt in this matter and free him from her influence."

The muted rustle of cloth and low murmur of voices filled the room. Master Ternan lifted his head a fraction to acknowledge the High Lady before letting it sink back to his chest.

She took her seat before continuing. "Master Ternan, what do you have to say in your defense?"

"I'm sorry," the man's voice cracked. When lifted his head to meet her gaze his eyes were red rimmed and his shoulders shook. "I've let you down. I never meant any of this to happen."

"Was the attack on me your doing?" she asked, her voice remarkably calm.

"She forced me. I couldn't stop her. I wasn't strong enough."

"And the other attacks in the keep, was that you as well?"

"Yes. All of it. She's used me horribly. I deserve whatever punishment you decide, as long as my torment ends."

"I understand." Lady Alystra regarded him for a long while before continuing. "We are not without compassion. What do you want us to do with you?"

He rubbed at his wrists behind him, tugging at the rope binding him to the chair. "Free me from her. Amul Dun and the world can't be safe until she's gone."

"I agree." Lady Alystra gave a solemn nod. "However, there is the risk that doing so might lead to your death, just as it did for Master Regulus."

"I understand. Should I die, then my punishment is complete." His head sagged back down as if he was too tired to hold it up.

The High Lady motioned to two figures sitting to the side of the platform. "Will you allow Master Aro and Master Firen to delve you?"

Master Ternan gave a resigned nod. The two masters approached the glowing cage and entered through an opening that resealed itself once they passed through. Katira almost didn't recognize Master Aro in his ceremonial robes. Gone were the mismatched layers. Gone were the dozens of pockets. The thick glasses remained perched on his head. He gave a polite bow to let Master Firen go first.

Of all the times Katira had watched the Head Healer work, she'd never seen him uncertain or unsure. Today, he approached Master Ternan cautiously, as one would approach a viper. It wasn't until he stepped behind the chair that his lines glowed to life and he dared touch the man. The delving only lasted a few minutes before he pulled his hands back to make his report.

"I found damage to the nerves, evidence of torture, and the corruption of his power similar to what I found with Master Regulus, all of which support the accusation of him being connected to an entity from the mirror realm." He stepped aside to allow Master Aro to come forward.

Masters Aro and Ternan regarded each other. If anything, Master Aro wore the expression of someone utterly disappointed in himself for trusting the man at all. When he touched the back of Master Ternan's neck, the man snapped rigid and he grabbed for the sides of the chair. It seemed Bender delving was anything but gentle. By the time he finished, Master Ternan struggled to catch his breath.

"Anchors have been set in place deep in his mind, the kind used to manipulate and compel. His power is not only corrupted, it's been realigned to accept both the Khandashii and the ancient Dashiian, which is why his lines have gone dark. The Dashiian doesn't shine white, but black."

The room erupted into whispers once again. Lady Alystra banged her staff to bring order.

"This evidence confirms what we had already suspected. Master Ternan has been compromised. His actions, though terrible, were not wholly his own." If anything, Lady Alystra sounded sad at the revelation, as if she held onto a secret hope he might be innocent, and it was finally dashed. "Do you think this can be reversed? Can he be freed?"

Master Firen stepped closer to the dais. "It will be difficult, but I believe it can be done."

"Can you force her to speak through him?" Bremin directed the question to Master Aro, leaning forward into his hand. "We need to be sure the extent of her treachery ends here."

Master Aro's brow twisted in thought. "I believe so. It won't be comfortable, but it won't harm him. We'll need access to the stone he was using. I believe she used it as a conduit from the mirror realm. It's the only possible explanation."

Lady Alystra signaled for Captain Edmont to open the box on the pedestal. "Proceed."

Master Aro lifted the stone from the box by its cord and replaced it around Master Ternan's neck.

Master Ternan fought against his bonds, shrinking away from the touch of the stone as if it were a live coal. "Please no, don't do this. Don't let her near me. She's too dangerous," he begged, flinching away from the ribbons of power flowing from Master Aro's hands.

Master Aro paused and looked to Lady Alystra for guidance.

"We have to know her intentions." She waved for them to continue. "I'm sorry, Master Ternan."

Next to Katira, Papan gripped the head of his cane hard enough that his fingers blanched white. He leaned forward as if meaning to object to the idea. Before he could say anything, Master Aro began to weave his glyphs. Master Ternan struggled and thrashed in the chair. Guttural cries broke through his clenched teeth.

"They shouldn't do this. It's not worth the risk." Papan stood and loosened his sword in its scabbard as if preparing for an attack to come pouring in any second. Across the room, Issa reacted the same way.

The ribbons pulled tight. Master Aro continued to weave more glyphs, strengthening and reinforcing the connection. "There, that should do it." He glanced to the Guardians around the circle. "Stay alert, watch for any change. Keep the shields strong."

Lady Alystra gripped her staff as if she had half a mind to beat someone with it. "Wrothe, I know you can hear this. What have you to say for yourself?"

Master Ternan snarled and sat straighter in the chair. "You are all fools. I won't talk." Wrothe's harsh voice came out of the man's mouth.

Hearing that voice scratched at Katira's bones. Every memory of fighting against her surged through her mind and made her pulse quicken.

"You will talk." Lady Alystra ordered. "Consider this your last chance to communicate with the waking world."

"You think you are in control here, don't you?" Master Ternan's body twisted and fought as the words emerged from his mouth. "You're not."

Shocked whispers erupted from the group of onlookers.

Lady Alystra thumped her staff on the floor, demanding order. "Those are big words for one bound to a chair. How long has Master Ternan been under your influence?"

"I will not answer. I will turn your whole world against you." Wrothe snarled again and the black lines on Master Ternan's arms glowed. Thin tendrils of her power snaked out from him, reaching, searching. Strange glyphs formed around the chair, ones Katira didn't recognize. They looked danger-ous. His bonds fell away and another sequence of glyphs formed in his now freed hands.

Master Aro stepped back, wildly forming and throwing glyphs to counter Wrothe's ever growing pattern "Maintain the shield, let nothing pass through!" he shouted.

"What's happening?" Lady Alystra demanded.

"She's breaking through to this world, forcing her way

through using the path I created. Guardians, protect the High Lady."

Papan wrapped his stone into his palm and drew his sword. Issa did the same next to Lady Alystra. Their markings flashed to life. The flash of heat echoed through Katira and throbbed at her temples.

Isben pulled at Katira's arm. "I'm taking you out of here."

She yanked herself free. "No. Not yet. He hasn't given the order."

"Please, Katira, no good will come from you staying here."

"Look!" She pointed to where the ribbons of power flowed around Master Ternan and the stone on his chest. "Her power is being focused through the stone. It's the pathway, not Master Ternan. It has to be destroyed."

Isben grabbed her arm again and dragged her another few steps toward the door. "Stones can't be destroyed. It will protect itself. It has its own power."

Katira yanked free again. "There has to be a way. Please. Think. You've studied with the Benders. Can motherstone be changed enough to no longer conduct power?"

"What?" The absurdity of the idea stopped his attempts to get her out of the room. "That's insane."

"Just think. Is there any way it can be done?"

Isben wrung his hands together. His gaze darted to the door then back to Katira. "It's dangerous. Even tinkering with it could be deadly. If anyone could do it, it would be Master Aro."

Sweeping tendrils of Wrothe's power chased out from Master Ternan's stone, seeking new victims. Master Aro struggled to maintain his shield all while working feverishly to cut Wrothe's connection to the stone.

"He's a little busy right now. It wouldn't have to be a huge change, just enough to break the connection. Do you think you could do it?"

A thin tendril darted past Master Aro's defenses and wrapped around his ankles. He stumbled and fell backward. In seconds, a mass of tendrils pounced on him, wrapping him up tight. He didn't even have a chance to scream.

Papan charged forward. "Open the shield," he yelled at the nearest Guardian. "Let me in. I can help him."

The Guardian didn't hesitate to make an opening in the cage. Papan slipped through. Missiles burst from his hand to push back the tendrils venturing too close to those maintaining the cage-like shield.

"Can you do it?" Katira asked again.

Isben took one look at the chaos and shook his head. "Maybe. But, not with all of this. I can't get close enough."

Inside the cage, Master Firen hurried to Master Aro's side, narrowly avoiding being snagged. "General, cut him free and I'll get him out," he shouted, dodging the tendrils reaching for him with a yelp.

Papan didn't spare a moment. He released a precise shot, severing the tendrils draining the Bender. Master Firen hoisted up the unconscious man by his armpits and dragged him to the closest Guardian who hurried to let them out. A yellow robed woman grabbed both Masters, and in a flash of light, they disappeared from the room.

The air filled with sharp cracking, small at first, but then louder and louder as the glowing cage started to splinter and break under the strain of Wrothe's attack. The Guardians standing in the circle frantically worked to reinforce the breaks, seal together the gaps. For each one they closed, another two cracks appeared. With one final heave, the massive shield shattered and fell into thousands of glittering pieces.

The room burst into chaos. Master Ternan's hands contorted and another more complicated glyph formed. More robed Stonebearers jumped forward, stones in hand, throwing out shields or counteracting glyphs to shatter what Wrothe was trying to complete. A sphere of red mist formed around the chair.

"Isben! Get Katira out of here!" Papan shouted over the noise as he swung his sword to cut down another searching tendril.

"You heard him." Isben grabbed her arm once more and hauled her toward the door.

Katira's power burned inside her, anxious and straining to be free. The Khandashii was so much bigger than the chaos that surrounded her, than her own fears, that she let it drown them out. She was a weapon forged by the power. Created not to save Papan, not even to protect Amul Dun, but for a much greater purpose that hadn't been revealed to her yet.

She stretched out her hands and allowed the power to flow through her. Dozens of glyphs leapt from her fingers, forming patterns in the air before bursting out into a shield in front of her. That intelligence hiding within the power took hold, urging her to follow, to trust. Together they were stronger. Together they could succeed where others had failed.

Katira grabbed hold to the offered trust. Unlike before, she now understood what it meant to wield this power. It wasn't submission, it was a partnership.

Isben leapt away from her flows, his own power flashing down the backs of his hands. "What are you doing?"

"Making a path so you can break the connection. Help me, Isben." Her voice sounded far away in her own ears as guided the power to work through her. "To do nothing is death. You and I both know it. Stay close."

A sphere of shining light formed around both her and Isben. As she guided him through the chaos, the power surging around her pushed away Wrothe's tendrils as if they were feathers in the breeze. Inside the sphere, the voices and shouting, the noise and screaming, died away. She led Isben next to Master Ternan and the blackened stone. The old master sat boneless with his head flung back over the chair and his mouth open. Only the twitching of the muscles of his throat showed that he was still alive.

"This is our one chance. Break the connection. I don't know how long I can hold this." As with the other times the power took control, she felt distant from herself, separated from reality.

Glyphs formed at Isben's fingertips and all of his focus shifted to the darkly glowing stone on Master Ternan's chest. "I'll do what I can." His flows of power wove in and out of the strands of Wrothe's connection before daring to touch the stone itself.

As with all Bending, Katira knew it would take time. She prayed she could give him enough. More of Wrothe's tendrils prodded at the bubble of protection she'd created, just as they'd done to Papan's shield. She could force them back, but not forever.

From the corner of her eye, Papan charged toward her, his face a terrifying mix of rage and horror. Power whipped around him in a storm of light. His flows still shone white. Wrothe hadn't corrupted him yet. He yelled what looked like orders to those close to him. Katira heard nothing.

Isben continued to work, his brow furrowed, now creating new chains of glyphs intended to transform. The other tendrils swirling around the room fell back suddenly and retreated into

Master Ternan like parasites. Katira had Wrothe's full attention.

A massive glyph formed over Master Ternan's head, dark and oppressive like a storm cloud. Katira braced herself as it sprang to action, strengthening the shield against whatever evil Wrothe might unleash next.

Dark streaks shot out in all directions, forming a new cage around them like the one she had shattered. The streaks widened and stretched until they formed a pocket of dreamspace inside the center of the hall. All the color outside her cage faded away. Those trapped outside the cage appeared frozen in place.

In the silence of the dreamspace, Katira heard her own harsh breathing too loudly in her head. The power thrummed and surged beneath her skin, awaiting the next step, the next need. Katira let her shield fall away. It didn't seem necessary anymore.

Isben worked steadily onward, too deeply involved in the process to notice the change. Papan was trapped inside with them, somewhere behind her. She didn't dare face him. She wasn't ready to see the anger caused by her disobedience. She'd ask for forgiveness when all of this was over.

A grating hiss erupted from the center of the strange bubble of dreamspace. Angry red lines marked the air as if they'd been made with burning claws. Wrothe strained to tear a new opening into the space. Given her anger, it wouldn't be long before she succeeded.

A new fear seized Katira even while deep within the calm of the Khandashii's embrace. Wrothe had tried to take her before, needing a body from the real world to inhabit. No doubt she'd try it again. If she managed it, she wouldn't need Master Ternan's stone, she would have direct access to the power she needed to destroy the entire tower and take what she wanted.

The clawed lines deepened, scraping and scratching until one broke through and those horrible tendrils spilled out of the cut. Wrothe wasn't stupid. By sending her tendrils in first, she could deal with her enemy without endangering herself.

Outside the bubble of dreamspace, the waking world shifted erratically with each blink. Issa and two of her guardswomen slammed glyph after glyph against the strange cage Wrothe had formed as they tried to force their way through.

Isben continued weaving bending glyphs one after another, keeping his head down and his focus locked on the work. The glyphs streaming from his hands grew more complex as they wove in and out of the blackened motherstone. If any of those tendrils reached him, it might destroy the work he'd done so far as well as their chances of stopping Wrothe for good.

Katira put herself between Isben and the growing tear between the two worlds. The power flowing through her responded to her need and surged to work, one part weaving the edges of the cut to close, the other pushing Wrothe back.

Papan worked his way closer, weaving glyphs of his own to join with and strengthen hers. "What is he doing? I told you to leave," he shouted over the noise.

"Breaking the connection." Katira jumped back from a seeking tendril that came too close to her ankle. Papan shot it back with a burst of light. "Keeping her from entering the real world."

"Do you think he can do it?" He deflected another tendril with a swing of his sword.

Katira's flows pulled and strained to close the tear. "It's the best chance we have."

A figure came into view through the chaos of glyphs and sizzling barrier strands. Wrothe approached the opening, hands outstretched, a wicked smile on her face.

"Is this the best fight you can give me? Two children and a spent Guardian? And here I worried Amul Dun might put up real resistance." Her hand passed through the tear and a series of dark glyphs began to form in rapid succession.

Papan met Katira's gaze, his eyes full of fire and steel. This was one battle he would not lose. "If we are to fight her, we do it together."

A piercing laugh shook Katira's resolve. Wrothe released her glyph. Dozens of spinning blades erupted from her hand, all aimed at Isben where he continued his work.

Papan flung a shield in a wild burst, blasting the attack away. The blades bounced off the shield and disappeared, but not before Wrothe started forming another attack.

"Concentrate your efforts on closing the tear," he told her. He held his sword high and bright blue glyphs ran up its length. "You're better at that than I am. I'll keep her off both you and Isben for as long as I can."

Katira refocused her flows back to her where her strength lay, healing. She examined the broken threads of the barrier, allowing her power to gather them up and knit them back together. She couldn't fight Wrothe directly, but she could keep her from coming any further.

Behind her, Isben grunted in frustration. Katira dared a single glance, worried that he'd pushed himself too far. Master Ternan's stone no longer shone inky black and was instead a dull grey. The change should have been enough, but a weak connection between the old man and Wrothe remained.

Papan deflected each attack with the studied grace and control of someone who had dedicated his life to fighting.

Each time he stopped her, Wrothe grew more and more desperate to break through. Her smile of victory changed to a grimace.

The tear shrank an inch at a time as Katira worked. With Wrothe too distracted to rip the opening larger again, she grew hopeful. This struggle against her might be the last.

Green glyphs flew from Isben's fingers as he worked to sever that last thin connection to Wrothe. The dull grey of the stone hadn't changed.

Only the last few inches of the tear remained. Wrothe's hand remained wedged in the gap, preventing it from shutting. More of her seeking tendrils swam through. If any of them grabbed and drained even one of them, it would enable her to break through the barrier again. They, however, would only grow weaker.

Papan saw it too. With a great shout, he bounded toward the cut, sword raised. He allowed the tendrils to grab him. With a mighty swing, he severed Wrothe's hand.

A shrill scream came through the gap only to be cut short as Katira yanked the remaining threads of the barrier shut tight. The tendrils fell away and vanished.

The last of Isben's glyphs settled into place, but the last thin connection between Master Ternan and Wrothe remained.

Isben gripped the stone in his hand. "I've done everything I can. It can't be broken. I'm sorry Katira. I failed you."

He let the stone fall from his hand.

It shattered when it hit the floor and the connection broke with it.

Katira grabbed Isben and wrapped her arms around him. "That's not what I call failure. You did it. I knew you could."

Papan leaned with both arms braced on the small pedestal, head bowed, breathing heavily.

"Everyone okay?" he asked in a low voice. His voice sounded too loud in the silent space. "Katira, talk to me. Say something."

With Wrothe gone and the connection broken, Katira's power no longer thrummed at her temples and beneath her skin. It retreated back into its vessel. "I'm okay."

"Isben?"

"Yeah. I'm good. Little shaky, that's all."

CHAPTER TWENTY-SEVEN

$\mathcal{M}$aster Ternan hadn't moved. After trying so hard to free him from that monster, Katira refused to believe he might be dead. She slid her fingers against the side of his neck, relieved to feel his heart still beating. Wrothe hadn't killed him. Small mercies.

"Is he...?" Isben started, but didn't manage to finish.

"Alive but unconscious," Katira answered.

"And you?"

"Tired, but okay." She held her hands in front of her. After all that had happened she'd expected them to shake, expected her head to be splitting in two from being overdrawn. It shouldn't have been that way. After what she did, she should have been on the floor alongside Master Ternan. Did the power grant her more?

Isben helped her lay the old master down on the marble floor to the side of the chair. As he straightened he stopped suddenly. "You need to see this. Something is really wrong."

Katira looked up from where she knelt next to the old

master. Outside the circle, the real world stood frozen and painted in tones of gray. Issa and two of her guardswomen were still locked in place as they worked to force their way through the unnatural barrier between worlds. Nearby, Lady Alystra and Bremin both appeared to be relaying orders to those nearest to them.

With each blink, the scene jumped forward.

The dreamspace hadn't retreated. Even with Wrothe's connection broken, something held the bubble of altered reality in place. On the far side near the great door, Cassim pointed to something behind them. He was clearly distressed

Katira turned.

Papan gripped the top of the pedestal, bloodless fingers wrapping around the edges. Sweat dotted his forehead as his face twisted in anguish. In the altered reality of the dream-space, dark vines wrapped around him and held him fast. A thick stalk grew from his chest, directly over his heart.

Katira's knees weakened at the sight of it. She hurried to his side and placed herself where his narrowed stare would see her. His eyes were glassy with pain.

"She has you, doesn't she?"

His gaze met hers and he nodded. The vines flexed around him and pulled tighter. After all they'd done, Wrothe had still found a way to anchor herself into him and use him. Damn that woman.

This was a battle he could not win, not alone. Unlike Wrothe's tendrils, cutting this vine away wouldn't free him. Every last fiber of the plant needed to be removed.

One of the vines slithered around her wrist, piercing and cutting as it went. Several others followed. She yanked it away, hugging her arm to her chest.

Isben pulled her back out of reach. "Can you help him?"

"I have to." The place where the vine touched her burned. A new vine split through her skin. Katira watched on in horror as it wrapped its way up her arm. She grabbed it and yanked it out, revulsion overriding the searing pain. She could not be caught in Wrothe's trap.

Papan's bad leg buckled. He fell to one knee. It was enough to rouse him to speak. "Get out of here," he forced out the words between gasps. "I can end her once and for all." He set his sword on the floor in front of him.

Katira knelt before him, avoiding the vines stretching to snag her. How could she save his life if he wanted to end it all? She set her hand over his. "You can't. I forbid it." He had to trust her, had to listen. "Let me save you. It's not too late."

"If I go, I'll take her with me." He sagged lower and his other leg folded beneath him. "You'll finally be safe from her. Let me do this, let me find my peace in it."

"Those words, they aren't you. Fight it. Fight her. Don't let her thoughts destroy you," she pleaded.

Isben pointed to the stone bound to Papan's open palm. "Look."

The edges swirled dark, like ink dripping into water. If Katira was going to act, she couldn't wait any longer. She wrapped her hand around his and filled herself with the power once more. If she joined with him, she could force him to see the truth.

When his power filled him in response, it pulsed in time with the frantic beats of his heart. "Don't watch. Leave me." His voice grew softer, brushing like feathers, cutting like a razor. "Get everyone out and seal the door to the Judgment Hall." When his gaze met hers, ink swirled in the whites of his eyes.

Another sprout grew out from her shoulder. She pinched

and yanked it free, leaving an open wound that bled down her arm. That's what she had to do. Burn the vines and weed out the roots digging themselves into his heart. With them gone, the overwhelming dread and grief burying him would dissipate like the lies they were. She could heal him. She could piece together his broken parts until he was whole.

With the connection to her father secure and strong, her words would carry the full weight of her desperation.

"This root in your chest, this is what is holding Wrothe here." She set the hand where her own stone was bound against the place where the vine pressed through his chest. "If we can get rid of it, then she has no way of returning here. The mirror realm will reclaim her and hold her there."

"It will kill me if you try. " He slumped forward when his arms were no longer strong enough to hold him up and rolled onto his back. "It's okay. I'm ready to go. This world and I are through with each other."

The walls he'd used to blocked her from reaching him crumbled. She felt the echo of those dark roots piercing deeper inside him, warping his thoughts, dragging him into darker despair. He sighed and let his head fall back. His eyes lost their intense focus.

A strangled cry burst from Katira's mouth and she bit it back.

"Do what you must. I've got you." Isben's hand radiated warmth on her neck, ready and willing to keep her strong enough to see this last trial through to its bitter end. "Trust yourself."

He leaned in closer, his curls brushing away the tear escaping down her cheek. "I know you can do this. So do you. You will keep him alive and put him back together." He pressed his lips to hers and for a brief moment her head was full of strawberries and music.

"What was that for?" Katira blinked in astonishment.

"In case things go wrong." His gaze dropped back to her father. "But they won't. You'll find a way. We'll find a way. I expect a kiss in return when all this is over."

Fortified with Isben's confidence, Katira sought out the deep calm within the folds of the Khandashii. It came to her rescue when the hounds came after her. It helped her to close the broken barrier. It saved both her and those around her so many times it felt like an old friend. It would help her now.

Buried within the power, Katira experienced Wrothe's crippling despair raging through Papan firsthand. It threatened to awaken her own raw grief. Her chest tightened with it, making it hard to breathe. This was why he wanted release, why he craved it all to be over and for oblivion to take him. Wrothe had battered and beaten his mind to shreds. He was barely hanging on.

She placed her hands on either side of the root and sent her awareness along its length into his body. The trunk was composed of hundreds of slender vines all twisted together into a firm rope. Sticky clinging fibers ran the length of its branching roots and firmly anchored it into place. She dug a single vine free from the trunk, allowing the power to burn the fibers away with a single thought in a flash of heat. In a smooth tug, the first of hundreds of vines slid free, leaving torn and broken flesh in its wake.

Even half senseless, Papan stiffened. His teeth clenched. The sooner she finished, the sooner this torture would be over. She redoubled her efforts, taking two and three of the vines at time, burning away the clinging fibers and working them free, then knitting the flesh back together behind them. It wasn't a perfect job, but it was all she had. Papan arched his back. Inarticulate noises forced through his clenched teeth.

"Hang on, please. Stay with me." She pulled another three and tossed them away, trying not to lose her nerve as his heart struggled and each labored breath shrank smaller. The best she could do was push through and finish the task as quickly as she could. She grabbed hold of more vines, cutting, burning, knitting in an endless loop.

Her head throbbed and her hands slipped and shook as she pared down the thick trunk of Wrothe's power and influence. Only a handful of vines remained. Behind her, Isben's warm hands had grown cooler, and he trembled ever so slightly as he continued to feed her his power. She reached for another pair of vines, needing to finish quickly.

The last vine remained, the thickest of all of them. She'd avoided this one until the end, knowing it pierced directly through the center of Papan's heart. If she pulled it and couldn't heal the resulting damage, he'd die fast.

If she didn't, Wrothe's last anchor would remain and all of this would be for nothing.

"Keep going," Isben urged. "Once this is done, it's over."

His last bit of encouragement held its own power, giving Katira strength to push past her fear. With one flash, she burned away the fibers and wrapped both hands around the thick vine. With a hard and steady pull, she worked it free and flung it away from them.

His chest flooded with blood. She raced her awareness along the edges of the jagged wound, weaving in healing knitting glyphs along each cut, each tear, channeling the blood back, and sealing it in. She forced his lungs to clear. Reassembled the broken bones. Reanchored the seven points of his power. Her own heart beat furiously with the strain. She couldn't catch her breath. So many tiny cuts and tears, so many rips. Papan's heart quivered, but refused to beat properly.

Stars started gathering around the edges of her vision. She guided her limping power to the last of the tears and carefully patched them back together. His heart continued to quiver instead of beat. It needed to remember, needed to find its natural rhythm once more. Despite everything, he still wasn't safe.

Katira refused to allow her thoughts to go down that path. Thoughts of Mamar came flooding back, discussions on how the heart worked, how the chambers needed to coordinate their efforts in order to pump blood efficiently. A presence filled her mind, one of warmth and comfort. It guided her hands, worked new sets of glyphs Katira didn't know with a calm reassurance everything would be okay. The quivering calmed, allowing the chambers to fill properly. A single bright pulse of power touched the muscle of the heart and it leapt to life with a single solid rhythmic beat.

Then silence.

One second.

Then two.

The presence hovered near.

Another bright burst, another rhythmic beat.

This time, it was followed by another, and another.

The sound of its steady throb was more beautiful than anything Katira had ever heard before. Color returned to Papan's face and as the presence withdrew, Katira could have sworn she smelled sanaresina. Somehow Mamar had come, had helped her.

Isben's gentle voice resonated through her sounding far away as she drifted off into the welcoming darkness.

CHAPTER TWENTY-EIGHT

*T*he smell of sanaresina tickled the edge of Katira's dream, summoning up memories of long pleasant evenings in the cottage during the long winter. In the dream, Papan relaxed in his chair, leaning back and half dozing with his stocking feet propped up by the fire. Mamar hummed as she measured herbs into small satchels at the long table along the wall. The rasp of a woolen blanket rubbed along Katira's neck as she pulled it tighter. This was comfort. This was home.

Mamar tied off the last satchel and joined Katira in front of the fire, wrapping herself into the fire warmed blanket. Somehow, Katira fit into her arms the same way she used to when she was very small. The curve of her back matched her mother's welcoming embrace, her head tucked beneath that regal chin.

"You did well today." Mamar whispered. "I'm proud of you."

The praise warmed Katira better than any fire. She clung to it, wishing the unending chill of each fear, each 'what if?' of her actions would melt away. "I was so scared. What if I had failed? What would have happened?"

"Shhh." Mamar stroked her hair. "You didn't. That's all that matters. Don't fret."

The edges of the dream curled up at the edges and light peeked in. Katira didn't want to wake.

She inched closer to her mother, breathing in her smell, bathing in her memory. "I miss you."

Mamar held her tighter. "I'm always with you, even when you can't see me. You carry part of my heart with you and always will."

"And Papan?" she asked as the dream retreated further.

The cottage in Namragan faded away, replaced with the bright airy light of Amul Dun's infirmary. In place of the comforting wool blanket, she was tucked in a bed made up with crisp linens smelling of floral soap. She pressed her eyes shut, holding tight to the last thread of the dream even as it slipped away.

"He's with me forever." Mamar's last words were felt rather than heard. Where Katira carried part of her mother's heart, Papan carried a part of her soul. They'd always have each other in thought, in memory, in dreams. With Wrothe's influence gone, he might finally be able to sense her once more.

A soft touch brushed against the side of Katira's face, urging her to open her eyes. She tried to ignore it, not wanting to let go of the moment.

"It's okay, Katira. You're safe," Isben murmured softly. "It's finally over."

The last of the dream floated away, leaving her at peace. She leaned into Isben's touch, wanting the closeness, needing the gentle reassurance of his presence. When she could stand the thought of opening her eyes, she found him sitting close to her bedside still wearing the gray rumpled robes from the day before. Now it looked as if he might have slept in them.

"You saved me." She slid her hand up to touch his.

The corner of his mouth lifted in a tired smile. "You asked me to. How could I refuse?"

"Why are you so good to me?"

"Because I can. Because you deserve it."

She pressed her lips to the side of his hand. "Thank you."

The familiar sound of Papan's quiet breathing drifted over from the bed behind Isben. Katira lifted her gaze, relieved to see him sleeping peacefully and quiet. With her free hand, she touched the stone at her throat. She needed the reassurance. She let her focus drift along the bond, seeking out the darkness she'd become accustomed to, seeking out those thin roots and was pleased to find none. After all these months of struggling, at last he could finally heal.

It was over. The people she loved were safe.

On Master Firen's insistence, Isben scooted off and finally curled up into one of the empty beds. In moments he was snoring gently.

The light shifted across the floor, dragging the rectangular grid of the glass panes with it. Papan stirred from his deep sleep just after the third bell. He awoke softly, tiny movements starting at his fingers and working up his body until his eyes fluttered open and he breathed a deep sigh. When his gaze met hers he stayed quiet for a long time before speaking.

"Did you feel Mamar too?" he whispered before coughing to clear his throat.

Katira nodded. "She helped me save you. I couldn't do it on my own."

"I asked you to leave me, asked you to let me die." His

voice trembled as the memory returned. "I would have done it. I would have taken myself to keep Wrothe away from you."

Katira left her bed and sat on the edge of his. "I wasn't going to let that happen. Not for her. I would not give her the pleasure of knowing she forced your hand. Not while I could do something about it."

He probed at his chest, gingerly touching at the point where the vine had sprouted. "I didn't realize she had sunk her claws so deep inside me." He sank back into the pillows on the bed and for the first time in weeks, he looked peaceful. "I feel lighter now."

"You should rest." She squeezed his arm gently before returning to her own bed. "Tomorrow is a new day."

Katira promised not to peek from under the blindfold, not even when Isben tugged her up several flights of stairs, not even when the brisk winter air chilled her face. He'd promised her a surprise but refused to give any clues. Now he was leading her somewhere she'd never been before.

He led her forward a few more steps before stopping and standing beside her. "Okay, take it off."

Katira slid back the blindfold and found herself standing on the rooftop of the keep. A low crenelated wall wrapped around her like a cottage fence. Ahead, a brilliant sunrise painted the clouds overhead. At her feet, Isben laid out a blanket. A basket hung from his elbow, smelling of fresh bread.

"It's beautiful." Katira settled herself on the blanket and wrapped her shawl tighter around her shoulders. "What's the occasion?"

Isben reached for her hand and she gladly took it. The past

few weeks had tested them both and because of it they'd grown that much closer.

"There's something I've been meaning to talk to you about. Something that deserved its own special moment." He released her hand to break open the warm loaf of bread and hand her a piece before setting out a crock of butter and a jar of berry preserves.

Katira inhaled the aroma of the bread, trying to calm her spinning mind. What was so important that he'd gone through all this effort?

Isben took both her hands in his, suddenly serious. "I've been thinking a lot about us. About how it's always felt right to be with you."

This was it; he meant to dive right in without waiting. Katira was glad for it. She couldn't get her heart to calm down. When she was with him it always felt right, like they fit together and filled in each other's empty spaces.

She traced a circle on his wrist with her thumb needing to say something, anything. "So much has changed that it makes my head spin. The only time I can get it to slow down is when I'm with you."

"There might be a reason for that." He turned away, taking in the pinks of the sunrise for a moment, as if what he wanted to say was difficult. When he returned his gaze to her, a tear glimmered in the corner of his eye. "I think we might be each other's match. That we're meant to be companions."

Warmth blossomed inside Katira's chest. Companions among the Stonebearers were more than love and more than devotion. They were two parts of the same soul finally reunited.

"Do you really think so?"

"It has to be. Whenever we're together, whenever we join,

there is a sense that I never want it to end. That I could stay there with you, forever. When companions find each other all their broken edges are healed in the other and they finally feel whole. I feel that with you."

He was being so careful, so gentle as he spoke. It made her realize her feelings had grown beyond those of friendship. She loved him. She loved how careful he was, how caring. She loved how he got lost in his books and fell asleep in the library. She loved that even now, after all they'd been through together, he wanted to make sure her feelings were held safe in his heart.

"We could find out right now, if you want to." His gave her hand a squeeze and there was an intensity in his gaze that Katira hadn't seen before. "Would you like to know?"

"I guess so." The butterflies in Katira's stomach leapt up and swirled her insides into a whirlwind. "What do I do?"

"Relax, it's simple. When we've joined before it was always because of a pressing need. One of us needed the other's help. With all the chaos and confusion, this was the last thing on either of our minds. We join with each other today, there will be no distractions. If we are matched, it will feel right, like it's meant to be. If we aren't, then the connection will be uncomfortable to hold for too long." He opened himself to his power and its heat pressed against the palms of her hands.

"I'm nervous." Katira opened herself to hers and allowed it to flow toward him, the motions reminding her of a dance.

"Me too."

The sensation was immediate, her power rushed to him and his rushed to her in return. There, alone on the rooftop, away from the press of duty, the danger of their world, and the uncertainty of youth, their souls aligned. The ragged edges of what fate had dealt them, of what the future had in store, of their time together, merged together into a seamless whole.

This was a place Katira would choose to stay forever.

Eventually Isben allowed his power to fade. Katira reluctantly did the same. Between the thundering of her heart and the way he made her soul sing, she found herself breathless in the best way.

"I think that was a yes," he said.

Katira smiled and reached up to touch his face. Her fingertips brushed the edge of his lip and he sucked in a tiny quiet gasp. She let her finger linger there, waiting to see what he would do.

His cheeks blossomed pink. "I'm sorry."

"About what?"

"At the trial, I shouldn't have kissed you. I thought there was real chance of something horrible happening—"

"Shhh." She quieted his flurry of words with her finger. "It's okay." She leaned in and caught his lips with hers and tasted sweetness there as she kissed him. Her heart fluttered, filling with butterfly wings and shining stars. When he kissed her back and his fingers tangled into her hair, those stars shot across the sky in brilliant arcs of light. After so many weeks of feeling lost and drifting, Katira finally found a place her heart could call home.

ACKNOWLEDGMENTS

When I began my journey of becoming an author, I never expected it to lead me to a unique community of wonderful people. Over the years I've found friendship, support, guidance, and so much more. They deserve my thanks. I literally couldn't have brought my dream of publishing books to life without their help.

There's only one group of people who have supported me more, and that is my family. They have been my support, my brain trust, and my inspiration throughout this whole process. An especially large thank you goes to my husband who made it possible for me to start my own small business with my writing.

The next thank you goes to my team of talented writers who made this book shine. To Jana Brown, my editor, thank you for fearlessly pointing out all my weak points and helping me make them strong. To Melissa McShane, thank you for your guidance, support, and mad skills to make my interiors pretty. To Fiona Jayde, thank you for creating another gorgeous cover for me.

A special shout out goes to all my wonderful friends in both The League of Utah Writers and Wednesday Writers Whatchamacallit. These writers have become not only great sources of inspiration, but greats friends as well.

To my fantastic beta readers Laura, Nicole, Emily, and Joe, thanks for putting up with me experimenting with news ways to get you your reading copies – we learned a lot together.

As always, thank you Mom and Dad for always listening when I ramble on about the ins and outs of the publishing industry.

And finally, to you, dear reader, thank you for lending your imagination to make my words take flight.

ABOUT THE AUTHOR

Jodi L. Milner, author of the Stonebearer novels, wanted to be a superhero and a doctor when she was growing up. When she discovered she couldn't fly, she did what any reasonable introvert would do and escaped into the wonderful hero-filled world of fiction and the occasional medical journal. She's lived there ever since.

These days, when she's not folding the children or feeding the laundry, she creates her own noble heroes on the page. Her award-winning speculative short stories explore the fabric of dreams and have appeared in numerous anthologies, while her novels weave magic into what it means to be human.

She still dreams of flying.

Connect with Jodi at JodiLMilner.com

• Facebook: @JodiLMilnerAuthor
• Instagram: @Jodi.L.Milner
• Twitter: @JodiLMilner

For exclusive deals and updates, come join Jodi's Fantasy Reader's Community:

https://www.subscribepage.com/jodilmilner